Powers of the Heart

Victoria Craven

Powers of the heart

By Victoria Craven

© 2015 Powers of the heart

Swartz Creek, MI 48473

Cover design by Clarissa Yeo

Printed in United States of America

Printed by

Tell-Tale Publishing Group, LLC
5174 Peri Street
Swartz Creek, MI 48473
www.tell-talepublishing.com

Dahlia Imprint

DAHLIA

From the author of **Immortal Love**

PROLOGUE

Weak and riddled with pain, Murdock's heartbeat felt slow and hollow. Yet he refused to die that night or any other.

Men stood around him in silence. No tears, no wailing, just waiting.

Screams echoed through the Great Hall. Murdock's sinister smile spread across his face. Fear would make her stronger, even more potent.

A guard dragged the young girl to his throne and tossed her at his feet. "Do it now, girl," he demanded, his voice barely above a whisper.

"No, I won't!" she shouted.

She was pulled to her feet by her hair. "I said do it now." The effort to speak caused a fit of coughing. He could barely catch his breath.

"I hope you die."

She was backhanded across the face, knocking her to the floor. Satisfaction came over him when he saw the fear in her eyes.

A soldier stepped forward to protest, but the sick man held up his hand. "If you help her you'll be hanged immediately." The man stepped back.

"Now heal me!"

Hate burned in her eyes. "No! Your men call you the Dragon because they think you brave, but you're a coward. Too scared to die like a man. I will enjoy watching your flesh rot from your bones."

"Perhaps you need to be persuaded." He wanted the intolerable brat to suffer and know real fear. She would be less likely to resist him again. He nodded to his guards and she was pushed on to the floor.

"No, no!" she screamed.

The rending of fabric torn to her waist ripped through the Hall. A whip cracked near her ear causing her body to shudder. The withered man waited in anticipation.

"Lord, have mercy. She is but a child," one of his guards pleaded.

"Silence, or you'll be on the floor next to her." Not another word was spoken.

She struggled from her captures. His deviant mind took pleasure in her panic. "Give her five," he hissed.

The girl bit down on her lip to keep from screaming, but her resolve didn't last. On the third strike her tears flowed freely, by the fourth she was pleading for them to stop.

"Do you yield, or do you require more *persuading*?" Murdock said with a sneer.

"I yield," she said weakly.

"You yield what."

"I yield to you, my lord."

"Then come here."

Raw and bloody, she crawled to his throne. She wrapped her hand around his ankle. Almost immediately he felt his body rejuvenate. He was getting stronger. Her powers of healing began to take hold. Closing his eyes he took a deep breath. One that would have been impossible before.

Once his body was renewed he pulled away and bent over the bloodied young girl. Grabbing her by the hair, he forced her to look at him. His anger burned strong. "You were wrong to think you could deny me, girl," he said through his teeth. This could have gone much easier for you. Now you'll pay for your insolence." He stood over her, strong and vital. Looking at his guard, "Give her five more."

CHAPTER I

Erik sensed Storm's need for freedom. The horse bobbed his head and stomped the ground with his powerful hooves, straining at the reins. His hawk perched equally impatiently on Erik's gloved arm. He stroked her sun-warmed feathers, and she let out a piercing cry. She demanded her freedom. The urge to break free was as strong within him as his horse and hawk.

Perhaps his own restlessness influenced them. Erik no longer remembered the first time he realized he could communicate with animals. His mind connected with and melded to theirs. He wasn't sure how it worked or why. He saw and felt everything whatever animal he connected with did.

Many people feared this ability, believing as his father did that Erik was the devil's own. But those closest to him called it a gift. He disagreed with them all. Being different was no gift for him, but he was certainly not evil.

He enjoyed the warm spring sun on his face as Storm entered the meadow. Celeste flapped her wings in anticipation. The fresh air lifted his spirit. The last few weeks had been cloudy, rainy and cold. Because of the foul weather, he and his men had been held up in the castle far too long and Erik's temper grew short. The night before, he'd promised himself that no matter the weather he would go out to hunt-- alone. Fortunately the weather was in his favor, but as he approached the woods on the other side of the meadow, an inner voice told him to move forward cautiously. He held steady on Storm's reins.

Celeste stood on one talon then quickly shifted to the other, rocking side to side, anxiously awaiting his signal to fly. Untying Celeste's hood, Erik closed his eyes, stroking the soft breast feathers. His mind reached out to her until they connected. When the connection was complete, he whistled extending his arm toward the endless ceiling of blue. When her wings caught a draft and stilled, he closed his eyes and rode with her on the wind. Forest then meadows rushed beneath her.

He smiled at her shrill screech of delight. He shared her elation. Soon she would find prey and bring it back to him.

Erik bent down toward his horse's ear. *Run!* He released his hold on the reins and let Storm have his head. They raced across the meadow. It was pure joy to experience such freedom.

Suddenly Celeste let out another cry, but not of delight. A warning! Seeing through her eyes, Erik observed five men on horseback, hiding in the woods ahead of him. Dressed in the colors of the forest they attempted to become invisible.

Erik drew his sword and broke connection with the hawk. Storm's anxiety at his master's quick reaction forced Erik to pull tighter on his reins. Realizing their victim knew they were there, three men rushed at him from the tree-line.

As soon as his legs tightened around its flanks the horse charged toward the first attacker. He was no match for Erik's swiftness or strength, and died with one swipe of his sword. The next attacker fell beneath Erik's downward blow, screaming in agony as he toppled from his horse. Erik turned and made one final thrust into the third man's heart.

The other two men rode out of the woods giving Erik little time to maneuver his horse around. He swung his sword wide, keeping the bandits at a distance, yet they slowly managed to edge forward.

He pulled away from his rising anger, which allowed him to fight with clarity, every stroke calculated and precise. Erik nearly unseated the man on his left, but the effort cost him. The other assailant moved in.

Through the corner of his eye, he saw a rider thundering across the meadow, sword drawn. Erik didn't have time to decide if it was friend or foe. He hoped the former, if he was to live out the day.

He clashed swords with the man on his right, spun his horse around, forcing the other riders to back off. This allowed him to turn so his back was not to the approaching rider. After countering another blow, he managed to glance up and felt a surge or relief. The rider reached his side and immediately engaged the

attacker on his left. This allowed Erik to
concentrate on the bandit to his right.

Unexpectedly, the brigand turned and drove
his sword into Erik's shoulder. Pain shot
through it like a fiery torch, yet with great
effort he forced his mind away from the pain
and focused on the fight. One of his greatest
skills was that he could fight with either arm
equally well. Grasping his sword in his left
hand, he turned his horse and caught his enemy
off guard. With one stroke, Erik sliced through
the man's midsection. The would-be assassin's
gasp of pain ended when his body hit the ground
with a solid thud. The robber's corpse was soon
joined by his final companion.

Celeste cried out above him. There was no
strength to answer her. When Erik looked down
he saw his tunic red with blood, not only from
his enemies, but his own. The world spun around
him as he too fell from his saddle, hitting the
ground like a sack of grain. Pain sliced
through his body like shards of glass. Celeste
landed beside him, screeching loudly. Storm
kicked the ground beside him, nudging Erik with
his soft muzzle, but he couldn't force himself
to respond.

As he lay on the cool grass, he noticed the
rider dismount. The large man knelt beside him.
With fascination Erik watched the warrior
remove his black helmet. Long black hair fell
around the face of an angel. Even though his
body was riddled with pain, he registered the
shock at what he saw. The warrior, who fought

so skillfully, was a woman. Surely, his mind was playing tricks on him.

"I must be dying," he rasped, "and you have come to take me to my Maker."

"You'll not die this day," she said, as she removed a dagger from her boot. She cut his tunic away from his shoulder. Blood pooled around the wound.

"I fear you're wrong. I'll be meeting God within the hour." It was becoming increasingly difficult to breath.

"You'll not die, for I won't allow it," she said, and placed her hand gently on his forehead and looked deeply into his eyes. She spoke as softly as a gentle caress. Calm washed over him.

She placed her hand over the wound and closed her eyes. He could feel the pain easing from his body, and a strange tingling sensation moved through his shoulder and down his arm. The fire was going out. He had heard tales of healers before, but never believed in them.... until now.

He studied her face with interest. Her teeth were clenched as though she were in pain. He regretted that they should share this agony, yet he was too weak to stop her. As soon as he was strong enough, he reached for her wrist and pulled her hand away. She opened her eyes in surprise. Her body was weary and drained.

"Enough," he said weakly.

She tried to place her hand back on his shoulder, but he held her wrist firmly. "The healing is not finished."

"I'm well enough to live," he said, rising into a sitting position, still holding her wrist. Looking down at his shoulder, he saw only a small gash where there should have been a gapping mortal wound. An ache remained where there was once a burning fire of pain. "You need not endure more. I'll heal the rest on my own." His eyes met with hers. She helped him as he struggled to his feet. He still felt weak, but was getting stronger.

Standing next to her he realized she was tall for a woman. She was only a few inches shorter than him, and he was no small man. He towered over most men, and so would she. Her frame was well formed. She didn't look frail like most women he knew. She was strong. Her eyes were the color of a frozen blue lake. For a moment he thought he might lose his soul in them.

Instead of taking power over his soul, she helped Erik to his horse. "Are you certain you're able to ride?"

"I'm fine." Erik couldn't resist running his fingers along her jaw. "Thank you for your help." His eyes held hers for a long moment. Reluctantly he lowered his hand and carefully mounted his horse.

Once he was settled he asked, "How is it you came to help me?"

"It was your hawk," she said, mounting her horse. "I heard her cry above me. She flew in a circle then dove at me. At first I thought I had stumbled onto her nest, but then I realized she was trying to tell me something, so I followed her and found you in trouble."

Erik stroked Celeste's feathers. He softly whistled and she answered him in return. The odd look on her face didn't go unnoticed. It was a look he had seen on many times.

He looked at the woman before him, awed by her beauty as she sat on her magnificent snow white stallion.

"I'm Erik, Lord of Alastair Keep. May I have the honor of knowing your name?"

"I'm Kiera."

"How is it you fight like well-trained warrior?"

A flash of anger sparked in her eyes. "I'm a warrior."

He held up his hand to ward off her anger. "Forgive me, but as you know, it's not common to find a woman who knows how to fight. Most women have husbands or protectors."

"I have neither."

Erik watched her wrap the reins tightly around her gloved hand. "How did you end up at Alastair?"

"I came to ask permission to make camp on your land."

"Are you traveling alone?"

"No, I travel with two companions. They're waiting for me about half a league from here."

His suspicion must have shone on his face, for she spoke before he could voice his concern. "No, there are no other enemies lurking around here," she said with exasperation. "Why would I save your life only to take it? I wish permission to stay for one night. Then we'll move on.

Profound relief washed over him. He wouldn't fare well in another battle just now. He gazed at her. He owed the woman his life and didn't want to see her leave without showing proper appreciation for his rescue.

"Where are you traveling to?"

The hesitation was only for a moment. "Godwin Castle to speak with Lord Dominick."

A shock ran through him like a lightning bolt. "Why do you want to talk to Dominick?"

"It's a matter I must take up with him, and only him."

Erik placed an edge of warning in his voice to make his point very clear. "Lord Dominick is a friend and ally. I'll not allow any harm to come to him."

Kiera raised her head slightly, "I mean him no harm, I seek his help," she said, quietly adding, "I can't tell you any more than that."

By the stubborn set of her jaw he knew no further information would be forthcoming. The coincidence that the woman should be here at this time was suspicious. "You are in good fortune. Dominick comes to my Keep in three days. You and your companions may stay here to await his arrival. You'll have a chance to meet his wife and son as well."

The arrangement was perfect. If she was lying about not harming Dominick he would be there to protect his friend. And no amount of mercy would protect her from him.

Kiera hesitated. "Very well. I must go and tell my friends we are to be your guest," She turned her horse toward the encampment.

Erik followed, watching her carefully, looking for any sign of treachery. Pain shot from his shoulder and down his arm with every step his horse made. Yet he wouldn't allow it to show on his face. If she knew he was in pain, she might want to heal him completely. Her touch was hypnotic, and he needed to keep his head clear.

They moved on to the campsite without talking, which gave Erik a chance to study the woman next to him. She rode her horse as though part of it, which somehow made Erik envy the horse. Tight leather breeches, and boots that laced up to each knee covered well-formed legs. She wore chainmail armor that must have been made specifically to fit her body. At her waist was a wide girdle, which held her sword. It wasn't a man's weapon, but lighter and more tapered. It was quite deadly.

Her black braid hung down her back past her girdle. Kiera's profile was magnificent. She had a straight nose, full red lips and long, thick, black sweeping lashes. She had a long neck and high cheeks bones. Her jaw was definitely defiant. Her entire manner was defensive. Erik suspected if she came across an obstacle, she would more likely go through it than avoid it.

He liked the woman's strength. The thought of her as a fierce warrior intrigued him. She was more than beautiful. He wondered what it would be like to see her eyes filled with passion as she lay beneath him. His body jolted. Such a thought surprised him. He felt himself becoming aroused and quickly pushed such thoughts away.

They rode into the small camp where the two men were waiting for her. An older man came forward and took her horse's reins. Erik pulled his cloak tighter around him knowing the sight of his bloody, torn tunic would cause concern.

"We've waited some time, Kiera. We were about to go searching for you." The older man looked toward Erik. "I see you brought someone with you."

"Marcus, this is Lord Erik of Alastair. Lord Erik, this is my friend, Marcus."

The older man nodded to him. He gestured toward the younger man. "My son, Jordan."

Jordan looked to be around the same age as Kiera. He wasn't quite as tall as Erik, but had a strong frame that required hard training. He had light brown hair with a tint of red in the sunlight.

Marcus was an older, stockier version of Jordan. They had the same eyes, except that there was more depth of knowledge and experience in those of the father. They also shared the same reddish brown hair, and Marcus' arms were equally massive from decades of wielding a sword. Erik saw that he would be a worthy opponent, but reasoned that he would make a greater ally. He wondered who this unusual trio was and where they came from. Most importantly what did they want with his friend,

Dominick. As his guests at Alastair Keep, he would find out.

"How is it you came upon Kiera?" Marcus asked.

"She actually came upon me. I was attacked by a band of outlaws, bent on my immediate disposal. She came to my aid and was quite remarkable," he continued. "I have rarely seen such skill from a man."

Marcus looked at her with pride. "She is a natural fighter with a talent that surprises even me."

Kiera dismounted and came around her horse. She looked directly at Erik. "I'm standing in front of you. Don't talk about me as though I'm not here."

"Forgive me. I was just curious as to why a woman would train for fighting as a man would."

"It was necessary for my survival." She quickly changed the subject. "Lord Erik has invited us to stay at Alastair Keep. He said that Lord Dominick is to be there in three days."

"I would be honored if you would stay in my home, in appreciation for her help."

Erik saw Marcus' hesitation. "You say that Lord Dominick will arrive in three days? Well it would be nice to sleep near a warm hearth for a change. We'll accept your kind invitation. Thank you."

Erik smiled. "No gratitude is necessary. I'm indebted to Kiera for saving my life." He gave her a knowing glance. He gazed in to her eyes then she turned away to helped Marcus and

Jordan break up camp. Soon all four mounted and rode for Alastair Keep.

CHAPTER II

Erik rode ahead toward Alastair Keep. She couldn't keep from staring at his back. His shoulders were wide, and his waist narrow. Muscles bulged out of his chest and arms. This was no pampered Lord. He worked long and hard to protect his land. There was a keenness in his eyes, an intelligence, unlike other noblemen she had known in the past. When she watched him fight, it had been with detachment and a ruthlessness that left no room for error. It had been sheer luck that one of the attackers ran his sword through his shoulder, yet he kept fighting with determination not to be defeated.

She wondered at the strange excitement she felt when he looked at her. He touched her face with such tenderness it startled her.

His face was ruggedly handsome. There were no soft lines in it, maybe with the exception of his mouth. It was not full, but his lips were somehow sensuous. She wondered what he looked like when he smiled. His eyes were the color of amber, and when he looked at her, she felt as if he were looking into her soul. Kiera never felt that way before, but she had never seen a man like him before. She'd been around men most of her life, but they all paled in comparison. He was larger than life.

Pulling away from her line of thinking, she reminded herself to be careful. Straying from finding Dominick and convincing him to help her was paramount. If she failed, she, Marcus, and Jordan would be destroyed.

She urged her horse forward then kept pace with Erik. "Don't tell anyone of my healing," she said, as she came up beside him.

He raised an eyebrow. "Why wouldn't you want me to tell anyone?"

"Because I don't wish to be accused of practicing witchcraft," she said with exasperation.

"Are you?"

"No, but people misunderstand, believing that the healing comes from evil."

He smiled. "You needn't worry. I won't tell anyone of your power."

She sighed then thought again, looking back at Marcus. "Don't even tell Marcus what I've done."

He gave her a questioning look. "Doesn't he know of your abilities?"

"Yes, but he will be angry that I used them."

"Why would he be angry?"

"For the very reason I told you. People don't understand. He feels in this matter no one can be trusted."

He turned to her. "I won't tell anyone."

She sighed with relief. "Thank you."

They moved on toward Alastair Keep. The sun was now setting. She could see the welcomed sight of the Keep in the distance. It would be good to sleep in a dry place after so many weeks of traveling in the rain and cold. She was used to the hardships, but it felt good to sleep with a roof over her head.

Kiera, Marcus and Jordan had been traveling from one place to another for years trying to stay one step ahead of the Dragon. Now they were very close to the end of their journey. Finally, the time had come to put things right. The years of running and danger must come to an end. If she could convince Lord Dominick to help them, she'd a future after all.

As they approached Alastair Keep, a feeling of safety seeped through her body. Somehow, she knew the Keep would be a safe haven where the Dragon couldn't reach them. Erik didn't seem the type of man who would align himself with a monster. He seemed to be an honorable man. She knew he felt he owed her a debt. And in some way, he would repay it. For that she was grateful.

She looked back at Marcus. He looked weary, and in need of a few nights out of the cold. They all did. A warmth of affection spread in her chest. Dear Marcus and Jordan. Without her friends she would have died years ago. They were more than just her friends. They were her family. Over the years Marcus became the father she lost and Jordan the brother she'd never had. She loved them with all her heart. Even when Marcus was stern with her, she knew he only meant to protect her from harm. He trained her as hard as his son, and more. When she felt she couldn't go on, he encouraged her. He gave her a sense of self-worth, and confidence.

As they approached Alastair Keep, they rode past small hamlets and fields starting to green with future crops. Upon entering the first wall to the Keep, a young man approached Erik.

"My Lord, we were about to send out a search party for you."

"As you can see Albert, I'm fine," Erik said, dismounting his horse. She watched him pull his mantle closer around him to hide the blood and his torn tunic. Probably to avoid questions that would surely be asked.

"I also brought some guests," he said as he walked toward Kiera's mount. Reaching up, he waited for her to slide in to his arms, as though she were a lady at court. His gesture was unsettling. She'd been dismounting horses on her own since Marcus taught her how to ride. Not knowing what to do, she looked to Marcus. He nodded his head. Sighing heavily, she moved her leg around to a sitting position, bent forward, and slid into Erik's arms. He held her for a moment. Kiera's heart hammered hard against her chest. His eyes were unreadable. Then before she could take a breath to calm her heart's frantic beating, he released her.

Her body bloomed with a flush of attracting too much attention. Looking toward Marcus, she could clearly see his disapproval. Jordan looked as though he would burst into a fit of laughter, at her discomfort. She glared at him, daring him to say a word.

Returning to his mount, Erik retrieved his hawk, whistling to her softly before handing her over to his falconer. She wondered at the strange affection he had for his animals.

"See to our guest's accommodations, Albert," Erik said, turning to his squire. He looked back at, Kiera, "Make sure they're comfortable."

Walking back to the small group, he addressed Marcus. "I'll leave you in my squire's capable hands. I have some business to discuss with my captain about those outlaws we encountered." He bowed to Kiera slightly. "I'll see you at the evening meal," then turned and walked away.

Albert signaled to two young boys standing nearby to take care of their horses. Marcus and Jordan dismounted and stood next to Kiera. The young squire turned back toward them. "Follow me please".

They followed him inside the Keep. She was amazed at the size of the Great Hall. It smelled clean and well cared for. There was a large hearth with a roaring fire in it. Heraldic banners trimmed in gold hung from the rafters. Colorful tapestries graced stone-walls, and tables were draped in fine linen. The Hall's appearance gave a sense of warmth and welcome.

Albert led them to a stairway that spiraled up to the second story and down a narrow corridor until they reached a large oak door.

The squire opened it to a spacious room. "This is where you'll be staying my er..." he stammered looking at Kiera's attire, "miss."

Marcus looked ready to pound the boy into the ground.

Quickly, Albert walked into the room. "I'm sorry, miss. It's just that I have never seen a woman dressed in warrior's garb before."

She followed him into the room. "It's all right Albert I'm quite used to it."

The boy was visibly uncomfortable. "Everything you need should be here. If there is anything else, just tell Alice. She will see to your needs."

"Thank you."

Albert nervously motioned to Marcus and Jordan. "I'll show you to your chambers sirs," then headed toward the door.

Jordan didn't move at first. "Will you be all right here?" Jordan asked, turning toward her.

She smiled, touched by his concern. "Yes, I'll be fine."

"Then we'll see you at the evening meal." He gave her a reassuring hug, before he and Marcus left the room.

She was finally left alone to her thoughts. Looking out the window, she could see the stables and cookhouse. People were moving about like worker bees. Everyone seemed to be in a hurry. There was an area that looked like a training field. She turned to look around her chambers. There was a large oak bed, with rich burgundy bed-robes and velvet curtains, standing in the middle of the room. The hearth was across from the bed, and an oak table and chairs sat to the right of the hearth. Tapestries hung on the walls, depicting battles of the past in rich vibrant colors. Never before had she stayed in a room so luxurious.

There was a knock at her door. A serving woman stepped into the chambers. "Hello miss, I'm Alice. Is there anything' ye be wantin' just yet?" She asked as she fussed around the room, dusting the table, and straightening a chair. "The master said you might be wantin' a bath so the tub will be comin' in shortly."

Alice was a middle-aged woman, plump with rosy cheeks and an easy smile. She couldn't help but smile back at her. "I left my things on my horse."

The servant made a flapping gesture with her hand. "Already been takin' care of," she said, as she looked into the hearth. "I'll be gettin' some firewood up here. We'll have a cheery fire in no time. The day may have been warm, but it promises to be a cold night." She turned to Kiera. "Is there anythin' I can get for ye in the meantime?"

"No, I'll be fine."

Alice smiled. "Well then, I'll be up shortly to help ye with yer bath."

"No!" her voice rose in panic. Alice gave her a questioning look. Composing herself, Kiera continued. "I mean, that won't be necessary, I can take care of it myself."

"Well, suit yerself. If ye be needin' me, just tell one of the men who bring ya yer bath, and I'll be here shortly. If not, then I'll come to get ye for the evening meal."

"That'll be fine."

Kiera breathed a sigh of relief as the maid left the room.

She turned back to the window, where she saw twenty men mounting their horses. She suspected they were going to search for more outlaws that may still be on Alastair land.

A knock came at her door and Kiera bid them to enter. A barrage of people walked in carrying a large tub and steaming water. Another man came in with an armload of firewood and proceeded to build a fire, and a young boy brought her bags from her horse. She thanked him as he went scampering out.

Finally, she was left to her bath. Kiera couldn't remember such a luxury. Usually it was a dip in an icy cold lake or stream, or a quick bath with a bowl of warm water. Quickly, she stripped out of her clothes and placed one foot in the water. The heat prickled her skin. Slowly, she stepped in until her body got used to the temperature. Once in the tub, Kiera let the warmth penetrate every pore.

A pot of scented soap sat next to the tub. She held it to her nose and let the aroma saturate her senses. She laid her head back against the tub and let the memory of being in his strong arms fill her mind. Her heart began to race again. It was difficult to breathe when he was close. When he looked into her eyes, she could feel it in the pit of her stomach. No man had ever looked at her the way he did. Most men found her manly ways offensive.

A warning bell sounded off in her head. Her feelings had to be guarded. She could ill afford to get involved when she was so close to her goal of defeating the Dragon--the man of her nightmares.

She washed her hair until it squeaked clean, and then she washed from head to toe. She couldn't remember the last time she felt so clean. She dried herself in front of the fire and dressed in a new tunic and britches Marcus had bought her. The tunic was soft white wool trimmed with gold thread. The contrast made her hair look black as night. Her breeches were supple black leather. At her waist was a wide leather girdle. Drying her hair by the fire, she swept the long tresses into a loose braid down her back.

As promised, Alice came to get her for the evening meal. Putting her sword on, she followed her out of the room, to find Marcus and Jordan waiting outside her door. The plump woman led the three of them into the Great Hall and took them to the master's head table where Erik was already seated. He stood, placing his hand on the back of the chair beside him. "Kiera will you do me the honor of sitting beside me. Marcus, Jordan, if you'll sit beside her."

Whispers filled the Hall and all eyes were on them. She knew they were curious about the woman who carried a sword. For the first time in many years she felt self-conscious. Usually, she took her evening meals in the kitchen or outside with her two friends.

Looking toward Marcus, who seemed to recognize what she was feeling, gently squeezed her hand. "This is not the first time, Kiera," he whispered. "They'll become accustomed to your attire soon enough."

He was right. Most times she never thought about the way she looked, but somehow, standing next to Erik, it was somewhat different.

On the other side of Erik sat a beautiful middle-aged woman who watched with a keen eye. She wore a scarlet gown and head scarf with a gold circlet. Her hair was a beautiful shade of white. Her eyes were a soft shade of blue.

Erik turned to Kiera. "I would like you to meet my Aunt Arelia." He gestured back to Kiera. "Arelia, this is Kiera. She saved my life today, for which I owe her a great debt. These are her companions, Marcus and Jordan."

She held her breath, praying that he wouldn't mention her healing power.

"She came to my aid when I was attacked by a band of outlaws," he said, giving her a conspirator's wink.

Kiera let out her breath. She felt the woman's momentary scrutiny before she smiled. "Then I too am indebted to you, for my nephew is very dear to me," she said, touching her nephew's hand. "It was fortunate you came along when you did."

For the first time she saw Erik smile. It was a beautiful transformation. His face beamed as warmly as the sun. His teeth were white and straight, and he had a dimple on each cheek giving him a boyish look. She wondered how many times that smile had gotten him out of trouble...or maybe into it.

"Erik told me you are here to meet Dominick."

"Yes."

"It's fortunate that he will be here soon. You must be fated to be here at this time, and thankfully in time to save my nephew."

Kiera felt her face grow warm. "I only did what I had to do. I saw a man in trouble, and couldn't allow him to be slaughtered."

"It was a brave thing you did, my dear. Don't make light of it."

The evening meal was brought in. Not used to complements such as she was receiving made her uncomfortable, and she was thankful for the interruption. There was more food than she had seen in years. Venison and partridge seduced her senses and made her mouth water. Boiled potatoes and pastries of every kind filled the table to its edges. She looked over at Marcus. He had already begun to eat with a relish she had rarely seen. Jordan too was deeply involved with his food. She ate with an appreciation of what was put before her as well.

Erik looked over at the unique woman that sat next to him, watching her hands as she ate. They were lovely hands. Not pampered hands, like the ladies of the king's court. He was sure hers were callused from wielding a sword, but her tapered fingers were very appealing. He could see them caressing his body. Heat in his groin began to rise. He looked back into the cup he was holding. He closed his eyes trying to put the image out of his mind, but the image imprinted itself in the back of his eyelids

"Are you feeling well?" Arelia asked.

He cleared his throat, "Yes, I'm fine, why do you ask?"

"You have barely touched your food." She pointed to his still full plate.

"Really? I hadn't noticed. I must not be very hungry...for food." He pushed his emotions deep, returning a look of indifference to his aunt. Not that she could ever be fooled, but he was in no mood for further questions.

Everyone ate their fill, and the evening meal was cleared away. Erik pulled out Kiera's chair when she rose to stretch her legs. She was taken by surprise. He suspected that she'd never experienced a man's attention before, despite her two traveling companions. They seemed to treat her as one of their own. Not as a woman, but as a warrior, like themselves.

Her awkward reaction was amusing. She mumbled her thanks and walked over to the fire. His curiosity, and so much more for her, compelled him to follow.

Marcus watched closely. "She'll be fine," said a voice from behind him. He turned around to find Arelia sitting next to him. "Erik won't do anything too inappropriate."

Marcus wondered if he had spoken his concerns aloud, for the woman indeed answered the questions he was asking in his mind. He turned back to Kiera and Erik. "I hope you're right. She's innocent to the ways of men. Jordan and I have seen to that."

"You needn't worry. My nephew will behave himself."

Looking back at the couple, he thought the doting aunt sounded more convincing than he felt. Never had a man looked at her like that before. It puzzled him what Erik saw in her that other men missed. Marcus knew she was a beautiful woman, but most men couldn't get past her manner of dress, or her skill.

"Where're you from?" His thoughts were brought back to Erik's aunt.

Marcus hesitated. He didn't like lying, but he couldn't divulge the purpose of their meeting with Lord Dominick. "We travel a great deal and have never really settled in one place."

Arelia eyed Marcus with suspicion. "You are being deliberately evasive."

"No," he said with a sigh. "It's just that since Kiera was a child we haven't belonged to any Keep or Manor." He braced his arms on the table and gave Arelia his full attention. "We hire out our services to anyone who may need them. When we're finished, we move on."

"I see." She looked over to Kiera. "Where are her parents? I'm assuming you're not her father."

Marcus was amazed at Aurelia's acute observations. "No, I'm not her father." He looked toward Kiera standing by the fire. "She and I are not related by blood, but she is no less my child than my son."

Arelia gave him a brilliant smile, and her eyes glowed with warmth. "How is it she came into your care?"

Uncomfortable with her questions, he shifted in his seat slightly. Jordan spoke for him. "Kiera was orphaned as a child. My father and I took it upon ourselves to take care of her, for she had no one else."

Marcus saw Arelia eye them suspiciously, knowing there was more than what they were telling her. Eventually they may tell their story. But now was not that time.

She placed her hand on Marcus' arm. "You did well in raising her. She is a fine young lady."

"It's kind of you to say such a thing, My Lady," he said. "She was not raised in the ways of ... but it was the only way I felt we could protect her." He dropped his hands in his lap, looking over to Kiera. "Many women have shunned her because of the way she dresses and her ability to fight. I know it's hurt her greatly. Many times my heart broke for the loneliness she felt. She has so many questions that as a man I can't answer." He sighed wearily. "I only hope that she will find a place for herself someday."

Arelia touched his hand as she rose to her feet. "I'm sure she'll find her place. She's a strong woman," she said glancing at the couple standing by the hearth. "It's getting late so I'll bid you good night, gentlemen. It has been a pleasure to meet you, and I'm glad you'll be staying with us during the festival."

Marcus and Jordan rose to their feet, bidding her good night. Marcus watched her cross the room to where her nephew and Kiera were standing. The woman had a presence he had rarely encountered.

--

"I'll see you two in the morning," Arelia said as she touched Erik's arm.

"Going to bed so soon?"

"Yes, it's been a long day." Turning to Kiera she reached for her hands holding both of them in hers. "It has been a great pleasure meeting you, and I'm glad you'll be staying with us," she said and kissed her on both cheeks. "Thank you for saving my nephew's life." She gave her hands a final squeeze and left the hall.

Kiera was touched by the woman's affection. She watched as the woman left the hall, admiring her natural grace.

"Your aunt is very beautiful, and very kind."

"You haven't seen her on a bad day," he said with a smile. "She can be an absolute bear. There have been many times I've felt her claws."

"I think you exaggerate," she said smiling.

"Cross her path the wrong way once, you'll see I speak the truth."

"I hope I'll never find out."

Erik looked into the fire clasping his hands behind his back, "Are your accommodations adequate?"

"Yes, thank you they're more than adequate. It's very kind of you to let us stay in your Keep."

"Nonsense it's the least I could do," he rubbed his shoulder as though remembering the pain.

"Does it still pain you?" she asked with concern. "I could finish healing it."

"Thank you that won't be necessary. It's but a dull ache." After a long moment he asked, "Where are you from, Kiera?"

She hesitated. "No one place, My Lord," she said finally. The answer was vague, and she went on to clarify. "Since I was a child Marcus, Jordan and I have traveled to many different places, so we couldn't call any one place our home."

Looking into his eyes she could see flecks of gold in the amber. She could so easily drown in their warmth.

"How is it in your travels no Lord or Baron kept the three of you for his warriors? You're a good fighter."

"No Lord would accept a woman fighter. I'm an abomination," she hesitated, and then went on. "Many times noblemen would hire Marcus and Jordan for their swords. They tried putting me in the kitchen where they felt I belonged." She sighed. "It never worked out. I'm a terrible cook."

Erik smiled down at her. She couldn't help but smile back. "What a waste of talent," he said.

"Thank you," she said, blushing at his compliment. "Later we kept the fact that I was a woman from other land owners."

"How was that possible?"

"Because of my height, with my helmet and armor on, most men don't question it."

"Eventually you would have to remove your helmet."

"Yes, but never in public," then she smiled. "Only after we have been paid and ready to leave, do I reveal who and what I am."

Erik smiled. "That must come as quite a surprise."

"Yes it was. I loved watching their faces when we were ready to leave. It was priceless."

"How is it you came to be with Marcus and his son?" He said, turning in their direction.

Kiera face sobered. She looked into the fire. Then, softly, "I was orphaned as a child."

"I'm sorry," he said sincerely.

"It was a very long time ago," she whispered, unable to keep the pain from lancing her heart.

Marcus came up behind her. Her heart jumped slightly when he cleared his throat.

"It's time we retire," Marcus said in a tone that didn't allow an argument.

"Yes it's been a long day," she said, somewhat grateful for the interruption. She was feeling things she couldn't put a name to, and needed to go to her room to get her feet back firmly on the ground. "Good night my lord, and thank you again," she said, and walked up the stairs to her chamber.

Erik watched her until she was no longer in his sight. He could feel Marcus and Jordan's eyes on him. Turning to them, he secreted what he was thinking.

"I want to thank you for allowing us to stay at your Keep," Marcus said.

"It isn't necessary," Erik said, waiving him off.

There was a long pause before Marcus spoke again. "I don't wish to be rude in your home, my lord, but it's my obligation to say this. In spite of her appearance she is an innocent. She's an honorable girl, not one to be trifled with. Am I making myself clear, sir?"

Erik stood straighter. "Very clear and let me put your mind at ease by saying I have no intention of insulting her. I owe her my life. It's gratitude, nothing else."

Marcus relaxed slightly. "Very well. As long as you assure us that no harm will come to her, we'll bid you good night."

Erik turned back to the fire, contemplating Marcus' words. "Kiera an innocent," he said to himself. He had no doubt. The way she fought he could believe no man would jeopardize his manhood. He smiled to himself. It would be an interesting challenge to woo her to his bed. As soon as that thought crossed his mind he dismissed it. He owed her too much to dishonor her. Still, he felt an attraction he couldn't deny, but it must be kept under control, for he still didn't know if she was his enemy or friend. He intended to find out soon enough.

Erik didn't want to think of Kiera as his enemy, but he couldn't let his guard down for a moment. She could have been sent by one of his enemies to the north to infiltrate his Keep. What better way than to save his life in a battle against a band of outlaws. Then use her unusual beauty to seduce him into letting down his guard.

With her under his roof he could keep a close eye on her and her friends. If she were his enemy he would make her pay dearly for her deception. With his resolve clear in his mind he left the Hall and headed toward his chambers.

CHAPTER III

Kiera rose early the next morning and readied herself to meet Marcus and Jordan on the training field. She wondered if Erik would be there. Would he feel differently about seeing her in training? It was one thing to see her in the heat of battle, not knowing who she was. It was quite another seeing her on the training field.

She couldn't explain the attraction she felt toward him. It wasn't just physical. She felt it deeper. Kiera was used to the company of men, but she had never before been drawn to one like this. Whenever Erik was around, she felt clumsy and self-conscious. Often, during the evening meal she found him looking at her, and it was unnerving.

Clearing her mind of those thoughts, she dressed in her hauberk and sword and went out to hone her skills. The sun was shining brightly. The weather was holding up, but the morning still carried the night's chill. It was always best to work out in the early part of day, before the sun rose high and became warm, too warm for full armor. Not that Marcus didn't train her in the heat of the day. Very often he would stretch her to her limits in the mid-afternoon sun. But she preferred to practice first thing in the morning.

Jordan was waiting for her, and smiled as she walked onto the field. "Are you anxious to be defeated today, milady?" he said with a courtly bow.

"Don't start with me. I'm in no mood for your heckling," she said raising her sword and making the first strike. "He was just being kind."

He chuckled as he countered her attack. "I'm not so sure about that. He seemed quite taken with you." He moved in for the next strike. "It's strange watching him pay court to you."

Her sword rang against his as they connected. "He was not paying court to me, and if he was, am I so ugly you think I'm not worthy of his attention?"

Jordan sobered, lowering his sword. "No, Kiera, if anyone was ever worthy of it, it would be you. You were never ugly to me. It's just that until now, I never noticed how much of a woman you have grown into. Being with you day after day one tends not to notice."

She'd never heard such words from Jordan. "Thank you." Playfully, she raised her sword, "but I'm still going to cut you to ribbons."

"So you may think," he said with a devilish grin.

Kiera made an aggressive move. Jordan was quick with a counter move. Men who were training across the field stopped to watch the two in mock battle.

Erik and Marcus walked out on to the training field. Swords were ringing through the crisp morning air. A crowd gathered in the center of the field. Kiera and Jordan were fighting, each displaying great skill. He watched the pair move and counter move. The woman moved with fluid grace. She was a true warrior.

"She's good," Erik said.

"Yes, she is, but they have trained together for so long they know each other's moves."

"Has she ever trained with anyone else?"

"Men find it beneath them to fight with a woman."

"Interesting." He knew Marcus was goading him into testing Kiera's skills, and he would oblige him.

"Hold!" he said, as he approached them. The two stopped. "I would like the honor of challenging Kiera." The men around them gathered closer.

"Be my guest," Jordan said as he sheathed his sword and left the field to stand next to Marcus. Erik caught them smiling at each other. They thought he was about to be trounced, but they were unaware of his own skill.

He turned to her. "Shall we make a wager before we begin?"

"That won't be necessary. I have nothing to offer should you win," she said standing proudly with her sword steadied in both hands.

"Ah, but that is where you're wrong, my Angel," his voice dripped with affection. "If I should defeat you all I ask for is a kiss."

Kiera's face paled momentarily, but recovered quickly. "And if I should beat you?"

"Ten gold pieces."

A murmur washed across the spectators. "Lord Erik need not worry about his gold." Kiera's body stiffened into an offensive stance. Determination set in her jaw.

She couldn't keep the smile from her face. The ten gold pieces were as good as hers. She'd make short work of the arrogant Lord and quiet the words of her defeat from the crowd. Even though she'd seen Erik in battle she was confident she could bring him down, especially since he was injured.

Raising their swords in salute, the fighting commenced. She moved in quickly, and he used his strength to force her back. She ducked when he swung high and jumped when he swung toward her knees.

Her mind focused on him as a whole, not just the sword, anticipating his next move. Adrenaline coursed through her veins. The thrill of the fight and mastery of the sword, made her heart race. All her focus was on her opponent.

Marcus came into view. The looked of pride swept across his face, as he clapped Jordan on the back, "That's my girl," he said.

Erik moved with precision, calculating every move. She saw that same detachment on his face that he wore when he fought the bandits the day before. He never took his eyes off her face. She knew he was looking for a weakness. A weakness she would never show him. She met him thrust for thrust, strike for strike.

As time wore on he used more strength. She was still strong, but she wasn't sure for how long. She grunted with the effort to keep him back. She swung her sword very close to his ear, and he backed away slightly, then moved in again.

Suddenly, he was on her, swords crossed at the hilt. She bent her knees, throwing her weight forward, but it was like leaning against a wall. Shifting forward, he pushed her back. Her heel caught in a rut causing her to lose her balance and fall flat on her back. Her sword flew out of her hands. Quickly, she rolled to pick it up, but Erik's sword came down as he stood above her, placing the tip close to her throat. "Have I won?" He said, standing over her with superiority.

Stunned by what just happened Kiera looked into Erik's face. It held no emotion. Not even one of triumph. Reluctantly, she nodded her head. He broke into a smile, and placed his sword in its sheath. He extended his hand out to her and as soon as her hand was in his, he pulled her up against him. His arms were wrapped tightly around her waist, as his lips came down on hers.

Surprised, Kiera didn't think to resist. His mouth pressed down hard, forcing her to part her lips. His tongue slipped into her mouth. Excitement washed over her as her heart pounded in her ears.

The crowd's shouts and jeers brought her back to the reality of her defeat. He was making a spectacle of her. Well she could give as well as she got. Wrapping her arms tightly around his neck, she pressed her body against his, and pulled his head down tighter.

Opening her eyes slightly she saw Jordan move toward them, but Marcus put his hand on his shoulder. "Let 'em be, lad. He defeated her fairly. It's his right. She agreed to the wager." But she knew Marcus didn't like much of what he saw. He would be burning her ears later for her behavior.

Erik relaxed his embrace, and gazed into her eyes intently. "Victory is sweet, my Angel," he said with a smile, "I shall have to challenge you again."

"You'll not win so easily next time, my lord."

"It was far from easy, Angel. You are a true warrior."

She smiled at the compliment.

"But can you be a true woman?" he said, releasing her. The fire left his eyes as he walked away.

Erik's blood boiled with desire. Her response shocked him to the core and he was clearly shaken. No woman made him respond like she did. When he entered the Great Hall he ordered wine to stop his racing thoughts.

Arelia saw him and sat next to him at the table. He loved his aunt but for once he wanted to be alone. Unfortunately she wasn't inclined to leave him. He looked up, wearing his mask of indifference.

"What's happened?"

"Nothing, why do you ask?" He kept his tone light.

"Erik, I know you better than that. You put that face on when you don't want anyone to know what you're thinking or feeling."

"I don't know what you're talking about." Not willing to endure any further interrogation, he stood and abruptly left the hall, leaving her behind.

He went to the falconry and retrieved Celeste from her cage. Storm was saddled and the three of them headed out the palisades gate. Once away from the Keep he connected with his hawk. *Let me fly with you,* Erik thought.

Trouble?

How do you know something is bothering me?

There is danger?

No, not from an enemy. Just let me fly.

She screeched and shook her head, flapping her wings.

He let go of her tether and she spread her great wings and flew into the morning sky. He felt her rise higher on the wind, a cool breeze on her face. He felt her freedom and took it on as his own. Taking deep breaths he expanded his chest letting go of what troubled his mind.

She flew beyond the meadow to the small village and over the crops greening with spring. He flew with her for the better part of the morning, but it was time to get back to the Keep.

He decided to take a small group of men to make sure they had routed out all the outlaws from the forest. He'd have Celeste search from above. She circled close to the tops of trees. Then he saw them. Kiera and Jordan were sitting together near a stream. Alone.

CHAPTER IV

Kiera stormed off the field. In long strides she climbed up the stairs to the Great hall where many people stopped to look at the unusual woman, dressed in a man's hauberk.

She entered her chambers and slammed the door behind her. She began to pace around the room. Her anger grew with each step.

"Who does he think he is," she said aloud? "Just because I'm not one of his mealy mouth little wenches, who swoon at his every word, doesn't mean I don't know how to be a woman."

She paced back to the window and watched the activity below. "When have you ever been a woman Kiera?" She asked herself. "Would you really know how to be one?"

Walking over to the table she reached for a goblet of water. The cup trembled. She quickly drew her hand away. "Control Kiera," she told herself. But she couldn't push her anger away. She felt the energy start to rise around her. She had to get it under control before something happened. She picked up the cup with shaky hands and drank the water, seeking to quench her rage, and the energy that rose around her. She closed her eyes. Her anger hadn't flared in months.

Since she was a child, she had known she was different. She had always had the power to heal people. But the power of energy had come a few years ago. It would only manifest itself through strong emotion.

Like the time they stopped in a small village to pick up supplies. As they walked through the village, Kiera noticed the people staring and pointing at her. She was used to this. It was her attire as a fighter, not to mention the fact that she towered over most women. She tried to ignore them, but everywhere she turned people were watching her. She turned to Marcus. He gave her a reassuring smile.

She heard a shout from somewhere in the crowd. Emerging in front of them was a little man in priest robes shouting at them. He came through the crowd to stand at the top of the stairs of a small church in the middle of the market place and called her an abomination against God. Her purpose in life was to be a servant his servant and to bear children. People started gathering, looking at her with angry faces.

"She has been taken in by the devil!" He shouted as he pointed a finger at Marcus. Men started yelling and shaking their fist at the three of them. A man from the crowed threw a clod of dirt, hitting Marcus square in the chest. The three of them drew their swords. They stood back to back as the crowed began to circle around them. Kiera's anger began to rise at the injustice.

"Silence little man!" Marcus shouted. The crowd gasped, then became silent.

"You dare to speak to a man of the cloth in this manner!"

"You are not a man of the cloth. You are a small minded little hypocrite, who uses your position for his own gain. You are a coward hiding behind your robes. Objecting to something, or someone, who may be different, because you're afraid they may see you for what you really are."

The priest turned red with indignation, stamping his foot, "Devil's spawn! He shouted, "You are the devil's agent sent here to confuse these good people as to the purpose of men and women." Pointing a finger at Kiera, "Child, come with me now and I'll show you the ways of women. Leave this devil, forsake him now, I'll show you your true purpose in life."

Kiera's anger rose to a fevered pitch. "Marcus is not the devil," she shouted, "you are!" The air charged around her. The wooden stairs to the church began to shake. The priest looked down desperately trying to keep his balance. He looked back at Kiera, his eyes filled with fear.

"Witch!" He shouted at her, "Burn her she is a witch!"

Just then the stairs collapsed. The priest climbed out of the rubble, "Burn her. Burn them all!" He shouted.

Jordan grabbed Kiera by the arm, "Run!" He shouted swinging his sword, parting the crowd.

Putting her sword back in its sheath, she did as Jordan said. All of her anger gone by the surprise of seeing the church stairs crumble. They ran to their horses and charged out of the village. They didn't stop until they were sure they were safely away.

Her thoughts came back to the present. She had to get herself under control.

She ran to the stables to saddle Snow. Fortunately, there was no one there. Walking through the stables, the straps and buckles banged against the stable walls. Horses whinnied feeling the energy around them. Kiera tried desperately to keep herself in check. She knew that only the exertion from a ride on her horse would do it. Rarely had she been so aware of her emotions If only she could be more like Erik, she thought, nothing bothered him, he was as cold as the steel in his sword.

"Damn his eyes!" She said aloud as she tightened the girth strap on Snow's saddle. Snow let out a snort in response. She realized she was being harsh and stroked his neck in apology.

Leading him out of his stall she mounted, and with a shout signaled him into a gallop out of the stables. As soon as they were through the palisade gate she gave him his head. Lowering her body, she and her horse moved as one. A few miles away, her mind began to ease and she started to feel the exhilaration of the ride. The wind whipped through her hair making it come undone. Her heart raced as the ground sped beneath them.

She let Snow run a little longer then slowed him to a trot then a walk. She dismounted and walked him to a nearby stream and sat next to him as he drank his fill. Her anger finally cooled. She was able to keep her temper under control and stay strong. Her mind eased. "I don't know what happened, Snow," she said. "He isn't like any other man I've encountered." She threw a stone into the stream."

The horse moved closer to her nibbling on blades of grass. She reached out and stroked his forehead. "So many years I've tried to make men take me seriously. Today I could almost feel their respect when they watched me fight him. Then my foot caught in that rut." She shook her head, "Next thing I know he was kissing me." She threw another stone into the stream, and watched the ripples in the water grow wider. "Well, it just undermined everything I was trying to do!" Rising she stood next to Snow stroking his neck. "Then to ask me if I can be a real woman." She sighed, "I know who, and what I am. No one has to tell me. And I'll not apologize to anyone for it. I won't become something I'm not just because his lordship wishes it."

She heard someone approaching threw the trees. She turned quickly, hand on the hilt of her sword, but it was Jordan. She should have known. Whenever her feelings were in turmoil he was there always there to comfort her.

She smiled as he approached.

"I see you are feeling better," he said as he dismounted.

"Yes, I just needed to get away for a while to think."

"Have you resolved anything?"

"Not really."

"Is there anything I can do to help?" He led his horse to the stream.

"I don't know. Why do you think Lord Erik treats me the way he does?"

"Kiera, you're a lady," he said, "You're the Lady of Dunsmore Castle.

"Yes, but he doesn't know that. No one knows that except you and Marcus."

"Kiera, you are a beautiful woman, any man who is not blind can see that."

"But most men ignore me, or are offended by my appearance."

"That is only because you scare them," he said with a smile. She was not smiling back. He let out a long sigh. "I don't know what is on the man's mind. He is very difficult to read," he said, pulling on a blade of grass. "Just be very careful around him. And don't make any more wagers. I don't want to see you get hurt. We don't know the man's purpose, but ours is very clear. We must seek the aid of Dominick and his brother Randolph to defeat the Dragon before he finds, and destroys us."

"I know."

"The Dragon seems always to be just one step behind us," he said.

"I know, but somehow I feel safe here. I don't think Lord Erik will let harm come to us."

"Don't be lulled, Kiera. The Dragon has many spies, in many places. He has proven that time and time again, and we have just narrowly escaped." He threw blades of grass toward the stream.

"But it feels different this time and..."

Jordan quickly grabbed Kiera by the shoulders, pulling her around to face him. "Please, Kiera, please," he said, "don't do this. You must keep your guard up at all times. Keep your eyes open and your purpose clear, for all our sakes."

She placed her hand on his. Looking back into his eyes, "I will. I promise, I will."

He pulled her up from the ground, "I know you will," he said kissing her gently on the forehead.

Just then they heard a team of horses break through the trees. Both had their hands on their sword. Looking up they saw Erik riding with a group of his men. His face was a stone mask that made her wary.

"Enjoying the scenery?" He said looking from one to the other.

Kiera didn't miss the contrast between the look on his face and the light friendly voice.

"Yes, as a matter of fact we are," Jordan said. "Alastair lands are beautiful." He stepped slightly in front of Kiera, when he noticed Erik hadn't taken his eyes off her.

"Yes, they're beautiful," he said still using the deceptively light tone. "But they're also very dangerous," making full eye contact with Jordan. "There are many enemies crawling around in these woods."

"We'll be sure to be careful," Jordan said.

Erik stared at him for a long moment, "Jordan would you be so good as to accompany my men," he said, shifting in his saddle. "There was a band of outlaws spotted just to the east of here. We could use a good swordsman such as you."

"Certainly my lord," he said, reaching for Kiera, "I'll just see Kiera safely back to Alastair."

"I'll see to her safety." The expression on his face brooked no argument.

Jordan stepped toward Erik, glaring into his face. "As I'm your guest, I'll be happy to accompany your men," he said placing his hand on the hilt of his sword. "And I entrust Kiera's safety into your hands. But if anything, anything at all, should happen to her I'll take exception and you and I will cross swords."

She saw Erik silently accepted Jordan's challenge. He sat on his horse looking down at him with eyes that would make most men tremble, but not Jordan, his purpose was clear. Kiera felt the tension between them. To avoid conflict she stepped between the two men, "Maybe I can be of some help my lord. I could also go with your men to look for this band of outlaws."

"That won't be necessary. I'm sure Jordan and my men are quite capable of handling this matter. Besides my sister and her husband have arrived, and I wish for you to meet them."

"Very well." She turned to Jordan reaching for his hand and squeezed it, "I'll not forget."

He squeezed her hand in return, then turned and mounted his horse.

Jordan looked back at Erik before placing his helmet on his head, then turned and led Erik's men away.

Kiera went to mount her horse.

Erik stopped her. "Wait, my horse needs water." He led his horse to the stream.

Kiera looked at the scenery around her. Jordan was right, for this was a beautiful place.

"Are you and Jordan lovers?" He said. His voice was like cold steel.

Kiera was so taken back she could only answer honestly, "No! We're friends. I owe Jordan my life."

"So you repay him with your body?"

So surprised, Kiera didn't even think about what she was doing. In a flash she took her dagger out of her boot and held the point to Erik's throat. "Don't cast dispersions on Jordan or me," she said, moving in closer. "I saved your life, don't force me to take it away."

The anger left his eyes and a smile grew across his face. Carefully, he nodded his head as he held up his arms in surrender. Forgive me, that was out of character and I do apologize for the slight. Your relationship with Jordan is none of my affair. Kiera placed the dagger back in her boot. As soon as it was safely tucked away, Erik attacked. Placing one foot behind hers, he forced her to the ground.

"No one holds a dagger to my throat," he said through gritted teeth.

She punched him in the stomach and forced him to expel the air from his lungs. It gave her the chance to slip out from under him. He was up on his feet grabbing her from behind. Another jab to his ribcage and he let go. Her training kicked in. He ducked her blows to the head, but she landed one hard on his shoulder. Erik gave as much as he got, and the two were in full hand to hand combat.

Kiera struggled to stay on her feet. Unexpectedly, she found herself in a bear hug she couldn't get out of.

"Hold, Kiera," he said softly in her ear. "This need not continue."

"Fine, then let me go."

As soon as his arms dropped to his sides she used leverage to push him to the ground. Lightning fast she was sitting on his chest and pressed her lips to his. He responded by returning the kiss. It was strong and feral and her heart pounded in her ears as the kiss deepened. She had never been kissed before, but instinct took over as her tongue dueled with his.

With great difficulty she pulled away and rose to her feet. "There should be no doubt now that I know how to be a woman. Too bad we didn't have an audience, as we did on your training field. Maybe your men would see me differently." She offered a hand to Erik and pulled him off the ground.

"Perhaps," he said brushing dead leaves from his clothes. "I concede that you have won this fight with a flaring finish." He gave her a courtly bow. "You're a fine warrior, Kiera."

With that said he mounted his horse. "My sister will be most impressed with you." Without a backward glance he rode through the trees.

She mounted her horse and followed him back to the Keep.

CHAPTER V

Reaching Alastair Keep, Erik dismounted his horse. This time he didn't help Kiera down from hers. She felt strangely disappointed.

"You may want to freshen up before meeting my sister, and her husband," he said taking in her appearance. She looked down at herself, not realizing until that moment she was still in her hauberk and her hair had come undone during her wild ride, "Yes, I should go clean up."

"I'll be waiting for you in the Great Hall." He pointed in the direction of a side entrance, "If you go through that door, there is a flight of stairs that will lead you to your chambers. I'll send Alice to help you." He had that same cold detached expression on his face that had become so familiar.

Kiera felt a tightening inside her chest. "That won't be necessary, I can take care of it myself," she said, raising her chin defiantly.

Turning she walked toward the entrance, not looking back. As soon as she was sure he couldn't see her, she ran up the stairs and into her chambers, as if the very devil himself were chasing her. Leaning back against the door, Kiera took deep breaths to ease the ache inside her. The sooner she and her friends were away from Alastair Keep, the better. But for now she would just keep her distance from the Lord of Ice.

Her head fell back against the door. She wouldn't allow herself to stray from her purpose, as she promised Jordan. She would seek Dominick's help, and move on.

Hoping to clear her mind, she walked to the washbasin and splashed water on her face. She changed out of her hauberk, putting on the soft white tunic she wore the night before. She combed and braided her hair loosely down her back. Sheathing her sword at her side, she was ready to meet Erik and his family in the Great Hall.

With her purpose clear in her mind she felt confident again. She would stay as far away from Erik as she possibly could. This way she would stay in control.

As she approached the Hall, she felt a hand grab her arm, spinning her around. Kiera was immediately defensive, jerking her arm out of the man's grip. She recognized him from the crowd of men who watched her mock battle with Erik earlier. He was a stocky man that reminded her of a small bull. He had no neck, bulky arms, and a wide girth. His height was only a couple of inches taller than hers. When she looked into his face, she saw contempt.

"Nice little show you put on," he said with a sneer.

"What do you want," she said impatiently, clenching her fists at her sides. This was not unlike other confrontations she'd had. But after today, she was in no mood.

"Maybe I want to make the same wager as his lordship."

"No thank you, I'm not interested." She turned to walk away.

Again he grabbed her by the arm, turning her around. Kiera clenched her teeth, trying to keep rein on her temper.

"Why not? You seemed pretty eager to accept his lordship's challenge. Maybe you think I'm not good enough. If you set your sights for him, you are wasting your time. He'd have nothing to do with the likes of you. You are just a common whore bedding down with that old man and his young buck."

Kiera drew her sword. "Shut your mouth, before I shut it for you."

The man drew his sword. "When I'm through with you, you'll know what it's like to have a real man in your bed."

Kiera swung first, high and hard. The man barely had time to stop the blow. With the swiftness of a cat, she swung her sword as she shifted her weight on the balls of her feet, pivoting so she could attack him from first one side and then the other side, testing for weaknesses. He could barely keep up. After a few minutes he was breathing hard, and staggering with her every blow.

Out of the corner of her eye, she saw a woman standing nearby watching her. Kiera didn't have time to think about her. She was too busy trying to dispose of this worm. She was making short work of him. She moved in close enough to kick him in the groin, knocking him to the ground. She was about to make him eat his words, when she heard, "Hold!"

She turned to see Erik standing there, with his hands on his hips. The same woman Kiera had seen out of the corner of her eye was standing beside him. Next to her was a man who looked to be about the same height as Erik, with a slightly smaller build. He was smiling down at her.

Kiera raised her sword away from the man's chest. She had no intention of killing him, just make him think twice before challenging her again.

"What's going on here?" Erik asked.

"She attacked me my lord," the man whined.

Kiera said nothing in her defense. She was sure she would be thrown out of Alastair Keep now. This vermin would see to that.

"She attacked me, and tried to take my head off."

The woman that stood next to Erik stepped forward. She moved with a grace and confidence befitting a Lady. She was small next to him. Her hair like spun gold, her eyes were the color of Amber. Kiera froze. This was Erik's sister. She couldn't mistake those eyes. She wished the ground would open up and swallow her whole. If Erik wanted her to make an impression, she was sure she had.

Erik's sister touched his sleeve. "Don't believe anything Olaf says." She turned toward Olaf who was picking himself up off the floor.

"He said the most vial things to her." She looked back at Kiera "She was provoked," she said.

Kiera was so surprised by the woman coming to her defense, she stood there speechless.

"What kind of things did he say," Erik asked. His tone was deadly. Olaf took a step back.

"It's not for a lady to repeat," Erik's sister said.

"Say it anyway, Bella," he said turning back to her. His expression brooked no argument.

She didn't hesitate. "Something about her being eager to accept your challenge. And about her bedding the old man, and his young buck." Erik visibly stiffened. Isabella continued. "He also said something about showing her what a real man was." When she finished she glared at Olaf.

"My lord, everyone knows she travels with two men, who are not her kin. She dresses like a man, showing off them legs of hers. She is nothing but a common whore."

Those were his last words when Erik planted his fist into the man's jaw. Olaf fell to the floor with the force of it. Kiera jumped out of the way.

"Guards!" Erik shouted. Two men came running. Olaf, still groggy from the blow, lay there moaning. "Take this scum out and have him flogged," he said.

Kiera finally found her voice. "No!" she declared.

"Kiera you are a guest in my home. I'll not tolerate this kind of talk about you." He gestured to the guards. "Pick him up and take him outside. I'll deal with him myself."

"No, wait!" She said trying to hold the guards back. "This is your fault Erik."

For the first time Erik's eyes lightened with surprise. He crossed his arms in front of him. "Tell me how this is my fault."

"You challenged me for a kiss."

Erik's sister turned quickly to look at him. The man next to her leaned one shoulder against the wall, grinning like a cat.

"I seem to remember, you agreed to that wager."

"Yes, well I guess it was my mistake too." Raising an eyebrow he waited for her to continue. "But you kissed me in front of your men. What did you expect to happen?"

He thought for a moment, she could see the questions his sister had, and was about to ask, when he raised his hand to stop her. He looked over to the man leaning on the wall. He was smiling, waiting to hear Erik's explanation. Erik gave him a warning glance, daring him to say a word.

"I guess I should have taken my victory a little more privately, but that is no excuse for Olaf to insult you. He shall be dealt with accordingly."

"Please Lord Erik, as you can see, I have seen to my own honor. I have beaten him fairly, and soundly. He will think twice before insulting me or any woman again."

Erik looked at the man for some time. "Olaf, until further notice, you'll be working in the kitchen."

"But my lord, that's a woman's place."

"Exactly, you have insulted a woman, and have been beaten by one. You shall work like one. Be grateful she came to your aid, or you would now be at the wrong end of a whip." He nodded to the guards. "Take him to the kitchen, and make sure the cook explains his new duties."

Olaf was shouting and sputtering as the guards took him away, laughing at his antics.

Erik and Kiera studied each other warily, until they heard someone clear their throat.

Her demand for attention acknowledged, he slipped his hand through hers and pulled her forward. "Kiera, I would like you to meet my sister, Isabella and her husband Ian."

Isabella came forward to take Kiera's hand. "It's such a pleasure to meet you," she said sincerely. "Arelia told me about you and what you did for my brother. I'm greatly indebted to you."

Kiera held her hand in return, never in her life has she had unconditional acceptance. "I apologize for meeting you under such circumstances."

Isabella waved her hand in dismissal. "Nonsense, it was quite entertaining. Olaf is such a bore. I never liked him anyway," she said smiling.

Ian stepped forward. He was a handsome man with a close clipped beard, dark brown hair, and smiling hazel eyes. Taking Kiera's hand, he placed a kiss on the back of it. She was too stunned to say anything. Erik glared at him. "Well done, my dear. It's about time someone knocked some sense into that ox." He put his arm around his wife. "Where did you learn to fight like that?"

"My friend Marcus, and his son Jordan."

"Remind me to talk to them about training some of my own men."

Erik stood next to Kiera. "Shall we go into the Great Hall? We can talk there."

Wine and cheese were brought in as the four of them sat down.

"Kiera and her friends are here waiting for Lord Dominick and Randolph to arrive," Erik said.

"What is it you want from Dominick?" Ian asked, as he popped a piece of cheese in his mouth.

"It's of a personal nature," Kiera said. Not willing to discuss it, she changed the subject. "How was your trip? The weather seems to be holding up. Marcus says it won't be for long. He says his joints are achy. That usually means rain." Her voice was high, and notably out of character.

Ian and Erik looked at each other, knowing she clearly didn't want to talk about her need to meet with Dominick and his brother. It made them both suspicious.

"Did you know Dominick has a wife and son?" Ian asked, not allowing her to stray from the subject, and making clear any romantic involvement with the Lord of Godwin would be out of the question.

"Yes, I know of his wife, and son," she said softly.

Ever since she was a child she'd heard stories of the two brothers, Dominick the Immortal, and his brother Randolph the Black Knight. In her travels, she would search for anyone who may have seen the two. Everywhere she went, there were always rumors, and stories, about the two great warriors.

The greatest one was of how Dominick got his name 'The Immortal'. She heard that the Turks during the holy wars had captured him. He was tortured beyond human endurance. Yet he survived.

Randolph, upon hearing of his brother's capture, led a rescue party. Finding Dominick barely alive, he was so incensed by his brother's condition, he ordered his men to kill everyone who lived in the palace. The walls were torn down, and nothing was left standing.

Dominick survived his ordeal in the Turkish prison, and many more battles after that. He and his brother were undefeated in tournaments. People began to believe he couldn't be killed. So he became known as Dominick the Immortal.

She heard that despite being born bastards, King William made Dominick a Baron, giving him Godwin Lands for his loyalty, and his ability to command armies. Randolph wishing to stay at his brother's side was given a considerable sum in gold.

For a long time she had heard nothing of the two brothers, until last year she heard Dominick was married, and had a son.

"Are you also a friend to Lord Dominick?" Kiera asked.

We are related by marriage. He is married to my cousin, and yes, he too is my friend."

"How long will you be staying at Alastair?" Isabella asked.

"I'm not sure, as long as it takes to talk with Lord Dominick."

"You must stay for the Spring Festival," Isabella said warmly. "People from all around come. We have been celebrating it as long as I can remember."

"We shall see." She was not sure if Erik wanted her to stay longer than was necessary. She could feel his eyes on her. She felt uncomfortable under his scrutiny. After today, he would probably like nothing better than to have her gone from here.

Isabella elbowed her brother in the side. She wasn't at all sure whether he heard any of the conversation. He looked down at her. "Wouldn't you like to have Kiera here for the celebration Erik?"

"Yes of course. I have already asked her to stay." He turned back to Kiera. "You must stay for the festival." Rising from his chair he said "if you would excuse me, I have some matters I have to attend to. I'll see you at the evening meal." He bent down, kissed his sister's cheek and left the hall.

"I'll go and see about the horses, and make sure everything is settled in for our stay," Ian said. Rising from the table, he took Kiera's hand, bending over it slightly, "It was a pleasure meeting you Kiera. I look forward to seeing you this evening." He bent down and kissed his wife firmly on the lips. Isabella blushed.

Uncomfortable, Kiera looked down at her hands. Erik left the room without giving her a backward glance.

"Kiera, I hope you don't mind me asking you to stay for a while here at Alastair Keep, but this place is much too dominated by men. It's nice to have another woman around."

Kiera smiled, never before had a woman approached her for companionship. "But you have your aunt, and soon the Lady of Godwin will be here."

"Yes I know. Lady Eleanor is a dear friend. You'll most certainly like her. She is a straightforward person. You know where you stand with her, right from the start."

"That sounds a little frightening." Kiera said raising her eyebrows.

"It can be, but if you are just as straightforward with her, she will be a friend for life."

"Isabella, you're not blind. The way I dress, and the fact that I carry a sword, is offensive to most people. So I don't have much hope for Lady Eleanor ever liking me."

"Nonsense, I like you," she said straightening in her chair, "I know Ian likes you and my brother likes you."

"I'm not so sure about that." Kiera said shrugging her shoulders.

"Really? Then what was the kiss all about?" It was Kiera's turn to blush. "See, besides, he wouldn't have asked you to stay for the festival."

"He did that because you prodded him to."

Isabella leaned forward across the table, capturing Kiera's eyes. "One thing you have to know about my brother. He never does anything he doesn't want to do."

Kiera kept silent. Isabella leaned back into her chair. "Yes, Lady Eleanor will like you, and the rest, "she said flipping her hand in the air in a gesture of dismissal, "they're of no importance."

Both women laughed. Kiera had never had a female friend. It felt good to laugh and talk with another woman. She felt she could be herself around Isabella, not always be on guard.

They talked awhile more. Later, Isabella looked out the window and said, "I didn't realize it was getting so late. I better see what mess the chambermaid has made of our cloths, but I'll see you at the evening meal." She stood to walk out of the hall, then turning around she said, "I really am glad you are here, Kiera."

"Thank you," was all was all she managed to say.

Powers Of The Heart

CHAPTER VI

Ian caught up with Erik near the stables, obviously anxious to talk to him about the unusual woman staying at Alastair Keep. "You know when I heard Arelia talking about a woman coming to your rescue I thought it was just another one of her stories. But after seeing her fight, I believe it. She is quite a fighter."

"I know," he said. "She's better than most of my soldiers." He sighed, looking toward the training field. "She wasn't so easy to beat this morning. I should have known. The bandit that felt her steel yesterday knew. Next time I won't take her so lightly."

"Will there be a next time?" Ian asked. Erik saw the smirk on Ian's face and chose to ignore it.

"Are you having a lot of trouble with outlaws?"

"On and off," he said leaning on a fence, "As soon as the weather breaks they seem to climb out from under their rocks. I sent a patrol out this afternoon with one of Kiera's friends."

"Can he be trusted?"

"We'll know soon enough."

"What do you know about the three of them?"

"About as much as you do. They're evasive about where they come from, or where they're headed. Kiera refuses to tell me her business with Dominick. Other than their fighting skills I don't know anything."

"What do you suspect?" Ian asked.

"I can't tell, they're a mystery. Kiera, even with her fighting skills is very protected by her two companions. She's running away from something or someone. He ran his hand through his hair. "One thing is for certain, we'll know soon enough what they're all about. That's why I'm glad you're here. If they try to hurt Dominick, or Randolph, we'll be able to intervene. And God help them if they try."

"While they've been here have there been any signs of treachery?"

"I only met them yesterday, it's too early to tell, but my people are watching them. I only wish I knew more."

Erik admitted to himself that that wasn't entirely true. He knew of Kiera's powers of healing. His promise to her wouldn't permit him to tell his friend. He also knew of her passion. She could be an addiction he could ill afford. He was angry with himself for his attack on her that afternoon, angry for losing his temper and control. He swore it would never happen again.

As if reading his mind Ian asked, "What the kiss all about?"

He shrugged. "I challenged her on the training field. It was a mistake I hope I'll not regret." He watched the men work on the training field.

"Was it good?" Ian asked, grinning from ear to ear.

Erik smiled back for the first time since they arrived. "It was sweeter than the nectar of a peach."

Erik watched the training field and saw Jordan carrying a heavy beam across his shoulders as he walked across the field. Silently he was impressed.

"God almighty! That man's strong." Ian said.

"Yes he is. I think I might have to add it to the training of my men." Erik clapped his friend on the back, "Come and see my new stallion. Unfortunately he's somewhat mean spirited. I have tried to reach him several times, but he continues to fight me."

"I don't recall you ever having a problem before. Losing your touch?" Ian said smugly.

Erik smiled, "It happens from time to time with an animal that's been abused. It takes some time to gain their trust."

"You talk of them as if they're human."

"They have feelings just as humans do, they just can't express them as we do. Now come see the great beast, and help me choose a name for him." As they started walking toward the stables, Erik saw Marcus headed toward them. He didn't look happy and Erik knew why.

"Marcus I would like you to meet a friend of mine, this is Lord Ian of Winfield, it's just south of Alastair."

Marcus bowed slightly, "My Lord."

"It's a pleasure to meet you Marcus. I see you training your son. It's quite impressive."

"Thank you, my lord." Marcus said, never taking his eyes off of Erik."

"I saw a display of your training when your pupil Kiera trounced one of Erik's soldiers this afternoon."

"I was just coming to talk to Lord Erik about that very same thing. May I have a private word with you my lord?"

"Ian why don't you check out the new stallion, I'll be with you in a moment."

As Ian walked away Erik turned toward Marcus. "Now what is it you have to say to me, or is it something I already know?"

"I'm sure you know what I'm about to say."

"Yes, you want to talk about this morning." Erik slapped his gauntlets on the side of his leg. "Marcus I regret my public display with Kiera, it was not in good judgment. I'll deal with any man harshly who tries to take advantage of her because of it. Hopefully Olaf will set the example. If not they will be dealt with more severely. I won't allow Kiera to be insulted again."

"But you don't apologize for the wager;" Marcus asked crossing his arms.

Erik's put on a mask of indifference. "No, I don't apologize for the wager."

Marcus' shoulders straightened. "Can you give me assurance that it will never happen again?"

Erik's eyes were hard. "I'll never make a wager of that kind with her again."

"Remember what I told you last night. Kiera is an innocent and will remain that way as long as she is under my protection. I won't allow any harm come to her."

"Marcus, I mean Kiera no harm, but you seem to be blind to one thing. Kiera is a woman, not just a warrior. She may have feelings you're unaware of. Maybe you should try explaining to her about a man and a woman. She may be confused by things she's feeling."

"And how would you know that?" Marcus said indignantly.

Erik remembered her response to him, and then the fear in her eyes, not understanding what she was feeling. "It's just an observation," he said, as he looked toward the stables.

Just then they heard the scream of a horse, then men shouting. Erik and Marcus ran toward the stables. A man shouted "My lord please, come hurry it's Lord Ian." Erik and Marcus ran to the stables, where they found Ian on the ground, his face contorted and sweating from pain.

"My leg, I think it's broken."

Erik kneeled next to him. He felt a sickening lump rise in his throat. The leg was indeed broken. It was twisted in an odd angle, and there were bloody patches on the fabric around the knee. Erik's mind raced as he fought down the desperation. His friend could be crippled from this kind of injury. He looked up at Marcus, "Bring Kiera to my sister's chambers."

In that moment, Marcus knew that Erik had knowledge of Kiera's powers. But Marcus didn't hesitate. He ran out of the stables and into the Keep.

Erik picked up his friend as gently as he could, wincing when Ian cried out in pain. "Hold on my friend." Erik said softly. He carried him to his chambers. He burst through the door with Ian cradled in his arms. Isabella turned when she heard the commotion at the door.

"My God! What has happened?" She ran over to the bed as Erik gently laid him down.

"It was my own ignorant fault," Ian said breathlessly. "I got behind the horse to check his hindquarters, not thinking, and he kicked me." Looking up at Erik with a grim smile, full of pain, "I know what we should call the horse now."

"What?" Erik smiled sympathetically at his friend.

"Lucifer!" Ian grabbed his leg in agony.

Isabella held Ian's hand. Tears ran down her face.

"Don't cry my love, it probably isn't that serious," Ian said.

Erik tore away Ian's pant leg to see that the bone was protruding out the side of his leg and there was a considerable amount of blood seeping around his knee. Erik feared for his friend's life, he was becoming increasingly pale. Ian clasped Erik's arm. Erik held his friend tight, foolishly hoping it would help ease his pain.

Kiera and Marcus came into the room. Erik took her away from the others. "I need you Kiera, I know I promised you that I wouldn't say anything, but I can't allow my friend to suffer, when I know you can help him."

For the first time Kiera saw the vulnerability in Erik's face. He was pleading for his friend. She couldn't deny him. She touched his hand, "Send everyone out of the room."

He did as she asked, with the exception of his sister, who refused to leave her husband's side. Kiera didn't argue. She knew Isabella wouldn't betray her.

She looked toward Erik and Marcus. "I need to straighten his leg first. You'll have to hold him down, while I do it." She looked down at Isabella who was still holding her husband's hand. "You have to let him go."

"I can't," she cried.

"You must," Kiera insisted. "I can't help him if you don't."

Hesitantly she stepped away. "What are you going to do?"

Kiera stepped over to her. She towered over the girl, holding her shoulders, "You can't tell anyone what I'm about to do... promise me."

Isabella was confused, she looked over to Erik, and he nodded. She looked back to Kiera, "I promise."

"Good." Kiera went back over to the bed. Erik and Marcus were on either side. She nodded to them. They bent over Ian, each holding down a shoulder and arm.

She tenderly touched his face, looking into his eyes. "Ian this part is going to hurt, but soon you'll feel the pain go away."

Ian could only nod. She moved down to his leg, placing her hands firmly around it she worked it into place. Ian screamed, nearly losing consciousness, but he held on.

Marcus and Erik stepped away. Kiera held his leg. She fell to the floor with the impact of his pain pouring through her senses, yet her hands held steady.

Erik went to her aid but Marcus held him back. "Don't touch her. You may kill them both." Endless minutes passed. Finally Ian's color started coming back.

Erik watched Kiera's face. She was pale, beads of sweat formed on her brow. He looked up at Marcus. He too, was watching with concern.

Kiera finally let go of Ian's leg. "God's Blood! What just happened?" Ian gasped.

"Your leg is healed." Kiera said wearily.

"How is that possible?" He moved it back and forth.

"I don't know" she answered honestly. "Just promise that you won't tell anyone of this."

Ian looked to Erik much the same way Isabella did. He looked back into Kiera's tired eyes. "Was it horrible for you?"

She wanted to say, "As horrible as it was for you," but she didn't. "No," she said quietly.

Ian held her hand and pressed it to his lips. "Thank you, Kiera," he whispered.

Erik saw her face blushed with embarrassed by Ian's show of affection.

"Just do me a favor, stay in this bed till morning, then walk around with a limp for the next couple of days."

Understanding her meaning, "I will."

Kiera started to rise, but her knees buckled underneath her. Erik was there to catch her. He held her in his arms, cradling her like a child. "I'll take you to your chambers now. You have had quite enough excitement for one day." He looked back over to Ian and Isabella. "I'll see you two later."

Marcus followed as they left the room. They entered her chambers, and he laid her gently on the bed and removed her boots. He tucked her under the blankets. Marcus watched the tenderness with which Erik handled her.

Erik sat beside her on the bed smoothing her hair from her face. "Thank you." He squeezed her hand. Rising from her bedside, "I'll be back later to check on you."

She nodded, barely able to keep her eyes open.

Erik walked to the chamber door where Marcus was standing. He patted Marcus on the shoulder and left.

--

Marcus stood there for a moment looking down at Kiera. She had grown into a fine woman. He wondered when it had happened. They had been running for so long, he didn't have the time to notice. He looked back at the chamber door. Erik certainly seemed to have noticed. He was right, he should explain how it is between a man and a woman. He taught her how to protect her body, now it was time to teach her how to protect her heart.

Thinking she was asleep, he bent down and kissed her forehead. As he stood up to leave he heard, "I love you Marcus." He smiled, "I love you too dear heart." And walked out of the room.

Downstairs in the Great Hall, Erik was there alone staring into the hearth.

"When did you learn about her healing powers?" Marcus asked.

Erik didn't look up from the fire. "When she rescued me, I had been wounded. She healed me."

"And you didn't say anything to anyone."

"I gave her my word." He said, still staring into the fire.

Marcus admired Erik's integrity. Most men, who knew of her power, wanted to use her for their own gain. Marcus watched him. Erik was a rare man. "Can your friend Ian, and your sister be trusted to keep this secret?" Marcus asked and took a chair beside him.

"I would trust them with my own life," He said with conviction.

They sat quietly for a while until Erik said "Is it always this bad for her?"

"It varies with the type of wound. Sometimes there is no effect at all, but most times when it's serious," he looked down at his hands, "yes it's bad."

"Is she ever afraid to use her powers?"

"Yes, most of the time, but she can't endure someone's suffering, so she puts her fears aside, and does what she knows she has to do." Marcus hesitated a moment considering what he was about to tell Erik, then said, "There is a time when she won't heal a person." Marcus had Erik's full attention, "When a person is close to what she calls the blackness. She's afraid they will take her into the darkness with them."

"I would never allow that to happen."

"I don't believe you would knowingly do it." He turned fully to face Erik. "Lord Erik, I'm not a man used to asking for things, but I ask you for Kiera's sake, don't ask her to heal again. If word should get out, people who don't understand her powers will try to hurt her, and I'm afraid one day, I won't be there to help her."

"Don't worry, I won't ask again."

Marcus was relieved. "Thank you my lord." He rose to leave the hall.

Erik stopped him. "Marcus, I would like you and Jordan on the training field tomorrow. I think that after the beating Olaf suffered today by Kiera, my men have gone soft with the winter. Would you mind helping me whip them into shape?"

Marcus smiled, "It will be my pleasure, my lord."

CHAPTER VII

Kiera woke the next day to the sun shining brightly on her face. It was mid-day. She was shocked to find she had slept so long. Stretching, her eyes moved around the room, to find Erik sleeping in a chair at the foot of her bed.

She watched Erik as he slept. He looked peaceful, and unguarded. The sunlight shone on his long blond hair, making it shimmer like gold. His hard jaw was softer, unlike awake, when it becomes rigid as steel, with his cold emotionless stare. His shoulders were wide, almost as wide as the winged back chair he slept in. His legs were propped up on the foot of her bed. They were long and muscled from years of battle.

He was so unlike other lords she had met. Pampered men who didn't know which end of the sword to hold.

She watched him for several minutes until he opened his eyes, as though he sensed her looking at him. She blushed, when he smiled. "How are you feeling?"

"I'm fine." She looked to the window. "How long have I been asleep?"

Straightening in the chair. "Since yesterday afternoon."

"Good Heavens! Why did you let me sleep so long?"

"You seemed to need the rest."

"How long have you been here?"

"Since last night."

"Last night! My God what will people think?" Putting her hands over her face, rubbing her forehead, "Marcus will kill me."

He rose from his chair. "I came in when everyone was asleep. No one will question my being here at this time of day, especially when I left orders for you not to be disturbed."

"Oh."

There was a light tapping on the door.

Erik walked over to open it. Kiera opened her mouth to stop him, but he was there before she could say anything.

Arelia came into her chambers with a bright smile, holding a tray of food, which made her stomach growl. "How are you feeling, my Dear?" She placed the tray on a table beside the bed.

"I'm fine, just a little tired."

"Well it's to be expected, you had quite a day yesterday."

Kiera looked over to Erik, his expression didn't change. She looked down at the bed covers as disappointment stabbed at her heart. He didn't keep his word about telling anyone of her healing ability. "Then you know," she said softly, looking down at her hands.

Arelia's eyes were filled with compassion. She sat down beside her on the bed, placing her hands on Kiera's. "I know," she said.

Kiera looked into Aurelia's eyes for some sign of condemnation, but she found none.

"Isabella thought it best I should know about what happened yesterday," Arelia said, patting Kiera's hands.

Kiera couldn't help showing her relief. She was happy that it wasn't Erik who had told Arelia about yesterday. He didn't break his word. It made her smile. Then she thought of all the other times when people were afraid of her. She looked back to Arelia, "You're not afraid?"

"No my Dear, I'm not," she held both Kiera's hands in hers, "There is a great deal of evil in this world. Healing people, and taking away their suffering is not one of them."

She felt a tightening in her throat. No one had ever thought of her healing as anything but evil. It was deemed a gift from the devil. She had to look away, she didn't want anyone to see how Aurelia's words affected her.

Drawing Kiera out of herself, "Now eat the soup, it really is very good. I think Olaf missed his calling when he became a soldier. Aurelia looked over to Erik, "Did you get any sleep last night?"

"Some," he said flatly. "I think I'll leave you two ladies alone now. I have things I must attend to," Looking over at Kiera, "You're in good hands. I'll see you at the evening meal." Then made a hasty retreat.

Kiera watched Erik leave, she stared at the door for some time, before Arelia squeezed her hand. She smiled, "Eat your soup Dear, it's really quite good."

Kiera tasted the steamy broth. "It really is good. Are you sure Olaf made it?"

"Yes, he did," she smiled cocking her head to one side, "Strange isn't it?" Kiera chuckled, at the thought of a man, as brutish as Olaf, able to cook such a fine soup. Arelia went around straightening Kiera's chambers. "I'll have more of Olaf's soup sent up."

Kiera laughed, "Don't tell him it's for me, he just may poison it."

Arelia chuckled, "Not if he knows what's good for him." She stopped for a moment. "I think he really enjoys being in the kitchen, even though he makes a lot of grumbling noises about cooking being women's work." She walked over to the bed, kissing Kiera's forehead. "I'll see you in the Great Hall, if you're up to it later."

Kiera was surprised at how natural it felt to have Arelia show her such affection. Erik's aunt was about to leave, when Kiera called out to her.

"Lady Arelia, thank you....for everything."

"Oh no my Dear, it's I who thanks you," she said, then quietly closed the door.

A few minutes later she tried to straighten her white tunic. It was wrinkled from sleeping in it. She looked down and sighed, there was nothing to be done about it. The other one was too dirty from her training yesterday. She would have to make sure it was cleaned by tomorrow, before Lord Dominick of Godwin got to Alastair. It would do no good if she looked like a beggar, instead of a soldier. She felt butterflies in her stomach. The thought of finally meeting Lord Dominick and Sir Randolph after all these years. What if they won't talk to her? She thought. She was sure a woman dressed as a warrior would offend them. Well, she couldn't worry about that. She had come too far, for too long. She would make them talk to her. How? She didn't know yet, but she would.

There was a knock on her door. Isabella stepped in. "May I come in?"

"Certainly," Kiera waved her in.

"Are you terribly upset with me for telling aunt Arelia what you did for Ian yesterday?"

"No," she said shaking her head, "but please don't tell anyone else. It's very important that few people know."

"I promise. It's just that Arelia knows of such things." She sat in a chair beside her. "She has her own kind of powers."

"Her own kind of powers?" Kiera shook her head in confusion, "What do you mean?" she asked.

Isabella thought for a moment, then let out a deep sigh. She leaned forward as though there were someone around to hear her secret. "She gets feelings about people. She says many people are like books, she can read them. She can tell when they're telling the truth, or lying. When Erik and I were children, it was so frustrating. We would get into more trouble for telling a lie than if we told the truth. Aunt Arelia says everyone has some kind of powers. But some are more developed than others."

Kiera sat thoughtfully for a moment. Isabella went on.

"Erik has his own special kind of powers as well," she said. Kiera sat motionless. "Surely you've noticed his closeness to the animals? His hawk, and his horse especially." Kiera shook her head. "He is able to communicate with them. He sees what they see, and feels what they feel."

Kiera thought about the day they met. His hawk and horse acted strangely. She had never seen such loyalty in animals before. She remembered Erik screeching and whistling to the hawk, as if talking to it. She didn't think much about it then. Many people talked to their animals as if they could understand them. She stared into the fire. It made sense to her now. His acceptance of her ability was because he had powers of his own.

Isabella took her hand, misunderstanding her silence. "Don't be afraid of him, Kiera. He's not evil, or a sorcerer, as some people think. He would never hurt you."

She looked back into Isabella's face. "I know that. I know what it's like to be feared by people. I'm not afraid of your brother."

Isabella was relieved. She held Kiera's hand tighter, "I can't thank you enough for helping Ian yesterday." Tears came into her eyes. "I have something I want to give you," Isabella said, as she pulled a bracelet with tiny silver bells on it off her wrist. She placed it into Kiera's hand.

"Oh no, I can't accept this," she protested.

"Please," Isabella said holding Kiera's hand shut, "as a token of our friendship, please take this gift."

She was so moved by Isabella's kindness, she agreed. Isabella took it from Kiera's hand, and put it around her wrist. Kiera looked down at the bracelet. She was amazed at its delicacy. The tiny bells made a soft sound as she moved. "It's beautiful." She looked back up at Isabella. "Thank you."

"You're most welcome." She stopped, as though suddenly remembering. "Oh, and here," she said unfolding a tunic that was sitting on her lap, "This is for you. Erik sent it. It might be a little big but he thought the one you have may need cleaning, so he sent this one for you to wear."

It was a soft wool tunic, black with silver thread embroidered around the neck. It was lovely. Kiera was grateful she didn't have to wear the wrinkled one she had on. "Tell your brother, thank you."

"You can tell him yourself, at the evening meal."

"Good Lord! Don't tell me it's that time already." Kiera looked out her window to see the sun sinking low.

"Well, you needed your rest, and we didn't want to disturb you."

"Yes... but the whole day." Kiera couldn't remember any time, when she had slept for an entire day. Marcus and Jordan must be worried sick. "If you don't mind I'll change right away, and go down with you."

Isabella nodded, but Kiera hesitated. As if reading her mind, Isabella turned her back to her allowing her privacy to change her tunic.

The tunic *was* large on her. She knew it was Erik's because it had his scent on it. Kiera closed her eyes and breathed it in. A wave of excitement went through her belly. She wondered what strange effect Erik had on her. She had to be careful. Being distracted from her purpose could be dangerous to her, and those around her.

A few moments later, Kiera announced she was ready, and the two women went down stairs, where they found everyone waiting.

Kiera saw Ian first walking with a cane. He headed toward her, making a big show with his limp. She blushed as her took her hand and placed a kiss on the back of it. She couldn't get used to such gallantry. He smiled and winked at her. She couldn't help but smile back. He took his wife's hand and led her to the table.

Next Jordan came up to her, putting his hands on her shoulders. He looked into her face for any sign that something might be wrong. "Are you all right?"

"I'm fine, you needn't worry." She placed her hand on his chest to reassure him.

Erik gaze held hers but his face was difficult to read. He walked over to them and took Kiera by the arm in a most proprietary way. She was startled by the firmness of his grip. "There is nothing to worry about. Kiera's fine," he said frostily. He started to walk her to the table, but Jordan put a hand on Erik's shoulder to stop him.

"She should never have done it," he whispered through his teeth.

Erik looked down at Jordan's hand. She didn't miss the icy expression on his face, yet Jordan was undaunted. He moved his hand away and clenched it at his side. "It was either that or let my friend be crippled, or even die."

"What if Kiera died?" Jordan said glaring at Erik.

"I wouldn't have allowed it to go that far. If I thought there was any danger I would have stopped it."

Kiera became angry, for they were talking as if she wasn't there. She pulled away from Erik and glared at both men. She looked over at Jordan, "I'm not a child anymore, Jordan. The decision to heal Lord Ian was mine. I was not forced to do so." Jordan started to protest. Kiera raised her hand to stop him. "I don't need your protection." Kiera could see the anger rise on Jordan's face. He stood there for a long moment staring into her eyes. Then turned and walked away. She felt guilty for snapping at him, but he had to realize she wasn't a little girl any more.

She turned to Erik, still angry for the proprietary way in which he dealt with her friend. "I have told you before, don't talk about me in my presence, as if I'm not there. It's insulting."

His face turned to the familiar stone. "I most humbly apologize.... *my lady*," stressing the last two words with the familiar timelessness in his voice. She stared back at him and was too angry to care. He held out his arm for her. Kiera hesitated a moment. She didn't want to make a scene and took it. They walked with him to the table. He sat her beside him once again.

By the time their meal was finished, Kiera's anger with Erik had cooled. She pulled on the front of the tunic, "Thank you for the loan of your tunic. I'll return it when my others are cleaned."

He took a sip of wine. "It's yours," he said simply.

"Oh, I can't....."

He put his hand on her forearm, "It's yours." His face brooked no argument.

"Thank you," she said, looking into his golden eyes.

"It's my pleasure." He held her gaze captive.

Kiera felt the intensity of his stare. Desperate to get away she saw Arelia and Isabella walking toward the hearth, and decided to join them. "If you'll excuse me." She stood and walked toward them.

For the first time she felt comfortable approaching women. She didn't have to worry about being shunned. They knew and accepted her for who she was.

Erik watched her walk over to his aunt and sister. It gave him great pleasure seeing her in his tunic. He could imagine her in nothing else except his tunic. He felt himself swell. He drank more wine to cool the desire building inside him, but it only made it more palatable. Her hair fell down the middle of her back. He watched the firelight dance across the silken strands. He watched her full red lips move, as she spoke. He imagined them on his body. The tightening was almost unbearable, he closed his eyes, trying to think of something else that would help him with his control.

"If you keep staring at her like that you're going to set her tunic on fire," came a voice from behind him.

Ian was just what he needed for distraction. "I don't know what you are talking about." He took another sip of wine.

"You can't fool me, Erik. I was waiting for her to go up in flames with the intensity your stare." Ian looked over at her. "She is quite beautiful. I can understand your attraction to her."

"She is a guest in my house, and I'm indebted to her, nothing more," Erik said bitingly.

"If you say that a few more times, you might begin to believe it."

Erik gave Ian a cold stare. He was undaunted. "She is very tall, don't you think?" Erik didn't answer. I think she's the tallest woman I have ever seen." Ian leaned one arm on

Erik's shoulder. Erik looked briefly at his friend. He didn't like what he saw.

"Can you imagine those long bare legs wrapped around your waist, and those long arms wrapped around your back, with her hands going down your body to your...."

Erik knew Ian was testing him. "Don't even think about it Ian, for I'd be forced to kill you," he said through clenched teeth.

Ian laughed, slapping Erik on the back, "That's what I thought good friend. Underneath that cool exterior of stone, beats the heart of a normal human being. It's good to know you're mortal just like the rest of us." He got up using his cane and walked over to his wife, kissing her firmly on the lips, to reassure his friend he was very much in love with his wife.

Kiera intrigued him. She was his equal as a warrior like himself. Unlike the mealy mouth maids he had had in the past. Kiera would never allow him to take her for granted. She was extremely independent.

Jordan walked up to her and Erik stiffened. He wanted to rip him away from her. Their familiarity unnerved him. It was a new emotion for him. One he didn't understand. He had met strong women in his past, but no one like her. He would have to keep his emotions in check. He could ill afford to have someone exploit them.

Kiera was restless. She had slept for a full day and couldn't get herself to relax enough to fall asleep. The walls closed in on her. She wasn't used to being inside for such a long time. She decided to go to the top of the tower for fresh air. It was a clear spring night. Only a few clouds marred the glittery sky. There was nearly a full moon. She took a deep breath and sighed at the tranquility of the night.

For the first time she felt safe. She felt at peace. Suddenly she heard a movement behind her.

"It's a beautiful night isn't it?"

Startled from her quiet solitude, she turned around quickly, immediately on the defense.

Erik stood in the shadows.

"Erik! I wasn't expecting anyone up here at this hour," she said. Her voice trembled.

"I'm sorry. I didn't mean to frighten you."

"I wasn't frightened, just surprised."

There was a gap in their conversation as they looked up at the stars. "What were you thinking about?" he said.

"Just about the night, and how beautiful it is," she said, trying to keep her voice calm. Her heart pounded so hard against her ribs, she was sure Erik could hear it beating.

He stood before her, looking at the stars. He looked down at her placing his hands on her shoulders. "You're trembling."

"It's just the chill of the night air."

He rubbed her upper arms, "Is that better?" She could only nod. He was too close to her. Her thoughts began to scatter.

"Yes, thank y...."

Before she could finish, she was in his arms with his lips pressed firmly against hers. She was so stunned that she didn't know how to respond. His lips were warm and soft upon hers she could feel the warmth growing in the pit of her stomach. With his urging, she parted her lips, and let his tongue explore her mouth.

She felt a wave of heat run through her body. He pulled her closer, wrapping her in his arms. She felt the heat of his body, and a moan escaped her lips. He moved her back toward the tower wall, pressing his body against hers. She held him tight not wanting him to let her go.

His mantle wrapped around them both. His hand slowly moved down her side, he didn't want to frighten her. Her kisses became urgent, but he wouldn't be rushed. His ran his hand over her breast. He could feel her nipple peak underneath her tunic. She pressed her breast in to his hand. She wanted more, but he held back, teaching her body how to respond to him.

He held himself back with ironclad control. It took all his strength, but he wouldn't rush her. He could feel the warmth of her hands through his tunic as they traveled down his back. He leaned his body into hers, crushing her between him and the wall. Her hips instinctively moved into his. It was nearly his undoing. He pulled his head away, closing his eyes, remaining in control. His hands moved down to her back and pulled her more fully into him. He heard her moan. Fearing she was frightened, he looked down into her face. He only saw passion in her light blue eyes and it encouraged him further.

He moved his hand under her tunic feeling her naked flesh. Her skin was warm and soft and her stomach was hard and flat. This time she was prepared when his hands moved up to fondle her breasts. She let out another small moan that went past her throat and into Erik's mouth.

He was consumed by passion. He ground his manhood into her woman's flesh. The blood was pounding so loudly in his ears that he barely heard the footsteps climbing the tower stairs. It became clear someone was approaching. Erik quickly removed his hand from under her tunic.

He pressed his lip over her ear, "Someone approaches," and he stepped back.

Kiera stood up straight as the footsteps came closer. It was Marcus.

"I see we all had the same idea about fresh air this evening," Marcus said, clearly studying the couple's face.

"I guess so," Erik said dryly, never taking his eyes off her.

Marcus looked at both of them. "Well Kiera I think we should be getting in. This cold night air may not be good for you after your ordeal yesterday."

Kiera couldn't find her voice. She looked at Erik.

"Yes Kiera, you should go in and get out of this night air," Erik said, knowing if she didn't leave he wouldn't be able to stop himself, and do something they both might regret.

"Yes, I better go," she finally managed to say.

"I'll walk you to your chambers," Marcus said. As he was leading Kiera to the stairs, he looked back at Erik, "Good night to you, my lord."

"Good night."

She only nodded her head then followed Marcus to her chambers.

Erik took in a long drink of the cool night air. His body still ached for her. He opened his mantle to let the night air cool the desire that burned within him. He closed his eyes, her face was before him. Never before has a woman stirred his blood so. He waited until his flesh prickled, and the fire dimmed in his body. Only then did he retire to his chambers.

CHAPTER VIII

Marcus followed Kiera into her chambers. She never looked up at him. "Kiera, please sit down, I would like to talk to you." She sat down in a chair near the hearth. He pulled one in front of her and sat down. "What happened up in the tower?" She started to protest, he raised his hand to stop her. "Don't deny it Kiera. It's written all over your face."

She knew she couldn't lie to him. She could never lie to him. As she looked at him her sight blurred with tears. "Oh Marcus, I don't know what I'm doing, or what I'm feeling. It's all so strange to me. I know I'm supposed to be strong, but when I'm with him I feel weak as a lamb. What's happening to me?"

Marcus kneeled before her and wiped the tears from her face. "Listen Kiera, tell me what happened up there. It's the only way I can protect you."

Kiera sniffed. How could she tell Marcus what happened? He and Jordan have protected her since she was a little girl. If there was any insult to her, they were always there to avenge it. Putting her face in her hands, "Oh Marcus, what have I become?"

Marcus pulled her hands away from her face, "Did he touch you in a way that was improper?"

She could see Marcus' face go red with anger. "I wouldn't know, Marcus, no man has ever touched me before, except in battle." She stood up walking over to the fire. "Yes he touched me." She turned to look back at him. He started to rise out of his chair, but she put her hand up to stop him, "But I wanted him to touch me. I...encouraged him to touch me."

She felt incredible sadness. He came to stand beside her. "What you're feeling is perfectly natural, but it must not be carried too far. There are consequences with such actions. I'll talk to Lord Erik and..."

NO! Marcus, please don't, I promise I'll handle it. I won't let it happen again."

"I'm afraid Lord Erik must be made to understand that you are not a whore to be trifled with."

"Marcus I promise, I won't let it happen again. Please don't say anything to him, it would be too humiliating," she said in desperation. "Tomorrow Lord Dominick and his brother Randolf will be here. We can talk to them about our business and then be on our way. I'm sure we'll never see Lord Erik again." Kiera nearly choked on her last words.

Marcus put his arms around her, offering her comfort. "Everything will be all right, my sweet. I promise."

Kiera pulled back and smiled. She felt an alarm cross her mind. "Marcus, please don't tell Jordan about what happened. I think he'll challenge Erik. I have no desire for anyone to get hurt because of my foolishness."

"I won't say anything. It would serve no purpose."

"Thank you," she sighed.

Marcus watched the sadness cross Kiera's face. He remembered what Erik had said the day before. Pulling her back to her chair, he sat down beside her. "Kiera, never forget that you're a woman. It's just by circumstance that you're a warrior as well. But you are a woman first, and what you're feeling, is a woman's feelings. Being a man I can't explain them to you. But understand that they're normal. I do know that you must not let things get out of hand with Lord Erik. You can't let him go too far." He saw her face redden. He knew she was uncomfortable with the conversation, but he had neglected his duty, as her protector, to tell her the facts between a man and a woman.

"Kiera, I don't wish to embarrass you, but there are things about men and women you should know." He was just as uncomfortable as Kiera was.

Kiera smiled for the first time since their conversation began. "Marcus I know where babies come from, and how it happens."

He sat up straighter, "How do you know?"

"Jordan told me," she chuckled.

"Why that upstart! I'll have his ears for that," he said angrily.

Kiera was still laughing, "I'm sure Jordan just felt I should know."

"Well it isn't decent to be talking about such things with a woman."

"I'm talking about it with you."

"That's different, you're like my daughter."

"And Jordan is like my brother," she said patting his hand. "I'm sure he just wanted to protect me, same as you."

"Well that may be, but he should have told me about it."

"I think he was afraid of your reaction."

"Regardless, I should have known, and I'll have a talk with him about it first thing in the morning." He stood. "Well it's getting late, and I should be letting you get your rest. We have a big day tomorrow. Just think our journey may be near an end."

"With all my heart, I hope so," she said. She gave Marcus a hug. "Thank you Marcus for your concern, I promise, I won't forget what you told me, and I will not forget our purpose here."

Chucking her under the chin, "That's my girl, I know you'll do the right thing," he said before leaving the room.

Kiera looked around her chambers. She suddenly felt very tired, as if a large weight was put on her shoulders. She thought about what Marcus said, she couldn't let what happened between Erik, and her, ever happen again. She must get away, and soon. If the Dragon ever found out where she was, and whom she cared for, he would use them against her. She could never allow that to happen.

Erik heard her scream in his sleep. Then there was a loud thunderclap. He came fully awake. He heard the scream again. In an instant his sword was in his hand and he was through the door, and into the main corridor. He heard the scream again, only this time it seemed to come from the Great Hall. He ran down the stairs, only to see Kiera running out into the night. He called her name, but she didn't seem to hear him. He saw the lightening through the door. He called her name again, but the thunder drowned out the sound of his voice. He ran to the door, but couldn't see where she had gone. Then the lightening lit up the sky, and he saw her running into the bailey. The rain was pouring down, but he didn't hesitate to go after her. He shouted her name again and again, but she didn't turn around. The lightening lit up the sky again, and he could clearly see her. She was wearing only her nightdress. He could hear her screaming. She ran as if the very devil were after her. Erik threw down his sword to give him greater freedom to run and catch her. In a last ditch effort, he lunged forward, bringing her down with him. She screamed fighting him off in desperation.

"Kiera!" he said shaking her, "Kiera! It's me, Erik!"

Her eyes were wild with fear, "No please, please don't hurt me! She begged.

"Hurt you?" The voice he heard was not Kiera's, but that of a child, it made his blood chill. Looking into her face, he realized she was dreaming. He shook her, "Kiera! Wake up, it's me, Erik. No one is going to hurt you!"

Her hands moved frantically over his bare chest, and arms, "Erik! Blood, there is so much blood." Her voice was now her own.   "No Kiera, it's only water." He held her hands, stilling them on his chest.

She looked around her, as though she were looking for something, or someone in the night. "The Dragon. He is coming. He knows where I'm. I have to run. I have to hide." She struggled to get away from him, but he held her tightly.

"There is no one here, Kiera." He held her face in the palms of his hands. "Wake up, I'm here, and you're safe." There was another clap of thunder, Kiera jumped and then he saw her eyes become lucid.

"Erik, what's happening? What are we doing here?"

"You had a nightmare."

He saw recognition in her eyes, the memories of the nightmare came flooding back. She put her hands to her face. She became silent and still. Her knees sank in the mud, as the rain plastered her hair to her face.

He drew her close to him. He felt her body tremble from the cold hard rain that was pelting them both. He stood bringing her with him, and wrapped his arms tightly around her. He walked her back toward the Keep, only stopping to pick up his sword. She buried her head in his shoulder.

Marcus and Arelia were standing at the door as they came in. Arelia held out a large blanket, wrapping them in it as they came through the door. "I'll get you both something to take away the chill."

Marcus walked over to the dying fire in the hearth and added wood to it and in a few minutes it was blazing. Erik walked Kiera to a large chair near the hearth, and pulled her down into his lap. He rubbed her arms, shoulders and back until her trembling subsided. He wrapped the blanket tightly around them, using the heat of his body to warm her.

Kiera was still silent. Erik looked up at Marcus, "How long has she had these nightmares?"

"Since she was a child, but she hasn't had one for some time."

Arelia came back with a steaming cup of cider, handing it to Erik. He looked down at Kiera, her lips were blue from the cold. He put the cup against them and she drank the soothing liquid. He wiped away the water from her face.

"We better get her upstairs, and get her out of those wet clothes before she catches a chill," Arelia said.

Erik agreed with her, even though he was reluctant to let her go. He walked her upstairs to her chambers and sat her near the hearth. He stirred up the coals, and added wood until the fire licked the new logs. He stood next to Marcus.

Arelia carried in more blankets. Seeing the worry on both Marcus and Erik's face, she wanted to reassure them, "She had a bad dream nothing more. I'll stay the night with her, and make sure she's all right." She touched Marcus' shoulder, "She will be all right, I promise."

Marcus nodded, placing his hand over Aurelia's. He gave her a long look then left the room.

Erik stood, watching Kiera. Her head down, her hair in a tangled mess around her shoulders and face. She never looked up at him. He felt helpless.

"Erik, go back to your chamber, and get out of those wet britches, before you catch your death."

Erik's head snapped up, "You'll call me if she needs anything?"

"Yes I will, but it was just a bad dream."

"It was more than a dream, Aurelia. It was a nightmare." Aurelia didn't argue.

He looked back at Kiera, her head still bent, silently staring into the fire. He turned and left the room.

He walked back to his chambers. Stripping out of his wet clothes. He thought of all the things that have happened since she came to Alastair. She came out of nowhere to save his life. She fought better than most warriors. She said that fighting was important to her survival. She wouldn't explain her need to talk with Dominick. She was as jumpy as a cat in the tower, her passionate response to him, and later her haunting nightmare. She was running away from something, hiding something, but what, he didn't know. She was a mystery to him.

Were they fugitives hiding in his Keep? Being kept in the dark made him furious. He felt he had no control of what was going on around him. But soon he would know everything. He pounded his fist into his hand, he swore he would. Tomorrow he would question Arelia, and hear what she thought of them.

CHAPTER IX

Murdock sat tapping his fingers on the arm of his chair as he stared down at the man kneeling before him.

"I found her, my lord." said the little man.

"Where?" His voice was deceptively sweet. The man broke into a sweat. The spy couldn't look into his lord's face.

"She's at Alastair Keep, my lord."

"Have you seen her?"

"Yes. Three days ago I was in the stables, trying to discreetly ask if they had seen a woman traveling with two men. One of the guests was checking out Lord Erik's new stallion. Quite a mean spirited beast. It kicked out as he was checking his hindquarters. I heard the snap my lord. The leg was not only broken but it was twisted and bleeding. Lord Erik came running in with a man behind him, looking like the man you described. Lord Erik bent over his friend. That's when I heard him tell the other man to have Kiera brought to them. I tried staying with them, but once she arrived, everyone was made to leave."

"So you did not actually see her heal this man?"

"No my lord, but the very next day the man was walking with only a crutch, and I know the man's leg was surely broken."

"You are sure it was not merely twisted, or strained?"

"No My Lord, it was broken."

"Was she dressed like a woman or a man?" He felt excitement pump through his veins.

"She was dressed exactly as you told me."

Murdock sat back in his chair smiling, "Good," he said on a long breath. "I want you to go back and keep an eye on them. Report back to me if there are any changes, or if they should leave the Keep."

Murdock came out of his chair, placing his dagger underneath his spy's chin. If you fail me, I'll have your eyes for it, do you understand?"

"Y...yes my lord," the man said trembling.

"Good, now go before your absence becomes suspicious."

The man rose, leaving at a dead run.

Murdock raised his head, and laughed loudly, "She doesn't know it but she's already mine."

Jordan and Marcus met on the training field the next morning. "You look as though you haven't slept all night," Jordan said.

"I haven't," he said simply.

"What's wrong?"

"Kiera had another nightmare last night."

"What! She hasn't had one for a long time."

"I know." Marcus ran his hands through his long gray hair.

"The only time she gets these nightmares is when Murdock or his spies are near." Jordan looked around the training field. "Do you suppose the Dragon knows where we are?"

"At this point anything is possible. Murdock has been just steps behind us. We may have been here too long."

"Surely they couldn't have found us yet? We left no trail."

"It doesn't matter. Murdock has spies everywhere. Quite frankly, I'm surprised we've survived this long."

"What do you intend to do?"

"I'll talk with Lord Erik, see if there is anyone new in his keep."

"He'll ask questions."

"Maybe it's time we confided in him. He may be our best hope for Kiera's safety."

"Father I don't know if he can be trusted. Murdock has many allies. We don't know if Lord Erik is one of them. Besides he used Kiera's powers for his friend, who's to say he won't do it again for his own gain."

"I have found Lord Erik to be an honorable man." He saw Jordan still had his doubts. "Look around you. Do these people look as though their master abuses them?

Jordan shook his head. "No they don't look like oppressed people, but I don't believe we can afford to trust him just yet. Lord Dominick and his brother Randolph will be here today. Maybe it won't be necessary to tell him anything if we can get their help."

Marcus thought for a moment, "Maybe you are right, it won't hurt to wait a few more days In the meantime look for anyone who may be suspicious. Keep your eyes open and leave the kitchen wench alone."

Jordan blushed, "You know about that?"

"I'm assuming that is where you were last night."

Jordan smiled, he could never get anything past his father. "And there is another matter I wish to talk to you about," Marcus said, as he held the steel point on his son's chest. "I understand you told Kiera all about men and women mating, and where babies come from."

Jordan paled, "She told you about that?"

"Aye, she told me about that."

Jordan blushed. "I only told her, to save you the embarrassment, and...and... I thought she should know in case she ran into any trouble," Jordan stammered.

Marcus pressed the point of his sword on Jordan's chest harder, forcing him to step back. "Mm hm...and don't you think I should have been the one to tell her?"

Jordan's shoulders squared. "You always treated her like one of your soldiers, or a child. You never saw her as a woman. I thought it was about time she learned."

This was the second time Marcus had been told he was blind to Kiera's womanhood. Maybe he was, but now his eyes were open and he would never close them to her again. He turned back to Jordan. A wicked smile crossed his face. "I think a nice run in full armor would be good training today."

Jordan just rolled his eyes.

"Maybe it will help you to think about telling me when you share such a secret."

Erik watched as Jordan ran by, acknowledging him with a nod. He walked over to Marcus. "Am I to assume this is part of your training?"

Marcus turned to Erik, "Yes, endurance training."

"Excellent! I'll have my men suit up in their armor and do the same." Erik slapped his gauntlet on the side of his leg. There was an uncomfortable silence between them. Then Erik said, "I would like to talk to you about last night."

"I want to thank you for your care of Kiera last night," Marcus said.

Marcus was deliberately changing the subject, but Erik was not put off, "No thanks are necessary. I want to talk about the nightmare Kiera had. What is she afraid of? Who are you hiding from?"

Marcus looked down on the ground. Erik saw that he was struggling with what he should say. "Lord Erik, I understand your concern, but for the safety of Kiera, and even Alastair Keep, I can't tell you anything at this time."

Erik's amber eyes turned cold. Most men looking into them would run for their lives, but Marcus stood his ground. "In a few day's everything will be revealed. But what I can tell you now is that we don't mean you or your people any harm, and we're not fugitives."

Erik straightened, "This is all you'll tell me?"

"I'm afraid it's all I can tell you now."

Erik studied Marcus' face. By the stubborn set of his jaw he knew Marcus wouldn't tell him anymore. "Very well then, I'll take you at your word." Erik moved in closer to Marcus "But make no mistake if I have been deceived, it will cost your lives."

"I have little doubt, My Lord."

Erik backed away. "In the meantime you are my guests, and I ask if you'll consider training my soldiers while you're here. I would be extremely grateful. They have turned soft over the winter."

"It will be my pleasure." Marcus smiled.

"Good, I'll assemble my men and you can put us through the paces."

"You, as well, my Lord?

"I can't expect to lead my men, if I can't stand beside them in battle." Erik turned and walked away.

A few moments later, Kiera came walking toward Marcus in full armor. She couldn't help notice the smile on Marcus' face. "What happened?"

"I have been asked to train Lord Erik's men."

Kiera patted Marcus on the shoulder. "Don't be easy on them. If my fight with Olaf is any indication of their skill, they need all the training they can get." Kiera was happy for Marcus, for this is what he was born and raised for, to train and lead men.

"Lord Erik is getting his men assembled now." He touched her arm, "Feel up to it?"

"Yes, I feel good," she said.

"I think some training will keep my mind off things." She spotted Jordan running in full armor around the bailey. "Is that Jordan?"

"I felt he needed a little reminder to keep his mouth shut when it comes to information about men and women."

"Marcus, you didn't." Watching him run she could see the anger in his face. He's going to kill me, she thought. She turned back to the Keep hoping there was some way she could make her escape, when she spotted Erik coming down the Great Hall steps, in full armor. Kiera's mouth dropped open, he was magnificent. The armor emphasized his form. He moved with authority, his golden hair shone as brightly as his armor. Kiera felt a tightening in the pit of her stomach.

He walked directly to her. "How are you feeling today?"

Kiera looked up at him, her mouth still hanging open until she felt a nudge from Marcus, "Ah, fine. Fine, thank you. I feel fine."

Marcus rolled his eyes.

"Good, will you be training with us today?"

"Y...yes."

Erik's men came up behind him. "Well I think we're all here, Marcus we are yours to command."

"Good, we will start off with a run in full armor, ten times around the bailey yard then come back here when you're finished."

The men started to groan, but when their master turned to look at them, they silenced immediately. Erik led them off first. Kiera was right behind.

They ran side by side for much of the time. His men were dropping like flies around them, yet Kiera still ran strong. "How about a race?" he said.

Kiera felt she needed to redeem herself after making such a fool of herself when he came out of the Great Hall. "I'm ready when you are."

"Good, when we reach the next wall we will start and finish when we reach Marcus."

"Done."

They came to the next wall at the same time, Kiera turned and pumped her legs in quick strides. Erik was right by her side. She couldn't let him win. This time it meant everything to her to win the race. She pushed herself and increased her speed. She gained slightly. When they turned the next corner, Erik's men were cheering him on, while she saw Isabella, Ian, Marcus and Jordan all encouraging her to run faster. She could feel Erik fast on her heels. She couldn't look back because it would cost her valuable time. She ran as hard as she could right up to Marcus and beyond. She did it! She actually beat him.

Isabella and Ian cheered her victory. "Well done!" Ian shouted. "Well done."

Marcus and Jordan clapped each other on the back, chests puffed out in pride.

Kiera and Erik walked in circles to cool down. Breathing hard, Kiera bent in half to catch her breath. Erik raised his arms in the air, expanding his chest. She gave it a try and noticed that she was able to breathe better. Even with his eased breathing, she could see by the quick rise and fall of his chest that he had not given her the race. Kiera felt an extreme sense of pride.

Still trying to catch his breath, he held out his hand in congratulations. She took it and felt it close around hers. When he didn't release it, she looked into his eyes.

"Well done, but next time it won't be so easy," he said still holding her hand.

Remembering what he said to her on the training field the first morning, she said, "It wasn't so easy." Then she smiled at him.

Those who were watching didn't miss their exchange. Isabella and Ian smiled. Jordan and Marcus worried.

CHAPTER X

Kiera sat in the steaming water of her bath soaking her sore muscles. Marcus had them train the entire morning and part of the afternoon in full armor. She sank further into the tub sighing as the warm water drifted over her shoulders. She smiled contentedly to herself. A few of his men had asked to be paired up with her, even asking her advice. When she looked over at Erik, he seemed to heartily approve. She was delighted that they finally thought of her as an equal, at least on the training field.

As she scrubbed mud off her chin, she grinned despite herself. Jordan had had his revenge. While she was occupied with another soldier, he snuck up behind her, and picked her up and threw her in the nearest pigsty. She was covered in mire. Everyone roared with laughter, with the exception of Erik. Kiera looked up to see his angry amber eyes glaring toward Jordan. He walked over to her and deftly pulled her out of the muck. "May I ask what that was all about?" His cold voice sent a shiver down her back. She quickly tried to smooth it over. "It was just a little revenge for something that happened last night." She tried to brush it off as something unimportant. "A family matter so to speak."

"But you are not family," he said wiping at the muck on her armor.

"Oh, but we are!" she contradicted. "We may not be related by blood but we're a family just the same." She looked back over at Jordan, who was now being berated by his father. "I've told you before, Jordan is like a brother to me."

"A brother, that's all?" he stared into her face intently.

Kiera looked confused. "What do you mean?"

"It's not important." He stepped closer, gently touching her arm. Kiera looked up into his golden eyes. "Would this have anything to do with what happened in the tower?"

Kiera felt the color rise into her face. She couldn't look at him. She looked down at her dirty hands wiping at the mud and only smearing it. She shook her head, "No, it doesn't have anything to do with what happened in the tower."

Clearing her mind she emerged from the tub feeling refreshed. Her skin was flushed from the heat of her bath. The day was warm so there wasn't need for a fire. Drying herself, the medallion she wore around her neck swung into view. Her mother had given it to her when she was a child. Her hand closed around it. "Today mother, today we'll all be together, just like you always wanted," she whispered. She took a deep breath to ease the ache she felt in her chest. How she missed her mother. She remembered her beautiful face. She had warm blue eyes, and hair that shone like honey in the sunlight. She remembered being held in her mother's lap, while told wonderful stories. What would she think of me if she could see me now? Kiera thought. In her heart she knew her mother would love her, no matter what she had become.

She turned to the bed where her white tunic laid cleaned and wrinkle free. She smiled knowing it was Isabella who had seen to its cleaning. Isabella had been seeing to all her needs since Ian's accident. They were becoming great friends. She didn't feel she had to protect, or justify herself. In a short time she was beginning to care about these people. When the time came for her to leave, it would break her heart. But she knew she had to leave soon. They have stayed far too long already. They must leave before Murdock found them. He would destroy the people she cared about if she were found. He must be defeated. She tightened her grip on the medallion. Only with Dominick, and Randolf could it be done. She only hoped she could convince them to help her.

Kiera rubbed the medallion one more time before she dressed, and readied herself for her meeting with Dominick. It wouldn't be long before she would come face to face with the legend of Dominick the Immortal and the Black Knight. His caravan was spotted a mile away from the Keep.

Her stomach tightened with anxiety. She closed her eyes for a moment, saying a silent prayer. Then putting the medallion under her tunic, she went down to the Great Hall.

There was a good deal of commotion by servants readying the hall for its visitors. Erik was waiting for her at the bottom of the stairs.

He pulled her aside, "Kiera, Dominick will be here soon. I would like to ask you to wait with your business until he and his family are settled in."

Kiera felt her anxiety rise. She was about to protest then thought better of it. She saw Erik's logic. It would be best to wait until Dominick was more receptive. She'd waited a long time to meet with him so a few more days wouldn't matter.

"You're right, I'll wait until the proper time to approach him."

Erik smiled. "Good." He looked out the Great Hall door. "It looks as though they're here now," he said as he held out his arm to escort her outside, as though she were a lady at court.

Kiera hesitated. She was about to come face to face, with two men she had heard horrific stories about. Stories that conjured up fear in the common man.

Erik responded to her hesitation. He gave her hand a squeeze, "It'll be all right. They haven't eaten anyone in years."

Kiera realized her fear was showing, and it wouldn't do to cower before Dominick and Randolf if she were to gain their help. She took a deep breath squaring her shoulders. She was ready to meet them.

As the party came through the gate, Kiera got her first look at the legends she had heard about all her life. Dominick was the first to come through the gate. He was the largest man she had ever seen. In the past, she thought the stories exaggerated his size. Now she realized they didn't do him justice. His features were dark with straight raven black hair that went well below his shoulders, giving him the look of a barbarian. When he dismounted his horse she saw that his legs were as large as tree trunks and his arms as thick as their branches.

Randolf rode into the bailey. They were cut from the same cloth only slightly smaller in build, but the same height. Kiera felt rooted in her spot as she watched the two men. The sight of them would bring fear into any man. Any army, for that matter.

Another mount came forward, carrying a woman and child. Kiera's mouth fell open. She was the most beautiful woman Kiera had ever seen. Her hair was of the palest yellow, her eyes the color of jade, and her full lips were the softest shade of pink. Dominick tenderly helped her from her horse. He handled her as if she were made of the finest porcelain. When her feet were firmly on the ground, he caressed her face. She looked up into his face with adoration. Standing next to Dominick, she realized the top of her head barely reached his chest.

Dominick handed down the little boy. He ran around Randolf's feet, releasing pent up energy from the long ride. Randolf picked him up and swung him in circles then let him down. He staggered for a moment and then chased the geese that had crossed his path. The little boy was a replica of Dominick.

Dominick came up the stairs with a smile. He and Erik grasped each other in greeting. Kiera noticed his smile lit up his face, taking away his fearsome look.

"Erik, it's good to see you old friend." His voice was deep and resonant.

"Good to see you too, Dominick. I hope your journey was an uneventful one."

"It was, thank you."

Seeing Dominick and Randolf's curious stares, Erik pulled her to his side. "I would like you to meet another guest of mine, Kiera. Kiera, this is Lord Dominick of Godwin, and his brother, Sir Randolf."

Dominick and Randolf stared at her for a moment. She knew it was because of her unusual attire. She never looked away, not allowing herself to be intimidated by them.

Erik spoke up. "Kiera is responsible for saving my life," he said. "I have asked her and her two companions to join us for the Spring Festival."

"I would be most interested in hearing how you were rescued by a woman," said Dominick, never taking his eyes off her face. She remained undaunted.

"Are you saying a woman can't rescue a man in an hour of need?" came a voice smooth as honey, behind the giant.

Randolf laughed, "Careful how you answer brother, or she'll have your ears for the evening meal."

Dominick smiled down at his wife, "I would never imply such a thing, since it's you who have rescued me." He reached over giving his wife a squeeze. "Kiera, this is my wife, Lady Eleanor."

Kiera bowed to her, "Lady Eleanor, it's a great pleasure to meet you."

Lady Eleanor smiled, "It's a great pleasure to meet you. And don't mind my brute of a husband, I'm sure he didn't mean to insult you," she said.

Suddenly the small child burst through the crowd, nearly knocking Eleanor down the stairs. Her husband gently held her in place beside him. The little boy jumped into Erik's arms. "Uncle Erik! I'm so glad we're finally at Alastair. Are you going to show me how to ride, while we're here?"

Erik laughed at the wiggling bundle in his arms. "Didn't I promise you the last time you were here? A promise is a promise." He gave the boy a squeeze. "Yes, I'll teach you how to ride while you're here." The little boy wrapped his arms around Erik's neck, and hugged him tightly.

It was the first time Kiera had seen Erik do anything spontaneous. It touched her heart to see him show such unguarded affection.

The little boy looked over at Kiera, "Who's the pretty lady, Uncle Erik?"

Kiera blushed.

"Derrick, I would like you to meet my friend, Kiera." He turned to Kiera, "Kiera this is Derrick."

"Pleasure to meet you Derrick," she bowed.

He wiggled out of Erik's arms grabbing hold of Kiera's hand. He bowed to her like a gentleman at court. He turned to his father. "She's pretty Papa, almost as pretty as Mama, wouldn't you say?"

Dominick cleared his throat, embarrassed by his son's outburst. "Yes son, she's pretty." He put his hand on the boy's shoulder, and said, "I think you should go find Albert and ask him to help us unload the wagons."

"All right, Papa." He turned back to Kiera. "Bye, pretty lady." Then he darted off into the Keep, in search of Erik's squire.

"Shall we go inside for some refreshments while your wagons are being unloaded?" Erik said, gesturing them into the Keep.

"That is an excellent idea, I could use a draft of ale about now," Randolf said.

The party moved into the Great Hall, where Isabella, Ian and Arelia joined them. The women exchanged hugs, and the men exchanged greetings. Kiera felt awkward, for these were old friends with pasts and memories that she wasn't a part of. Isabella came to her rescue, pulling her into a conversation with the three of them. A few minutes later, Marcus and Jordan joined them.

Erik saw the two men come into the Great Hall. He waved them over to meet his friends. "Dominick, Randolf, I would like you to meet Marcus, and his son Jordan. They're the two companions that are traveling with Kiera."

Dominick and Randolf gave each other a long look that wasn't missed by Kiera. She held her head higher, trying not to let what the two men thought disturb her. But it did.

Erik saw the look the two men exchanged. But until he knew what her business was with his friends, he couldn't defend her. They would know Kiera in time. "Marcus is training my men. They are in dire need of rigorous training. If today's training was any indication, Marcus will have them in shape by mid-spring."

Dominick stood next to Erik, leaning one arm on his shoulder. His hand holding a cup of ale. "My soldiers could use some good training while we're here, any objections to my men training with you as well, Marcus?" Dominick asked.

"It would be an honor, my lord." Marcus bowed slightly.

"Good, I'll have my men on the field in the morning." Dominick slapped his hand on Erik's back. Turning toward Kiera, "Now I would like to hear how this woman saved your life."

They all sat down at the table now set with food. Marcus and Jordan took their places beside Kiera, before Erik continued.

"A few days ago I was set upon by five outlaws. I was able to dispatch the first three, but the remaining two had me pinned down. When I looked up there was a knight barreling down on the three men. The knight made short work of one bandit, while I finished off the last one."

"That still doesn't tell us how Kiera was responsible for saving your life," Dominick said. Kiera stiffened.

"When the knight removed his helmet, you could understand my shock to find I had been rescued by a woman."

"You're pulling our leg," said Randolf. "This girl defeated a man as desperate and vicious as a bandit?"

"I didn't believe the story either," said Ian. All eyes turned to him, "until I saw her beat Olaf."

"She beat Olaf? But he is one of your best swordsmen!" Dominick said in surprise. "Erik, you're right, your men have gone soft."

Erik saw Kiera's hands tighten around the arms of her chair. He reached for her hand to try and soothe her, but she would have none of it. Isabella was about to come to her defense, but Kiera beat her to it. She jumped out of her chair, looking down at Dominick. "If you don't believe them, maybe I could show you what I'm capable of tomorrow on the training field."

"Is that a challenge, my dear?" Dominick asked calmly, his black eyes boring through her. Trying to intimidate her.

Erik saw that she wasn't going to back down. "Take it however you wish, I'll be waiting on the field tomorrow." With that said, she walked out of the Hall. Everyone heard her chamber door slam.

"Dominick! How could you have been so rude to that woman?" Eleanor snapped.

"Believe me, my dear, it wasn't intentional," he said sipping his ale.

"I think you should go up there and apologize to her."

Erik smiled. Only this slip of a woman could bully his great hulking friend. "I think it would be best to leave things as they are. You'll be astounded by her ability tomorrow. And don't plan to go easy with her because she'll take advantage of it, and hand you your head."

"I look forward to seeing this phenomenon."

Marcus excused himself and went up to Kiera's chamber and gently rapped on her door. When she opened it, he could see she'd been crying. He held his arms out to her, and she ran into them. "Oh Marcus, what have I done? I can't make an enemy out of Dominick. All this time, all the waiting and planning, and in one breath I have destroyed it all."

"There, there child, Lord Dominick didn't seem at all put out with your challenge," he said patting her back. "This may be your opportunity to show him what you're capable of. Maybe this will be the best way to win him over."

She sniffed, pulling away. "Oh Marcus, do you think that truly possible?"

"I do," he said confidently.

She smiled, he saw hope come back into her eyes. "Then I'll give him the very best I have."

"That's my girl. You have defeated bigger giants than him."

Kiera laughed, "When have I ever defeated someone that size? There is no one that size in all of England."

Marcus laughed, "Well maybe not, but you'll defeat him just the same. Just remember everything you have heard about his fighting skills, and you'll have a greater chance."

Kiera hugged Marcus tightly. "Thank you Marcus, you always know how to make me feel better."

"It's my pleasure darling." He held her at arm's length. "Are you ready to come back down stairs?"

"No, I don't think so. I think I humiliated myself enough for one day."

"Suit yourself, it's getting late anyway and I want you on the field at dawn tomorrow."

"Oh, wild horses couldn't keep me away tomorrow."

"Good night then. Don't let what happened tonight worry you too much."

"I'll try not to. I'll see you tomorrow."

He turned to the door. "Sweet dreams," he touched her face closing the door as he left.

Kiera felt better after talking to Marcus, but in the future she would have to keep a lid on her temper. There was another knock on her door. When she opened it, gasped in shock.

"Lady Eleanor!"

"May I come in?"

"Yes, of course," she opened the door wider gesturing her in.

"I must apologize for my husband's rude behavior."

"That's not necessary. I don't know why I became so upset, it's happened to me many times, most of the time I'm able to ignore it. I don't know what came over me."

"My husband can be somewhat overwhelming, but behind that gruff exterior lies a kind and just heart."

"I have always heard that he is a fair man," Kiera said gesturing Lady Eleanor toward a chair near the hearth.

"Well none the less he upset you this evening, and for that I apologize," she said, sitting down.

Kiera took the chair next to hers. "Thank you for your concern."

"Are you really as good as Erik claims you are?" Lady Eleanor's eyes sparkled.

Kiera's face reddened, "I don't know how to answer that, except I have been fighting since I was twelve years old. I was raised and taught by the best trainer in England. I guess I will just have to wait and see tomorrow."

"Good," she said, "Because I'll be cheering for you."

Kiera nearly fell out of her chair in surprise. "You will?"

"Yes," Eleanor said touching Kiera's hand. "My husband needs to be taught that not all women are made out of glass, and that they can fight side by side with their men if trained properly."

"Most women don't feel the way you do, Lady Eleanor."

"I know it's not popular thinking, but women are not as fragile as men think. My husband treats me as though I'll break, and I feel you can change his way of thinking."

"I thank you for your support, Lady Eleanor."

"Just call me Eleanor, I think we are going to be great friends."

"I would like that very much."

"So would I," she said as she walked toward the chamber door. "I'll leave you to your rest now. Tomorrow is a big day." She reached for her headscarf handing it to Kiera, "For luck," she said and left the room.

Kiera leaned on the door, smiling. She looked down at the fabric in her hands. It was silk in a soft jade color that matched Lady Eleanor's eyes. She felt like dancing her way to the bed if she only knew how to dance. She changed for bed and snuggled down into her blankets. She held her mother's medallion, "I'm close mother, so very close."

CHAPTER XI

Kiera was already on the field as Dominick approached. Word had gotten around the Keep about her challenge. The field was crowded with both Dominick's and Erik's men.

Marcus and Jordan stood on either side of her, each rattling off instructions on how to handle Dominick the Immortal. She could hear nothing except the pounding of her heart. She knew the only way to defeat his brawn was with speed. She shook her head. Who was she kidding? She would never beat the giant. The best she could hope for was to keep her head on her shoulders. If he didn't pound her into the ground with those great arms of his.

As Dominick approached she had to fight the urge to step back. He towered over her as they stood face to face.

"So you still plan to show me what you're made of are you?" he asked, staring down at her with his intense black eyes.

Kiera stiffened. "Yes, My Lord," she said flatly.

"I'm glad to see you have courage. It's unusual for a woman," he saw her about to protest. He held up his hand, "and for most men," he conceded. He looked down at her sleeve. She was wearing the scarf that Eleanor had given her. He fingered the cloth tied around her arm. He turned toward his wife. She watched Eleanor cross her arms in front of her undaunted by her husband's stare. He turned back to Kiera. "I see you have the support of my wife."

"Yes, I do," she said proudly.

"Honor is a difficult thing Kiera. You'll find yourself always having to defend it."

"I have been doing it most of my life."

Dominick's squire handed him his sword. She unsheathed hers from her belt. Marcus stepped forward her helmet grasped in his extended hand. She took it and started to put it on, when Erik called out to her.

"Wait!" he shouted as he trotted over to her side. "I would like a word with Kiera before you proceed," he said turning to his friend.

"As you wish," Dominick bowed slightly.

Erik pulled Kiera away, so others couldn't hear. "You don't have to do this."

Kiera looked over to the crowd. She saw Lady Eleanor smiling back at her. Isabella, Aurelia and Ian were standing next to her. Ian gave her thumbs up. Kiera smiled back at him. "Yes I do Erik. Everything I am must be known to this man."

"Why is this so important?" His eyes fixed on her face.

"I can't tell you now."

He turned her to face him fully. "Will I ever know Kiera?"

"Soon, I promise, I'll tell you everything."

He gazed into her eyes, then before she knew what happened he kissed her fully on the mouth. The crowd cheered and whistled. Kiera's anger rose for the spectacle he was making of her. She tried to struggle away, but he held her firmly, his lips still pressed to hers. Her ears rang with the shouts from the crowd. She thought if she could reach her knife she would cut him to pieces.

Finally he let her go, but his hand still held the back of her neck. He could see the fire in her ice blue eyes. "Are you angry?"

"Yes!" she tried to struggle away, but he held her tight.

"Good, then use it." he released her abruptly, and walked back toward the crowd.

She looked toward Dominick, "Men!" she shouted, and put on her helmet. She walked over to Dominick. He held out his sword, she tapped it with hers then took her stance.

Dominick was the first to swing with one arm. She countered with two. Her hands stung with the power of his first blow. She gripped the hilt of her sword tighter. Their sword singing as they clashed. He came swinging after her. She backed up crossing his every move. She used speed against him. He jumped back when she swung wide toward his mid-section. His sword came down again. He swung toward her left shoulder and she rolled her body to avoid it. Again she became aggressive, thrusting forward. He moved to the right, she narrowly missed his left side. He brought his sword up and she countered, knocking his away. "My God! You're almost as fast as Randolf."

"You think so?" she said through gritted teeth, countering another blow, as he swung again. "His speed is legendary. I will take that as a complement."

Kiera was surprised that a man so large, was so agile. Her ears began to ring from the sound of swords meeting. She raised her sword high, and as she came down, he came up in one stroke, knocking her sword out of her hands. It flew behind her.

Every one stopped cheering thinking the battle was over. She never took her eyes off Dominick. He moved forward to claim his victory. Her chest heaved from exertion. Then in a blink of an eye, she did a back flip, flying in the air, and landing just behind her sword. She picked it up and raised the tip to his throat in one motion.

"Do you yield?" she said breathlessly. There was no sound from the crowd. The only thing heard was the bleating of nearby sheep.

Dominick stood for a moment then smiled. He stretched out his arms. Bowing his head, he said, "I yield." Then to her surprise, he winked at her, and added, "This time."

"It will be my pleasure to show you again," she said lowering her sword.

"At this time it won't be necessary." Then he did the most unexpected thing. He took her hand and bowed deeply before placing a kiss on the back of it. The crowd was jumping and cheering. She even saw Olaf cheering and clapping loudly.

"You were magnificent," Dominick said as he straightened, placing her hand in the crook of his arm and escorted her off the field. He led her to Eleanor who kissed her on both cheeks. She mouthed the words, 'thank you'. Then he moved her on to Randolf who also bowed before her hand, placing a kiss on it. Kiera smiled back at him.

They moved on to Marcus and Jordan where Jordan promptly picked her up swinging her around in a big bear hug. Upon seeing this Erik made a move toward them, but Aurelia held his back.

When Jordan finally put Kiera down she was dizzy and out of breath. Marcus reached out to steady her and placed both hands on her shoulders. "I'm proud of you, child."

She hugged him. "Thank you, Marcus."

"Marcus," said Dominick's deep resonating voice, "you're truly a master trainer. Never have I seen such timing and skill."

"I can't take all the credit. She has a natural ability, she inherited from her family."

"You have trained her well."

"Thank you, my lord," said Marcus with pride.

"If you could help my men in anyway, I would be most grateful...and generous," he said, placing a hand on Marcus' shoulder.

"It will be my pleasure, my lord."

Erik came up behind. "So the kiss worked."

She turned around, still angry for the way he humiliated her. "No, my skill worked."

"Put your claws back in, Kiera, I'm only teasing you."

She looked into his eyes. They were warm like liquid amber, and he smiled. She couldn't help but smile back, "Well, maybe it helped a little," she said.

He gave her shoulders a squeeze. "You know after seeing your last move, my men are going to be jumping around the field like acrobats at the fair."

Kiera laughed. Erik turned to Marcus, "Well Marcus, no time like the present. Why don't we split the men up in groups and start our morning training."

"Yes, but first we'll have our run. Ten times around the court in full armor, including helmets. The men around him groaned.

Dominick shouted, "Twelve! And if I hear any more complaining it will be fifteen," he looked back at Erik, "Is that acceptable?"

"By all means," Erik said.

Kiera just rolled her eyes. Sure he would be agreeable to that, he didn't just fight a giant. She placed her helmet on her head and started to follow the men around the court. She saw Ian standing there itching to get into the training. *One more day,* she mouthed, holding up one finger. He smiled to acknowledge her.

Randolf ran next to her. "Well done, Kiera."

"Thank you."

"I don't wish to sound like I'm bragging, but I have rarely seen anyone with the same speed that would rival me, and yet I have rarely been able to defeat my brother in a mock battle. That was quite a brilliant move. I would be most grateful if you'll teach it to me."

"Certainly, Sir Randolf."

"Just Randolf, please."

"Randolf." She tested the name on her tongue, secretly smiling.

They continued to run side by side, until Dominick ran up behind them. "Care for a race brother?"

"Nothing would please me more."

She dropped back. "Kiera you give us the word," Dominick said.

She waited until the two men were side by side, "Go!" she shouted, and the two men took off. They ran around the bailey walls with amazing speed, yet Randolf was clearly faster and won by two lengths.

Erik came up to her, "It seems speed beats brawn today."

"Today I believe it does," she said rounding their last lap. When she came to Marcus she made a great show of collapsing on the ground. Sighing, "Marcus, I'm done."

Erik sat beside her on the ground. "Nonsense, you have a lot more in you girl," Marcus said. Looking down at her, "I would like you to take a group of men, and show them maneuvers on a horse."

"Is there anything she can't do?" Erik asked.

"She can't cook," Marcus said smiling down at her.

Jordan came and sat down on the other side of her. Erik stiffened, yet said nothing. She could feel the tension between them.

"Jordan I want you to take a group of men and work with them on the cross bow."

"Yes Sir," Jordan never took his eyes off Erik.

"Kiera, it's time for you to mount up." Marcus said, with a keen eye on the three of them. She jumped at the chance to get away. She followed Marcus to the stables.

The two men were silent for a while. Then Jordan spoke. "You're reckless with her."

"What do you mean, reckless?"

"You don't know how she thinks, or feels."

"And you do," Erik said flatly.

"You had her heal your friend, Ian without considering the danger to her."

"I told you, if there was any danger I would have stopped it."

"How would you know when she was in danger?"

Erik couldn't answer. He wasn't sure when he would know, he just felt he would. They were silent again. "She's an innocent, yet you kiss her in front of your men like she was a common whore. Don't make any further advances toward her." Jordan shoved his hands into his gauntlets. "I have told her the way it is between a man and a woman, but I couldn't convey the emotions. Kiera feels things very deeply and she may be confused about what she's feeling about you. Don't take advantage of that."

"Do you think that's what I'm doing?" Erik asked, raising one eyebrow.

"I'm not a mind reader. I can't tell you your motives, but I can tell you, if you hurt her in anyway, I'll kill you." With that Jordan stood up and walked away.

Erik remained where he was. He couldn't fault Jordan for wanting to protect Kiera. Hell, he wasn't even sure of his own motives. Every time he came near her, he couldn't keep his hands off her. He'll have to make a conscious effort in the future. He was a man who never let his emotions control him, and he never would.

He looked toward where Kiera was training a group of men on horses. They watch her avidly. He smiled to himself. They now respected her skills as a fighter. He wondered if they would follow her into battle. Possibly.

"May I join you?"

Erik looked up to find Isabella standing next to him.

"Please," he said giving her a hand down beside him.

"Quite an exciting day, wouldn't you say?" she said brightly.

"Yes quite," he said distracted watching Kiera on her horse.

Isabella noticed, "She's very good, isn't she?"

"Yes very."

"Are you going to talk to me, or just repeat everything I say?" she asked, smiling at him.

"I'm sorry, what is it you want to talk about." He looked at her directly.

"What would you say, if I asked Kiera to teach me how to fight?"

"Not a chance!" he said flatly. His eyes bore into hers.

"Why not? She's no less of a woman than I am, I feel I could learn a lot."

"You have men to protect and care for you."

"Maybe I don't want to be protected," she said crossing her arms. "If I should ever find myself in trouble, I would like to know I can take care of myself."

"What kind of trouble could you possibly ever get into?"

"I don't know, but looking at Kiera and her ability to take care of herself makes me feel....vulnerable."

Looking in her eyes he wondered why this was so important. "Has someone been troubling you?"

"No! I just think it would be good for me to know how to defend myself."

Erik understood her point, it may not be a bad idea if Kiera showed her a few ways to protect herself in Ian's absence. "Did you talk to Ian?"

"No, I wanted to know what you think first."

"And also gain my help in convincing him it's the right thing to do."

"Well, yes," she said slyly.

"I know you so well," he smiled back at her.

"Of course you do, you're my brother."

Erik looked back at Kiera. Hadn't Jordan said the same thing about her? He knew her well after the years they spent together. Erik was jealous of Jordan's time with Kiera. He shook his head. He wouldn't let the train of thought continue. He cleared his mind. Looking back to Isabella he said, "I'll talk to Ian, but I don't think it will be too difficult to convince him, he is one of Kiera's biggest supporters."

"Can you blame him? She faced possible ridicule, and danger in healing him."

"I know. It was a selfless act."

Isabella hesitated then asked, "How did you know about Kiera's ability to heal people?"

He thought for a moment, since Isabella already knew of Kiera's power of healing. He explained what happened on the day they met.

Isabella's eyes were bright with tears. She held Erik's hands tightly, "There will be no end to the debt I owe this woman. I only hope one day, I'll be able to repay it."

Erik stood up bringing Isabella with him. "Again, don't tell anyone what I've told you, it may endanger her life."

"I swear her secret is safe with me." She reached up and hugged her brother tight. "I'll forever be grateful to her," she said and walked away.

Erik watched her as she ran back into the Keep. He turned to a group of men who were learning hand to hand combat, and decided to join them. It would do him good to throw some one around for a bit. He needed to get Kiera off his mind.

CHAPTER XII

Kiera worked with the men on their horses most of the day, stressing balance as opposed to strength. "If you can keep your balance no matter how strong your opponent is he can't unseat you." She called one of the men over, "With your sword I would like to use all your strength to unseat me." The man gave her a wicked smile. He raised his sword and brought it down on her. She rolled her body to one side, clamping her knees to Snow's sides. The young man nearly fell off his horse with the force he was using. He raised his sword again. In a blink of an eye, Kiera kicked him in the mid-section, knocking him off balance and off his horse. The men roared with laughter. "You see, balance and agility are the keys. Watch," she said, leading her horse away from the group of men. She started galloping her horse around the training field. Everyone was watching including Erik. She brought her feet up into the saddle. While the horse was still galloping, she stood up. Mouths dropped, as they watched her ride her horse while standing. She went once around the field then dropped back in the saddle. She trotted back toward the men, "Balance," she said, when she reached her group of men.

No one said a word. Their mouths hung open. "Now, I want you to pair up and try rolling away from the sword, as opposed to hitting it head on. Try avoiding it. The men paired up. She sat on her horse watching them lean back and forth. Some were unseated and fell to the ground. She shouted an occasional instruction, but for the most part they were learning to keep seated on their horses under attack.

Erik came over to her side. "Care to take a rest," he said looking up at her.

"Yes, I could use some water."

He reached up to help her down from her mount. She hesitated for a moment and looked around the field. No one was paying attention. She shrugged her shoulders. Her men were too busy trying not to fall off their horses to give her any worry. She slid down into his waiting hands. When her feet touched the ground, he promptly stepped back.

"Why do you do that?" she said, her face flushed.

"Do what?" He deliberately misunderstood her question.

"You know what, help me down from my horse. I have been dismounting horses since I could ride."

"It's what a gentleman does for a lady," he said, matter as a matter of fact.

"No one's done it for me, I'm not exactly what you would call, a lady," A stable boy came to take her horse's reins.

"Of course you are. It's just that you're not a conventional one," he said, as they walked off the field.

"Many people would disagree with you."

"You don't strike me as the type who would care what people think."

"I didn't until I came here," she said looking down on the ground. "Now, somehow it matters what people think."

He turned her to face him. "What's different now?"

She felt awkward. He was standing to close. She discreetly took a step back. He watched her face too intently. She tried to shrug it off. "People here seem to accept me for who I am. It's difficult to put up barriers when people are nice to you."

"So in the past, people treated you badly."

"No that isn't it." She tried to explain. "Most of the time, people just tried to avoid me, or pretend I'm not there. They were sometimes cruel. Those people I didn't care about. Things they said rarely bothered me." She looked down at her hands.

"Yet, I can see that it bothered you from time to time."

"Yes," she said looking into his eyes. She saw the warmth in them. She was drawn into them. She forced herself to remember her purpose. Pulling back, she looked around her, breaking the spell she was under. Then turning back to him, "Erik, I don't know what's going to happen in the next few days. But I would like you to know how much I appreciate your kindness and your family's kindness." He was about to say something, when she held up her hand, she rushed on. "Never before, have I been treated with unconditional acceptance." She placed her hand upon his chest. "Thank you for making us feel so welcome." She could feel her face burning. She never had to thank anyone before.

"It's I who should thank you for saving my life and that of my friend. For that you are most welcome to stay in my home for as long as you wish," he said sincerely.

"Unfortunately that's not possible." She watched his face turn expressionless.

"Why would that be Kiera?" his voice turned cold.

"Erik...." she started to say but he held up his hand to stop her.

"I know, you can't tell me right now," his face became harder. He turned and walked away.

She felt somehow disappointed. Why couldn't she bring herself to tell him? He deserved her trust, but she spent too many years not trusting. What would he do if he did know? He would throw her out on her ear, for all the trouble she could bring down on him, and his family. No, she had to wait a few more days then she would be gone. She sighed. Somehow that made her feel worse.

She felt a tap on her shoulder. It was Olaf. He handed her a cup of water. "Olaf! Thank you."

"Yer welcome," he said. He hesitated for a moment, then said, "I would like to apologize for the other day." His face reddened, not used to apologizing to the gentler sex.

"I'm sorry, I lost my temper," she said taking another sip of water.

"I deserved it. I have had time ta think about it. Ye were very kind t' save me hide, after all the things I said to ye."

"You're forgiven, I'm sorry you were sent to the kitchen."

"It was the least that could have happen to me." He leaned over, whispering in her ear. "Secretly I'm enjoyin' it. But don't be tellin' anyone."

"Your secret is safe with me." She smiled at him. "By the way your soup was excellent the other day."

"If ye think that was good. Wait till ye see what I have planned this evenin'. It will be in yer honor," he said smiling.

"Oh Olaf, that's so kind of you." She leaned over and kissed his cheek. His face turned red as an apple.

He touched his cheek where she had kissed him, smiling like an idiot he walked back into the Keep.

Kiera sat on the front steps for a long time absent mindedly watching soldiers on the field thinking about the people at Alastair. The longer she stayed the harder it would be for her to leave. She would talk to Dominick tonight. She had no choice. The longer she stayed the more danger there would be for the people there.

With her mind made up, she went back to the men she was training.

CHAPTER XIII

Kiera dressed in the tunic Erik had given her. She wrapped her arms around herself, breathing in his scent. She wanted to remember everything about him. His touch, his smell, his eyes that could warm her soul. She didn't know how much longer she would be at Alastair Keep, but she had to leave soon. She reached for her medallion and held it between her fingers and closed her eyes, "Courage mother, give me courage."

Placing the medallion back under her tunic, she took a deep breath and walked out of her chambers and down to the Great Hall.

Dominick was the first to see her coming down the stairs, he held out his arm and escorted her to her chair. She smiled up at him, "Thank you," she said, as she sat down. She liked being treated like a lady.

He bowed slightly to her, "You are most welcome." Then looking up he saw his wife coming down the stairs and promptly went to escort her to her seat. Derrick was at his mother's side. He ran over to Kiera as soon as he saw her. "My Papa says you're a soldier, just like him."

Kiera smiled, "Yes, I'm a soldier, just like your Papa."

"But how can that be? You're a woman. Women aren't supposed to be soldiers," he said plainly confused.

"Anybody can be a soldier, even a small boy like you," she said, tapping the tip of his nose.

Without hesitation he climbed into her lap, clearly curious about her. "Do you think so?"

"I know so. You are young, and strong, and handsome, all the main requirements to be a really good knight."

"Do you know any other women that are warriors like you?"

"No, I don't, but I'm sure there are some out there somewhere." She couldn't resist touching his cheek.

"My Papa says you're good. So if there are any more women soldiers out there, I bet you're the best." He jumped down off her lap, and went to sit by his mother's side.

She just shook her head, and smiled. She watched the young boy as he chattered away to his mother. Her head bent as she patiently listened. Eleanor looked up and smiled at her. She couldn't help but smile back.

Erik came and sat down beside her. He gave her a chilly acknowledgment. Clearly, he was still angry about her secretiveness.

She felt the same disappointment she had that afternoon, when he left her on the steps of the Keep. She looked over at Jordan and Marcus. She wished she could join them. Because of the new guests they were moved to another table. She looked down at her plate. She didn't want to see the frozen expression on Erik's face.

Isabella sat next to her. "You were wonderful today."

Kiera turned toward her giving her a half smile. "Thank you," she said looking down into her plate.

"I watched you most of the day. I especially liked the way you stood on your horse and rode him. Where did you learn to do that?"

"Jordan taught me on a dare." She was being pulled out of her self-pity. "When we were kids, we would see who could stay on a horse the longest."

"How long can you ride like that?" Isabella was fascinated.

"As long as I need to win," she said smiling.

"It was very exciting to watch." Isabella turned completely toward Kiera. "Do you think you could teach me how to fight?"

"Why would you want to learn how to fight?"

"I feel a woman should know how to defend herself if a man isn't around to protect her," she said, looking back at Ian. "And Ian has agreed."

"Why don't you ask Ian, or your brother, to show you?" Kiera asked.

"They don't have time. They both spend their time with their men, hunting or scouting for outlaws." She looked at Kiera in earnest, "Please Kiera, so many times when Ian is gone I feel vulnerable. I have been protected all my life, and I just want to know I can protect myself."

She looked into Isabella's face. She couldn't bring herself to tell her no, even though she might not be staying long enough to accomplish anything. "All right, meet me on the field tomorrow, and wear something appropriate, you are going to get very dirty."

Isabella was as excited as a child. "Thank you, Kiera," she said earnestly.

"Save it for tomorrow. You may not feel the same."

The two women chatted about the training while the meal was served.

"Erik," Ian said, "I think you should have sent Olaf to the kitchens long ago." He patted his belly, "This is magnificent."

"It is good. I just may extend his punishment to keep him in the kitchen."

"It's not a punishment, he likes it there." Kiera forgot her promise, to keep Olaf's secret.

For the first time that evening, Erik looked at her. "How would you know that?" he said, his tone flat.

"He told me today," she said, raising her chin.

"Olaf had the nerve to talk to you." His voice rose slightly. She saw Erik's jaw clench.

"He apologized to me."

Ian nearly choked on his wine. "Olaf apologize? I think the heat in the kitchen has turned his brain into gruel. He never apologizes to anyone, especially a woman."

Kiera stiffened in her chair. "Well he apologized to me, and it was sweet."

Ian nearly rolled off his chair laughing, "Sweet! Olaf? Kiera what effect do you have on men, that could make the meanest man tame?" he looked over to Erik, "or a man with ironclad control, lose it."

Erik glared at Ian, a penetrating message that would make most men whither. Ian just smiled back at him.

Kiera took a sip of wine. "I don't know what you're taking about." She watched Erik over the rim of her cup.

For the remainder of the meal, the silence was intense. Erik barely spoke a word to her or anyone else.

The meal finally ended. Most of the party moved toward the fire across the chamber, conversation resuming. Erik did not leave his seat yet he still wouldn't talk to Kiera. Dominick came to sit down across from Ian.

"So how are things at Godwin, Dominick?" Ian asked.

"Blissfully quiet, I'm glad to say." He took a sip of his ale.

"No more problems from your northern neighbors?"

"None, Randolf and I negotiated a deal with them. We agreed they could hunt and fish on our northern borders, as long as they kept the peace."

Randolf came and sat down next to Dominick.

"Do you think the McPhearson clan will hold to their word?" Ian asked.

"I believe they will. They want peace as much as we do. Like us, they want time to rebuild their lands. It can't be done while they're fighting. I believe Liam McPhearson is a good clan leader. He's a reasonable man."

Ian saluted Dominick with his drink. "I salute your success. You have fought many battles and won. You gained favor with the king, were awarded land no other lord could manage. Your land flourishes and you have managed peace in a time of war. It's a great feat for a bastard son."

Kiera watched Dominick's face. He didn't seem to resent Ian's statement. Dominick didn't keep his heritage a secret. He was proud of what he'd became, and what he and Randolf had accomplished in spite of the fact that they were considered bastards. But Kiera was there to change all that.

"He's not a bastard," Kiera said very quietly, taking a sip from her cup. Only those around her heard. Dominick turned his head sharply and looked at her with intensity.

"What do you mean by that?" Randolf said. He looked at Kiera with suspicion.

"Just what I said," She looked at Dominick just as intently. "Neither one of you are bastards."

Erik sat very still. All present waited in stony silence for her to explain.

Dominick walked over to her and stood beside her chair. Even with his great size he didn't intimidate her. She looked directly into his eyes, "You are the son of Lord Alfred Wolfingham and Lady Hanna Pinochet."

Dominick looked at her with surprise. Kiera continued, never taking her eyes off his face. "Even though your father was married to another woman it was in name only. Lord Wolfingham loved your mother with all his heart, and despite the fact that he was married to another, your mother and father lived together. Is that not correct?" she asked.

Dominick stood very still. "Yes," he answered quietly.

"Five years after Randolf was born, you were both fostered out to Lord Harold Landau where you grew up and received most of your training. You and Randolf left when you reached maturity. You and Randolf felt the only way for a bastard to achieve wealth was by selling your sword arms. The two of you built a reputation for yourselves. So much so that it attracted the attention of the King. You were commissioned and earned the honor of knighthood, and fought in the war against the Turks. For your heroics you received Godwin Castle."

Dominick held up his hand, "I know what I have done. Please continue with why you don't think I'm a bastard son."

."I don't think it, Lord Dominick, I know you are not." She pushed back her chair and rose, locking her eyes to his. "One year after you were fostered out, your father's wife died. Six months later, Lord Alfred married Lady Hanna and petitioned the King to make you and

Randolf his legitimate heirs. Since there were no children from his previous marriage, the petition was granted."

"God's teeth!" Randolf said, crossing the room to stand next to Dominick. Dominick looked at the girl in front of him. "How would you know all of this?" he said placing his hands on his hips, "and where is the proof of this marriage and petition?" There was a cold chill in his voice.

Kiera felt no fear in the face of the warrior. She pulled her medallion from underneath her tunic. It was round with a sapphire stone in its center. Kiera held it out to him, "Do you remember this, Dominick?" she asked.

He gazed at the medallion as though he was hypnotized. It was his mother's. He remembered how she used to let him play with it when he was a child. She held him on her lap and sang to him with her long blond hair shimmering in the sunlight. Dominick reached for the medallion. He fingered its shinny surface then he closed his hand around it. He tugged it bringing her closer to him. He glared down at her. "How is it that you are wearing my mother's medallion?" he said, dangerously calm. "Who are you?"

She raised her chin, never taking her eyes off his. "While you were away, Lady Hanna and Lord Wolfingham had another child." She was silent for a moment. "Me."

The room became very quiet. Erik sat very still, yet Kiera could feel his stare. She didn't look his way. She had to make Dominick and Randolf understand who they were and what she needed from them.

"So you're claiming to be our sister?" Dominick said looking down at the medallion, rubbing it between his fingers. Randolf stepped forward and looked at the medallion. "I seem to remember this. I also remember our mother singing and telling stories, but how do we know Kiera's telling the truth?"

"She is your very image, Randolf." All eyes turned toward Erik as he rose to stand beside them. "You can't see it for yourself?" he said. "For the past few days I have looked into her face, and felt I have seen it before. Now I know why it's been so familiar." He stood beside her and touched her hair, holding it between his fingers. It unnerved her. "Her hair is as black as the night, like yours, Dominick." He raised her chin toward Randolf. "And look at her eyes. They're the same ice blue as yours, Randolf. An usual and rare color." He touched the side of her cheek, running his finger down along her jaw line. "She also has a cleft in her chin." He dropped his hand, finally releasing her from his touch. And only a sister of yours would be so tall. Looking into her eyes, "If you don't believe her, why don't you ask Aurelia."

Aurelia walked over to her "Would you like to know the truth, Dominick?" she asked.

"I feel I already do," he said gazing in Kiera's eyes. "But to be sure, I would like you to confirm it."

Dominick and Randolf took a step back. "Are you the daughter of Lady Pinochet and Lord Wolfingham?" Dominick asked.

"Yes," she said confidently.

He turned to Aurelia, "She's telling the truth," Aurelia said.

"Are you telling me the truth about our legitimacy?" he asked.

"Yes," she said without hesitation.

Again he turned to Aurelia, she nodded in confirmation.

"That will be all Aurelia, thank you."

Dominick looked back at Kiera, as if seeing her for the first time. Randolf moved forward. "God's teeth, Dominick! We have a sister."

Dominick stroked his chin. "Why do you come to us now?" he asked, eyeing her suspiciously. "I want to know it all." He took her arm and led her to the table. Dominick took a chair on one side of the table and indicated that she was to take the one across from him. Randolf sat next to her. Erik sat next to Dominick.

Marcus moved to stand behind Kiera, as well as, Jordan, to add their support to her.

"Tell me everything, from when you were born to how you came to be here," Dominick said.

"It's a very long story my lord," she said, raising her eyebrows.

"We have all night," he said crossing his arms and leaned back in his chair.

Lady Eleanor returned from putting her son to bed, sitting beside her husband, she looked at his stern face, "What's happened? You look as though you're going to eat Kiera alive," she said.

"We have just found out we have a sister," Randolf said.

"It's about time you realized it," Eleanor said.

"What do you mean?" Dominick asked in surprise.

"You men can be so blind sometimes. I knew she was related to you the first time I saw her. She mirrors the two of you. How did you finally realize Kiera was your sister?"

"She just told us," Randolf said.

"We're about to find out all the details," Randolf said, and turned back to Kiera. "Please start from the beginning."

Kiera took a deep breath. She could finally talk about what she kept secret. "I was born two years after you and Randolf left. Mother and father were very happy together. But there was also sadness. She missed the two of you terribly, and always worried about your fate being raised as bastards, outcasts so to speak. So father went to the King, and petitioned to make the two of you his legitimate heirs. He knew it would take time for this to happen. So in the meantime, he sent the best fighting trainers to Lord Harold to make you men who could stand on our own."

Kiera stopped briefly to take a sip of her wine and swallow the lump in her throat. It was difficult to talk about her parents. "We have an uncle, Murdock, who strongly opposed what father was doing. Without legal male heirs from our father he would inherit his land and title. Our father knew this. He took great care in keeping your whereabouts a secret until he could bring you back to our home and claim you as his legitimate sons. When the petition was granted, he made a will stating that in the event of his death you and Randolf would inherit everything.

Our uncle has many spies, and our father knew this. He trusted no one. He kept the documents hidden.

One day I followed father down to the secret chamber, where he hid the documents. They're inside the castle and I'm the only person who knows where they are. Not even our mother knew. I believe he felt it would be best for her safety." The room was silent as Kiera continued her story.

"When Murdock found out that the petition had been granted, he became enraged. A spy told him a messenger had been sent to return you and Randolf to our home. Murdock had him murdered before he could reach you." Kiera spoke very quietly, "You were to never know of what our father had done to secure your birthright.

Murdock plotted against our father," Kiera said gazing at Dominick, but not really seeing him, as she slipped back into the past. "One afternoon our father decided to take mother and me for a picnic in a meadow near our home to celebrate your eminent homecoming. Mother was so happy, thinking that any day you and Randolf would be coming home.

Father was holding me in front of him on his horse when we saw two men riding out of the woods toward us with swords drawn. Father rode over to the nearest tree and told me to climb in it and stay there no matter what happened. He rode toward the men to fight and protect us. He yelled for mother to hide in the woods, but she refused to leave his side. Suddenly four more men came out of the woods. There was no time to defend themselves. I could see everything from where I was. Father was run through the heart, and our mother...." Kiera felt a hand on top of hers. She looked over to see Randolf. She took a deep breath. The memory was too much to tell. "I couldn't save them, there was so much blood." Kiera started to choke, realizing what she was about to say.

"Of course you couldn't save them, you were only a child." Dominick said sympathetically.

She looked over at Erik. He sat very still gazing into her eyes, silently reaching out for her. He could feel her pain almost as if it were his own. Yet he stayed in control.

Marcus put a hand on her shoulder. She put her hand on top of his. "Marcus was one of father's men. It was he who found us. He took me home, but it was no longer my home. Murdock took over the castle and land. There was no proof there were any legal heirs and you never knew what happened."

Erik could see his friend's pain. Dominick stared at his hands for some time. Randolf sat thoughtfully drinking his wine. Everyone was silent after Kiera's tale. The only sound was the crackling of the fire.

Finally Dominick spoke. "All these years I thought our father had forgotten us," he said looking at Randolf. Erik knew that his friend kept his feelings about his parents abandoning them close and rarely talked about it.

"I never questioned the trainers that came to the Landau Manor. I always thought Lord Harold commissioned them. So many years I hated our father for abandoning us. Then when I heard they died, I couldn't bring myself to go back."

He reached over the table taking Kiera's hands, "Thank you Kiera, thank you for taking that burden away. How can I ever repay you?"

She looked squarely into his eyes, "Kill Murdock," she said with dead calm.

Erik looked into her eyes. He heard the venom in her voice.

"I beg your pardon?" Dominick said releasing her hands.

"I want you to kill Murdock and take back what is rightfully yours." She sat very still in her chair.

Randolf waited for his brother to speak. Dominick looked at Kiera for a long time. He turned to his wife and took her hand. "Why would you want me to do that?" he asked calmly.

Kiera's mouth flew open, "Why!" she shouted "To take back what was stolen from you. Your lands, and your title."

He shifted forward in his chair, leaning his arms on the table, looking into her bewildered face. "I have more lands than I can manage, and

I already have a title. Why would I need Dunsmore Castle?"

Slamming her fist on the table, Kiera screamed, "That monster has no right to those lands!"

"You are asking me to fight for something I don't care about, Kiera." He leaned forward trying to make her understand. "I have spent most of my life fighting one battle after another. I've finally restored peace to the land I now hold. I don't wish to be torn away from my family for another war."

Kiera tried to calm herself. "But that man murdered our parents."

"Another war won't bring them back. I can't waste time, money, and men, for another battle."

Erik saw the volcano of emotions rising in her. She fought hard to keep from exploding. Her breath came in short gasps. She stood up swiftly and knocked her chair backward. She ran out from the hall. He followed, catching up with her in the tower. Her head was pressed against the wall.

She jumped when he touched her back. Seeing her distress, he rubbed her shoulders. "Calm down. Take deep breaths."

She threw her head back. He watched her breath in the frosty air.

Erik kept talking softly, rubbing her shoulders and waited for her to calm down. Finally when her breathing returned to normal, he released her. "It will be all right, Kiera."

She quickly turned around. "It will never be all right Erik, never!" she snapped. She stared out into the black night. He's out there, waiting to strike."

"Who's out there?"

She continued as if she didn't hear him. "All the hope, all the planning is gone. I was such a fool to put faith in Dominick and Randolf. I thought they could save me, but now it's over, it's all over." She pulled away from him.

Erik reached for her, turning her to face him. "Who is out there, Kiera? What are you afraid of?" A tear ran down her cheek. He wiped it away. He wanted to assure her that she was safe, but he wasn't sure how. He couldn't resist kissing her where the tear had trailed down.

Kiera held on to his tunic. He felt her respond. Wrapping her arms around his neck she pulled his mouth down to hers. He moaned with wanting her. She kissed him again, harder, and held onto him like a lifeline. Her kisses became more frantic. He held her tightly, kissing her mouth, her cheek, and her neck. He was consumed by her. His hands moved down to her lower back, pressing her into him. She held on just as fiercely. "I need you," she whispered on his lips.

He kissed her again. Her hands were on his belt, frantically unfastening it. The heavy metal buckle fell to the tower floor, making a loud clatter. He felt her cool hands on his warm flesh. Her hands traveled to his chest. He moaned and held her tighter. He moved his hands down her lower back, pressing her into him. He kissed her neck and face. He unfastened her belt. She was warm and soft, her breasts ripe as she pressed them into his hands.

He felt the wet tears upon her cheek. He froze. Her hands went around his back. "Please, Erik, please. I need you," she said through her tears.

He pulled her away, holding her at arm's length. "I can't take you like this." His voice vibrated from the force he was using to hold on to his control. "You are too raw, too vulnerable. I won't take advantage of that."

Kiera's eyes filled with new tears. Erik held her tightly, gently rocking her as she cried.

"What the hell is going on here!" shouted Jordan.

Erik stepped away from Kiera. Jordan took one look at Erik and Kiera's disheveled appearance. "You son of a bitch!" Before he could react, Jordan planted a fist into Erik's jaw, knocking him to the ground. Jordan quickly jumped on top of him and tried to pummel him. Erik diverted the blows.

Kiera wrapped Jordan in a headlock and pulled him off Erik. "Jordan! What are you doing?"

"That bastard was all over you." Jordan shouted, pointing to him. Erik held down his anger." I have warned him before about taking advantage of you."

"Taking advantage of me?" Kiera raged. "I went after him, and he would have no part of it. I was crying, and he was consoling me."

Jordan looked to him, then to Kiera. His shoulders slumped. "I'm sorry. I thought he was molesting you."

"No. It was the other way around. Men! I'm sick of all of you." She ran from the tower, fresh tears running down her face.

Erik was silent. Jordan was clearly embarrassed. "I'm sorry, I didn't know."

Erik felt his anger pump through his arms and in a blink of an eye, Erik's fist connected with Jordan's jaw, knocking him to the ground. Erik quietly stepped over him and walked out of the tower.

CHAPTER XIV

His spy shook with fear as he kneeled before his master.

"What news do you bring?" Murdock demanded. His voice, a suppressed whisper, was intended to solicit fear, like a cold breath on the back of the shaking man's neck.

"My Lord, Lord Dominick and Randolf have arrived at Alastair Keep.

Murdock sat very still for a moment. His mind went dark. With the speed of a striking cobra he kicked the footstool in front of him, sending it across the room. The man barely had time to move out of the way. In the next instant he calmed himself. "Do they know who she is?"

"I can't say my lord, I came as soon as Lord Dominick's entourage arrived."

Murdock snapped his fingers at his Captain, Lacerta. "Send out your men and bring her to me, now!"

Captain Lacerta gave him a wicked smile. He and Lacerta were of the same mind. Capture their enemies and destroy them.

The captain left the hall. Murdock turned to his spy. "Get back to Alastair and find out what Dominick knows." Angus turned running out of the hall. Murdock was still shouting, "Those bastards won't have what belongs to me. I'll kill them first."

Erik sat in front of the hearth in the Great Hall absently rubbing his sore jaw, replaying in his mind what had happened that evening.

Kiera was Dominick and Randolf's sister. A sister they never knew they had. Her business with them was revenge. But was it only revenge? Kiera was a strong woman, but in her unguarded moments she looked haunted. Tonight he got a closer look at her suffering. She was frightened. She had been frightened for a very long time. He wondered what would happen to her now that Dominick and Randolf knew they had a younger sister. Would they feel an obligation to protect her?

As if materializing from his thoughts, Dominick sat next to him, handing him a draught of ale. "It's been quite a night, my friend."

"Yes, it has," Erik said talking into his cup.

"I have a sister I never knew existed. I find out my father didn't abandon me and my brother, and that they were murdered.

"It's quite a bit to take in." Erik turned to his friend. "Are you truly not interested in your father's lands?"

"Honestly, I would like to claim them, but not at the price it would cost me." He sighed looking into the flames of the hearth Dominick continued. "I have seen too much fighting, Erik, too much blood. I didn't realize the horrors of war, until I met the tranquility of my wife. She taught me how to build, instead of destroy. She showed me the happiness of peace. I want to spend my life tending my lands, and raising my family. To build something I can be proud of. I can't do that and fight another war. It would tear what I've built apart.

"Is Randolf of the same mind?"

"I can't say. His soul is still very restless. He searches for something yet I can't tell what he's looking for, nor can he."

"Do you think he will stay at Godwin?"

"I can only hope. I believe he turned down King William's offer for land, because he didn't want to be tied down to it."

"Be assured Dominick, Randolf will find himself in time."

"I'm sure you're right," he said drinking his ale.

Ian came to join them and pulled up a chair next to them. "Quite an exciting night."

"Yes, quite," said Dominick.

"How do you feel about having a sister?" Ian asked as he settled in his chair.

"I haven't had time to think about it." He looked back into the fire. "I'm confused about what she's doing here. Shouldn't she be with her guardian, this Murdock."

"Apparently she hasn't lived with her guardian since she was a child," Erik said.

"But why?" He shrugged his shoulders, "Why would she leave the protection of Dunsmore Castle?" Dominick asked.

"Maybe she wasn't safe," Erik said remembering the fear he saw in her eyes that night.

"Do you think Murdock tried to harm her?" Dominick asked.

Erik shifted in his seat, to look more directly at Dominick. "Kiera claims he murdered your parents. He may well have tried to harm her."

"Why?" Dominick threw his hands wide. "The land is his, there's no proof for anyone to dispute it."

"I can't say. All I do know is that she's running away from something or someone and is scared to death, but she won't tell me what she's afraid of." Erik spoke with vehemence.

The two men watched Erik as he spoke. Erik saw their stares and quickly put on his mask of indifference. Dominick and Ian looked to each other, then back at Erik. They knew their friend well.

"Where did she learn how to fight?" Dominick asked.

"I believe she learned everything from Marcus and his son." Erik said, turning back to the hearth. "She traveled to many places with them, like you, selling her fighting skills to whoever would hire them."

"None of this makes any sense. I want to know why a girl would leave her home to run around the country with two men who are not even her relation."

"You needn't worry about her relationship with Marcus and Jordan. They have protected her all these years." Erik thought for a moment then continued, "She told me they're like family to her. Marcus is the father she lost and Jordan her brother."

Dominick sat quietly. Erik could see he was thinking about Kiera, and what to do. "Erik, I'm at a loss as to what to do now. I have a responsibility to a sister I don't know."

Ian patted Dominick on the back, "Don't worry my friend, Eleanor will help you through it."

Erik sat thoughtfully drinking his ale. For some strange reason he didn't want Kiera to leave yet he knew when Dominick and Randolf left, they would be taking Kiera with them.

Suddenly they heard a piercing scream. The three men jumped up in readiness. The scream came again. It came from upstairs. Erik knew instantly it came from Kiera's chambers. He was the first up the stairs, crashing through her chamber door. The other two men were right behind him.

Erik saw Kiera thrashing around on the bed. He turned to Ian, "Get Aurelia, and have her bring a sleeping draught. Ian immediately left her chambers. Erik ran to the bed, trying to wake Kiera from her nightmare.

"Kiera!" he shouted, shaking her hard. "Kiera, wake up, it's me, Erik."

"No, no, please don't hurt me!" she said thrashing about.

Erik's blood went cold, "No one is going to hurt you, Kiera, wake up." He shook her again.

Her eyes opened, but he knew she wasn't seeing him.

"He's coming. He's going to find me." She scooted out of Erik's arms huddling at the bed post, tucking her head onto her knees, as though trying to make herself small enough not to be seen. "No! No please don't put me in there, please!" she sobbed.

Erik could feel his heart wrench. What tortures did she endure as a girl to cause them to haunt her in her nightmares? "He's not going to find you Kiera? I swear," he shouted, but she did not respond.

She looked down at her hands. "Blood! There's so much blood!"

Erik grabbed her hands. "There's no blood Kiera, wake up!" He shook her hard once more, Erik saw Kiera's eyes become lucid.

"Erik, what...." she put her hand over her face. "Not again." She didn't cry as she had before, she just became silent, so very silent. It worried Erik even more.

He turned to Dominick who seemed transfixed by what he had just witnessed. "Who did this to her?" Dominick asked, his deep voice full of pity.

"I believe your Uncle Murdock is responsible."

Dominick's hands clenched at his sides.

Erik went to put his arms around Kiera to comfort her, but she resisted. Jumping off the bed, "I have to leave here, now." She walked to the chair where she'd laid her clothes. She started dressing not caring that there were two men standing in the room.

Erik quickly grabbed her arm before she could put her britches on. "You aren't going anywhere."

She tried jerking away, but Erik held firmly onto her arm. "I have to leave, please let me go!"

He turned her toward him holding both her arms, "Kiera, you are safe here, there's no one here to harm you."

She tried struggling away. "He knows I'm here, he'll be coming to get me."

"Who, Kiera?" Erik insisted.

"Murdock!" she shouted. "I can't be here when he finds me. I have to leave." She struggled against him.

His face became hard, his voice firm. "You're not leaving here."

She struggled harder against him. "Marcus!" she screamed, "Jordan! Help me!"

Erik wrapped his arms around her, pinning her arms at her sides. She tried kicking him, but he avoided her blows.

Marcus and Jordan came running into her room with swords drawn, ready to fight. Dominick jumped in front of them.

She saw them enter the room. She started screaming for them to help her.

The two men moved forward, but Dominick clearly was not going to let them come to Kiera's aid.

"She had another nightmare. She's trying to leave the Keep." Erik said breathlessly, as he tried to keep her subdued.

Marcus and Jordan lowered their swords. "We can't leave Kiera, it's too dangerous. We will be safer here." Marcus said.

"Dominick, grab her feet and help me carry her to the bed."

Kiera fought wildly. She kicked out at Dominick. He moved his thigh to avoid a kick to his groin. He quickly grabbed her ankles, before she had time to try kicking him again.

"No!" she pleaded, "you don't understand, it's too dangerous for you and your family if he finds me here."

They got her on the bed. Erik straddled her, pinning each wrist over her head.

"I'll worry about my family, and you'll stay here, even if I have to tie you to this bed. Is that clear?"

She was tiring from her struggle. Ian came in with Aurelia. She ran over to the bed. "What on earth is going on here?" she shouted.

"She was trying to leave," Erik said, through gritted teeth.

"Leave, why?" Aurelia asked.

"I'll tell you later. Just give her the draught," he said, as she struggled underneath him.

"You'll have to sit her up."

He looked down at Kiera, "I'll release you, but don't try fighting me again, or I'll do as I promised. You'll be spending your days here, tied to this bed."

She nodded her agreement. He slowly rose up, lifting her with him.

Aurelia held out the drink for her, but Kiera refused to take it.

"Jordan, go and find me some rope," Erik said, never taking his eyes off her.

She jumped at the tone of his voice. Looking up she glared daggers at him. He only smiled back at her. Kiera took the draught from Aurelia. She looked into the cup for a moment then drank it down all at once and handed the cup back to Aurelia. She looked back at Erik. She thought she would see satisfaction on his face, but she saw no expression at all. She felt helpless, she looked down at her hands.

Aurelia sat down by her side, brushing her tousled hair away from her face. "Now dear, it isn't all that bleak. You'll see, when you have had time to rest and think about it."

Kiera looked into her beautiful face, Aurelia's eyes glowing with warmth. "Nothing will change, it will all be the same tomorrow," she said quietly.

"You'll be safer here," Erik said, his arms crossed in front of him.

"There's no place safe for me." She looked back down at the floor.

Erik watched her head droop as the sleeping draught took effect. He gently laid her back on the bed. Aurelia tucked her in. "I'll stay with her awhile," she said, stroking Kiera's hand.

"Do you think her nightmares come from seeing her parents being killed?" Dominick asked.

Still stroking Kiera's hand, Aurelia looked into her face. "It goes much deeper than that," she said, distantly.

Marcus and Jordan looked to each other. The three other men didn't miss it, but none of them chose to pursue it.

They all quietly left the room.

CHAPTER XV

Kiera awoke at dawn. She was furious about her treatment from the night before. She quickly dressed and went down to break her fast. In the Great Hall were the five men who were responsible for keeping her at Alastair Keep.

"Good morning, Kiera. I trust you slept well," Erik said as a matter of fact.

"I slept as the dead, as you are well aware of."

"I'm sorry, but you were a bit out of control."

"I was not out of control, I just wanted to leave."

Erik raised one eyebrow, "In the middle of the night? Where would you go?"

"Away from here."

"Kiera, you can be better protected here."

He spoke as if speaking to a child. This incensed her. She slammed her hands on the table, standing up and leaning over at him, "Don't talk to me as if I'm addle brained. I don't need your protection! The three of us have been faring well on our own before we came to your Keep, and we will continue to do so after we leave."

Erik was undaunted by Kiera's outburst. "Sit down, Kiera, and eat something."

"I'll not sit down. I'm not one of your soldiers to command!" she shouted, moving closer to him.

"Kiera, sit down!" Marcus shouted. Surprised by his outburst she did so without thinking. "I'm ashamed of your behavior. Now, Lord Erik has offered us his protection, the least you could do is be courteous if not grateful. Your brothers are here with their men, so for now this is the safest place for us all."

Kiera was silent. Marcus was rarely ever cross with her. Maybe she was being ungrateful, but last night her dream seemed so real.

"Kiera," came Dominick's voice from across the table. "We have just found one another, please give us the opportunity to know you. There are many things about our parents Randolf and I would like to hear. Please give us that time. You're our sister, which makes you our responsibility. From this day forward, you'll have our protection. As long as you are with us, I vow to keep you safe."

Looking into her brother's eyes, she knew she couldn't leave. Her mother and father would never forgive her if she didn't take the time to be a family at last. Her heart broke as she thought of her parents. She wished they could be here and see what two fine sons they had. They would be proud. She sighed, still looking into Dominick's face. "It was our parents' most ardent wish that we could be family. If I walked away now, it would dishonor their memory." She looked over at Erik. Her skin still prickled for his high handedness. No one but Marcus has ever taken control of her life and it galled her that she had to be gracious to his lordship. "Forgive my thoughtlessness, my lord," she said quite formally, "I know you have my best interest at heart. Thank you for allowing us to stay in your Keep." She stood up, bowed deeply to him, then walked out of the Great Hall.

The five men watched her stride through the large doorway, her boots clicked on the stone steps. Her back was straight and her long black braid swayed with each step.

"What was that all about?" Ian asked.

"She's still angry about last night. Control is the only thing that makes her feel safe. She puts a wall up between her, and whoever she is angry at," Jordan said.

Toying with an eating dagger Erik listened carefully to what Jordan had said. If she thinks to put a wall between them, he would make her think again. "If you gentlemen will excuse me," he said. He stood and followed Kiera out of the Hall.

He saw her rounding the Keep, heading toward the training field. Before she could reach the field, he caught her and swept her to a nearby wall, pinning her shoulders against the hard surface, commanding her full attention.

"Erik," he said deeply. "Say my name, Erik." His voice vibrated with intensity. He never took his eyes off her.

"This is ridiculous," she started to move forward, but he held her in place with one hand splayed across her chest, leaning into her.

"Put my name on your lips. Please." She again started to protest. He held up one finger just inches from her face, stopping her instantly. "Only my name. That's all I ask of you." He reached around her neck and pulled her into him as his mouth came down in a passionate kiss. She did not fight him. He felt her body respond the moment his tongue slipped between her teeth. Her arms involuntary moved around his neck. He pulled her in tighter molding his body into hers. With great effort he pulled away and looked down into her face flushed with passion "Say my name."

"Erik," she whispered finally.

He smiled, "Never, ever, forget what is between us, Kiera. And don't use such formality with me again, or I'll be forced to remind you of the passion that burns between us." He finally released her and without a backward glance walked away.

Kiera couldn't believe how her body betrayed her. Her skin flamed with his touch. She felt flush from her toes to her hairline. Anger seeped into her bones. But she was reluctant to admit it was anger toward herself. It was his fault she reacted this way. If he hadn't kissed her like that she wouldn't respond in such a manner. She resisted the urge to go after him, and give him a piece of her mind. It wouldn't do any good if she confronted him now, in her present state of mind. She might try to cut out his heart...if he had one.

"Kiera, here you are. I was looking for you on the training field." Kiera jumped at the sound of Isabella's voice. "I'm sorry, I didn't mean to startle you." She looked into Kiera's flushed face. "Are you all right?"

"I'm fine, just deep in thought." Her eyes widened in surprise. Isabella was dressed in a tunic and britches with leather boots, and her hair hung in a long braid.

"Well, how do I look?" she asked, holding her arms wide turning full circle.

"You look like a warrior."

"With one exception. I have no sword."

"We will worry about that at another time. Today we will learn how to use our body in combat.

"What does that mean?"

"It means, learning how to fight without weapons."

They walked to the training field. All eyes were on the two women. Kiera knew Erik's men had become accustomed to her dress, but to see Lady Isabella, Lord Erik's sister, was another matter. Yet Isabella chose to ignore them. Kiera had her undivided attention.

"With hand to hand fighting, a woman has to be trickier, even a little meaner than her attacker. She has to make up for his strength. The first thing you'll learn is what stops a man in an instant. Kiera held Isabella's shoulders to demonstrate her move. "If a man tries to attack you from the front, you take

your knee and jam it into his groin like this,"
she made the motion with her knee.

"And that's supposed to stop them?"

"It will make a man weep, my dear." Ian's
voice came from behind them. He stepped up to
Isabella, wrapped an arm around her shoulder
and placed a kiss on the top of her head.
"How's the training going?"

"We've only just started." Kiera couldn't
conceal the sharp edge in her voice, since he
was also responsible for keeping her here.

"Good. I thought I could be of some
assistance. Maybe if you had someone to throw
around you could work off some of that venom."
He turned back to his wife, "Isabella, Kiera
and I'll show you some maneuvers and counter
maneuvers, and then you can try them."

"What a marvelous idea." Isabella winked at
her husband.

"Very well, it would be better for me to
show her by example. Rush toward me." She
looked at Isabella. "Watch what I do. If he
comes forward and you bring your knee...." as
Ian came forward, Kiera brought her knee just
short of her target. Ian jumped out of the way,
just in case she missed.

"Play nice," Ian said wagging a finger at
her.

Kiera couldn't resist his smile. Her anger
with him dissipated. She chuckled back at him.
"Now, how about attacking from behind."

Ian stood behind her and when she was ready
he wrapped his arms around her shoulders.
"Isabella, when someone grabs you from behind,

you take your elbow and as hard as you can ram it into their stomach. It will knock the wind out of them, giving you time to get away." She demonstrated on Ian in slow motion so Isabella could see how it was done.

Ian, Isabella and Kiera, practiced for the better part of the morning. Kiera had many opportunities to throw Ian in the dirt. She felt much better. Ian took it all in stride. She wondered if Ian ever became angry. He was always polite and jovial, unlike his friend Erik.

Isabella had her opportunities as well. She learned fast. At one point she knocked Ian to the ground. He held onto her as he went down. She fell on top of him. He quickly rolled, pinning her under him. "Don't get any ideas of trying this in the bedroom, for there I'm still the master.

Isabella couldn't contain a giggle. "Yes, master."

He kissed her hard on the mouth then helped her off the ground.

Kiera smiled. They were truly happy together. Then her smiled faded. She would never see her future as bright as theirs. She never looked toward the future at all. Living moment by moment had been her life.

Ian and Isabella were too wrapped up in each other to notice Kiera's sadness. "Have you had enough for one day?" Ian asked Isabella.

"Yes, I think I have."

"Good. If you have any questions, we can continue your lessons tonight--alone." Ian squeezed his wife tightly. He looked back at Kiera. "Thank you for your help today. We'll see you later at the evening meal." They walked back into the Keep arm in arm.

Kiera watched them until Randolf caught her eye. He walked toward her. "Good afternoon, Kiera."

"Good afternoon." She stared up at him, amazed at how much he looked like Dominick with the exception of his striking blue eyes.

"I understand you had a bad dream last night."

She couldn't reply. She was too embarrassed that anyone should know about her nightmares.

His eyes reflected only compassion. "Is there anything I can do?"

"Only if you could erase the last nine years of my life."

He touched her arm. "I would if I could." He looked up into the bright clear sky. I thought about you most of the night and I feel that something has been stolen from me."

She looked at him puzzled. "I don't know what you mean."

"Until yesterday, I never gave my parents a thought. I was very young when they sent us away. Too young to remember them very well. Dominick I know has always felt an empty place because he was older when we left. But me, I never cared. Then suddenly overnight I have a sister. A sister I was cheated out of ever knowing. All the memories of our parents are in you and I never knew of your existence. A part of my life has been taken away without me ever knowing it."

Touched by his words, Kiera squeezed his hands. "We have time, Randolf. Whatever you want to know, I'm here for you to ask."

"I think it will do me good to have a little sister to protect."

"Little sister!" she said in mock surprise, "I'll have you know I'm not so little, or in need of your protection. If you care for me to demonstrated."

"Lead on," he said, gallantly bowing, extending his hand to the center of the training field.

When she reached its center she drew her sword. Randolf drew his. After they saluted each other, they commenced fighting. She was as fast as he was. Their swords rang as the afternoon sun shone down on them. Soldiers gathered around. They never took their eyes off one another. They were both smiling, trying to catch the other off guard. Finally, both too tired to continue, called it a draw. Breathing heavily, they began to laugh. Neither one knew why.

"You nearly took my head off!" Randolf said.

"You nearly cut me in half."

"You two are too dangerous for your own good." Erik said walking up to them, glaring at them both.

"Don't worry Erik, we were just playing," Randolf chuckled.

"You could have killed her with that speed of yours." Kiera was surprised to hear the anger in his voice.

Randolf stopped smiling and looked at both of them. Kiera couldn't imagine what he was thinking. She saw Erik's amber eyes glaring down at Randolf.

Randolf shrugged his shoulders and put a protective arm around Kiera. "I'm in need of refreshment, Kiera, how about you?"

She nodded in agreement. She examined Erik's face. Was that fear she saw? It was only for a moment. Then it was hidden behind his anger. She was unsure of what would anger him so. He had seen her fight before, including a mock battle with him. She didn't understand.

"Will you excuse us, Erik, we'll take our leave and have some wine."

Erik didn't answer.

Randolf led her into the Keep. After the wine had been poured, he asked, "What is between you and Erik.

She looked up at Randolf in surprise. "What do you mean?" Her voice was a little too high.

"I mean he watches you like a hawk and is as protective as a bear protecting her cub."

Raising her chin, "I don't know what you're talking about. There's nothing between us." Erik's words echoed in her mind. *Never forget what is between us, Kiera.* She sipped her wine to swallow the lump that grew in her throat.

Randolf raised his cup to his lips and watched her over the rim. He was about to say more, when Derrick came bounding into the hall and jumped into his uncle's arms. "Hello, little tadpole. What mischief have you been conjuring up today?"

"I just came from the stables. Have you seen Kiera's horse, Uncle Randolf?"

"No, I haven't had the time. You haven't been in the stables alone have you?"

"No, Papa and Uncle Erik were with me. Uncle Erik showed me Kiera's horse. Uncle Randolf, it's snow white and at least a hundred hands tall!"

Randolf laughed at the boy's exaggeration. "Is that so? Well, I'll have to see this phenomenon later today."

Derrick wiggled out of Randolf's arms to stand beside Kiera. "Would you take me for a ride on him?" His eyes were pleading.

Kiera couldn't resist those big black cow eyes. She smiled and touched his cheek. "Yes, I'll take you, but I have to ask your mother first."

"I'm sure she won't mind. Thank you, Kiera, thank you, thank you, thank you!" The boy hugged her neck tightly. Then bounded back off to the stables.

"It looks like you found a new friend."

"I hope so. He's such a sweet child."

"You just caught him on a good day. Wait until you see him when he is a real terror."

"I'm sure he can be."

Draining the last of his wine, Randolf stood to leave. "Well, I better see to my own horse. I'll see you at the evening meal."

"I look forward to it. I better find Lady Eleanor, and ask her if I can take Derrick for the afternoon."

"I'm sure that won't be a problem." He bid her farewell and walked out of the Keep.

She smiled as she watched him walk out of the Great Hall. He moved as graceful as a lion. Every step confident and strong. She sent a silent prayer to her parents. *If only you could see him. He is the best parts of you.* She felt a sense of pride. This was her family. She blinked back a tear. Remembering her promise to Derrick, she went in search of Eleanor.

CHAPTER XVI

Albert was walking through the hall. "Albert, have you seen Lady Eleanor?"

Yes ma'am, she is in her chambers," he said politely then scurried out the door. *Everyone was always so busy around here*, she thought.

She ran up the stairs to Lady Eleanor's chamber and knocked on the door. Faintly she heard a voice bid her to enter. As she stepped in she saw Lady Eleanor being fitted for a new gown.

"Oh, I'm sorry, I didn't know you were busy. She started to turn and leave, when Lady Eleanor stopped her.

"Please don't leave. I need your opinion on this gown." She was wearing a violet silk gown. The fabric accented her jade green eyes. Kiera gazed in awe. Her bother's wife was so beautiful. Kiera felt awkward in her presence. "It beautiful," she said sincerely. Eleanor smiled back at her. She pointed to the bolts of fabric on the bed. "Would you help me pick out fabric for a mantle to compliment it?" Kiera was stunned that a woman would ask her opinion on such things.

As she sifted through the fabric, a bolt of royal blue velvet fabric caught her eye. She was drawn to it. Kiera ran her hands over it without thinking. It felt as soft as the breast of a dove.

"It would look wonderful on you," Eleanor said. She jumped not realizing what she was doing.

"I'm sorry, I didn't realize," she stammered. "It's just that not since I left Dunsmore, have I seen such beautiful things." Eleanor picked up the fabric and held it up to Kiera's face.

"Yes, I think this will look quite nice on you," she said.

Kiera's eyes widened. "Oh no, I can't!" Kiera said nervously. Besides what would I need a gown such as this for?" She looked down at Eleanor, "I would look foolish. I'm too tall."

There was a light rap on the chamber door. Aurelia walked in. "I'm here to help you with your hem." She looked up in surprise, "Hello Kiera, how are you today?"

Kiera blushed, "I'm fine, thank you."

"Good, you look very well," Aurelia said brightly.

Eleanor turned to Aurelia. "What do you think of this fabric for Kiera?" Eleanor said, holding up the fabric to Kiera's chin.

"I think it's most becoming."

"I'm too tall," Kiera said.

"Nonsense," Eleanor stated firmly. "You are one of the most beautiful women here. And as for this bolt of fabric, Dominick would want you to have it."

Aurelia crossed the room standing beside Kiera. "I think this fabric will make her eyes sparkle like sapphires.

Kiera blushed with such a compliment. "I have a silver circlet that will go nicely with it," Aurelia said.

Kiera smiled. Although she loved Marcus and Jordan dearly, she didn't realize until now how lonely she was for female companionship. She couldn't help the tears from slipping down her face as the two women buzzed around her.

Eleanor looked into Kiera's face. "Oh dear, what's the matter?"

Before Kiera could answer, Aurelia touched her hand, "she's happy."

"I'm sorry," Kiera said sniffing. "Not since my mother was alive have I been pampered like this."

"Well you better get used to it," said Eleanor, feigning firmness, "because you are the sister of Lord Dominick the Immortal, and the Black Knight. And that makes you my sister as well."

"Thank you," she whispered.

"There's no reason to thank me, it's what families do for each other." Eleanor turned back to the matters at hand. "Now we have just three days to get this gown ready in time for the festival. So we're going to need all the help we can get." She turned to "Aurelia, "I think we are going to need Isabella's help on this."

"She would be more than pleased," Aurelia said. "She is quite the seamstress."

Eleanor and Aurelia started fussing over Kiera with plans for her new gown. Suddenly, she remembered Derrick. As much as she wanted to stay with the women, she promised her nephew to take him horseback riding. "I almost forgot, I promised to take Derrick for a ride this afternoon," she said. "I came to ask you permission."

"Yes, of course," Eleanor said. "Just wait until we take a few measurements.

When the women were finally done with her, she left Eleanor's chambers in search for Derrick. She found him in the bailey chasing the same geese he had chased the day he arrived. One of them turned around, hissing at him. Derrick was undaunted. She stopped him just before the goose was ready to strike. They walked to the stables, Derrick chattering all the way. Kiera smiled at the boy's energy.

Kiera mounted Snow, pulling young Derrick up in front of her. She had to hold tight to the little creature wiggling in front of her.

Slowly they moved past the palisades gates, out into the bright warm spring day. They rode past the small hamlets and fields, into a meadow, not unlike the one in which she and Erik first met. How that day had changed her life, she thought. Never would she have imagined she would be riding with this young boy that was her nephew, the son of Dominick of Godwin. What a lovely boy he was. He had an intelligence and wisdom that was beyond most boys his age.

"Papa says you're his sister," Derrick said, twisting around to look at her.

"Yes, I am," she said, smiling down at him.

"That would make you my aunt."

"Yes, it does." She felt the bond building between them. She was going to feel the loss when it was time for her to go. She bent her head and kissed the top of his head, lightly breathing in the scent of his hair. She felt the pang in her heart. Yes she would miss him.

Turning completely around to get a good look at her, he said, "You look like my Papa, only prettier...like a girl."

She rubbed the top of his head. "I am a girl, Derrick," she said, "I just dress differently."

"Uncle Randolf thinks you're pretty too. He said you fight better than most men."

"I have had a lot of training."

"But why? Girls aren't supposed to fight like men."

It's a very long story. When you're older, I'll tell it to you."

"Why do you fight now?" he said turning back around. "My Papa and uncle will protect you."

"It's not that simple, sweety." How much she wished it could be. How much she wished for a normal life. She wanted to be able to put her sword down forever and not have to constantly look over her shoulder. She held Derrick tighter. What she wouldn't give to have a family of her own.

She thought of Erik, what kind of father would he make? The thought of him holding their children brought a longing in her heart. But it could never happen. She was too different, unlike any women he has ever encountered. She thought of his kiss, and how it set her body on fire. She felt weak and vulnerable in his arms.

"Will you teach me how to fight?" Came the small voice, bringing her out of her thoughts.

"Don't you think it best to have your father teach you, or your Uncle Randolf?" she asked.

"I would ask, but they're so busy most of the time," he said.

She looked into his large, hopeful eyes. She smiled down at him. "Well I suppose I could show you a few things," she said.

They moved to a grassy area, where Kiera dismounted, helping Derrick down. She found two long sticks and handed one to him.

"Now, put one foot slightly in front of the other." She showed him. He took the same stance. "Make sure you have your balance, because you can't swing your sword without it." He bent his knees the same way she did, bouncing up and down. "Now, swing your sword like this." She made a swinging motion, arms straight in front of her. Derrick did the same thing. She made a downward motion, he followed her movements.

Kiera smiled at the intensity on his face. "Move in closer to me, but keep your balance and your head up."

He did as she said, and soon their sticks were hitting each other. The mock battle went on until Kiera opened her arms slightly so Derrick could move in. He pressed his stick into her middle. She dropped her stick, pressing her hands where Derrick had jabbed her. She faked a cry of pain, and went down to her knees. "You have run me through you knave! You are truly a great warrior," she said and collapsed to the ground.

Derrick began to laugh. She opened one eye, and in a flash she had him around the waist, bringing him down to the ground with her, tickling his sides. Derrick was helpless. "Do you yield?" she said.

"No!" he said, laughing, trying to breathe.

She tickled him more. "Do you yield?" she said again, laughing almost as hard as he.

"Yes!" Derrick said, laughing and squirming. She stopped and helped him to his feet.

Kiera looked at the beauty that surrounded them. There were wild flowers everywhere. She looked back to Derrick. "You know, to become a great Knight you must know more than how to wield a sword."

"What else do I have to know?"

"You must know how to woo women," she said with a smile.

"Yuck!" he said with a grimace, "I don't like girls."

"You like your mother," she said.

"Yes, but that's different, Mama isn't a girl."

"None the less it's essential to your training," she said with mock sternness. "There are some flowers over there. Why don't you go over and pick some for her. I'm sure she will be wooed off her feet.

They walked into the field of flowers. After Derrick thought he had picked enough, he turned to Kiera, who was making a wreath of flowers, and placed them on her head.

"Do you think I have enough?" he said holding them out for her to inspect.

"I believe you do," she said looking at the bunch he had in his hand. "You'll woo your mother to tears."

Snow whinnied. Kiera looked over in his direction. She could hear the thundering of hooves. She looked over to her right, in the distance she could see three men on horses riding fast toward them. They were moving too fast to be friendly. She had a bad feeling about it. "Derrick come to me," she said, running toward him. She grabbed him around the waist and threw him on to Snow's back, mounting behind him in one leap.

She looked toward Alastair Keep, it was too far away to try and out run them. They would be overtaken before they had a chance to reach it. She couldn't stand and fight risking, Derrick's life. She looked back toward the forest. They had a better chance of losing them in there. She kicked her horse into the direction of the trees. When she felt she had enough cover she turned Derrick toward her.

"Derrick, I want you to climb this tree and hide. Be very, very quiet. Don't come down until I call for you, do you understand?"

Too frightened to speak, the boy nodded.

"Good boy," she said lifting him to the first branch, watching him climb out of sight.

She could hear the men coming through the forest. She dismounted her horse and quietly urged him to move away, further into the woods. Then she hid in some brush.

"They're in here, I saw em' ride in," she heard one man say.

"Well, spread out, we'll find them faster that way," she heard another man say.

She moved deeper into the woods. One was moving toward her, but still too far away to see her. She climbed up into a tree, waiting for him.

Her heart pounded. The man was almost directly underneath her. She pulled her dagger from her boot. Jumping, she caught him by surprise, knocking him off his horse. He let out a yell, just before she thrust the dagger into his heart. His eyes went blank.

"Over here!" one voice shouted to the other. Kiera quickly got to her feet, running back into the brush.

"I thought I heard something," one man said. They found the body of the third man. One man got off his horse, checking the body on the ground, concluding he was dead. He looked around. "Find them, they can't be far," he said.

Kiera crouched lower into the bushes. She had to outsmart them if she was going to get Derrick safely back to the Keep. She could hear the men moving around her. "I found their horse!" one man shouted.

"Good," the other man said, "Then they can't be too far away. Keep looking."

As long as they kept talking Kiera could keep track of them. She was afraid to leave her hiding place, for fear of them hearing her.

There was silence. She waited, her breathing became rapid, and her heart hammered. She was sure it was going to pound right out of her chest. She tried to remain calm, for Derrick's sake. *Where are they?* she wondered.

Suddenly she heard the snap of a twig behind her. Turning swiftly, all she saw was a fist that came down on her cheek. Everything went black.

She woke to someone slapping her face.

"Well now, sleeping beauty awakes," said one man standing over her.

She quickly tried to rise, but one man placed his foot on her chest and pinned her to the ground. "Not so fast, dearie," he said. The other man pulled her up and held her arms firmly at her sides, like steel bands.

Kiera looked at the man in front of her. He was an ugly man with greasy hair and two front teeth missing. He had a long scar on the right side of his face that ran from his forehead to his chin.

He came closer, and she kick out at him, but he jumped out of reach. He grabbed her chin pulling it close to his face, his breath was sour. "Try that again, dearie, and I'll cut you from here to here," he said taking his dagger and ran its tip down her middle.

"What do you want?"

The man holding her tightened his grip. Kiera grimaced.

"Lord Murdock wants to see you."

Kiera nearly blacked out with fright. He found her just like she knew he would. He would hurt Derrick if they were to find him, and take him back to Dunsmore. He would use Derrick to manipulate her. She had to get away somehow. Her fear for Derrick fueled her strength. She struggled against the man holding her.

The man in front of her moved in closer. "Such a beauty. Too bad it will be wasted on a man like Murdock," he said, and ran his hand under her chin. She glared at him. Undaunted, he rubbed his thumb along her lips.

Kiera took the opportunity to sink her teeth into his thumb. He jerked his hand away and held it for a moment. She could see it bleeding. Grinding his teeth he backhanded her across her face. She felt the sting in her lip. She could taste the blood in her mouth.

"You'll be sorry for that," he said menacingly. "Ooooooh so sorry."

The man from behind gripped harder on her arms, while the other man tore her tunic down the front. He stared down at her naked breasts and licked his lips. She struggled fiercely against the man holding her. The man in front of her placed his grimy hands on her breasts. She felt the bile rise to her throat. She screamed in anguish, as the man fondled her.

"Leave her alone!" cried a small voice.

The two men looked up at the small boy. Kiera saw her opportunity. She kicked the man in front of her in the groin. He fell to the ground like a stone. The man behind her loosened his grip in surprise. Kiera brought her heel down hard on his instep. Crying out in pain he let her go. She turned with the swiftness of a cat. With all her strength she slammed her fist into his jaw. He went down the same as the other man.

She drew her sword, making short work of disposing of the two men. Quickly she grabbed the reins of her horse. She mounted her horse, tugged her torn shirt together and stuffing the ends in her pants to secure it, and went to the tree Derrick was hiding in. She signaled him to come down. He jumped into her arms and hugged her tight. She wrapped her arms around him, needing as much reassurance as he did.

"I was so scared Kiera," he cried.

"I know, little one," she said breathlessly, "So was I."

"I know you told me to be quiet, but when those men hurt you, I couldn't be quiet anymore," he said sniffing.

"You are a very brave boy. Like a true knight, you saved both of us."

"You mean I did a good thing?"

"Yes," she said, "but it doesn't mean that in the future when you're given a command that you can ignore it. Like any good knight you have to obey orders."

"I will."

She hugged him again. "Good, we have to hurry. There might be more of them lurking about."

She moved Snow out of the woods then rode at a full run toward Alastair Keep.

When they arrived at the Keep, Erik and Dominick were walking toward the stables. They saw her ride in. Snow was breathing hard from their wild ride.

"God's teeth!" Dominick said and ran toward the two with Erik right beside him.

"What happened?" She felt his stare and pulled her tunic together tighter. She wanted to hide her humiliation.

"We were attacked in the north meadow."

Derrick jumped into his father's arms. "Papa! Kiera fought them and won," he said with pride.

"You endangered my son's life!" Dominick shouted.

"No Papa, she hid me in a tree and when they caught her I yelled at them, even though she told me to be quiet. I couldn't let them hurt her. I surprised them and--"

"Hold on little man," he said placing his hand on the little boy's mouth. "Let's get you inside, and the two of you can explain what happened, and why you were outside the keep without support." Dominick carried Derrick into the Keep.

Erik never took his eyes off her. He held out his arms to her and she eagerly slid into his arms. She could feel the heat of his body as he held her tight. He wrapped his arms around her and placed her head on his shoulder. "Are you all right?" he asked softly.

She couldn't bring herself to talk. Her brother's words had struck home like a dagger. If anything had happened to her young nephew,

it would have been entirely her fault, the
fault of her own arrogance and stupidity. She
knew Murdock had found her. What was she
thinking? Her new family security was making
her soft, and careless. She merely nodded her
head.

"Did they hurt you?"

Looking into his face she saw his concern.
She looked down at her tunic. "No." She
couldn't bring herself to tell him what
happened.

She wanted to vomit when she thought of the
dirty pig that touched her. For him to be the
first man to touch her in such a personal way
disgusted her. If only she could kill him
again. Erik drew her in closer. He untied his
mantle and swung it around her shoulders. He
looked at her bruised cheek and cut lip.

His jaw tightened. Kiera could see the anger
in his face. He rarely let his face reflect his
emotions. Her eyes filled with tears. She
couldn't help herself. "It was Murdock," she
cried. "I was right. He has found me."

"Are you sure?" he said holding her tighter.

"Yes, they said they were taking me to him."

He pulled her tighter into his arms. "I
won't allow this to happen again. I promise
you." He kissed her forehead. "I'll keep you
safe from him, I swear."

Kiera clung to him, "But who will keep you
safe from him?"

Jordan ran out of the Keep upon hearing the
news of the attack. "Kiera, are you all right?"

"I'm fine," she said, raising her head to look in his direction while wiping her tears away, "I'm just a little shaken."

He gently touched her chin, turning her bruised cheek toward him. "Good Lord!" he said clenching his teeth. "Dominick said you killed the men who attacked you."

"Yes."

"May they rot in hell," he said with rancor.

Erik pulled his mantle closer around her. "Would you see Kiera to her chambers? She needs a bath and some rest, we all can question her later."

"Yes, of course," Jordan said putting an arm around her shoulder and walked her up the steps of the Keep.

Kiera turned back toward Erik. He was stroking her horse's neck. He was using his ability to communicate with the animal to see what happened. His body went ridged and she knew what he was seeing right then. She felt suddenly ashamed and unclean. She turned away, walking with Jordan into the Keep.

He stroked her horse's neck and reached into his mind. He saw what the horse saw of the battle and the men who attacked her. His body went ridged when he saw the two men attack her. He felt sick inside when he saw the man touched her breast. He wanted to race to Dunsmore and kill the devil that hunted her. He pulled back on his rage so as not to frighten the animal. *Thank you for allowing me in.* Storm bobbed his head in acknowledgment. He handed his reins to a waiting boy.

Reaching the Great Hall, he saw Derrick reach in his tunic, and retrieve the flowers he picked for is mother. Even after all they had been through he still held on to the flowers.

Eleanor took her precious gift, going down on her knees and hugged him tightly. She looked at Kiera, mouthing the words, *thank you*.

Derrick pulled away. He pulled a flower out of the bunch his mother was holding. Walking over to Kiera, he held it out to her. "This one is for you," he said, handing it to her. "I picked it because it matches your eyes."

She went down on one knee, taking the flower. He threw his arms around her neck. "I love you, Aunt Kiera."

I love you too, my brave knight. You have passed your test for wooing women," she chuckled, kissing him on the forehead.

Erik swelled with pride. Kiera was capable of great love as well as being a great warrior.

"All right, son, go with your mother while we talk to Kiera for a moment," Dominick said gently.

"Yes, Papa," he said taking his mother's hand.

Dominick reached for Eleanor's hand as she passed by, giving her a reassuring squeeze before she left the hall. Erik felt a small bit of jealousy. Dominick and Eleanor had a special bond. He hadn't realized how much he longed for the same kind of relationship until now.

Dominick turned to Kiera. She looked at him wiping the tears from her face as she stood up. He looked at her for a long moment. Then to Erik's surprise Dominick opened his arms to her. She ran into them, nearly knocking him off his feet. She held him tightly, crying like a child. Erik realized she was no longer alone.

Her brother led her to the chair by the hearth. Randolf followed. Dominick held her hands to comfort her. Randolf was squatting beside them, rubbing her arm, and holding her hand.

"Shhh," Dominick said, stroking her hair. "Everything is fine now. You're safe."

"I was so scared," she sobbed. "Not for me. I am accustomed to war. But when those men had me, all I could think was how I was going to get Derrick out of there. He's so little. And if Murdock got his hands on him…." She stopped short, shaking at the thought.

"You did very well," Randolf said.

"Actually if it hadn't been for Derrick yelling at them, causing a distraction, I don't know how things would have turned out," she said.

The mantle she was wearing fell open. Dominick and Randolf both eyed her tunic. Erik ground his teeth.

"Did they touch you?" Dominick asked in a low growl.

"No, Derrick shouted in time," she said visibly blushing and pulling the mantle closed.

"I wish I could have killed those bastards myself," Randolf said.

Dominick brushed her tears away. "I'll take you to your chambers now. We'll talk about this after you have rested. But this time we will talk about it, and we will expect the entire truth." He pulled her out of her chair and led her to the stairs. His arm was tightly around her. Erik wanted to follow, but this was a moment for Kiera and her brothers.

"I'm quite capable of walking," she said.

"Indulge me please," he said. "It's nice to have a little sister to spoil."

Taking her to her chamber, Dominick set her carefully on the bed. A bath had already been drawn, and a warm fire glowing in the hearth.

"Will you be all right now?" Dominick asked, moving her hair out of her face. The bruise was growing darker, her lip was swollen. She held his hand to her cheek, closing her eyes.

"Thank you for my son's life," he said, "I'm proud to call you my sister, but next time, please don't try to take on such danger alone. You are no longer alone, Kiera."

Her eyes filled with new tears, "I have always been proud that you are my brother."

"Well, you get some rest now. I'll see you at the evening meal.

"I will see you then."

Once alone, Kiera sat for a moment staring at the fire. She couldn't believe that her brothers accepted her as she was. "But they don't know everything, do they?" she said out loud. What would they think if they saw her heal someone? What would happen then?

She removed Erik's mantle, lifting it to her face. She took in the smell that only belonged to him. The memory of his embrace made her warm inside. It comforted her. She placed it carefully on the bed. She couldn't allow herself to feel those feelings. She couldn't allow herself to hope, it was too dangerous for her, and for him. Murdock knew where she was. He will do anything to have her. She had to leave....and soon.

She finished undressing. Climbing into the tub of hot water, she scrubbed herself thoroughly, trying to wash away the memory of her ordeal. Looking down at the bruises on her arms, the memories came flooding back. She reached up, touching her cheek, wincing with the pain. She moved her hand to her lip that too was swollen and painful. She flexed her hand. Her knuckles were raw and bruised, from punching her attacker.

She laid her head on the back of the tub. As much as she wanted to, she couldn't turn the healing power into herself, for there would be questions, and suspicions. They would have to heal in their own time. She probably looked ghastly, but she couldn't take the chance.

She got out of the tub, dried herself off, and put on an under tunic. She picked up the torn tunic lying in a heap and threw it in the fire. There was a knock at her door and when she opened it Marcus was on the other side.

"Oh, Marcus, he found us."

"If he comes, we'll be prepared, and I think this time he is the one who will have regrets."

"He'll use my family to get to me."

"Dominick and Randolf are powerful warriors. He held her face in his hands and looked into her eyes." Do you think after all these years of fighting that they could just be taken by a man like Murdock?" She shook her head. "We're talking about Dominick the Immortal and the Black Knight. They've never been defeated. They can't be defeated. Besides, Dominick is a friend to the King. What do you think would happen if the King should hear of their capture?" He stroked her cheek. "Murdock would be hung for treason. Don't worry, you'll be well protected. And Murdock won't dare try to hurt Dominick, or his family."

He pulled her forward, kissing her forehead. "You are the daughter of my heart, and I cherish you," he said. "I won't allow anything to happen to you, or your family."

Touching his face, she looked into his eyes, "I love you, too. You will always be family." He kissed her hand. "I'll never be able to repay you for stealing me away from that awful place."

"I'm the one who is grateful to have such a loving child as you." He looked into her face, as if seeing the bruises for the first time. He stroked her cheek. "Why didn't you heal yourself?"

"I don't want my brothers to know," she said. "They might ask questions."

"They might understand. They seem to understand everything else."

"Not now. I want them to get to know me for who I am first. Besides I think it's enough to adjust to, finding out they have a sister.

"You may be right. I'll talk to Erik about his staff. Someone must have told Murdock we're here. We'll find out if there are any new people in the Keep."

"I hope so," she hugged her knees tighter.

Marcus saw her fear, "Aw Lamb, I'm sorry I wasn't there to protect you."

"It wasn't your fault," she said reaching for his hand. "I didn't think he would find us so fast."

"You're safe here, my love," he said.

"Yes, but for how long. We can't stay here forever, and when we leave he'll be waiting."

"We'll deal with that when the time comes." He squeezed her hand tightly. "Do you feel ready to come down for the evening meal?"

"I'll be ready in a few minutes," she said, giving him a final squeeze. "You don't need to wait for me."

"I'll see you in the Great Hall shortly then."

"Yes."

"Good," he kissed her forehead and left the room.

CHAPTER XVII

Kiera was almost afraid to leave her room. She no longer felt safe at Alastair Keep. Murdock knew where she was. His men will be waiting for an opportunity to snatch her away. Then her nightmare would really begin.

She heard a commotion outside her window. A large group of soldiers mounted on horseback. They were heavily armed. Erik was giving orders before they departed.

They were a patrol to search for any more of Murdock's men. They wouldn't find any. Murdock's men could blend anywhere, as anyone and no one would suspect them. The Captain of Murdock's guards taught them well. She shivered at the thought of him. He was an evil man. He delighted in people's pain and suffering, just as his master did. She saw too many lives lost to his sword in the name of duty. Ha! More like the name of pleasure. She knew if her life fell into his hands, there would be no mercy.

Turning away from the window, Kiera dressed in her white tunic. Looking at her reflection it somehow made her bruised face more grotesque. She brought her hand to her swollen cracked lip, wincing at the touch. How she wished she could heal herself, but there would be too many questions. Her brothers would never understand. She thought of staying in her chambers, but that would be hiding like a coward. Too many years had already been spent in hiding. She won't do it any longer. She turned away from the mirror. Staring at her chamber door she forced herself to walk to it. Taking a deep breath she swung it open. She jumped with a start. To her surprise, she found a guard standing just outside her door.

"Ma'am," the guard said, bowing slightly. "I'm to escort you to the Great Hall."

Kiera put her hand on her chest trying to calm herself. Thank you," she said breathlessly.

"I'm sorry if I frightened you."

"I'm all right. I just didn't expect you."

Erik wanted to make her feel safe by posting a guard at her door. But Kiera knew Murdock too well. Nothing would keep her safe now that he had found her. His men would run through anyone who was in their way to get to her. She would have to talk to Erik about releasing his soldier from his duty. It would be better to have Marcus, or Jordan, who knew more about Murdock's treachery. She was safer with them.

When she reached the bottom of the stairs the guard left her side. She saw Erik standing alone by the hearth. There was no one else in the hall. She watched him for some time. He was deep in thought as he stared into the flames. His amber eyes reflected in the bright firelight, like a great cat. His long blond hair fell over his shoulder. He flexed his arm, and the muscles bulged through his tunic. It sent a wave of desire through her. She crossed the hall unable to resist touching him. She lightly ran her fingers down his arm. He placed his hand over hers. When he turned to her she nearly gasped with the anger and the intensity of his glare.

He saw the images of her attack and near rape. She was mortified, and pulled her hand away, lowering her head, unable to look in to his face. The thought of his seeing what they had done to her made her feel ashamed.

He saw her despair. "Kiera, it wasn't your fault, there was nothing you could have done. You fought bravely against those scum." He grabbed her arms and looked her in the eye. "I swear nothing like that will ever happen to you again."

She winced when his hands grew tighter around her upper arms. He quickly released her, moving her sleeve up her arm. Seeing her bruises dark clouds of anger moved over him. Further evidence of what had happened to her.

After a long moment, he said, "Can't you turn the healing into yourself?"

"Yes," she said softly, "but too many people saw me when I came in. There would be too many questions."

He saw her reasoning, but still felt helpless at her suffering.

Still holding her wrist, he heard the soft sound of tiny bells on her bracelet. He thumbed her wrist gently.

"Isabella gave it to me for helping Ian."

He looked up into her face. "It becomes you. You should be adorned in more women's finery."

He was still holding her wrist, when he heard someone clear their throat. Erik dropped her hand, stepping away. "I must be growing deaf," Erik whispered to himself.

Dominick and Eleanor were at the bottom of the stairs. Eleanor came forward, and gently touched Kiera's bruised cheek. Erik winced when he saw Kiera jump with pain.

"You poor dear!" She pulled a jar out of her pocket. "I brought you a salve that will help bring the swelling down, and ease the pain." Gently as she could Eleanor applied the salve to Kiera's lip. She winced slightly. Erik clenched his teeth, seeing her pain.

"You'll need to apply some to her arms, as well," Erik said through his teeth.

Realizing he was being watched by Dominick, he turned his face into detachment then turned back toward the hearth.

Turmoil rolled through him. His world was spinning out of control. He needed to stop it. Control was how he lived. It was something he depended on. He swore he would get it back, and God help those who tried to take it away from him.

Aurelia came in to the hall escorted by Marcus. Everyone watched as they entered the room. She gracefully held Marcus' arm. They were completely animated with each other as they entered the hall.

Seeing Aurelia on Marcus' arm, reminded Erik that his aunt was indeed a beautiful woman. Many times he wondered why she never married, but never thought to ask. He supposed it was because she was too busy raising him and his sister after their mother had died. Then when they grew up, she may have felt she was too old. It was his father's duty to make a suitable marriage, but then again his father neglected his responsibilities when it came to his family. Looking at her now smiling at Marcus she looked younger than her years, even radiant.

The tables were now turned. He was responsible for his aunt and he wouldn't allow her to be hurt.

"How are you feeling?" Dominick asked, turning to his sister, kissing her lightly on her good cheek.

"I feel better, thank you." She tried giving him a reassuring smile, but couldn't.

"You are definitely my sister, to be such a fierce warrior." Dominick took Kiera's hand and looked down at her bruised knuckles. "It must have given you great satisfaction when your fist connected with that bastard's jaw.

"Dominick!" Eleanor said.

"Sorry, my dear," he said properly chastised.

"Bastard is too good of a word for those sons of bitches," she smiled.

Dominick laughed. Even Erik smiled. "My Dear we are going to have to talk about your language."

Ian and Isabella came down the stairs with Randolf right behind. Randolf was dressed completely in black. He looked dark and mysterious. His long black hair was pulled tightly away from his face, tied in back with a strip of black leather. His features were made sharper, his face bronzed from long hours working out in the sun, which was in stark contrast with his brilliant blue eyes. They were hypnotic. Mouths were hanging open on every serving woman in the hall. But Randolf was oblivious to their presence.

He walked over to Kiera and placed a light kiss at her temple. She could hear the sighs of the women around them. Isabella laughed. "You always make a great entrance, Randolf," she said.

"Not enough to impress you," he said, smiling back at her.

"You were always too handsome for me. I couldn't stand up to the competition," she said teasingly. "Besides my heart was already taken from the time I was four years old."

She hugged Ian's arm tightly.

Ian shrugged his shoulders. "What can I say, I was charming even as a child," he said smugly.

Randolf slapped him on the back. "As I recall, that so called charm nearly got you killed by a serving wench's husband, a few years back," he said mischievously.

Ian threw up his hands, "I never touched the wench! It was all a misunderstanding." Isabella gave Ian a hard elbow to his ribs. He let out a low grunt. Everyone began to laugh. Kiera held her mouth to keep from smiling.

Aurelia went to Kiera and looked into her face. "I have some herbs that will heal those bruises in no time," she said loud enough for everyone to hear. "In a couple of days you won't look as if you had a mark on you." She gave Kiera a conspiratorial wink, having given her the means by which to heal herself.

They sat down at the evening meal. Kiera inquired about Derrick. "He will be fine," Eleanor said. "I put him to bed early. I think he had enough excitement for one day."

"You're probably right. If you don't mind I would like to check on him later."

Eleanor smiled. "That would be fine. I think he would like that."

Kiera turned back to her meal. She was unable to enjoy it. Her mouth throbbed with every bite. Erik poured her wine, but it stung with every sip. She tried eating again, but it was impossible. When she couldn't tolerate any more, she pushed her plate away in disgust, but continued drinking her wine. After a while it didn't sting as much.

Erik touched her hand.

"I wasn't that hungry anyway." She began to feel the weight of her day. "I'm tired. I think I'll retire early if you don't mind."

"I'll walk you to your chamber," he said. He helped her with her chair and gave her his arm. He looked down at Dominick who had one eyebrow raised. "I'll just see her to her room. I will be back down shortly."

They briefly checked in on Derrick. He was curled up in his bed, sound asleep, without a care in the world. Kiera stood over his bed lightly brushing his hair from his face.

A few minutes later, Erik led her up to her chambers. When they entered he searched for any unwanted guests. When he was satisfied there were none, he went back to Kiera and placed his hands on her shoulders. "You'll be safe tonight. I'll have a guard posted outside your door."

"Erik please, don't do that. If Murdock wants me he'll have me. He will cut down anyone who stands in his way."

"Murdock is a man, Kiera, not a ghost. No one can get into this room without someone knowing about it."

"You don't know him like I do. He has spies everywhere," she said, exasperated.

"And I'll find them. But until I do, I'll feel better if you have a guard outside your door."

She couldn't argue with him. He would do whatever he felt was necessary to protect her.

He wrapped her in his arms. She could smell the scent of the soap on his skin. She committed it to memory. "You'll be all right." Bending so they were eye to eye. "Is there anything I can get you?"

"No," she said, shaking her head, "I'm just very tired, I think sleep is all I need now."

"I'll see you in the morning."

She nodded, as he turned to leave the room, she could see through the open door that the guard was already posted.

Kiera barely had the energy to change out of her clothes, and climb into bed.

Erik returned to his friends and family down in the Great Hall. He joined Dominick and Randolf who were talking about the attack on Kiera. "What do you think we should do about her, Dominick," Randolf said.

"I'm not sure," he said thoughtfully. "Marcus told me this isn't the first time Murdock's men have tried to take her. He told me this is the reason they've been on the run for so long."

"Did he tell you why Murdock was after them?"

No, he wouldn't say, and I couldn't push him. I believe for her safety we should take her back to Godwin as soon as possible."

"I don't think that would be a good idea at this time," Erik said.

Both men turned to him. "Why wouldn't you think so?" Dominick asked.

Erik leaned forward and looked around making sure the women couldn't hear. "You only have a few men with you. If there were a spy here at Alastair, Murdock would have already been informed that you are here and planning to take her back with you. His men would be out there in numbers to ambush you as soon as you leave the Keep. And if I were to send my men with you, it would leave Alastair unprotected."

"What do you suppose we should do? We can't stay here indefinitely," Randolf pointed out.

"First we must find the spy. After he's caught, we could send one of your men to Godwin to bring an army for your escort."

"That sounds like a good plan," Dominick said, "but what do we do about protecting Kiera in the meantime?"

"I have a guard posted at her door now. I also have patrols out looking for any more of Murdock's scum. If they try to take her again, we'll be ready for them." Erik sat back in his chair and took a drink of his ale.

"Good," Dominick said. "In the meantime one of us will be with her at all times. She won't be allowed to leave the Keep without an escort, whether she likes it or not."

Erik and Randolf nodded in agreement. The three men stood up to say good night. Dominick and Eleanor were the first to leave the hall. After the others left, Erik sat at the table absently stroking his dogs thinking and planning ways to keep Kiera safe.

Jordan approached him. "Lord Erik," he said clearing his throat. He looked up. "I want to apologize for the other night, when I saw Kiera in your arms. I thought the worst.

"There's no need to apologize. I would have done the same thing if I were in your shoes," he said, turning back to the animals.

"Well maybe. I also want to thank you for all you've done to see Kiera safe. She's not your responsibility, yet you have done a great deal for her, for all of us."

Erik turned back to Jordan, seeing his sincerity. "She was not your responsibility, yet you protected her."

Jordan stopped and stared off for a moment as if deep in thought. As if he had made up his mind about something, he said quickly, "Murdock thinks if he has Kiera, he will become immortal."

"Why would he think that?"

"Because of her power to heal. He feels she can cure aging and disease. With her he would fear nothing."

Erik dropped his hand, "So he will do anything to have her."

"Exactly. No matter how far we run, he seems to be right behind us. He has spies everywhere. There has been no place for us to hide. Many times we have barely escaped. His men are very devious. You never know who they are, or where they're hiding. We have learned to trust no one."

"We'll find the spy he has here, I swear to you Jordan."

"And he will send another one." Jordan stood straighter, his expression sober.

Erik looked back down at his dogs, scratching one behind the ear. Jordan stepped closer. "We never expected Dominick to become a man of peace. By not taking what belongs to him, he has signed our death warrants."

Erik thought for a moment. "Jordan would you swear fealty to me, along with your father. You'll have the protection of Alastair Keep."

"I'll swear fealty to you, but it will do no good. Murdock's men know where we are. It's just a matter of time."

Erik watched the hopelessness in Jordan' face. He stood, putting his hand on Jordan' shoulder. "Jordan I promise it's not so bleak. Together we'll find a way to make all of you safe."

Jordan smiled back, "I hope so. I truly hope so." With that Jordan left the hall, leaving Erik deep in his thoughts.

How his life had changed in the matter of a week. Before he had nothing to care about except his sister, his aunt and his land. Then one day by a twist of fate a woman saved his life. And now he was responsible for hers. Yet he wasn't sure he would have it any other way. He was strongly attracted to her. She was unlike any woman he ever met before. Besides her strength, there was a passion he never knew in another woman. Just being near her made his pulse race. Even her battered and bruised face didn't deter his wanting of her. It made him all the more willing to hold her close, to lay down his life to keep her from any further hurt or pain.

No matter how many battles he fought, or bandits that attacked his home he had never been frightened. But his attraction to Kiera scared him to death. He straightened himself up. He would see about this spy at Alastair first thing in the morning. If he wanted his household alert, they needed their rest. In the meantime he would send out a few men of his own. He would fight fire with fire. He would find out what this Murdock was all about, find his weakness, and destroy him.

With his plan set he left the hall, intending to retire, but first he would look in on Kiera.

CHAPTER XVIII

She woke up with a start, sitting straight up in her bed, her heart pounded hard in her chest.

In the darkness she heard Erik's voice, "It was just a dream, Angel." There was a striking of a flint as he lit a candle beside her bed. His features glowed in the warm light. He sat down beside her on the bed and held her hand.

"Erik, what are you doing in here?"

"Just making sure you're all right," he said rubbing the top of her hand. "Go back to sleep."

She sighed, "I can't."

"Would you like me to get something to help you sleep?"

She held his hand tighter. "No, I don't want to sleep."

He brushed her hair from her face. "Why?" he asked gently.

"Because every time I close my eyes, I see him, and my nightmare begins."

"You need to rest."

"I know." Kiera looked down noticing his tunic was open halfway down his chest. She could see his muscles flex when he moved his hand. She watched the pulse beat in his neck.

She couldn't resist the urge to place a kiss where it throbbed.

When her lips made contact, she jumped buck. She had forgotten about her bruised lip.

Erik looked into her eyes and touched her tender face. "Heal yourself, Angel." He kissed her forehead, then her neck. "I want to feel your lips on my skin."

His warm breath on her neck sent a spear of excitement through her. She looked into his eyes. They were glowing like a cat's in the night.

She needed to be close to him. She felt a hunger she couldn't define. There was so little time left. For once in her life she wanted to feel cared for, as only a man could care for a woman. Lying back down on the bed, she closed her eyes, turning the healing into herself. Erik watched the bruises fade. When her eyes opened there was no evidence of her battle.

Erik leaned over and gently brushed her lips with his. She wound her fingers in his hair, deepening their kiss. A feeling overwhelmed her. A moan escaped her lips as he laid his body next to hers. His warmth fueled her passion.

He kissed the hollow of her throat, running his tongue up her neck then lightly tugged on her earlobe. It made her skin prickle. A burning need bloomed between her thighs, a need she didn't understand.

She kissed his neck and nipped it with her teeth. He held his head beck, giving her greater access. Her hands moved to his chest, as she kissed his shoulders. Wanting to touch more of him, she reached under his tunic and pulled it over his head. She stopped for a moment, awed by his strong powerful body. Her fingers flexed into his flesh, sending shards of desire through her.

He pulled her down beneath him kissing her full red lips. His hand moved down her neck to her chest, then to her breast. For a moment she froze, remembering the attack.

He put his lips to her ear. "Open your eyes, Kiera, it's me touching you, me making love to you," His thumb gently brushed across her nipple.

Hearing his voice pulled her back to him. He unlaced the front of her nightdress, and pulled it open. He fondled her nipples to hard peaks. Her back arched into his touch. Kiera was nearly insane with desire.

His hands moved down to her thigh. Her muscles were firm from years of riding. He pulled her nightdress up over her hips. His hand caressed the inside of her knee, then ran it up the inside of her thigh. He gave the other side the same attention, making her hot with need.

Kiera ran her fingers in his hair, as he raised her nightdress above her waist. He ran his tongue along the inside of her thigh and kissed the back of her knee. He came back up and pressed a kiss on her lips. His tongue explored her mouth.

His body completely covered hers. She loved the feel of his weight on her. His manhood was rock hard.

His hand moved between them to the soft curls between her thighs. Kiera could barely catch her breath. His hands moved to the inside of her knees, and spread them wider. He touched her woman's core, stroking it gently. Desire tightened her muscles low in her belly. Kiera nearly came off the bed.

"Slowly Angel, slowly," he whispered.

Holding on tightly she said, "Erik, I don't understand what I want. It's so strange to me," she moaned. Her nails dug into his chest.

"You will, Angel, you will." He slipped one finger inside her. She nearly screamed. Her hips moved of their own accord with every stroke. Her body dismissed her will.

A need grew between her legs. "That's it, Angel." Her breathing became rapid and shallow. His hand moved faster. She climaxed. It felt as though her body was rising then crashed through a wall of passion and beyond.

Erik held her tightly as her body shuddered. When she finally began to calm down, he moved back on top of her and pressed his manhood into her tender center, sending a final shot of desire through her already sensitive core.

He hadn't yet removed his britches. "Kiera open your eyes," he said holding her face in his hands. "If you want me to, I'll stop now."

At first Kiera didn't grasp his meaning. Then her eyes widened in understanding. "Erik, I need you, I want you, please don't stop," she whispered. She kissed him hard on the mouth, moving her hips into his groin. He broke away, throwing his head back. A small groan escaped his lips. She ran her tongue along his jaw, nipping his chin.

He was about to move off the bed, to remove the rest of his clothing, when Albert came crashing through her chamber door. Kiera screamed, covering herself with the blankets. Erik was off the bed in an instant and grabbed Albert by the tunic. But before he could thrash him soundly, the squired yelled, "My Lord, it's Lady Aurelia, she's been hurt! She's in the stables."

Kiera was off the bed and out the door before Erik could stop her. He turned to Albert. "You saw nothing, understand?" she heard him say as he ran after her.

Kiera ran to the stables. She had to work her way through the crowd that surrounded Aurelia. She saw her on the ground deathly white. Marcus was kneeling beside her. Blood stained her gown. She swallowed hard. The memories of her nightmare that afternoon came flooding back.

Marcus had his hand pressed to Aurelia's side trying to stop the flow of blood. Tears ran down his face. Marcus was in love with her. Her heart broke for him. He looked up, seeing Kiera standing there, "Kiera, please," he pleaded. The wound was mortal. She was afraid, but she bent down, touching Aurelia's arm. Kiera felt the darkness rising from within. She jumped back. "She's too close to the blackness," she said, shaking her head. Marcus' face showed his devastation. It tore her heart apart. He wept, holding her tightly as he rocked her back and forth. Kiera couldn't stand to see Marcus suffer so. She looked into Aurelia's face. This woman had always been kind to her. She accepted her the way she was. No one since her mother cared for her as Aurelia had. Tears ran down Kiera's cheeks, as she moved Marcus's hand away.

Marcus tried to stop her. "No Kiera, you can't do this, it's too dangerous."

"Marcus, I have to help her. Please step back."

"No Kiera, you said she was too close," he said desperately.

"I love her too, and it's because of me she's dying."

Marcus' eyes widened, "You don't know that."

"I do," she said with conviction.

Erik and Jordan stepped through the crowd just as Kiera placed her hands on Aurelia's wounds.

Erik tried to stop her, "Kiera, no!" he shouted, but Jordan held him back.

Erik struggled against him, until Marcus too held him back. When she touched Aurelia's side, Kiera felt the burning pain. It tore through her body like a torch. The blood stopped flowing beneath her hand. After a few minutes Aurelia's eyes opened. Finally, Kiera pulled her hands away.

She didn't move. Still on her knees, her head down, her shoulders slumped.

Aurelia sat up, realizing what had happened. She put her arms around Kiera, and hugged her tight, but there was no response from her. Marcus pulled Aurelia away.

Erik slowly walked over to her and kneeled in front of her. He looked into her pale face. Raising her chin, he was shocked to see that even the color in her eyes had paled. She looked at him without recognition. He felt fear twist in his gut. "Kiera," he gently called her name.

She slowly raised her head to look at him. Her eyes rolled back as she collapsed into his arms. He touched the pulse in her neck, it was very weak.

Lifting her he carried her through the crowd. Many people crossed themselves as he walked by. Dominick and Randolf just stared, as he walked between them. Eleanor was the first to recover and ran after them.

When they reached Kiera's chamber, Eleanor turned down the bed, then he gently laid Kiera in it. Eleanor tucked the blankets around her. He sat on the bed beside her and held her cold pale hand. Eleanor brought more candles over to the bedside table. He could see the dark smudges under her eyes. It was like looking at a ghost.

Eleanor placed her hand on Kiera's forehead. "She needs more blankets. We have to keep her warm."

"I'll get them," Dominick said.

Erik looked up just in time to see him walk out of the room. He was back in just moments, with Randolf behind him carrying firewood. Randolf started a blazing fire, while Dominick laid blankets on top of Kiera, tucking them around her.

Kiera lay still as death. Erik sat there watching her, hoping for a flicker of an eyelash, or an involuntary flex of a finger. There was nothing. She lay there as if her life had been completely drained from her body. It was then Erik understood her power. She poured her life's energy into a wound and made it heal. The more severe the wound, the more life it took. He swore he would never allow her to do it again.

He felt Eleanor's hand on his shoulder. "You can leave now Erik. I'll stay with her."

"No, I want to stay," his eyes never leaving Kiera's face.

"You have more important things to do," she said firmly.

"Such as?" he turned to her.

"Such as finding who did this," she said harshly.

He felt as if someone had just thrown a bucket of cold water on him. He stood up abruptly and turned to Eleanor, "Help her, please."

"I'll do all that I can."

Erik quickly ran to his chambers, yelling for his squire. Albert was there before Erik reached the door, awaiting his orders.

He dressed in full armor and hurried down to Aurelia's chambers. Isabella was there along with Ian and Marcus. "Tell me what happened." His tone flat.

"I went to the stables with Marcus. He was showing me his...ah, horse." Aurelia blushed. "I saw Angus, our new stable hand lurking about. I could feel something strange about him, but I didn't say anything to Marcus, because I wanted to make sure. Later, I went back to the stables. When I saw him again I knew he was the spy. Angus knew I knew. That's when he attacked me."

Marcus patted her on the shoulder and turned toward him. "Later I asked one of the serving girls if they had seen her. She said Aurelia headed toward the stables." Marcus nearly choked on his words. Clearing his throat he said, "That's when I found her."

Aurelia stood out of her chair, "I must go to Kiera."

Ian put out a hand to stop her. "You must rest, Aurelia, you have had a terrible shock."

Erik's body hardened. "I want you to rest," he said. "You need not worry about Kiera, Eleanor is with her now."

Marcus put his arm around Aurelia's waist as she looked down at the floor in despair. Erik stood watching the intimacy between them. Anger grew inside his mind. Because of their rendezvous in the stable, Kiera was lying motionless in her bed. He could hardly look at his Aunt without condemnation.

"I'm going after Angus," Erik said sharply.

"I'll come with you," Marcus said.

"No," Erik stopped him. If Marcus came near him he was sure he would kill him. "I need you here in case he should come back. I'll take Jordan with me."

Ian stepped forward, "I'm coming with you," he said.

"Fine." He turned back to Marcus. "When I come back, you'll marry my aunt," he said in a deceptively calm voice that masked his irritation.

"What?" Aurelia said. "Erik how dare you just hand me over like I was some kind of cattle. I'm old enough to be your mother."

"Then you are old enough to be responsible for your actions," he said, frowning.

Marcus' back stiffened, but he kept silent.

"You must know you have been compromised by being alone with him in the stables." He turned back to Marcus. Anger pumped through his veins. "You'll marry her, or you'll be hanged."

"It would be my honor to marry her," Marcus said, standing stiffly.

Erik turned and left the room without acknowledging Marcus' reply. Ian followed him out, wisely keeping silent for once. Dominick and Randolf were waiting for Erik and Ian in the Great Hall.

Not a word was said as the four men walked into the bailey. Dawn was breaking. Jordan was waiting with their mounts.

Erik's dogs and hawk were brought to him. He stroked his hawk's feathers, "We have a new prey, my love," he said. Closing his eyes he brought Angus' face to mind. *Find him.* A piece of Angus's bedding had been brought for the dogs to catch his scent. Albert held on tight to their leashes as they became excited, sensing the hunt.

They rode out of the palisades gate. Erik unhooked his hawk and released her into the brightening sky. He nodded to Albert to unleash the straining dogs. They took off, yelping and barking. His horse bounded after them. The others followed suit. Hooves thundered and dogs barked. Anyone who saw them would think they were an army from Hell.

The sky was ablaze with an orange glow as the night folded its purple blanket to reveal the new morning. The hawk flew high into the sky, while the five men rode hard across the meadow after the dogs. Upon entering the forest, the dogs separated, but still kept moving forward. Erik slowed Storm as his dogs sniffed the ground, frantically looking for the scent. Once found, they exploded forth with their noses close to the ground. They came upon a stream. The dogs started baying. They had lost the scent and became confused. Randolf and Ian walked their horses further downstream hoping to find something. Jordan moved across to the other side of the stream.

He closed his eyes, clearing his mind. He reached out to Celeste, as she circled above them. Through her he saw Angus crossing the meadow to the north. He yelled for Randolf and Ian to join them. They crossed the stream and carefully picked their way through the dense forest. The dogs followed and soon found the scent they sought.

As they broke through the trees, he saw a lone man a few hundred yards in front of them. Upon hearing the dogs, Angus turned. Seeing the five men on horses barreling down on him, he started to run. Erik urged Storm into a deadly chase. The dogs were barking behind him.

He pulled his mount alongside Angus and kicked out, knocking him to the ground. The dogs were quickly on him. Angus shrieked. Erik called them off.

"My Lord! What brings you out so early in the morning?" Angus asked, pitifully trying to hide his fear.

"Hunting," Erik said. He steeled his emotions. Deadly calm, he waited for Angus to speak again. The other four men caught up to them, their horses circled Angus.

The man looked around him as the five armored men looked down at him. "Hunting?" he said nervously, hunting for what?"

"Spies."

"Spies?" There are no spies here."

"I think differently," Erik said, dismounting his horse.

Angus's eyes widened with fear. "My Lord, please, I was only following orders." Angus got to his knees pleading. "Please, My Lord, he would have killed me if I didn't do as he said."

He walked to Angus, glaring down on him. "Who gave the orders?"

Angus bowed his head, "Lord Murdock. He sent me out to look for the girl, and her companions, that's all."

"Why didn't you just leave when you reported her the first time? Why did you come back?"

"I had to My Lord. Murdock wanted to know of any changes. He promised to take my eyes if I failed him."

"Then you tried to kill Lady Aurelia when she discovered you."

Angus trembled. "It-it was an accident, My Lord. I was just trying to get away when she came after me. Somehow the dagger slipped."

Erik turned to Jordan, "Tie him up." His anger settled into a pool of calm.

Angus went pale. "Please, my lord, please, I'm sorry. Please don't do this. I could become your spy," he said desperately, as he saw Jordan dismount his horse with a rope. "I could tell you what's going on at Dunsmore Castle. Please, Lord Erik, he would have killed me, I didn't have a choice."

Erik mounted. Looking down on Angus he said coldly, "Neither do I."

Jordan threw Angus across the front of his horse, and mounted behind him. Angus pleaded and cried all the way to the nearest tree. He jerked Angus upright so he could place the rope around his neck. Throwing the other end of the rope over the thickest branch on the tree, he pulled up the slack. Jumping to the ground, Jordan tied the end of the rope around the trunk. He pulled on the knot to make sure it was secure. Angus quivered and cried, begging for his life.

Jordan looked at Erik. He nodded and Jordan slapped his horse's hindquarter sending him off. They heard the snap of Angus' neck as he was snatched off the horse by the rope. His body jerked for a moment, and then became completely still.

Jordan went to cut the body down, but Erik stopped him.

"Let the vultures have him, and let Murdock receive that message." He turned his mount, and rode back toward Alastair.

CHAPTER XIX

The five men returned to the Keep in silence. Even the hounds were quiet. Erik called his hawk out of the sky and handed her over to his falconer. He dismounted and entered the Keep, not stopping until he reached Kiera's chambers. There he found her just as he had left her, pale and lifeless. Eleanor came across the room.

"There's been no change," she said, looking back at Kiera. "Give it time."

Erik couldn't bring himself to respond. He left her chambers without a backward glance. In his chambers he found a bath being drawn for him. Albert removed his armor. "Do you need help, My Lord?"

"No, thank you Albert," he said as he sank wearily into the tub. "I want you to bring the chaplain to me, however. Then find Alice, and have her prepare Lady Aurelia for her wedding. Ready the church with flowers and tell Olaf to cook a wedding feast." He knew Albert had questions, but he was trained well enough not to voice them.

Erik laid his head on the back of the tub and tried to calm himself. He had let his emotions become too involved. It frightened

him. He told himself it was simple lust he felt
for her. First opportunity, he would find a
buxom serving girl, and spend his lust without
any emotional complications. He would get Kiera
out of his mind. Once she left with her
brothers she would be forgotten, like so many
other women he had known. He took a deep
breath, trying to shake loose the tightness in
his chest. Kiera's blue eyes were imprinted on
the back of his eyelids. He took deep breaths,
but he couldn't force her out of his mind.

He was nearly out of the tub when Aurelia
stormed in. He sank quickly back into the
water. "So you think I'm going to go along with
your wedding plans, do you?" she said with her
hands on her hips. "Well think again, my boy,
I'll not be forced by anyone to marry!"

Erik was nonplused. "Aunt Aurelia, I'm in
the middle of my bath."

"I raised you, don't think I haven't seen
you naked before," she said angrily pacing back
and forth.

"Not since I was a boy, and yes you'll marry
Marcus, unless you would like to see him
hanged."

Stopping in her tracks, she cried, "Erik,
you wouldn't do that!"

"Wouldn't I?" he raised his eyes to hers.
"Don't doubt me capable of anything just now."

Aurelia stepped back. "Why, Erik? Why would
you do this?"

He thought at first it was to punish the
couple because their indiscretion had harmed
Kiera. Now he thought clearly and it was

unreasonable to think Aurelia was responsible. Erik's eyes softened, seeing his aunt's distress. "To insure your happiness."

"What makes you think forcing me to marry will insure my happiness?" she said, throwing her hands up.

He wiped soap off his shoulder. "I don't think I have to explain it."

"Yet you won't change your mind," she said as a fact rather than a question.

"No," he said simply.

He saw the resignation on her face. "Fine." She left his chamber not looking back at him as she slammed the door.

Drying himself, he saw faint red marks on his chest, left by Kiera's fingernails during their lovemaking. The thought of her passion hit him like a hard blow to his stomach. For distraction he thought of the wedding at hand.

He dressed quickly in his best finery for Aurelia's wedding. He wore a green tunic with gold and red embroidery around the neck. Brown deer skin britches, with matching leather boots. His mantle was forest green. He wore a wide brown leather belt, with an ornate buckle, his sword in its sheath at his side.

Ian walked in. "So you really plan to go through with this."

"Yes."

"May I ask why?"

"I thought I explained it last night," Erik said looking at Ian directly.

"You were angry last night. I didn't think you would go through with it, once you had time to think about it."

"What has changed since last night?" Erik asked. "My Aunt was in the stables with Marcus alone. She was compromised, and I'll see her properly wed. It is my duty as head of the family."

"Or maybe you wish to get Marcus out of the way as Kiera's protector so you can take his place."

Erik gave Ian a cold hard stare. Neither man said a word for a moment, then Erik spoke. "After Spring Festival, Dominick and Randolf will be going back to Godwin. Kiera will be going with them. She'll be under their protection...not mine," he said flatly.

"So you're going to crawl back in that shell of yours. Is that what you want?"

"Most heartily yes. I want nothing more than my life to go back to normal."

"By normal you mean, being an unfeeling selfish bastard?"

He refused to be goaded into an argument. He started to leave the chambers when Ian grabbed his arm to stop him. "When are you going to realize to be truly happy you have to let someone in? You're going to have to actually give into your emotions."

Erik pulled away from him. "I can't," he said and left the room.

He met Aurelia in the chapel. She was beautiful in her dazzling scarlet gown.

He remembered she was only fourteen when she came to live with them. She was not an old woman. He remembered her comforting him when his mother died. She took care of him when he was sick, nurtured him when his father left. She cared for his every need. It was time for him to care for hers. He knew he was doing the right thing marrying her to Marcus. Marcus was a good man. He may not be of the same status, but he knew Marcus would take care of her, and cherish her the way she deserved.

Erik offered his arm. She reluctantly took it. He could feel her trembling as he walked her down the chapel aisle, but she won't look at him. He was sure by nightfall he would be forgiven.

He saw Marcus at the altar with Jordan standing beside him. Marcus never took his eyes off Aurelia. His eyes even became misted when Erik gave him her hand. The ceremony was short. Tears ran down Aurelia's cheeks as she spoke her vows. Marcus held her hands tightly. When he was finally allowed to kiss his bride it was more than just a ceremonial peck. It was downright possessive.

Marcus' chest puffed out as he walked his bride back up the aisle. He nodded to Erik as he passed by. Jordan was right behind them, and gave Erik a quick wink.

A great cheer rose up as the couple came out of the chapel. Everyone loved Aurelia and her selflessness. They were all truly happy for her. Marcus gave his new wife a hug. "All will be well my love, you'll see."

"You're not angry that Erik forced you to marry me?"

"Angry! I'm truly grateful that he should allow someone like me to marry such a beautiful and honorable woman. No man could be as lucky as me."

Aurelia hugged him and cried. "It's I who is lucky, to finally find a man I can truly love with all my heart."

Marcus kissed her passionately. The cheer from the crowd was deafening. When Marcus finally released her, she laughed, wiping the tears from her face.

The bridal procession went into the gardens where there were tables set up for the wedding feast. Albert had outdone himself. There were flowers on every table. The head table was decorated with scarlet streamers with a great canopy over the top.

Olaf had prepared a great feast in a short amount of time. There were soups, fresh game, vegetables, potatoes, breads and pastries of every kind.

Erik looked over at the bridal couple. They were completely absorbed with one another. He smiled to himself. "You made the right decision," said Isabella, handing him a cup of wine. "She would never have married, if she wasn't forced to do so. She always put us before herself. It's good to see her so happy."

"I hope so Bella, after so many years of sacrifice she deserves it."

Isabella turned to him, "So do you brother."

He touched her face, "Seeing my family happy makes me happy."

"Maybe isn't enough for us."

"What do you mean?"

"We want to see you happy and settled down. It breaks my heart thinking of you alone."

"I'm not alone. I have the Keep."

"The Keep can't climb into bed with you on a cold winter night to keep you warm. It can't warm your heart, or breathe life into your soul, as a woman who loves you could. It can't give you children to love and cherish." Her voice cracked. "It will never be a home without someone inside it who loves you. It's merely stone."

He held her tightly in his arms. "I promise you Bella, I'll be all right."

She finally pulled away from him. "You better be, and count on the fact that I'll be hounding you the rest of your days until I see this Keep filled with your children." She smiled as she walked away toward Ian.

Erik felt the pull to go to Kiera's chamber. He bounded up the stairs and opened the chamber door. Alice was chatting away to Kiera's still body, brushing her hair. Alice hadn't noticed him come in. He chose not to disturb them. He watched as Alice talked with every stroke of the brush.

"A great thing has happened, my lady. Your friend Marcus and Lady Aurelia have married this morning. They're so happy. I haven't seen my Lady look that radiate in years. That Marcus of yours has added ten years to her life, he has. Such a handsome couple. You must wake up soon. You're missing a great bridal feast Olaf prepared despite such short notice. I hear he has become quite a tyrant in the kitchen, demanding perfection. Let me see, what did he prepare? Roast venison, cooked outdoors over a great pit, spiced as though for the table of the gods. There's partridge and peacock, various game hens. He made the most mouth-watering rabbit stew, and the pastries, my lady, none in the land could compare. You must wake up. Olaf would be disappointed if you didn't try them. Besides you're scaring poor Lord Erik to death. He is worried sick about you. Today he caught and hung the spy who was responsible for this. You're safe now, so you can wake up. Lord Erik is so strong he will always keep you safe. Please My Lady, won't you try and open your eyes. I know you're in there. Find your way out of the darkness and come back to us." Alice continued to brush her hair.

Erik cleared his throat. Alice nearly dropped the brush. "Oh, My Lord! You nearly scared the life out of me. I didn't know you were here."

Looking over to the bed he asked, "How is she?"

"Her color is looking better, and I think her breathing is getting deeper. It's just my opinion my Lord, but I think talking to her helps. It just may give her a direction to follow in bringing her back."

"Thank you Alice, I'll keep an eye on her for a while." He patted her on the shoulder.

"Why don't you go down and join in the celebration."

"Thank you my Lord." Before she left, she turned back to him. "Keep talking to her, it may bring her back."

He stood and watched her breathe. Her color had gotten better since he saw her last. He walked over to her window and opened the shutters wider to let the bright sun shine upon her face. He could hear the music from the celebration below. He hoped she could hear it too. He walked back over to her bed, and sat beside her. He took her hand. It felt warmer. He touched her face. That too was warm. He stroked her chin.

"Kiera I want you to open your eyes. I want you to follow the sound of my voice and come to me. Can you hear me? Come toward the sound of my voice." He held her hand to his face. "Feel my face?" he rubbed his cheek against the back of her hand. "Do you hear the music? Come to me Kiera and we'll dance together." He leaned closer to her, his face just inches above hers. He gently blew on her lips. "Do you remember last night when I held you in my arms? Do you remember my hands on your body? My very breath upon your face, filling you with desire?"

He felt her hand twitch. He jumped. "That's it. Kiera come back to me. Come toward the sound of my voice." Her eyes fluttered, but didn't open. "Come to me Kiera, hear me, I'm waiting for you." He moved closer. Her eyes fluttered slightly then closed again. "No

Kiera! You've had enough sleep open your eyes. Now!"

Kiera's eyes fluttered open to find Erik's golden orbs gazing back at her. She smiled up at him and touched his face. He brought his mouth down on hers. She could feel life pouring into her veins. He looked back into her face then kissed her again. When he finally pulled away he stared at her as though she would disappear before him.

She heard the music outside. "What's happening? It's not Spring Festival already?"

"No, it's a wedding," he said smiling.

"A wedding? Whose wedding?"

"Marcus and Aurelia's, they were married this morning," he said as if it were no exception.

"Marcus and Aurelia's! My God, what happened while I was asleep?"

"It's a long story. I'll tell you when you're stronger."

Kiera nearly cried with disappointment.

"What's wrong?"

"They were married and I missed it."

He sat for a moment. Then he stood up abruptly and wrapped her in blankets. "Erik! What are you doing?"

He picked her up off the bed. "I'm taking you to a wedding celebration."

"Erik, put me down, I'm not dressed for it."

"You look fine. Alice was grooming you all afternoon."

"What?"

"Never mind," he said as he carried her out of her chamber, and into the garden. Everyone shouted their delight when they saw Erik coming with Kiera in his arms.

Aurelia was the first to reach them. "Oh my Dear, thank God you're all right." She pressed Kiera's hand to her cheek. "I'll never be able to thank you for what you've done." She held Kiera's hand until Erik lowered her to a chase lounge underneath a great oak tree. Aurelia kissed her forehead. "I'll be right back."

Marcus was next to come to Kiera, tears filled his eyes. He held her face in the palms of his hands. "My life would be over if I lost you."

Kiera arms wound around Marcus' neck. "You have a new life. One of great possibilities, enjoy it, you deserve it. I'm so sorry I missed your wedding." Joy for her friend made her eyes mist with tears.

He hugged her tight. "At least you're here for the celebration."

"You are going to have to tell me how this all came about in just one night." Then she thought for a moment. "Oh dear, it has been just one night hasn't it?"

Marcus laughed, "Yes only one night, but you gave us quite a scare."

Aurelia returned with a bowl of Olaf's rabbit stew. Eleanor followed with a cup of ale. She bent over kissing her cheek. "You look wonderful," Eleanor said.

"Thank you." Kiera drank the ale and ate her stew under their watchful eye. She was embarrassed to have so much attention.

One by one they all came to inquire about her health. Erik left to refill her cup when Dominick came and sat on the ground beside her. Even sitting on the ground he was still eye level with her. He looked out at the wedding party without talking. She felt uncomfortable by his silence. His was the last face she saw before everything went dark. He knew about her powers to heal. She looked down at her hands, expecting him to cast her away. His big hand covered hers. Surprised, she looked into his face. "The reason Murdock hunts you, is for your ability to heal. Is that correct?"

She nodded her head. "When we return to Godwin you shall join us. You'll be safer there under my protection."

She shook her head. "No Dominick, I can't."

"Why do you say that?" he asked. "You'll be with your family."

"It's too dangerous. I don't want anyone I love to be hurt."

"Nothing can happen to you at Godwin. It's well guarded."

"It will be a prison. I don't wish to be guarded and watched all the time."

"None the less, until a solution can be reached you'll come back with us."

"No! Dominick," she said adamantly.

His back went straighter. "I'm your brother and head of the family, you'll do what I think is best."

"You don't have proof of that. Without it, I'm not obligated to follow your orders."

"We shall see." His voice was firm. He sat for a moment. "If you didn't come with us, what would you do?"

"I don't know yet. I do know I can't stay here. The attack on Aurelia was proof of that. I can't allow anyone else to be hurt because of me."

"Marcus is now married and Jordan has sworn fealty to Erik. You can't leave here alone."

"I'll think of something. I can't keep on running," she said half to herself.

"And if you don't run, what will happen to you then?"

She didn't answer. Murdock would find her then suck the life out of her. Dominick must have read her thoughts. "The look on your face betrays you Kiera. I can't allow you to be unprotected. You'll come with us to Godwin, proof or no proof. If I have to tie you to a wagon, you'll be accompanying us."

She sat quietly for some time, thinking. Then the idea hit her. Proof! She needed the proof that Dominick and Randolf were the legal heirs of Dunsmore Castle. Dominick was a friend to the King. He will see that Dominick gets what is rightfully his. She could take the documents to him. With his help, Murdock could be destroyed. The only problem, was that the proof was in Dunsmore Castle. She would risk a great deal by going there, but she knew exactly where the documents were. She would have to think on it further, but she knew that was what she had to done. She just needed a plan to escape from her brothers and Erik's watchful eye.

Dominick saw that she was not paying attention to him. "Kiera, did you hear what I said? You'll be joining us at Godwin."

"Yes Dominick I'll join you," she said turning her attention to Marcus and Aurelia dancing. Someday, she thought.

"Good." He brushed himself off, "This is the best way Kiera," he said.

"I know," she said blushing. Kiera felt guilty lying to him, but it was the only way to distract him. With her mind made up, she would have to plan her trip very carefully.

Erik came back with another mug of ale. He sat down next to her, and watched the musicians play. Derrick came running up to her and without preamble climbed into her lap, sitting quietly. She stroked his hair absently kissing the top of his head. He snuggled in tighter then fell asleep in her arms. He knew she would make a good mother. When Dominick took her back to Godwin he would see her properly wed. He looked away, his hands clenched at his sides at the thought of another man touching her. He pushed the feelings down deep. It was what had to be. He turned back to her and saw the weariness on her face. He rose and called Randolf over to take Derrick out of her arms. Then in the next moment she was lifted back into his arms, and taken back to her chambers.

She watched him as he carried her up the stairs. He wouldn't look at her. And when he placed her in bed he gave her a polite bow and left the room. She wondered what caused him to be so distant all of a sudden. She could feel him drawing away. She looked down at her hands. Oh well, she thought to herself, it's better this way. She would be leaving in a few days anyway. It would be difficult enough as it was without the entanglements of her feelings toward him.

She laid back on her pillows and watched the sun set out her window. She hoped the weather would hold out until she left. Then she would pray for rain to hide any trace of her.

Later the three women came into her chambers bringing her a piece of wedding cake. Aurelia carried a cup of tea with special herbs. She looked beautiful and happy. Eleanor fussed over her like a mother hen, straightening her bedcovers, fluffing pillows while Isabella chatted about the day's activities. Kiera loved these women with all her heart. To leave them would be near impossible, but for their protection she had to go.

Isabella and Eleanor left and Aurelia stayed behind. When the door closed, Aurelia gazed at her. She reached for Kiera's medallion and held it in her hand, her thumb rubbed the center stone. "Do you miss her?" Aurelia asked.

"Every day of my life."

Aurelia stared at the stone. "I lost my mother when I was very young too. I felt a great void in my life. Then a few years later I lost my sister. We were very close. I thought I wouldn't live through the pain, but I did. I took on the responsibility of raising her two children. They filled the void, and eased the pain of the ones I lost. Their need for me made me happy. Then they grew up and they didn't need me so much anymore. Then you came brining me someone else to love. And above all that you saved my life at the risk of your own, giving me a second chance to be happy. How can I ever repay you?'

She put her hand on top of Aurelia's. She was still holding the medallion. "It's not a debt, it's a gift...to Marcus. He loves you deeply, he was nearly destroyed when he saw you on the ground bleeding, near death." Aurelia's head lowered, tears running down her face. "I owe Marcus my life. He saved me from a monster and put his life and his son's in peril. Now I had the opportunity to repay his love and support of me. He filled the void of the loss of my father, and I love him dearly. My gift to him was you, Aurelia. The only thing I ask is that you love him back and make him happy."

Aurelia hugged her tightly. After a few moments she sat back up wiping way the tears. "The only thing I hope for is that I may be able to ease the loss of your mother and you'll come to love me too."

Kiera touched her cheek. "I already do."

Aurelia kissed her forehead. New tears ran down her cheeks. "Oh my, all this crying, and it's my wedding day." She stood to leave, "I better let you get some sleep, I'm sure you'll feel better in the morning." Aurelia straightened her gown. "Well, my husband awaits." She shook her head and chuckled. "That sounds so strange, *my husband*. I never thought this would happen to me after so many years."

"You'll get used to it." Now go, Marcus doesn't like to be kept waiting. Take it from someone who knows," she said chuckling.

"Yes, well, good night dear. I'll see you in the morning." For the first time she was looking forward to a future. That is if her plan worked. She was going into the dragon's den and she only hope she would survive.

CHAPTER XX

Kiera woke early the next morning. Her arms and legs felt heavy, but she didn't feel as lethargic as the night before.

She washed and dressed thinking about her plans to get the documents from Dunsmore Castle.

She braided her hair down the back, looking at her reflection. The bruises were gone. A tight feeling came across her stomach. She brought her hand to her lips remembering the kiss she placed on his neck. She loved the feel of his muscles rippling beneath her curious exploration. His hands. His hands had stroked her into a climax that shattered her into tiny bits of blinding light. She closed her eyes, breathing deep with the memory. She didn't feel ashamed. Their lovemaking seemed right. Sadness stabbed at her heart. She was foolish. There was no chance for them as long as Murdock stalked her. If he captured her she couldn't bear the loss of the future she and Erik might have had. It was better that she left now.

Jordan and Marcus had new lives. They deserved a chance at happiness, not a life on the run. She could leave them with a clear conscious.

She decided to leave the following night. It was the first night of the Spring Festival. There would be too much celebration for anyone to miss her. She would be long gone by the time they realized she'd left. No one would suspect where she was going.

With her mind made up, she went downstairs to break her fast.

Everyone was at the morning meal except Erik. Kiera felt a pang of disappointment, but dismissed it. Isabella told her he was out on patrols with his men.

She finished her meal and headed for the stables. She and her horse needed exercise. She saddled Snow and took him to the training field for maneuvers. She practiced most of the day.

She rubbed Snow down and gave him a bag of oats. She returned to her chamber. Bathed, brushed her hair, and dressed in her white tunic. She went down for the evening meal. Erik wasn't there. Again she pushed her feeling of disappointment aside. She and Isabella talked about the next day's activities.

Erik came down after the meal was already being served. His hair was wet and he smelled of the soap she loved. She had to resist the urge to lean toward him. Her face flushed, remembering the smell. She took a deep breath to pull back hard on her need.

Erik looked at her briefly. "Are you well?" he asked politely.

"Yes, I'm fine, thank you," she said with the same politeness

Erik turned away. They were like two strangers. Kiera sat straighter in her chair pretending it didn't matter. She didn't understand the distance he was putting between them. She felt embarrassed when everyone watched Erik's treatment of her. She pushed her food away no longer having an appetite.

"I think we should go on a hunt tomorrow, bring back some fresh game for the Festival," Erik said.

"Whatever you say, Erik," he said smartly, drinking his ale.

She was sure he couldn't have missed Ian's dry tone of his friend. "Good, we will leave at first light."

"Fine." Isabella leaned forward, "Kiera I want to talk to you about tomorrow."

She saw Isabella give her brother a hard kick before she stood up. He grunted, grabbing his shin and turned to glare at his sister. Ian smiled. Isabella pulled Kiera away from the table to stand her next to Jordan. She looked back to see if Erik was watching....he was.

"What is it you want to talk about?"

"Oh....um..." Kiera saw that Isabella was trying to think of something to say. "Do you know how to dance?"

"What?" She was caught off guard. "No, I'm afraid I don't."

"Well you must learn. There is going to be so much dancing tomorrow you have to learn, tonight."

She and Jordan looked at each other thinking Isabella had lost her mind.

Ian came to stand beside his wife.

"Don't you think Ian?" Isabella asked, drawing him closer to her.

"Think what, dear?"

"That Kiera and Jordan should learn how to dance,"

Kiera didn't miss the wink Isabella gave her husband. They were up to something.

"Yes, of course, it's a must that you learn." He took Kiera's hand and wrapped his arm around her waist and spun her around. When he stopped, he gave Isabella a sly smile, "I'll go rally the musicians."

Isabella took Kiera's hand and put it into Jordan's, then took Jordan's hand and placed it on Kiera's waist. "Now this is what you have to do. Jordan you step forward, Kiera you step back. Watch Ian and me." Ian expertly glided Isabella around the floor. She couldn't have felt more self-conscious. All eyes were on her and Jordan. They encouraged the two of them try. Jordan shrugged his shoulders and proceeded to follow Ian and Isabella's lead.

Soon they were gliding around the room. Eleanor and Dominick joined in, so did Marcus and Aurelia, along with many other couples of the Keep. She started laughing when Jordan nearly tripped.

She watched Isabella give her brother a triumphant smile. His when his jaw flex, then he stood suddenly and left the hall. Her heart sank. As soon as it was polite she pleaded fatigue and left the hall.

She changed for bed and brushed her hair. Disappointment was hard to swallow, yet she refused to cry. It wouldn't serve any purpose. She climbed into bed and laid in the darkness trying to force herself to sleep, but it wouldn't come. She tossed and turned most of the night. She thought about her plans to leave Alastair, and mostly about Erik. She kept telling herself it was better this way, it would be easier for her to leave. But she couldn't convince her heart.

She watched the sun rise. She had dozed on and off throughout the early hours of the morning. Finally, giving up she splashed water on her face attempting to revive herself.

Dressing, she went down to the Great Hall. Isabella, Aurelia and Eleanor were already there. The men left early for the hunting party.

Aurelia and Eleanor were planning to pick herbs and flowers for the celebration. Isabella asked her to help with the preparation of the hall, and setting up the tables in the garden. Earlier she had taken supplies and hidden them in the stables for her departure that evening.

Isabella kept her busy most of the morning, setting up tables and chairs and arranging place settings. Kiera was happy for the distraction.

The men returned from hunting with venison, two wild boars, ducks and various game hens. They were immediately turned over to Olaf for preparation.

She was in the hall when Erik walked in. He gave her a curt nod.

She didn't expect anything from him. But to be treated as a stranger was beyond reason. This time Kiera wasn't hurt, she was angry. She hadn't done anything to warrant this kind of treatment. She had saved his life, helped his friend, and risking her life, to save his aunt.

Well if he wanted to ignore her that was fine. She was leaving anyway she told herself. The rage exploded inside her. The cups and plates rattled on the table. The sound startled her. She looked around the Hall to see if anyone was near to see the phenomenon. Her anger cooled. The dishes became still. She had to remain in control.

She ran up to the sanctuary of her chambers, to find a bath waiting for her. Perfumed oils were sitting beside the tub. It was like nothing she had ever smelled before.

She quickly got out of her clothes and sank into the hot water. She washed her hair thoroughly then poured the scented oil into her bath. The smell filled her senses. She felt pampered, and something else, less familiar, that she had no name for. Her skin came to life.

She was drying herself with a towel, when she heard a knock on her door. She barely had time to wrap herself in it, when the door flew open. Isabella was the first to come in followed by Aurelia and Eleanor.

Eleanor was holding a blue gown. Clutching the towel in front of her, Kiera slowly

approached it. The fabric she'd seen a few days
before was transformed into a beautiful gown,
trimmed in silver. She was stunned at its
beauty. She ran her hand over the rich fabric.
She couldn't bring herself to say anything.
"Well girl, we better get you ready before the
celebration starts," Aurelia said.

Isabella handed her silk undergarments.
Kiera went behind the changing screen. When she
came out from behind the screen, Aurelia
slipped the gown over her head. Aurelia tied up
the laces in the back. She ran her hands along
its velvety sides. The gown fit her body like a
second skin. She looked down and smiled, even
the length was right.

Eleanor pulled her medallion out from
underneath her gown. The blue stone shone
brighter on the blue fabric. Isabella wrapped a
silver girdle around her waist, encrusted with
sapphires. She gasped at its beauty. Aurelia
then handed her blue satin slippers. They fit
her perfectly. She looked at Aurelia.

"I had Albert trace your boot for the right
size."

Eleanor pulled her over to a stool, and
began working on her hair. She brushed it till
it shined. "I think we'll leave it down
tonight."

Kiera felt something being slipped on her
head. The three women stood in front of her.
They all smiled at their handy work. Aurelia
pulled her to the mirror.

She couldn't believe her eyes. A silver
circlet with a large sapphire in its center was

placed on her head. Her hair shone blacker, her eyes brighter. She was filled with awe that she could look like the woman in the mirror. "This is not me," she said.

"Yes, it is," Isabella said squeezing her shoulders. "It's the woman inside of you."

Kiera couldn't take her eyes away from the mirror. "Now for the final touch." Isabella dabbed perfume on her neck and wrists. "Let's go downstairs and make the men glad we're here."

She wanted just one man's heart to skip a beat at her entrance, but she doubted he had one.

"You are beautiful," Eleanor said.

Kiera squeezed her hands. "Thank you, all of you. I feel like a princess."

"You look like a queen," Aurelia said. "We'll go downstairs first, so you can make a grand entrance." She suddenly felt panic.

Aurelia, I don't know if I can do this."

The older woman patted her hand. "You'll be fine, my dear."

She'd been a warrior in many heated battles, but she was never as frightened as she was right now.

The women gave her a reassuring hug and left the room.

Pacing back and forth, she caught her reflection in the mirror again and stared at the woman before her. She was amazed at the transformation. She brought her wrist to her nose, breathing in the sensual perfume. She looked back at her reflection. She *was* a woman she told herself. No matter what she wore she would never forget it again.

She walked out of her chamber door. When she reached the top of the stairs, she took a deep breath then started her descent. Halfway down the stairs, she could almost feel the hush that fell around the Great Hall.

Erik was bringing a cup of wine to his lips, when he spotted her coming down the stairs. His hand froze. He had always thought Kiera beautiful. But now she was a vision, beyond his dreams. All around the room mouths hung open. Kiera moved with grace as she came into the Hall.

Randolf was the first to rise and escort her to the table. "You are the most beautiful woman I have ever seen," he said kissing her cheek.

Her smile was brilliant. His pulse raced. He watched the gown float around her as she walked toward him. The sapphire girdle emphasized her small waist. The color of the gown made her eyes sparkle. His breath caught in his chest, and surged the beat of his heart. Her hair was undone, and gleamed like a raven's feathers. He exhaled slowly as she came to the table. He stood without thinking, and held out her chair.

Randolf kissed her cheek before she took her place beside Erik.

He took his own seat. He again tried to ignore her, but her perfume was intoxicating. He was drawn to it. He could feel himself growing hard. He tried pushing his feelings down, but they kept surfacing. He thought to leave, to escape her strange magnetism that made him feel helplessly drawn to her. He was rooted to his chair.

Erik raised his knife and looked down at his empty plate. He couldn't remember eating.

She was talking and laughing with Marcus and Aurelia when Jordan came over and asked her to dance. She readily agreed. She curtsied to him as he bowed. Then he swung her into a lively dance.

Ian stood behind him as he watched Jordan swing Kiera around the floor. He patted Erik's shoulder. "What goes around comes around, my friend," he said and pulled Isabella up for a dance.

He didn't respond. He watched as Randolf accepted Kiera's hand from Jordan and began to dance with her. Next, she danced with Dominick. His braver soldiers even asked her to dance. She took time to dance with Derrick, laughing the whole time. Her laughter was like music from the heavens, but she wasn't laughing for him.

He watched as Marcus took his turn. Erik felt his mood turn blacker. A beautiful young serving wench reached around him to pour him another cup of wine. He wanted to prove his lust could be settled on anybody. As she was reaching for the cup, he ran the back of his hand down her arm, giving her a knowing glance. She smiled back seductively.

He was going to ease his lust and get Kiera out of his mind, permanently. He looked back to see her still dancing with Marcus. He stood, and pulled the wench closer to him, then walked her out of the Great Hall.

Kiera saw him leave with the woman in his arms. She felt as if the wind was knocked out of her. She stopped in mid-motion, watching him leave.

It was one thing to be ignored, quite another to watch him seduce another woman.

"It means nothing Kiera," Marcus said.

She could only nod, too close to tears to say anything. Marcus pulled her away from the people dancing. Jordan came to her side. "The bastard!" he said harshly.

"Jordan, he's your liege," Marcus scolded.

"That doesn't mean I have to agree with all that he does."

Kiera finally found her voice. "It's of no importance. There was no hope in the first place," she said, straightening. "I'm very tired. I think I'll go to my chambers now. Thank you both for everything." Her eyes pooled with tears. She hugged them both, as though it were the last time.

Marcus and Jordan looked at each other, as she ran up the stairs.

She ran into her chamber and slammed the door behind her.

How could she be in love with a man who pretended she didn't exist? She stopped short. Love? She covered her face with her hands, in despair. Why now? Why this time in her life?

She dropped her hands in resignation. Well it didn't matter now that she was leaving.

Noticing her reflection in the mirror, she sighed. "This is not me," she said to herself, and removed the circlet. She unlaced her dress, and slipped it down her body. Lifting it, she folded it gently and then carefully laid it on the bed. She changed into her black tunic and britches, and braided her hair.

Then, ready and resigned, Kiera sat down on the window seat, staring out into the bailey, waiting for the Keep to settle down for the night.

There was a light rap on her door. She bid them enter. Isabella came into her chambers. She seemed surprised at Kiera's appearance. "Why are you dressed like that?"

"I'm more comfortable in this. I can't pretend to be something I'm not."

"You were beautiful tonight, Kiera. Please don't let what my brother did convince you otherwise," Isabella pleaded.

"I'm not. It's just that I wished for something that was impossible."

"No! Please don't say that. I know the two of you could be together. It just takes time."

"I don't have time, Isabella. My time is running out."

"What do you mean?"

"Murdock knows that I'm here. He's waiting for an opportunity to take me."

"Kiera, you're safe here. Erik will protect you."

"Erik made it clear he doesn't want me," her voice cracked.

Isabella put her arms around her. "Erik does care."

"He showed me how much he cares when he walked off with that serving girl," she sniffed.

Isabella held her tight. "Erik has a hard time expressing his feelings. Ever since our father left us he's been this way. I think he is afraid of rejection. He doesn't allow people to get too close. People have to prove themselves to him before he lets them in."

Isabella pulled back looking directly into her face. "His own father accused him of being possessed by the devil."

"That may explain the way he is, but it doesn't change the fact that I must go away for the safety of everyone here."

"Kiera that's not true. We are all safe."

"As safe as Aurelia was when she was attacked?" Isabella thought, but didn't say. "Isabella, I know this man, he is relentless. He will send another, then another, and another, until he finally has me."

"Your brothers are great warriors. They will find a solution."

"Their only solution is to lock me up and keep me guarded in the name of safety. I have been there before and I don't wish to do it again."

Isabella couldn't argue with her. "Kiera, promise me you won't do anything without talking to Erik or your brothers first."

Kiera only nodded, she didn't want to lie.

"Well I should let you get some sleep, the celebration continues tomorrow." She hugged Kiera tightly. "Try not to worry, things will work out."

"I hope you're right," she said. As Isabella was about to leave the room, Kiera stopped her. "Isabella, you have been the greatest friend a woman could ever have."

Isabella looked confused. "Thank you. I feel the same way about you. Good night, Kiera," she bid her, hesitating as though uncertain if she should say something more. Apparently deciding against it, she turned and left, pulling the door shut behind her.

Kiera turned back to the window, perhaps even more troubled than before.

CHAPTER XXI

She threw supplies onto the back of her horse. Grabbing the reins, she walked Snow through the palisades gate. Luck was on her side. A serving wench from the kitchen distracted the guard and she went through unnoticed.

Her chest tightened with the weight of her worries. It was the first time she'd gone out alone. Marcus and Jordan had lives of their own and she couldn't be part of them. Her focus was to get the documents out of Dunsmore and to the king. If the Dragon had no land, he had no power. He would no longer be able to hurt anyone ever again. It was worth the danger she was facing. She didn't want to think about what would happen to her if she were captured. She prayed her brothers would find out and come after her.

She continued walking her horse away from the Keep until she was sure she couldn't be heard. Once mounted, she headed toward Dunsmore Castle. It would take her three days to reach it. She shuddered at the thought of what would happen should the Dragon catch her. She could still feel the sting of his whip, but she was committed to her purpose. She would ride through the night, finding shelter during the day.

Erik paced back and forth in his chambers. He berated himself for the way he had acted that evening. As soon as he left with the serving wench, he knew it was a mistake. The moment he kissed the girl, he realized it was Kiera's lips he wanted to kiss. It was Kiera's body he wanted next to his.

He apologized to the woman and walked directly to his chambers. How could he have treated Kiera so badly? She hadn't done anything but help him and his family, risking her own life to save his aunt. What kind of fool would treat someone as badly as he did her?

He made up his mind that he was going to apologize to her...right now.

He gently knocked on her chamber door. There was no answer. The second time he knocked the door swung slightly open. He pushed it further. He entered the chamber, to find her bed empty. It looked as though it had never been slept in. He searched the room. His anger started to swell. His first thought was Jordan. He swore if she was with him, he would kill them both.

He stormed down the hall to Jordan's chamber. Too angry to think, he kicked the door open. Jordan was out of bed in an instant, sword in hand.

"Where is she?" Erik growled.

"Where is who?"

"You know perfectly well, who. Kiera."

Calmly, pointing to the bed. "Well, she's obviously not here."

Erik began searching the room.

Hearing the commotion, Dominick, Randolf and Ian, were at Jordan's door. Marcus and Aurelia came shortly after.

Dominick looked to Jordan. "What is he looking for?"

"Kiera," Jordan answered.

Dominick crossed his arms glaring at him. "Please tell me she's not here."

"She's not."

Dominick turned to Erik, "Have you checked her chambers?"

"Yes, she's not there," he said looking under the bed. He finished his search, satisfied that she wasn't in the room.

Isabella came up behind Ian, tying her robe together. "What's going on," she asked.

"Erik can't find Kiera," Ian said.

"Why would he be looking for her in Jordan's chambers?" Ian gave her a knowing glance. "Ah, I see. She isn't in here is she?"

"Apparently not," Ian said.

Isabella turned back toward Erik. "Oh my God!"

Everyone turned toward her. Erik came to stand directly in front of her. "What is it?"

"I went to see her earlier this evening. She was dressed in her tunic and britches. She said she felt better in them, so I didn't think much of it. Then she talked about how everyone would be safer if she left Alastair. I told her that she was wrong. I thought I had convinced her to wait until she talked to Dominick first." Isabella thought for a moment. "That's why she said what she said."

"What did she say," Erik asked.

"She said I was the best friend a woman could have." Her eyes widened. "My God! She was saying goodbye."

Erik ran past her, dashing out of the Keep and into the stables. Her horse was gone. He ran to the gatehouse. The guard was surprised to see him.

"My Lord, what are you doing here this time of night?"

"I was about to ask you the same thing," Erik growled.

"I don't know what you mean, My Lord," he said clearly confused.

"I thought my orders were that no one was to leave or enter without my expressed permission."

"Yes, My Lord."

Erik's anger grew, "Then can you tell me where Lady Kiera might be?"

"In her chambers?" the guard said, questioningly.

Erik's fist connected with the guard's jaw, knocking him to the ground. "You idiot! She's missing, and the only way out of Alastair Keep is through this gate."

"I'm sorry My Lord. I saw no one leave."

Erik calmed himself. "I'll deal with you when I return." He came back to the hall, where everyone was waiting.

"Well?" Dominick asked.

"Her horse is gone."

Dominick turned to Randolf, "Tell our squires to ready our horses."

"No!" Erik shouted. "I'll go after her myself. I'm a better tracker and I can travel faster alone." He didn't wait to argue, he ran out of the hall and up the stairs to his chambers. Albert was already waiting. In a matter of minutes, Erik went back down to the hall where the others were waiting, armed with his sword, his face intent.

He walked directly to Dominick. The girl is ignorant to her safety. I'll bind her to me, and my authority. Do I have your approval?"

Dominick looked at Erik for a long time. His hand stroking his chin. He turned to Marcus, then back to Erik. Kiera is my sister, but I have known her for a very short time. The approval you seek is not mine to give. You must ask Marcus' He has been like a father to her, and has ensured her safety for her entire life."

Dominick was right. He turned to Marcus. "Marcus, she needs me. By our marriage she will have the house of Alastair to protect her, along with Godwin and its allies."

Marcus thought for a long time. "You hurt Kiera deeply tonight. I don't wish to see her hurt again." Erik was about to say something, when Marcus held up his hand to stop him. "But, I can't argue that she will be safer here than wandering about on her own." He nodded his head, "Aye, I'll agree to this marriage, for

Kiera's safety." Erik started to breathe a sigh of relief, when Marcus grabbed the front of his tunic, and pulled him closer. "But be assured this. Hurt her again, and you'll have to deal with me." Erik nodded.

Isabella stepped forward. "After the way you've been treating her, I don't think she will have you," she said coarsely.

Hastily, Erik turned and walked toward the door. "She will have no choice," he said. Then turned to Dominick, "and neither will I," slamming the door behind him.

CHAPTER XXII

It was mid-afternoon when Kiera approached the boundary of Dunsmore. She came upon the edge of the forest, where she could see the castle loom before her. She would keep to the forest until well past nightfall. She moved back deeper into the woods, to wait.

She had time to think. She thought about her newfound family and friends, and their complete acceptance of her. For so many years she'd had to hide who she was.

The further she traveled, the more her heart ached to go back. But her mind was set. She had to get the documents and go directly to the King. Being her brother's friend, she was sure he would help, and she would be free.

Or was it all a fantasy. Maybe she'd never be free of Murdock.

Erik never left her thoughts. The pain of seeing him hold another woman was more than she could bare. She would never go back to Alastair. But then she thought of Marcus and Jordan. If she never goes back she would never see them again. She fought back the tears. It was for the best.

The sun was setting. In the three days she traveled, she had formulated a plan. She would leave Snow tethered in the forest, and approach the castle on foot to its northern wall, where she would go unnoticed. She would stay close to the wall and enter in a secret entrance that was on the east side.

Night fell. Kiera waited at the edge of the forest. She looked to the sky. The moon was high, it was time to go. Quietly, she slipped out of the trees and ran as fast as she could to the north wall.

Her dark clothing made her virtually invisible. She made it to the castle wall and flattened herself against it. Her heart was pounding. It had been nine years since she was there last.

The memory of Murdock terrorizing her came flooding back. She was nearly paralyzed with fear.

By shear will, she moved on, her hand on the hilt of her sword. She felt along the wall to where she knew a small door was located. Her hand bumped and then wrapped around the handle. She pushed gently on the door with her shoulder so to make as little noise as possible. It gave way. There was a faint pool of light from a distant torch. Pressing into the wall, blended with the shadows. There were voices in the distance. She reached down into her boot and pulled out her dagger, never taking her eyes off the corridor.

She crept slowly forward and listened for every sound. Her heart pounded fiercely with every step. Suddenly she heard voices coming from behind her. She ran to the end of the corridor and turned the corner again pressed against a shadowed wall. She held her dagger, ready to fight. The two men were laughing as they passed her by without seeing her. Her ears drummed with the beat of her heart.

She moved cautiously to the small stairway leading down to the dungeons. She remembered the way to her father's secret chamber as though he had showed it to her yesterday. Loss twisted in her gut. The pain was always with her when she thought of her father. It was her constant companion when she thought of her parents. Even now it made its way through her fear.

Moving down the stairs, she could feel the cold dampness penetrate her skin. She shivered. The place frightened her as a child, and as an adult too, she admitted to herself.

As Kiera approached the end of the stairs she saw several torches lit on the walls of the dungeon. There was only one guard in sight, and he had his chair propped against one of the stone walls. He appeared to be sound asleep.

Slowly, Kiera moved into the room. There were twelve cells along each wall. She reached the one that was in the furthest left hand corner. She prayed there was no one in it. As quietly as she could, she removed one of the torches from its holder, never taking her eyes off the guard sleeping in the chair. She moved silently toward the cell door. Halfway across the floor, the guard shifted in his chair. She froze and held her dagger ready. The guard never opened his eyes. The door to the cell was bolted on the outside. Carefully, she pulled it back. The door groaned as she opened it. She stopped to look over to the guard. He shifted again but still never woke up.

She went to the center of the cell, brushing away the straw with her foot to find the trap door hidden beneath it. Reaching the handle, she pulled up on the door that led down to a secret chamber. Kiera climbed down and placed the torch in a sconce on the wall.

Looking around the room, she felt reassured to see that everything was the same as it had been ten years ago. There were four large chests along the wall, where her father hid his valuables.

She opened one of the chests. In it were her father's personal belongings, a golden amulet, and a silver armband set with three sapphires in its center. She placed them in a pouch that she had slung over her shoulder. She found her father's sword. Holding it, she could feel his essence. Pain swept through her. She shook her head and cleared her mind. She had to stay focused. She had to find the documents. There was a false bottom in the chest. She pulled on it and moved it to the side. In the bottom she found what she was looking for. She placed the documents in her pouch. She went to replace the false bottom when something shinny caught her eyes.

Kiera reached down and pulled it out. It was her father's ring. Tears ran down her face. She clenched the ring in the palm of her hand, rocking back and forth. She held her fists to her lips.

"Papa, oh Papa!" she cried softly. "I'll avenge your death, I swear." She kissed the ring reverently, placing it in the pouch.

She now had all the items she came for. Wiping her face, she put the false bottom back in place. She reached for the torch and climbed the ladder. With her back to the cell door, she lowered the trap door, covering it again with the straw.

"Well, well, what do we got here?" said a voice from behind.

She quickly turned around. The guard that had once been sleeping stood in the doorway.

"Ye don't look a common thief," he said moving closer. "Now what would a wench as pretty as ye be doing' down here?" He nodded toward the trap door. "Nice little hidin' place ye got. Master would be glad to know of it too, but he'd be sleepin' now." He moved closer. "It could wait while you and me have a little fun, eh?"

He reached for her, and in one swift move she sent her father's sword through his middle. The only sound he made was expelling his last dying breath. She jumped over the body, bolting the door behind her. She made her way through the dungeon and up the stairs. Cautiously she moved along the wall of the corridor, frequently looking behind her. She made it through the secret entrance door and into the darkness. Keeping to the wall she crept back to the north side. From there she ran as though the devil himself was after her. She didn't stop until she got to her horse. Mounting him in one jump, she urged him into a gallop.

After what seemed only a few short minutes, she heard horse's hooves coming up fast behind her. She couldn't believe anyone had seen her leaving Dunsmore. There was no sound of alarm. The pounding behind her came closer. She urged her horse faster. The moon lit up the trail as the trees thinned up ahead. She was able to dodge trees and bushes that were in front of her, but she couldn't get away from her pursuer. When she looked back he was gaining on her. He was almost next to her. She was frantic. If the Dragon should get his hands on her, it would be the end of her life.

Suddenly, hands reached out for her. She fought them back, edging her horse away from him, but his horse moved with hers. She was fighting for her life. A hand came around her waist, and lifted her off her horse. Kiera fought her attacker, swinging her arms until she connected with her assailant's ribs. She heard him grunt with the blow. He tightened his grip until she could hardly breathe.

Warm breath caressed the side of her neck, and then, "Be still, Angel."

She spun around and looked up. Even in the moonlight she could see his eyes. Those amber eyes glowing in the dark.

"Erik! What are you doing here?" She grabbed the front of his tunic, "I thought you were someone from Dunsmore." She pulled him to her, instinctively, flooded with relief. Finally safe? Could it be possible?

She noted the stiffness of his chest beneath her cheek. A chill ran down her spine. Pulling back, she looked at him carefully and saw that his face was as cold as stone.

"We must move on," he said, his voice sharp.

The momentary safety she felt was gone. She knew he was more dangerous now than any enemy she could encounter. Her eyes never left his. "Yes, just let me get to my horse," she said.

His arm tightened around her waist. "You ride with me."

CHAPTER XXIII

They rode until the first signs of daylight broke through the trees and came upon a deserted cottage. Erik dismounted, helping Kiera down. He hadn't said anything to her throughout the night. His silence made her uncomfortable.

The cottage had been recently abandoned. Erik moved to the hearth to get a fire started. When it was blazing he turned to her. "I'll tend to the horses."

She became increasingly nervous. In Erik's present mood she didn't know what to expect. "I don't belong to him. He has no right to be angry. I answer to no one," she said out loud, trying to calm her fears. She almost felt a sense of comfort, until he walked back in the door. His expression had changed from stone, to one of anger. He held her father's sword with blood still on it.

He held it out to her. "This is what you risked your life for." She flinched as he threw it on the ground before her. He glared at her then crossed the distance between them. She backed away until she felt the wall behind her. He grabbed her upper arms, pinning her to it.

"You little fool! What were you trying to prove by running away, and going back to Dunsmore?" he said through gritted teeth.

Her first instinct was to fight. She tried grabbing the hilt of her sword, but he leaned his body into hers, pinning her completely. "Don't fight me Kiera, you'll never win," he growled. "I want an answer now, or you may regret not being captured by Murdock."

She struggled against him. I don't belong to you! I don't owe you an explanation."

No sooner were the words out of her mouth then his lips clamped down on hers. She was taken by surprise. His kiss was like fire on a cold body. Her blood began to warm. She could hear her heart pounding in her ears. She was clinging to him for dear life. When he finally released her, she had a firm grip on his tunic.

He looked down at her hands. "We shall see if you belong to me or not," he said with venom. "There is something we left undone. I intend to correct that now." He kissed her again, this time it was punishing. She tried to pull away, but the more she tried, the angrier he became. He pulled her to a pallet on floor, she tried to resist as he pushed her down, covering her body with his. His mouth came down in a brutal assault. She heard the tearing of her tunic down the front. His hands were on her breasts. The way he touched her reminded her of the two men in the woods.

She started screaming. "Erik no! Please, please, not this way, please," she cried. She fought him with all her strength, tears running down her cheeks.

He looked down into her face, her cheeks wet from crying. "My God, Kiera, what am I doing?" She saw the naked torment in his eyes. "I'm sorry," he said softly and rolled off her. He wiped away her tears. "Forgive me," he gently whispered. He turned his back to her. He ran his fingers through his hair and bowed his head.

His regret was tangible. It rattled a frame rigid with self-restraint. Cautiously, she ran her hand up his back. He turned to her. His amber eyes were filled with turmoil. She touched his face. He turned his head to plant a kiss on her palm. She got on her knees and kissed his face. He gently touched hers and kissed her lightly. She allowed him to deepen the kiss. Her arms wound around his neck. She pulled him down on top of her. Her hunger for him grew stronger. She needed to feel his skin against hers. She pulled his tunic over his head.

His warm flesh pressed against hers. His hands moved up and down her side. Her body quivered at his touch. He lightly stroked the side of her breast, while he placed a kiss on its other side. He ran his tongue up the side of her neck, nipping at her throat. She moaned and moved her head to the side, to give him greater access.

She ran her hands along his back, and felt the muscles ripple as he moved. His manhood hardened as she moved her hips into his groin.

He groaned against the side of her neck and then continued the downward journey of his lips, sweeping the curve where her neck met her body and outward to press tender caresses upon the top of her shoulder.

He moved further down her body, taking one of her nipples in his mouth. She held his head to her breast as he suckled. She was hungry with her own needs. Erik's hair tickled down her belly as he ran his tongue along her ribs, then down her stomach. He unlaced her britches and pulled them down her hips before removing them completely. She watched him remove his clothes. His magnificent naked body stood before her. This is what she wanted, this was what she needed. He came back down beside her.

She moaned as his tongue coaxed her to welcome him into her core. Her legs opened of their own accord. His fingers caressed her with gentle, circular motions, and then penetrated her. He kissed her nipple again, flicking his tongue over its ripening peak. His fingers moved in and out of her then stroked her eager center. He kissed her mouth as his hand moved faster and faster. She exploded, screaming out her orgasm.

She was ready for him as he moved on top of her. She looked at him with a need for completion. He penetrated her slowly. He was filling her with his body and she wanted more. "Slow down Angel, we'll get there." She watched the muscles in his jaw flex as though he were trying to hold on to his control. She wanted to break that control. He lost his battle. She felt her maidenhead tear as he penetrated her deeply. Their fate had been sealed.

Looking into his eyes, she melted with their intensity. Nothing else existed at that moment but them.

She brought her hips up with each thrust. Her head moved side to side. She was climbing again. Her nails dug into the back of his hands. He released his own control and they both came in an explosion at the same time. Collapsing on top of her, he managed to prop himself up on his forearms well enough not to crush her.

"That was wonderful," she said breathlessly.

His smile was genuine, and he replied softly, "No regrets?"

"Only one," she said. He stilled. "That we didn't do this sooner."

For the first time, she saw him genuinely laugh, his body shook with it. It warmed her heart, making her smile.

He slowly pulled out of her. She saw her virgin's blood on him. "Here, give me your tunic, and I'll clean us up."

"No Erik I can take care of it myself."

"Kiera, we just made love, there's nothing to be embarrassed about," he said as he pulled her torn tunic down. "Mother of God!" He pulled the tunic completely off her. She wrapped her arms around her knees. He saw the evidence of her beatings and it made her feel vulnerable. His finger trailed one scar down its path. "The man who did this to you will die!"

"No, Erik! Please don't say that. It will mean facing the devil himself. He has taken everything away from me, I couldn't bare it if he took you away too," she said lowering her head.

Erik ground his teeth seeing the horror displayed across her back. He didn't say anything. His rage was hard to contain. He left her for a moment bringing her pouch to her. She quickly pulled out another tunic, and slipped it on while he wet the torn one with water. He gently wiped the blood away from her body. When he was done, they both quietly finished dressing.

Erik brought over their provisions, and handed her some bread and cheese. They ate in silence. When they finished, he packed everything up then laid himself down on a palette next to her. "Can you tell me what happened?" he asked

"No," she said, and her eyes pooled with tears.

He pulled her closer to him kissing her forehead. "Sleep Angel, you're safe."

CHAPTER XXIV

Lacerta knocked on Murdock's chamber door. A young serving girl with a fresh bruise on her cheek answered. "I need to see Lord Murdock," he said as he pushed his way past her. Murdock was lounging in his bed. The girl returned to his side. He stroked her tender cheek. She visibly flinched, but was too frightened to protest. "Lord Murdock," the captain said, bowing slightly.

"Captain Lacerta, it must be extremely important for you to disturb me at such an early hour," he said with a sneer, as he continued to pet the girl.

"It is, My Lord. One of my men has been murdered."

"And why would this concern me? These men are your responsibility Captain," he said, finally turning to Lacerta. "Handle it."

"Lord Murdock, it was a dungeon guard. He was found in one of the cells."

Murdock sighed loudly. "Why are you bothering me with this? Just kill who is responsible."

"That's the problem, he was killed with a sword and no one was in that cell. The door was locked from the outside."

"Then one of the prisoners must have gotten the guard's sword, killed him with it and escaped." Murdock made a dismissive gesture, "The man was incompetent, and he deserved to die."

It took all of Lacerta's control not to roll his eyes in front of his Lord. The man was an idiot. He would have to spell it out for him. "The guard was locked in a cell that was empty. There had never been a prisoner in it, and the guard's sword was clean at his side."

Murdock rose from the bed, "What are you saying Captain?"

Captain Lacerta stood straighter. "I believe someone went down there with a purpose. When we pulled the body out of the cell, we discovered a trap door to a hidden chamber. In it are four chests, each filled with treasures, and documents."

Lacerta had Murdock's full attention. He quickly jumped off the bed. "I want to see this chamber." Murdock threw his mantle around him, not caring that he was still in his nightclothes. He all but ran down the stairs, which led him down to the dungeon. Lacerta followed closely behind.

There were two guards outside the cell holding torches. When Murdock entered the cell he saw the trap door still open. He turned to Lacerta, "Has anything been disturbed?"

"No, My Lord."

Grabbing a torch from one of the guards, Murdock descended the ladder to the secret chamber. Lacerta followed behind.

"My God! How long has this been down here?"

"I believe since the castle was built, My Lord. The stones are the same as the rest of the castle. It looks like your brother hid his valuables down here." He pointed to the dusty chest that showed signs of recently being disturbed. "It looks like someone came for something specific. The treasure still seems to be there."

Murdock went to the chest throwing open the lid, ransacking its contents. He found jewelry and a few documents, but not what he was looking for. He searched the other three, ransacking them as well. "They're not here!" he shouted.

"What is not here, My Lord?"

"The documents, the documents proving the legitimacy of my brother's bastards," he said, looking down on the chests. "This is where my brother would have hidden them and they're not here."

"That's what the intruder came here for, and the guard must have discovered him, and he was killed."

Enraged Murdock backhanded his captain across the face. Lacerta stiffened, clenching his hands at his side. "Your men are incompetent!" he shouted, his face turning crimson. "How could someone come into my castle without being noticed? Kill one of my men, and escape without being seen? Can you tell me that Captain?" Murdock shoved him hard into the wall, with his forearm pressed against Lacerta's throat. "Kiera did this. She was the

only one who could have known about those
documents, and where they were hidden. And now
she has them. Find her Lacerta. Find her and
bring those documents back to me before she
gives them to that bastard Dominick. If you
fail me so help me I'll nail your entrails to
the wall, before I slit your throat." He shoved
him again then left the chamber.

Lacerta rubbed his throat. Then wasted no
time. His fury rose. As soon as he was out of
the chamber, he ordered his gatehouse guards
whipped. He took a group of fifteen mounted men
out of Dunsmore, and into the woods. He would
find the bitch and make her pay dearly for
disgracing him. Up until now he had Murdock
under control. With her capture he vowed he
would have it again.

Kiera woke at sunset. She felt cold,
realizing Erik was no longer beside her. She
turned to see him putting supplies back in the
pouch. Sensing she was awake he said, "We must
hurry now. The person you killed has surely
been discovered by now, and they will be
looking for you. We'll keep to the forest as
much as possible and stay off the main roads."

Kiera rose off her palette. She helped him
pack up their things. Neither of them talked to
each other. She picked up her father's sword.
Taking a piece of her torn tunic she wiped away
the blood. She looked at it for a moment. This
was the first opportunity she'd had to really
look at it. The hilt was overlaid with gold, in
its center was a large sapphire stone. Toward

the bottom was the family crest, a sword with a climbing rose whose leaves and vines entwined around it. It symbolized her mother and father. They had loved each other deeply. Their love never failed them, and in the end they died as they lived, together. Kiera didn't realize tears were falling down her face until Erik came and wiped them away.

"It will be fine as soon as you get home," he said.

"I have no home," she sniffed.

He put his arm around her. "Everything will work out, you'll see," he said, giving her shoulders a squeeze.

She shrugged him off. "It will never be all right until Murdock is stopped and the land is returned to my brothers. That is the only way I'll ever be free."

The pouch that carried the documents and her father's sword was tied to her horse's saddle. She was about to mount, when Erik grabbed her from behind and lifted her on his horse then mounted behind her. "Erik! Let me down."

"You haven't told me where you planned to go after leaving the Keep and I don't think you planned on coming back. This way I can make sure you do."

"Erik, this is ridiculous, just let me get back on my horse," she said, exasperated.

"I'm in no mood for a chase." He bent down and stroked her horse's neck. He was communicating with Snow. Suddenly, her horse went bounding through the forest.

"Snow!" she shouted.

"He'll be waiting for us at Alastair." he pulled her tighter, "Now are you going to tell me why you ran away?"

"I didn't run away. I went to Dunsmore Castle to retrieve the documents proving my brothers legitimacy and their right to Dunsmore properties."

"And did you get those documents?"

"Yes," she said simply.

"What did you plan to do with them?"

She hesitated to answer, but he gave her a slight squeeze, encouraging her to answer. "I planned to take them to the King," she said finally. "Dominick is a loyal friend to him, so I thought he could help me."

"Kiera, your brother is no fool. Don't you think he can protect you from Murdock?"

"My brother's solution is to lock me up in Godwin. I have been imprisoned before. I don't care to have it to happen again."

Erik's hands clenched tightly on the reins of his horse. Seeing her back and now hearing about her treatment, he felt rage rising to the surface. He pushed it down. Breathing in the scent of her hair, the memories of their lovemaking dowsed the fires of his anger and renewed his desire.

The night grew chilly. Erik wrapped his mantle around her. He settled her safely in his arms, thankful he had found her in time.

As they journeyed deeper into the forest wariness began to prickle his skin. Woodland animals were disturbed and scurried around in

the darkness. Storm's ears twitched. *Danger.*
When he began to charge forward, hands dragged
him off his horse. Kiera screamed as men pulled
her down as well. Four men had seized him, and
forced him to the ground. A leather noose was
wrapped around his neck and tied his hands
behind his back. A man took his noose and
pulled him along in the darkened woods.

Kiera was bound hand and foot, then slung
over Storm's back. After walking some time he
could see a campfire in a clearing through the
trees. They were taken further into the forest.
When Kiera was handed down to another man, she
made a futile attempt to get away. She was
thrown over a man's shoulder then tied to a
nearby tree. Erik was pulled down and tied to
one next to her.

"Are you all right?" he asked calmly.

"I'll be fine," she said confidently.

He was relieved when he heard the warrior in
her voice.

His mind reached out deep into the darkness
and found what he was looking for.

"Well, well. You have grown up into a fine
looking woman," he said, raising her chin into
the light. His voice. She jerked her head away.
She wasn't the frightened child he used to
torment.

One of his soldiers came over to them.
"Captain, there are no documents on them."

He rose before the man, and struck him
across the face. "Look again you idiot, they

have to be somewhere." The man didn't hesitate to get out of the captain's sight.

Lacerta knelt closer to her, grabbing her chin, forcing her to look at him. "Where are those documents?" he said sweetly.

Defiantly, she glared at him. "Where you'll never find them."

When he smiled his teeth shone brightly in the moonlight. With the swiftness of a snake he slapped her hard across the face. Pain ripped through her mouth as her lips were pierced by her teeth. Warm blood trickled down her chin. She looked directly into his eyes and she used her powers to heal herself.

He watched as the cut on her lip disappeared. "Your powers have grown stronger I see. It may take more persuasion to get you to talk."

She looked over at Erik. His eyes were closed and he was breathing deeply. She hoped he hadn't been hurt during his struggle with their attackers.

Kiera jumped when she heard the loud crack in front of her. The sound of the whip made her heart stop, then explode into a furious rhythm. She forced herself to calm down. She wouldn't give him the power to see her fear. He snapped the whip again, closer to her ear. She flinched slightly, but kept her body as still as possible.

He rolled the whip in his hand. He ran the handle along her chin. She refused to back away. "I'm not that same terrified little girl, Lacerta. I see you for what you really are,

just an overbearing coward who likes to torment
women and children. That's all you can really
handle. If you had to fight a real warrior, you
would run with your tail between your legs."

He grabbed her face and dug his fingers
deeply into her flesh. "Maybe I could show you
what a real man is." He pressed his lips
against hers in a punishing kiss.

The urge to struggle nearly overcame her
iron will. She gritted her teach to remain
still. It was what Marcus had taught her. Never
show her opponent fear. When he moved away, she
spit in his face. He wiped his face, and in the
same motion slapped her hard across the face
again.

She glared at him, "Coward," she sneered.

"I'll show you who's a coward. By the time
I'm through with you, you'll be groveling at my
feet."

As he raised his whip to strike her, an
eerie howl broke through the night. Lacerta's
hand froze. Kiera quickly looked toward Erik.
Her hair stood up on her neck. Again Erik
howled. Moments later another howl was heard.
This time it came from the forest. There was
another howl, then another, then another. The
unearthly noise surrounded the camp.

She looked over at Erik and his eyes
appeared to glow. He looked as though he was
possessed by a demon. Lacerta backed away.
Looking around the surrounding trees she saw
many eyes glowing around the camp.

A large gray wolf stepped out of the
shadows, baring his teeth. Other wolves came

out of the forest, their eyes focused on the men in the camp. Deep growls rolling in their throats. In the blink of an eye, Erik was out of his ropes. He threw off his noose, and ran to Kiera and untied her.

"How did you get loose?"

"Wizardry," he said pulling her off the ground, "Come on, we have to get away from here."

They ran to his horse. Their captors were still backing away from the very real threat still snarling and salivating with the eager anticipation of predators approaching a kill.

Erik mounted and reached down to draw her up behind him. She held him tightly as they bolted into the forest. As they rode away she could hear men screaming as the wolves attacked. Storm ran hard until they crossed a river.

Erik helped Kiera dismount and tightly wrapped his arms around her. Both of them were trembling. Kiera finally pulled away. "You brought the wolves."

His shoulders squared. "Does that frighten you?"

"No." She held him again. "Isabella told me about your ability to communicate with animals the day after Ian's accident. When she told me of your powers it made sense why you could so readily accept mine."

"Why didn't you say anything?" he asked in surprise.

"What was I supposed to say? Have you gossiped with the geese lately?" She shrugged her shoulders. "How do you approach something like that?"

He threw his head back and laughed. "I suppose you have a point." He kissed the bridge of her nose, obviously relieved that she wasn't afraid. He gave her another hug.

"Could we go now? I think it better to put ourselves as far away from Lacerta's men as possible."

They rode the rest of the evening and most of the next day until they were on Alastair's border.

Before they reached the meadow he stopped his horse and dismounted before she could ask questions. He pulled her down into his arms. "I want a kiss before we continue. I don't know when we'll have the opportunity again." He pulled her into his arms, kissing her passionately on the lips. Kiera responded instantly, melting into his body. His kiss was a long and passionate one. Their tongues dueled together until she was senseless. He moved his lips along her neck, nipping her with his teeth, like a stallion nipping his mare. As he suckled her neck, she moaned with pleasure. He'd undone her hair winding his fingers through it. Kissing her hard again on the mouth. When he withdrew, her lips felt swollen from his kisses.

"We have to go now. Your brothers are probably sick with worry." She did want to stop and attempted to kiss him again. He held her back. "We'll finish this tonight." He stroked his thumb across her cheek. He picked her up by the waist and put her on his horse, mounting behind her.

As they came out of the woods, she saw Snow waiting in the meadow. "Why didn't he go on to the Keep?

"I told him not to. It would cause alarm to find your horse without you on it.

Kiera was overwhelmed with relief as they approached the gate. But she couldn't allow herself to enjoy those feelings for long. Soon she'd have to leave the Keep and everyone in it behind. It would be far too dangerous for them if she stayed.

As they entered the courtyard, they saw Dominick and Randolf on the steps of the great hall. Instead of looking happy to see her, they looked like two judges ready to execute. They never took their eyes off her. She flushed under their scrutiny.

Erik helped her dismount. She went over to Snow and gathered the pouch and her father's sword and walked toward her brothers. Their arms crossed in front of them. She knew they were angry, but she tried to keep her tone light. "Hello, my brothers."

Neither one acknowledged her greeting. "Come into the Keep, Kiera," Dominick said, his black eyes boring into hers. She instinctively wanted to cringe, but her pride wouldn't allow it. She followed both men into the Keep with Erik right behind her. When they didn't stop in the Great Hall, Kiera questioned Dominick. "Where are we going?"

He turned to her. "Where we can't be overheard." She felt as though a rock had dropped in her stomach. She tried to calm herself. This was not Murdock she was dealing with. Besides Erik wouldn't let anything happen to her.

They walked up the stairs to her chamber door. Dominick held it open and signaled her in. She walked in to find Jordan, Marcus and Ian standing there. She would not be intimidated.

Dominick was the first to speak. "I want to know why you left Alastair Keep without telling anyone."

She straightened. "First of all, I'm not a child and can go anywhere I please. Second I went to Dunsmore Castle to retrieve the documents proving your legitimacy and ownership of Dunsmore lands."

"I've told you before, I don't want Dunsmore," he said coldly.

"I know what you've told me, but that changes nothing for me. As long as Murdock holds the land I'll never be free. I was going to take the documents to the King. Knowing he's your friend I thought maybe he would help me, since you're not inclined to do so." She saw him stiffen. She was treading dangerously on thin ice, but after what she'd been through she didn't care. She held out her father's sword. "I took this. It was our father's," she said, handing it to him. "It's now yours." She reached deeper into the pouch, "This is our father's ring," she added, and placed it in

Randolf's hand. Randolf turned it over in his hand to look at it. "And these are the documents I went for." She held them out for Dominick to take.

He handed the sword to Randolf, and took the documents from her. Unrolling the parchment, he examined the documents. The muscles worked at his jaw.

"Murdock had stolen everything away from you, including our parents."

Dominick looked back up at Kiera, and gazed at her for a long time. She began to squirm under his scrutiny.

He slowly approached her. This time Kiera unconsciously took a step back. He towered over her. She flinched slightly when he reached for a strand of her unbound hair and moved it behind her and pulled the fabric away from her neck.

"You bare Erik's mark."

She quickly put her hand on her neck, and turned toward Erik. His face was still as stone.

"Did you make good your vow, Erik?" Dominick said turning toward him. His tone was flat. "Is my sister no longer a virgin?

Without hesitation he answered, "She may even now be bearing my child," he said simply.

Kiera felt as though a stone dropped into her stomach. She couldn't believe that he would betray her like that.

"Then the two of you'll be married immediately," he said.

"What!" Kiera shouted. "You can't order me to marry him. I refuse. This is not going to happen."

Dominick placed his hands on his hips, staring down at her. "These documents you were so eager to retrieve prove that I'm your brother, and the head of this family. By risking your life for them you have sealed your own fate, and you'll do as I say" he crossed his arms with authority.

"No, I won't!" She tried walking out the door but Marcus and Jordan blocked it. "I thought you were my friends, how could you go along with this!"

"It's in your best interest, Kiera." Marcus said. "After running away, you showed a lack in judgment. You need the protection of Lord Erik and his Keep."

"I don't need his protection." She turned to Jordan, "Jordan, help me," she pleaded.

"I'm sorry Kiera, I can't."

Ian came to her side, "Kiera it's for your own good, when you have a chance to stop and think about it you'll see it's for the best," he said, as though he were talking to a child.

"I wish everyone would stop saying that! It's not for the best. Two people should be in love when they get married. We made a mistake, why do we have to pay for it for the rest of our lives."

She felt Erik at her elbow. "Don't touch me!" she shouted. "This is all your fault. You did this on purpose. Why? So you could firm up your alliance with the Great Dominick the

Immortal and the Black Knight, is that what this is about? Or is it some debt you feel you owe me? I'll not marry a man who feels indebted to me. It's over, you owe me nothing."

Erik grabbed her by the shoulders, shaking her hard. "Kiera stop it! The debt will be settled when I say it's settled."

She broke out of his hold. "No! Don't you understand what is at stake here?" She looked at all the men around her. "Because of me, Murdock will wage war against you to get to me." She pointed her finger at her chest. "I'm the one he wants, not you. It's immortality he wants, not just Dunsmore and he will stop at nothing to have me. That's why I have to leave and get as far away from you as I can."

"You forget who we are, Kiera." Dominick stepped closer. "Like you, we are warriors and we can keep you safe."

She glared at him. "How? By keeping me locked up where he can't get to me?" She stood straighter with her fists clenched tightly. "I'll never be put in a prison again."

Erik turned her toward him. "I'll not allow you to wander about putting yourself in danger. There is nowhere you can go where he can't find you. Then you'll be in his clutches forever."

"I'll kill myself before I let that happen."

"You'll do no such thing. We are going to be married and you'll be under my protection."

"I'm not going to be someone else's burden."

"Did I say you would be a burden?"

He stared at her for some time. She felt her will begin to crack. These men weren't going to let her leave. Her eyes filled with tears. She put her forehead against his chest, defeated and intelligent enough to realize it. "Please don't do this," she pleaded one last time.

"It's the only way to keep you safe. I'll do all I can to prevent you from regretting it. I swear."

CHAPTER XXV

Isabella burst into Kiera's chambers filled with excitement. "Kiera this is wonderful news. I can't tell you how happy I am," she said. She stopped abruptly. She must have seen the despair on Kiera's face. "What's wrong?" she asked.

"Your brother trapped me," she said bitterly.

"I know, Ian told me."

Kiera looked down at her hands. "Did he also tell you that I'm against this?"

Isabella ran to her side, taking hold of her hands. "Yes, but you'll feel differently, I promise," she said, squeezing her hands in reassurance.

Kiera pulled away, rubbing her hands across her face, turning toward the window. "I'll live in constant fear, Isabella. Murdock will hear of my marriage, and try to hurt Erik to get to me. I can't allow that to happen. First chance I get I'll go back to Dunsmore and Kill Murdock myself."

"You mustn't talk like that, Kiera! You'll most certainly be captured or killed," Isabella said with alarm.

"It's better than living with this fear. I have been living with it all my life. I can't endure it any longer. Erik doesn't realize he has become my weakness. If Murdock killed him I couldn't bear it."

Isabella was very still, absorbing what Kiera had said. "Then you do love him."

Kiera turned to her, "I-I never let myself think about it that way, but yes, I guess I do."

"Kiera. You are marrying the man you love. That is rare."

"He is only marrying me to fulfill a debt he feels he owes. He doesn't love me. A part of me will never truly be whole without it," she said sadly.

"Erik has never done anything he doesn't want to do. He cares for you. I know he does."

"I wish I could believe that."

"Just give him time Kiera. You can break down the walls he's built around himself. He needs you."

"Erik doesn't need anyone."

"That's not true. He does need you." She stood up and placed her hands on Kiera's shoulders. "You make him human. You have made him feel emotion. Whether he likes it or not, I see the walls coming down. Give him time, Kiera. Give him time."

Isabella went to the wardrobe, pulling out the blue gown. "This will be very appropriate for your wedding." She laid it out on the bed.

As her bath was being prepared, Kiera's mind was in turmoil. Murdock will most surely be more desperate now that Dominick has the documents. She will have to constantly be on her guard. She had to protect her family. They had no idea what the Dragon was capable of. Fear knotted in her stomach. She undressed without thinking. Isabella turned toward her before she had fully submerged into the tub.

"My God, Kiera, your back!" Isabella shouted.

She froze for a moment then lowered herself into the water. Isabella ran to her, pushing her forward to get a better look. She could have kicked herself for not thinking about Isabella being in the room. "Isabella, it's nothing, it happened a long time ago."

"Nothing! Oh Kiera, how you must have suffered," Isabella said, close to tears. "Has Erik seen this?"

"Yes," She lowered her head.

"Did Murdock do this?"

"Yes."

Isabella turned Kiera toward her, staring intently into her eyes. "I swear to you, Kiera, Erik will never allow anyone to hurt you again. You'll have the protection of Alastair, and my husband's home, the house of Winfield. You need never fear that monster again."

Kiera kept silent, for she knew only Murdock's death would take away her fear. She finished with her bath and wrapped herself in a bath sheet. Isabella helped her with her gown, lacing it up the back. Her hair was left down. Isabella brushed it until it shone. Both women were silent with their own thoughts. The circlet was placed on her head, and again she was transformed to an ethereal beauty.

Eleanor and Aurelia came in, both kissing her cheeks, and telling her how happy they were for her. She gave them a fleeting smile. Eleanor saw her reluctance at her upcoming marriage. She placed her hand on both sides of Kiera's face, "I too had my doubts about marrying Dominick, but in time I learned of his kindness, and generosity. I could never be happier. You too, will one day know these things about Erik. It's only a matter of time. It will work out, you'll see."

Kiera squeezed her hand, "I hope so Eleanor, I certainly hope so."

The women walked her out of her chamber door. Marcus was waiting. "Am I forgiven?" he asked.

Kiera rushed into his arms, hugging him tightly. "Oh Marcus, I could never be angry at you. At least not for long," she added with a smile.

"I feel in my bones that it's right."

"It's not me I worry about. It's Erik."

"I'm sure he can take care of himself. He has many allies. He is also the son of an Earl. Murdock wouldn't dare hurt him."

Feeling slightly reassured, Kiera smiled at him. "How our lives have changed. Who would have thought a few weeks ago we would both be married?" she laughed.

"I couldn't be happier," he said looking at Aurelia. He turned back to Kiera, "Now, to the matters at hand. Dominick felt that it should be my responsibility to give the bride away."

She smiled, "You have been my father, and my protector. It's as it should be."

He took her hand and placed it in the crook of his arm, walking her down the stairs. They proceeded to the chapel. She was on Marcus's arm, and the three women followed behind. It was a glorious evening. The sun was falling on the horizon. Its fiery glow settled on the Keep. But Kiera felt as though something dark hovered over her. She was afraid to be happy. She tried telling herself she was marrying the man she loved. That it should be enough. But she wasn't sure it could be.

They walked into the chapel where Jordan was waiting. He handed her a bouquet of spring flowers. She leapt into his arms, hugging him tightly. "Be happy Kiera," he said.

Her eyes held his, "It will never be the same again, will it?" she said, as tears clouded her vision.

"No, it will be better," he said kissing her cheek.

"I feel as though I'm losing my best friend." Tears streaming down her face.

"I'll always be here for you Kiera, never forget that. If you should ever need me, I'll be by your side as always."

She hugged him again tightly, "You have been like a brother to me," she said. "You have been the best part of my life. Promise me things will never change between us."

"I'll always be your brother, and you'll always be the sister of my heart. That I promise will never change." They held each other for a long time.

Marcus whispered to her, "Kiera it's time."

Jordan kissed the top of her head. She straightened herself, wiping away the tears. She was ready.

As she walked down the aisle, she saw Erik dressed in the same color blue as her gown. The color made his amber eyes more striking. His blond hair was pulled tightly back, accentuating his high cheekbones and squared jaw. He wore a silver amulet around his neck. His blue mantle was trimmed in silver.

She looked over at her brothers standing in the pews. Dominick and Randolf smiled, and gave her a reassuring nod. Randolf did the same. She calmed as she took Erik's hand. Looking into his eyes she resigned herself to what was happening. She couldn't change things now. She looked around her. Family and friends surrounded her. She felt stronger. She squeezed Erik's hand. He turned to her smiling. Yes, she would allow herself to be happy that day.

The ceremony was brief. Kiera could barely remember saying the words that she would take Erik as her husband. Erik placed a heavy gold band on her finger, with the Alastair seal. When they were pronounced husband and wife, he kissed her soundly on the lips, taking her breathy away. He pulled away staring into her sparkling blue eyes.

"Swear to me in front of God, that you'll never leave me or Alastair Keep again." His golden eyes were intent.

"Erik, I...." she said, looking around her.

He squeezed her hand tighter, forcing her to look at him. "Swear it," he said, firmly.

Would he ever forgive the lie? "I swear," she said lowering her head.

Pulling her chin up, he kissed her again. "Never forget this vow to me Kiera," he said, then turned her toward their guests. Everyone was smiling back at them. She only wished she felt as optimistic as they did. He led her out of the chapel to her cheers of the people of Alastair. They walked arm in arm through the crowed. Men were clapping, and the women were weeping tears of joy.

Dominick and Eleanor were the first to congratulate them. Dominick wrapped his big arms around her, lifting her off the ground in a great big hug. They both laughed as he put her back on the ground. "Still angry at you big brother?"

"No, you only did what you felt was right.

"You're a great warrior, Kiera, and an honorable woman. But you still need protection. As your brother I had to see it done. Erik too, is a great warrior. He will keep you safe."

"But who will keep him safe?" she asked.

"I believe that responsibility is yours." Kiera was surprised by his answer. He hugged her again tightly. "It will work out," he said, then left to dance with his wife.

She looked over at Randolf, who had three women standing around him and staring up at him like lovesick sheep. He looked at her, his eyes pleaded for her to come and rescue him. She had to lower her head, so he wouldn't see her laughing. She walked over, grabbing his arm, "Will you excuse us? I have a few things I would like to talk to my brother about." The women looked on with disappointment as she led him away.

"Thank you very much," he said, wiping his brow.

"You are the first man I have ever met who didn't like the attention," she said.

"Don't get me wrong, I love the attention, but sometimes it can be a bit overwhelming."

"Oh poor baby, it must be hell to be so handsome," she sighed mockingly.

"Watch it, you're not too big to turn over my knee."

"Try it and you'll be at the wrong end of my sword," she said, smiling. She looked down at her wedding band. Her smile faded. "Randolf, what am I going to do? I don't know anything about being a wife. I don't know how to manage a household, or lead servants. I don't even know how to cook. All I know how to do is fight. Marcus never prepared me for this. I never thought I would have a home, much less a husband. What do I do?"

He put his hands on her shoulders. "Now don't panic, you'll be just fine. Isabella is here to help you and so is Aurelia, and for a little while, Eleanor. I'm sure they'll help you through it," he said. He bent down kissing her cheeks. "Everything will be all right."

"I wish people would stop saying that."

"Why?"

"Because when people say everything is going to be all right, that is usually when everything goes wrong."

"You are being superstitious."

"No. I have a history of things going wrong."

"That's not true. You came to Alastair Keep, found your brothers, made new friends, and married the son of an Earl. That doesn't sound like things going wrong to me."

"Put that way I can hardly argue." Looking over at Erik, she saw him watching her. "I pray you're right, I couldn't bare things to go wrong now. I never thought I would have a family besides Marcus and Jordan. It was easier that way. Now there are so many people to care for. I'm scared."

"We love you too, don't forget that. We'll look out for each other. Together we are strong and no one can tear us apart."

His words comforted her. She hugged him. "Thank you Randolf." She looked back toward Erik, "I better get back to Erik before he thinks I'm ignoring him."

"Ignoring him will keep him on his toes." he leaned further into her. "A bit of advice. Make him come to you." They both laughed.

She saw a red haired serving girl staring at Randolf. He didn't miss the seductive look the girl gave him either. "I think you should go over there and start enjoying the celebration."

"I think you're right," he said squeezing her hand. "Save me a dance later?"

"I will. Go," she said pushing him forward, "enjoy yourself." She watched him for a while. She saw Erik walking toward her. He laced his fingers between hers.

"Have I told you how beautiful you look?" he asked.

Kiera blushed, "No, you haven't."

"Then I have been remiss on my husbandly duties, you look ravishing," he said kissing her cheek. Kiera was so surprised by his compliment she didn't know what to say. "Would you care to dance?" He led her to the center of the garden. Erik's movements were smooth and strong as he led her around the garden. Later others joined in.

The celebration lasted well into the night. Olaf got drunk and fell over one of the musicians when he tried to toast the bride and groom. Everyone roared with laughter. One of the soldiers picked him up and carried him away. Little by little people left offering their congratulations.

Isabella and Ian came up to them hand in hand. Kiera thought them truly in love. She longed for such a relationship. For just a moment her heart felt heavy.

Isabella tugged on Erik's tunic. "How do you like my wedding present?" she said. "I was in luck that Eleanor had more than one bolt of the fabric. I made it along with Kiera's gown.

"You are a hopeless romantic," He said kissing her cheek.

"I just want you to be happy." She turned to Kiera. "Do you need help readying for bed?"

"I'll ready her for bed, you needn't worry," he said.

She blushed furiously. "Erik sometimes you can be so crass," Isabella berated. She kissed them good night and left arm in arm with Ian. Ian turned back and winked at Erik.

"Shall we retire my Lady?" he asked holding her hand.

She looked into his face. His eyes glowed. She felt the desire building in. "Yes," she answered breathlessly. They headed up to his chamber. It was decorated with rich gold and burgundy colors. There were lush tapestries hanging on the wall, of lions and wolves, and knights doing battle. A large hearth with a fire blazing cast a soft glow around the room. Several large windows led out to a small balcony. Candles were lit around the bed like an altar.

Erik came up behind her moving her hair over one shoulder kissing the small of her neck. It made her skin prickle. "Let me help you remove this," he said as he started unlacing her gown. He pulled it down her shoulders, and trailed kisses across them. His hands caressed her hips, moving it further down. He helped her step out of it. He turned her toward him kissing her lips, his tongue explored her mouth. Her head pressed against his shoulder, as he held her tight. Moving his hands down her back he ground her hips into his groin. His manhood hardened, sending desire through her veins. He moved his hands up her rib cage to her breasts. His thumbs stroked her nipples into hard peaks through her chemise. Kiera moaned with excitement.

She removed his girdle, letting it fall to the floor with a loud clang. Her hand reached under his tunic and stroked his warm skin, feeling the muscles beneath her hands. She stroked his chest, loving the feel of the soft hair curling around her fingers. She followed his example by running her thumbs across his nipples. She heard his sharp intake of breath and smiled at the power she felt. Kissing his corded neck, she ran her hands down his washboard stomach, feeling the muscles contract with her touch.

Grabbing her hair at the back of her head, he pulled her lips back to his kissing her hard and long until she was dizzy with passion. He quickly removed the rest of her clothing then carried her to his bed. His muscles rippled as he removed his tunic. He unlaced his britches, pulling them down his hips. She watched the hard muscles in his belly moved as he bent down to remove them. His bronzed skin glowed in the candlelight. Her eyes moved further down. His buttock was firm, his legs flexed as he turned. Her eyes moved back up to his large shaft, jutted out.

Her blood burned white hot with desire. Her arms reached up to him, no longer willing to wait. He climbed in beside her and wrapped her tightly in his arms. His lips found hers, and pressed her hard against the pillows. The full weight of his body was on top of hers, his manhood pressed into her belly. A moan escaped his lips when she rose her hips.

His hot breath caressed her breasts. He suckled each one until they turned into hard peaks. He moved down to her navel, licking it with his tongue. Kiera held his head as he moved further down. He looked up into her face, flushed with passion.

"I'm going to take you to paradise." Gently, his hands parted the lips between her thighs as his tongue stroked her woman's core. Kiera nearly came off the bed. His tongue stroked her again. Her fists clenched tightly on the bed. She thought she couldn't endure more, but he held her still, sliding one finger inside her sheath as his tongue licked and stroked her. She couldn't catch her breath. All thought washed away with the tide of passion. She screamed when the climax crested. Her muscles contracted in spasms of delight.

Erik came up quickly and slid his body into hers as her body shuddered. He slowly moved as her body calmed. "Open your eyes Kiera," he commanded. Looking into his eyes her passion was fueled again. His hair came down around his face, his eyes glowing in the firelight. He slipped one hand behind her knee, bringing it up to his side and buried himself deeper. "Feel me, Kiera, I'm the only man who will ever possess your body." He thrust hard into her, driving his point home. She felt the desire burning between her thighs again. She brought her other leg up wrapping her thighs around his waist. When she climaxed again, he let go of his own control and moved faster until his released.

He held her kissing her cheeks, eyes, and lips as they both came back to earth. Slowly, he rolled off of her breathing heavy. He brought her hand to his lips and kissed it reverently.

"Your passion runs deep," he said as he rubbed his thumb along her knuckles. You make love with abandon and inhibition. He tucked her in at his side. "Did you make it to paradise?" he asked still breathless.

"To paradise and beyond," she said, slinging her arm across his chest.

"We are a good match," he said stroking her arm.

CHAPTER XXVI

Lacerta dreaded his confrontation with Murdock. He was an unreasonable and unpredictable man. He would have someone hung for a minor infraction. Lacerta had spent years making himself invaluable to him. Murdock depended on him. But with the loss of those documents, and Kiera, Murdock may very well have him killed.

Lacerta's arm throbbed furiously. The large gray wolf managed to bite and claw him several times before he was able to run his dagger through the beast's heart. That sorcerer was responsible for it. Lacerta swore he would make him pay dearly.

He was not at all pleased that Kiera didn't fear him. If it was the last thing he did, he would have her on her knees groveling before him. He would make sure the warlock watched before he killed him. His cock hardened at the thought. She had turned into a fine looking woman and he would enjoy training her to his needs.

As he approached, Murdock's his phallus went limp as the cold feeling of dread pumped through his veins.

"Where is the girl?" Murdock demanded.

"She's not here, My Lord," Lacerta said calmly, as he bowed. "We had them but we were attacked by a pack of wolves. They escaped. Many of my men were wounded some killed.

"I want the girl Lacerta not excuses," Murdock said crossing the floor. "Your incompetence doesn't suit you Captain." Murdock started pacing then without warning he struck Lacerta. His ring cut across his cheek.

Without flinching Lacerta wiped the blood away.

"Most certainly by now those bastards have the documents. We must have her as a hostage to keep them from attacking us." he continued to pace. "We must bring her back here."

"We?" Lacerta asked raising a brow.

"Yes, *we* Captain. I can't allow you to fail me again."

"As you wish My Lord."

"You are dismissed, Captain."

Lacerta quickly turned and left the hall. "The bitch will pay for this," he whispered to himself.

Erik flew his hawk into the morning sky. He watched the ground race below her when he connected to her. He searched the outlying meadows and forest looking for any sign of Murdock's men. So far there was nothing, but Erik kept up his vigilance

Every morning he flew with Celeste, but at night he took his owl. Nothing was taken by chance. Secretly, he hoped that Murdock's captain made an attempt to cross his boarders.

The thought of killing the man would be greatly satisfying.

While looking for Murdock's men, he and his soldiers routed out robbers that plagued the village, as well. There was no way Murdock's men could get passed the borders of his land without him knowing it.

He thought of Kiera and her bravery when she was in the clutches of danger. It made him proud. She was so much more than a worrier. She was a woman of passion. A combination that nearly consumed him. His thoughts of her were always close to his mind. Something he could ill afford if he had to go to battle. He tried to distance himself, but he kept being pulled back to her by a force unknown to him. When he was away he longed for her breath on his skin, the feel of her warm hands on his body, and the sweet scent of her skin as they made love. The last few days were surreal. Never in his life would he have believed he would find peace in a woman's arms.

He called Celeste out of the sky and rode back to Alistair. Now that Kiera was in his life could he really ever let her go?

The next few days at Alastair, passed blissfully. One morning she woke up to find a rose on her pillow. The next she woke with bolts of fabric in every color piled high on a nearby table.

She would be walking down a corridor, or around the stables when she would be quickly swept up in his arms passionately kiss her.

"Just exercising my husbandly rights," he would say, and walk away leaving her breathless with anticipation for the night ahead.

Whenever she rode her horse outside the palisades gate she was heavily guarded. It was only at night in Erik's arms did she feel truly free. They made love falling asleep in each other's arms.

During the day she trained hard with Marcus and Jordan, to fine tune her skills. Not for a moment did she believe Murdock would give up and she wanted to be ready.

Dominick's men had arrived and in a few days he would be departing. The hall was filled to capacity between the quest and the fighting men.

Isabella ran around frantically trying to find accommodations for everyone. Many of Dominick's men camped outside Alastair walls. Kiera's job was to help with the arrangements for food, and to try to keep Olaf calm.

She learned how to make bread, and many kinds of soups. He taught her about spices and how to use them.

Eleanor showed her how to make candle wax, while Aurelia showed her how to make the fragrant soap Erik used and how to handle the Keep's accounts. By the end of the day Kiera's head was spinning. She wondered how one woman could manage it all. Aurelia kept assuring her she could.

She had three new gowns made for her. All enhanced the blue of her eyes, and the blackness of her hair.

Each night Erik took her to the tower. Absorbed with each other they watched the stars, and basked in the moonlight.

They rose together one morning, Kiera putting on her tunic, britches and armor. Erik raised one eyebrow. She saw the question on his face. "If I'm to be your knight I must train."

"I suppose you're right, but I was getting used to you wearing gowns," he said disappointed.

She walked over kissing his lips briefly, "I'll wear one for you at the evening meal." She started to braid her hair when he stilled her hands.

"I'll do it for you." He wrapped his fingers in the thickness of her hair. She rubbed the back of her head into the palms, loving the feel of his hands running along her head. He braided it down the back and planted a brief kiss at the nap of her neck. They walked down to the Great Hall to break their fast.

After their morning meal, Erik went with Dominick to see to the provisions for his journey back to Godwin. Kiera met Marcus and Jordan on the training field. As they were talking, Kiera watched a man shouting at a woman from the corner of her eye. Marcus tried to divert her attention to other matters, but she kept watching the man and woman.

The woman was visibly afraid. She coward as the man moved closer to her, more threatening.

"This is none of your concern Kiera," Marcus said.

"Stay out of it," Jordan said holding her arm. She shrugged it off.

The man raised his hand and struck the woman across the face and knocked her to the ground. Kiera started running, with Marcus and Jordan right behind.

"Kiera, no!" Marcus shouted.

"Kiera!" Jordan shouted trying to catch up with her.

Erik and Dominick heard the shouting, and turned in time to see Kiera running toward the man, who was about to strike again.

"You son of a bitch!" Kiera screamed. The energy pumped through her veins. She was twenty feet away when she extended her arm and a burst of energy shot through her fingertips. The man flew through the air and knocked to the ground, as though a horse had kicked him.

Erik stopped, stunned by what he had just seen. "God's teeth," Dominick said.

Kiera continued to run toward the man who was clearly shaken. He started to rise off the ground when Kiera's arm extended again. She knocked him into a nearby wall. He crumbled to the ground.

She was drawing her sword when Erik tackled her to the ground. "Enough Kiera!" But she couldn't hear him. She was blind with rage and her eyes were glazed over in fury.

Jordan and Marcus ran to her side. "Hold her Erik, she's out of control!" Erik could feel the energy around her. Every hair on his body stood on end. His skin tingled. It took all his strength to hold on. Marcus and Jordan helped Erik hold her down. Dominick stood nearby, stunned by what he saw.

Aurelia heard the screaming and ran over to help. The three me struggled to hold her.

"Erik try to reach her mind," she said.

"I have my hands full right now Aurelia," he said struggling to keep Kiera from striking him.

"Relax your hold, the others can hold her down. You have got to get into her mind. Use your ability with animals to reach her."

"It only works for animals."

"She has the mind of an animal right now."

It was worth a try. He took a deep breath, clearing his mind. Placing his hand over her forehead. He reached out and to his surprise he felt them connect. *Calm, Angel* he told her. He felt the energy decrease. He moved in deeper. *Rest your mind.* Her body started to relax. *Calm,* he said again. Her eyes began to focus, and her body became still. She looked first at Erik then to Dominick.

Rationality took hold. "Oh Marcus, what have I done!" she cried. "Please tell me it didn't happen again!" She started to cry in earnest. "Please Marcus! Please say I didn't do it again!" she pleaded.

"Hush, my pet, it'll be all right," Marcus said in a soft tone. "No one was harmed," he said, stroking her hair.

Erik looked to Marcus. "You'll explain this," he said firmly.

"Aye," Marcus said.

Kiera was sobbing, when Erik picked her up and carried her up to their chambers. The others followed. He tried laying her on the bed, but she wouldn't let go.

"I'm going to get Eleanor, she may be able to help," Dominick said solemnly and left the room.

Erik rocked Kiera back and forth trying to calm her down.

"This always happens after she loses control. She goes into a fit of crying," Jordan said. "Just like the healing, everything is taken out of her."

Dominick walked into the room with Eleanor and Aurelia. Eleanor had a small bottle in her hands. She filled a cup of water then placed just a few drops in it from the bottle then handed it to Erik. "Here, get her to drink this."

Erik took the cup and pressed it to her lips. "Drink," he commanded softly. She did, when she finished she was immediately quiet. A few moments more she collapsed in his arms. He laid her gently on the bed, and turned toward Aurelia.

"She'll be fine, she's only asleep. We'll take care of her."

The men looked at Kiera one more time then left and went down to the Great Hall. They sat at a table each man in their own thoughts.

Erik had seen many things, but nothing like this. He was overwhelmed by what he saw. Emotion rolled around in his mind unable to settle on one.

"What demons live inside her?" Dominick asked bewildered.

"It's the rage." Marcus said.

"Where does it come from?" Dominick asked.

"I don't know for sure," he said evading the question.

"Does this happen every time she becomes angry?" Erik asked.

"No," Marcus said. "Something has to trigger it, something familiar, such as that woman's abuse."

"You said something familiar, what do you mean?" Dominick asked.

Just then Randolf came into the hall. "Good God! You all look as though you had just seen a ghost. What's happened?"

"We just found out our sister is a witch," Dominick said.

"What!" Randolf shouted, placing his hands on his hips.

"She's not a witch!" Jordan shouted as he stood up out of his chair. "If you knew half of what she's been through, you would understand."

"Will someone please tell me what's going on," Randolf demanded. He looked toward Dominick, "What do you mean our sister is a witch?" Jordan was ready to jump him. Randolf held up his hand, "Or not. What's happened?"

Erik looked down at the table. In all his life had never seen anyone who possessed so much rage. He felt it when he connected with her mind. A black fury that scared even him.

His thoughts were interrupted as Dominick relayed what happened, to Randolf. "I can't believe it," he said sitting down. The men fell silent. Aurelia walked into the hall. "You may come into the room now, she's resting comfortably. There is something we wish to show you."

Erik knew what it was that Aurelia wanted to show them, but kept silent.

They stood around her as she laid on the bed, motionless, her breathing steady.

Marcus kneeled beside the bed stroking her hand. Eleanor moved in front of Dominick, "I would like you to see something." She looked at Marcus. "If you'll please turn her on her side."

He looked at Eleanor and then looked back to Kiera, "Forgive me," he whispered and pulled her on her side. Eleanor pulled down blanket to Kiera's waist bringing a candle closer.

"My God!" Dominick said through clenched teeth.

"Whoever did this shall pay with his life," Randolf said.

Dominick looked to Marcus as he laid Kiera back down. Eleanor moved back to Dominick placing her hand on his chest. Erik knew he was remembering his own beatings. The anger was welling up inside him.

"We saw this when we were preparing her for bed.

Dominick turned to Erik, "Did you know about this?"

"Yes," Erik kept his anger close to him. His tone was flat and emotionless.

"Why didn't you tell me?" he growled.

"What would you have done if I had? Torment yourself for not being there for her? Until two weeks ago you didn't even know she existed. There was nothing you could do."

He stared at Marcus before, "Tell us what happened, and tell us all of it."

Let's go down stairs first. Marcus looked down at Kiera before he left. His eyes misted as he looked back toward Dominick. "After your parents were killed, Murdock moved into Dunsmore Castle. He is a sadistic man. One day, one of the stable boys had fallen from the loft breaking his arm. She was there when it happened. The boy was wreathing in agony. Instinctively, she went to the boy and touched his arm. The boy quieted. When she finally pulled away and he could move his arm freely. The break had been completely healed.

Murdock was in the stable when it happened. He made the boy swear not to tell anyone. He took Kiera back into the castle, locking her inside the tower. Later they found the boy's body in a nearby lake.

That evening, he brought a serving girl to Kiera, and right before her eyes, he cut the woman's wrist. Heal her," he said. Kiera so horrified she grabbed the woman's wrist. The bleeding stopped and her wrist was healed.

He kept her locked in the castle. She wasn't allowed to go anywhere outside the walls. He assigned a guard on her at all times. She was a prisoner. But that wasn't the worst of it. He thought to exercise her powers and the beatings began. But it went beyond beatings, he humiliated her, as well. He would strike her in front of his men. He would have her bend on all fours while he beat her with his whip. She would cry and plead for him to stop. The more she cried, the more he enjoyed her torment.

Then he became ill. A debilitating disease swept through his body. She would cure him, but in time the disease came back. She healed him over and over until her strength was waning. Three years of this horror she endured." He looked up into Erik's face. Erik remained motionless. Marcus continued.

"I watched her go from a happy normal little girl, to an empty shell of a child. She walked in the shadows, hoping she wouldn't be seen. She started at every sound and cringed from anyone's sudden movements. My heart ached for her. Murdock wouldn't allow anyone to talk to her. When she was beaten she would turn her powers inside herself to heal her wounds. She was usually well in a day or two.

One night Murdock was drinking and was in a foul mood. She tried to hide from him, but it was no use. One of his men found her in the kitchen, hiding underneath a table. When brought her to the Great Hall she was beaten for no reason other than the man's foul mood. Her screams were unbearable to me. I ran like a coward to the stable taking my horse out, and ran fast as I could into the night. When I returned, the castle was quiet and everyone was asleep. I went to the tower to check on her. She was barely breathing. Her back was torn, and there was so much blood. I knew she was dying. She had lost her will to live. She wouldn't turn her power onto herself. This time she endured too much. In a moment I knew what I had to do. I wrapped her in a blanket and quietly carried her out of the castle. I had my son gather supplies and two horses. We shod their hooves so they wouldn't be heard, and left through a secret entrance from the castle. I held her in my arms for what seemed like an eternity, all the while trying to convince her to turn her powers inside herself. But she couldn't hear me.

We finally came upon the village I grew up in as a child. They offered us shelter. A fever had set in on her. I feared the worst. All night swore I would never let anyone hurt her again. That I would keep her safe. Somewhere in her delirium she must have heard me because the next day her fever broke. She was still too weak to heal herself completely. That's why she has the scars. But every day she became stronger." Marcus rubbed his eyes.

Erik was finally able to speak. "So you taught her how to fight."

"Yes. The only way to keep her safe was to teach her how to defend herself."

"She's a very good student." Erik said with some pride.

"I believe it's a legacy of our family," Randolf said.

"Has she always had this power to move things?" Dominick asked.

"No. It developed over the years. And it only happens when she's extremely angry."

"This explains why she attacked that man. When he struck the woman, it must have brought back her memories of abuse," Dominick said.

Aurelia stepped forward. "We all have a certain power within us. Even you Dominick. For a long time you were able to communicate with the dead. Often it saved Eleanor's life." Dominick looked toward Eleanor without saying a word. "You have the instincts of a warrior, unlike I have ever known. You shouldn't have survived that prison, yet you did. How?" He couldn't answer. "Your name, *The Immortal*, tells the story in itself. People believe you can't die. You have survived battles that couldn't be won. Yet here you stand before us."

She turned to Randolf. "I believe you possess the same powers of healing as Kiera does." Randolf shook his head. Aurelia held up her hand. "Your brother was dying. Yet you were able to nurse him back to health. As I said we all have some sort of power within us. Some are not as obvious as others."

The silence grew thick in the room, each with their own thoughts.

Erik's thoughts were in turmoil. Hate, anger and wanting revenge. "How long is she like this?"

"It varies to how much energy she spends."

Dominick turned to his wife, "Will she be all right?"

"I believe she'll be fine," she said, reaching out for her husband. "Don't worry, she just needs some rest." She pulled Dominick toward the door, "Come, you and Randolf have a lot to think about.

Marcus looked as though a great burden was lifted off his shoulders. He began to the door leave the Hall when Erik put his hand on his shoulder looking into his eyes, silently thanking him for what he'd done for Kiera.

"No one will harm her ever again." He remembered her words on the day they met. "For I will not allow it."

Ian and Isabella came into the Hall. Dominick relayed what had happened to them. Isabella ran upstairs to check on Kiera.

Randolf paced back and forth clearly enraged by what he had learned. "Never in my life have I heard of such evil. Torturing a child is beyond comprehension. What kind of monster would do such a thing? He ranted.

"Kiera calls him the Dragon, because he wears a dragon on his tunic and armor," Marcus said.

"This dragon ought to be slain," Ian said.

Eleanor came into the Hall, each man looked up at her. "She's resting peacefully. Isabella and Aurelia are with her now."

Erik ground his teeth. His heart broke for what Kiera endured. Never had he pulled so hard on the reins of his anger. His forehead broke out in a sweat with the effort to keep it inside.

"Erik what are you thinking?" Dominick asked.

"I'm thinking that I'm going to kill Murdock, and release Kiera from her fear forever."

Dominick looked to Eleanor. "I release you from your vow to me," said Eleanor. "This man needs to be destroyed, and your sister and parents avenged." Dominick took her hand and kissed the back of it reverently.

"I'll send a message to the King explaining what has happened, and what I plan to do," he said.

Ian crossed over to Erik. "I'll send for my men. You'll have my support as well."

Erik was grateful, but it wouldn't be enough. His spies had returned telling him of the fortification, and the armies at Dunsmore Castle. It will take more men to defeat Murdock and Dunsmore.

The evening meal was a quiet one. Everyone was in deep in thought. As soon as Erik finished his meal he went up to his chambers. Isabella sat in a chair next to the bed.

"How is she," he asked.

"A little restless, but she'll be fine." Isabella rose, "I'm glad you're going to kill him." Erik looked at her in surprise. "I only wish I could do it myself."

"I never realized how blood thirsty you are," he chuckled, trying to make light what they both felt. She didn't smile back.

"She is my friend and my sister, and she has suffered and endured what most people wouldn't, and all because of one man. He has to be destroyed."

Erik kissed her forehead, "He will be Bella, I promise. Go get some rest we'll talk about it in the morning."

She left, leaving Erik to his thoughts. He stared down at her as she slept. He made a vow to keep her safe and he intended to keep it no matter the cost.

He sat down at his table to pen a letter. When he finished he called to Albert. He would see it delivered.

After that was done he quietly undressed and slipped under the covers, pulling her into his arms.

"Erik!" she said, awaking with a start.

"I'm here." He kissed her gently. "Go back to sleep."

She fell back into a contented sleep. He laid awake through most of the night, thinking, and planning, all the while stroking her hair. He wondered how he was able to communicate with her mind. He had only been able to communicate with animals. But then he thought her mind was like an animal, with her instinct to protect, and defend. He felt the rage her rage when he connected with her mind. He would never forget the horror he felt mixed with that rage.

He fell into a restless sleep, dreaming of dragons, fire and blood.

CHAPTER XXVII

The next morning Erik rose not disturbing Kiera. He watched her chest rise and fall, her breathing deep and even, as she slept soundly. Convinced her sleep was natural he quickly dressed and went down stairs. After his morning meal, he went to start readying his men for the battle against Dunsmore.

He later met up with Ian, "How is Kiera this morning?"

"She's still sleeping."

"This has been quite a turn of events, hasn't it my friend. What are you going to do?"

Erik looked up at him. "What do you mean?"

Ian stood directly in front of him. "Erik your men saw what Kiera did yesterday. They're afraid of her. I'm not sure they will follow you into battle for witch."

Erik threw his head back breathing in deeply then let it out slowly. He knew there would be a problem with his people. They accepted Kiera's ability to heal, because it saved their lady Aurelia. But this other power may not be so readily accepted. Erik looked back at Ian. "Are you afraid?"

"The devil's eyes, yes, I'm afraid." Erik began to speak then Ian held up his hand. "Yes,

I'm afraid. This is unlike anything I have ever seen. It's not an unreasonable fear. But I know in my heart Kiera is a good woman, with a tortured soul. A woman with a black heart, wouldn't have done what she had done for me, and wouldn't have risked her own life to save Aurelia. This is not the heart of a witch. I owe her a great deal. That's why I have dispatched a messenger, sending for my men at Winfield. There will be at least three hundred to ride with us," Ian said with conviction.

Erik placed his hand on Ian's shoulder with a firm grip. "Thank you my friend. Thank you for your understanding and your support." Erik dropped his hand. The two men started to walk toward the stables. "The more men we have, the more likely Murdock will surrender Dunsmore, Erik said. He looked over at the palisades wall deep in thought. Ian could sense something troubling him.

"What are you thinking, Erik," he asked.

"I'm thinking with all the men we have, it may still not be enough. The spies I sent out have come back to report that Dunsmore is heavily armed and well-fortified. A siege could last for months. Murdock is no fool, if he knows that Dominick and Randolf have the documents proving Dunsmore is rightfully theirs, he'll be waiting for us. Worse I fear that he will become more desperate and try to take Kiera as hostage to use her against us."

"How could he get near her? Alastair is surrounded by soldiers."

"There are so many people here, and more to come, it will be hard to know if Murdock's men are among us. It's only a matter of time before they try."

"What do you intend to do?"

"Strike as soon as possible with a team of men, before Murdock gets wind of what we have planned and the armies we intend to mount against him. Marcus said there was a secret entrance, we could take a team of men and strike from within."

"It sounds like a good plan, count me in."

Erik slapped him on the back, "Thank you but I can't risk it." Ian was about to argue, but Erik held up his hand. "I need you outside with your armies in case we're captured."

"Who will you take in with you?"

"Marcus and Jordan of course. They know the layout of the castle. And the two spies I sent to Dunsmore.

"What about Kiera?'

"She will stay here, heavily guarded. I don't want her anywhere near that castle until Murdock is dead."

"So your intention is to kill him, not take him before the King."

"That man will die for what he's done to her," he said with venom.

Ian smiled, "That sounds like a man in love to me."

Erik's face hardened into indifference, "I'm avenging my wife. It's my duty as her husband nothing more."

Ian grew angry, "So noble are you," he said, his voice thick with sarcasm. "If you keep it to duty, you won't have to feel anything. Keep everything at a distance." Ian took a step closer to him. "I have seen you fight the fiercest warriors, go into battle with odds against you coming out alive. I thought you then the bravest man I have ever known. And now I know the truth. You are a coward Erik." Erik clenched his fists. No man had called him a coward and kept standing. He pulled tight on his temper. "I tell you now, Erik, it's an empty life you lead." He turned and left Erik without another word.

He stood there watching his friend walk away. He knew Ian was right, but the cast had been set. Emotion was not something that came to him easily...if it came at all.

He returned to the Keep. He realized he hadn't seen Kiera throughout the day, which was unusual. He found Isabella in the Great Hall, "Have you seen Kiera today?" he asked.

"No, as a matter of fact I haven't. I thought she was training with your men."

"No, she isn't there." Isabella gave him a puzzled look as he climbed up the stairs to his chamber.

Upon entering he found her in the window seat staring down into the garden. She was dressed in her scarlet gown, her hair hung in a loose braid down her back.

He stood there watching her. She had a sad faraway look on her face. Already he missed her smile. He crossed the floor. She turned as she heard him approach. "Why aren't you downstairs with the others?"

"I can't face them after what I've done. Surely they must think me a witch or sorceress," she said softly looking down at her hands. "I'm surprised you haven't locked me up in your dungeon. Aren't you afraid of me? I'm sure my brothers are probably ready to burn me at the stake for what I did."

He gently laid his hands on her shoulders, "What you did was defend a woman who was being abused."

"We can't pretend it wasn't more than that," she said. "You saw what happened I was going to kill that man." She turned back to look out the window. "I lost control of my temper. I didn't know who I was, or what I was doing. I just felt rage."

"This power you possess, do you know where it comes from?"

"No," she shook her head. "It happens rarely. It's something I can't control, and only rage will make it happen. It's as if all the energy of that anger forms around me. I feel my heart pounding, and I'm blinded by a white hot anger."

"Kiera, I'll admit this power of yours concerns me, but it doesn't frighten me. I don't believe you're a sorceress, or that you're evil. Things that happened to you, most people wouldn't survive, much less a child. This force that manifests inside you, I believe is your one true defense. Don't let it control you. You must gain control of it yourself. If you feel it come on, concentrate, harness it then let it fall away. If you don't, I fear one day, it could destroy you."

Kiera eyes filled with tears. "Dominick saw what happened, didn't he?"

"Yes," he said frankly.

He watched a tear roll down her cheek. "He must think I'm a berserker, or worse a witch. He will have nothing to do with me now. I'm sure he and Randolf will go back to Godwin, never to acknowledge me again."

"That's not true." He bent on one knee to face her. "Dominick was shaken by what he saw. He didn't understand it, but he didn't judge you. He understood better after what he saw had happen to you."

Kiera shook her head, confused. "What do you mean, after what he saw happened to me?"

"They saw the scars on your back. Eleanor saw them and thought your brothers should see them. Marcus felt it was time for them to know."

She put her face in her hands, "How will I ever face them again?"

He cupped her chin and raised her face to look at him. "Why wouldn't you be able to face them?"

"I don't want their pity." She pulled her face away, and walked toward the hearth. "If you want to annul our marriage, I'll understand."

He came up behind her. "When I reached your mind Kiera, I saw the rage and I felt your horror. This anger you feel, you're entitled to. Purge these demons that haunt you Kiera, for no one will hurt you again, I swear." he rubbed her arms, "I don't wish to annul our marriage. I made a vow to protect you, a vow I intend to keep." he turned her to face him.

She wrapped her arms around him, breathing in deeply. "Thank you Erik. Thank you for all you've done for us. You have been a true friend."

He couldn't help the wicked smile that spread across his face. "Just a friend?"

She smiles back, "More than just a friend."

His face moved closer to hers, "Are you sure?"

"Yes," she whispered as his mouth came down on hers. He teasingly nipped her bottom lip then wrapped her completely in his arms for a long and passionate kiss. When he pulled away a pink flush rose to her cheeks.

"If we keep this up we won't get much accomplished this afternoon," he said as he pulled away.

"I don't mind," she said smiling.

He touched her cheek, "What kind of insatiable woman have I married?"

"One that loves the feel of your body next to hers," she said pulling him into her arms.

"Woman, you make it very hard to leave these chambers."

"That's my intent," she said boldly.

"Never the less, you and I have duties to perform," he said with mock authority.

"Yes, My Lord," she said sarcastically.

He playfully swatted her behind, "Don't take
that tone with me young lady, or it won't go
easy for you this evening."

"Promise," she said smiling.

He sighed exasperated, for the wanton wench
she had become. "Let's go while I can still
stand up," he said grabbing her arm and pulling
her out of the chambers.

He felt her reluctance to leave their
chambers, but didn't resist as he led her down
the stairs to the Great Hall.

Kiera saw Isabella, managing the staff. She
felt ashamed, that she had left her duties upon
Isabella's shoulders. She would try in some way
to make it up to her. When Isabella saw them
coming into the Hall she immediately went to
Kiera's side, taking her hand.

"How are you feeling today?" she asked.

Kiera didn't see any sign of condemnation on
Isabella's face, only concern. She looked at
her no differently than she had the day before.
Isabella accepted her unconditionally. It
filled Kiera with emotion she never experienced
before. Never, had she expected this. All her
life, she'd been ostracized by people who knew
less about her. It humbled her.

"I'm much better, thank you," she said,
sincerely. "And thank you for taking care of
things in my absence.

"Nonsense, you needed some time, that's all
there is to it. I'm sure if there comes a time
I should need you, I'm sure you wouldn't
hesitate to help me."

Kiera gave Isabella a big hug. "Count on it."

Dominick and Randolf came into the Hall. Eleanor was on Dominick's arm, with Derrick tagging behind. As soon as Derrick saw Kiera, he came running up to her. She scooped him up in a big hug and kissed him on the cheek. "How was your day today, any big adventures?" she asked.

"Uncle Erik taught me how to ride today on a pony he gave me," he said excitedly. He held up his forefinger, "I was chasing one of the geese and he turned around and bit me," he held it so she could get a closer look.

"Aw...poor lamb. Aunt Kiera will kiss it and make it better." She kissed his finger then held it down at his side, where he couldn't see her heal it. "Did you slay any dragons, or save any damsels in distress?"

"No," he said dejected, "I had to take a nap."

She put him down, "I'll tell you what, tomorrow you can show me how well you ride, and maybe we can find some damsels in distress. How does that sound?"

"Great! We can go first thing tomorrow."

"First thing," she laughed, as he scampered away.

"It's good to see you smile, Kiera," Dominick said solemnly.

She turned to him, giving him a long silent look. His gazed into her eyes. She breathed in deeply, struggling not to cry. She swallowed hard before she spoke. "I'm sorry if I caused you concern yesterday."

He looked down at her hand before he took it in his. He rubbed the back of it with his other. They completely engulfed hers. "I've thought about you all night." he still didn't look at her. "I'm the one I who's sorry. If I hadn't been so stubborn when I heard about our parent's death, I would have come to Dunsmore, to properly mourn their passing. I would have found you, and I would have taken you away from that horrible man. You wouldn't have suffered as you did." Kiera stood silent. He stroked her knuckles with his thumb. "Because I neglected my duty to our parents, this evil man has placed a demon in you." He paused for a moment. "I have always considered myself an honorable man, but what had happened to you, there was no honor."

Kiera finally spoke. "You couldn't have known, Dominick. For all you knew, your father abandoned you. No one could blame you for your hate." She put her hand on top of his. "What is important is that we are together now, just as our parents wanted. I have loved you and Randolf all my life. Being your sister is the greatest honor. Don't berate yourself for what has already happened. I know in my heart that if you had known about me, you would have found me, and taken me away."

Randolf stepped up to her. "Your pain will be avenged Kiera, along with the murder of our parents. Murdock will lose his life for it, I promise."

"What do you mean?"

"We have called for more men from Godwin. We've also sent a message to the King, and asked for his help," Dominick said. "We're going to reclaim our land."

Isabella stepped forward. "Ian has also sent for men at Winfield. They should be here soon."

Kiera stood with her mouth open, as she looked at the people that stood around her. Her years of pain and heartache melted away. She was no longer alone.

Erik led her to the head table in the Hall. "There is a bit of business we still have to tend to." Erik nodded to Albert. The boy left the hall.

Soon the man who she attacked was bought in with irons. He glared at her with a jaundiced eye. The woman he struck came meekly to her side. The woman was beautiful, with dark brown hair, with large brown eyes and long sweeping lashes. She bore a large bruise on one cheek. Kiera's heart went out to her.

Her confusion must have shone on her face. "He's here for you to pass judgment on him."

"But I attacked him," she said with astonishment.

"You were only defending the woman he attacked, therefore you'll pass judgment on him, and it'll be carried out."

Erik was giving her control to make up for the time when she didn't have any. He was giving her the opportunity to right a wrong. She straightened in her chair. "What's your name?" she said to the young woman.

"Meghann, my lady," she spoke softly.

"Who's this man, Meghann?"

"He's my husband," she said, lowering her head.

She already knew the answer to her next question, but felt compelled to ask. "Has he beaten you before?"

"Yes, my lady," she answered. Shame clearly on her face.

"What do you think we should do with him?"

Meghann looked up at her in surprise. "I....I don't know my lady. It isn't my place to decide."

"I believe it is since the wrong was done to you. What would you like to see done with him?" He glared at his wife, trying to intimidate her. Kiera came quickly to her defense. "I would be very careful how you look at your wife Sir. If she wants to have you castrated, it'll be done. So I would look a little kinder upon her." The man quickly turned away.

She turned back toward Meghann, her brown eyes glistened with tears. "I would like to see him work from sunrise to well into the evening hours without so much as a kind word. I want him to feel the same humiliation I do."

Kiera's understood the woman's fear and humiliation. "Very well," she said turning back to the man. Looking into his face she saw a deep purple bruise under his chin, and his eye was slightly puffy. It gave her a sense of satisfaction. "What's your name?" she asked the man.

"Gerald," he said gruffly. One of the soldiers nudged him hard, My Lady," he said finally.

"Well Gerald, for the next month you'll rise before the sun, cleaning out the stables. Then you'll clean out the pigsty, scrub the floors and help in the kitchen. You'll work well into the evening. And you'll sleep where the hounds sleep," she added for humility.

She came out of her chair to stand in front of him, looking directly into his eyes so there would be no mistake about her meaning. "And if I hear of you ever striking your wife again, it will cost you your hand. And if you strike her a second time, it will cost you your life."

Gerald's eyes widened, turning to Erik, he struggled against the soldiers holding him back. "My Lord, you can't allow this. There's no law against keeping your wife obedient," he shouted.

Erik walked up to Gerald. His expression was the same as the one he had when he was set upon by the bandits. Gerald took a step back. "I don't condone anyone to abuse those weaker than themselves. It's the act of a coward. You are not worthy to be one of my soldiers. You'll be my example. If anyone should abuse another, who's under my protection, they shall have to deal with me." Be grateful my wife only has you shoveling out muck. If it were me you would be a guest in my dungeon." He took Kiera's hand and walked her back to their chairs, sitting down he signaled for the soldiers to take him away.

"Thank you, my lady," Meghann said.

When they left, Kiera reached for Erik's hand. "Thank you".

"You were much too lenient with him," he said.

"I agree," Randolf said.

"Not if he should strike her again," Kiera said. All three men nodded in agreement.

They walked over to the tables where the evening meal was being served. She couldn't take her eyes off Erik throughout the evening. Even when she was talking with Isabella and Eleanor her eyes wandered back to him. Strangely so did his. She could feel the bond between them. His eyes were like flames licking at a log ready to consume it. Eventually she couldn't take it any longer. She bid good night to everyone, giving Erik one long look. Her eyes conveying her message to him.

In their chambers she lit the candles around their bed. It was warm in their chamber. She opened all their shutters to the windows to let the cool night breeze in. The candles flickered, and the room danced with the soft light. She undressed and let her hair down. It felt luxurious on her bare skin. She dabbed perfume at her throat and trailed it down between her breasts. She smiled wickedly dabbing it between her thighs.

She climbed into bed and waited for Erik. She didn't have to wait long. She rose on her elbow, and pushed the blankets to her waist. He had full view of her voluptuous breasts. She watched him undress. She couldn't get used to her magnificent body. When he climbed in beside her, she leaned over and kissed him long and hard. He sucked in a large breathed deeply. When she pulled back, her body lit with a passion.

"You gave me control this evening. Will you give it to me now?"

"What do you mean?" he said warily.

She moved her body fully on top of his. He became very still. She kissed him again, then ran her tongue along his bottom lip. He remained silent.

"Yield to me, Erik," she whispered, as she ran her tongue along his jaw, nipping his earlobe, and ran her tongue down his neck. He was still holding on to his control.

She sat up looking down into his eyes. "Now you bare my mark." A smile spread across his face. He reached up to fondle her breasts. She captured his hands, pushing them down on either side of his head. "This time I'm in control. Release your hold Erik, concede your will to me," she whispered, as she came down planting a kiss on his chest. She ran her tongue around his nipple, as he had done to her so many times before, then gently blowing on its tender peak.

His teeth gnashed together. She was relentless as her lips moved down further. She placed tiny kisses down his rib cage, to his flat hard stomach, where she ran her tongue inside his navel.

"Kiera don't go further," his voice rasped.

She placed her fingers on his lips, "My warrior, I won't hurt you," she said playfully.

She moved further down stroking his manhood with her tongue. His body trembled. She took him fully into her mouth. Erik groaned his fingers wound tightly in her hair.

"Where did you learn to do such things?" his voice strained.

"From you my lord. I only follow your example," she said, licking him once more. She kissed his stomach then sat up. He let out a long slow breath. She straddled him and took him fully into her.

He clamped his jaws together. He tried to place his hands on her breast, and she slid them down her hips.

"Release your control, Erik," she said, as she started moving up and down him. She reached behind his neck, and pulled him up to her. She held his face looking into his eyes. "Give your will to me," she whispered. She tighten around him and a growl rolled from the back of his throat. "I love the feel of you deep inside me," she said, as she moved up and down, throwing her head back. He placed a kiss on her neck. She looked back into his burning amber eyes, and knew he was close. "Let go of your control." She moved down deeper on him. His hips began to push inside her. "Yes," was all he said, his control shattered. His fingers dug into her hips as he shouted with his release.

Her heart nearly burst with joy, that she could bring him such ecstasy. She held him tightly, then laid him gently back on the bed and stroked his chest until his breathing returned to normal. When he recovered, she moved off him and slid out of bed. She returned with a goblet of wine, and a cool wet towel. While he drank the wine, she cooled his body with the towel.

Placing the goblet on the table near the bed, he touched her face and caught her full attention, looking deep into her eyes. "You do more than heal the body Kiera, you heal the soul." He placed a light kiss on her lips. She smiled back at him, pleased with his words.

He raised one eyebrow. "Fighting is not the only skill you learned well."

She blushed, "I never do anything half way my lord."

He stroked her face smiling, "I guess not." He moved his hand to her throat, firmly pressing his fingers, "See that you never apply what you've learned to anyone else," he said.

His possessiveness brought a small thrill to her stomach. "That is a promise I'll keep till the day I die."

He kissed her passionately. He reached for the goblet on the table, holding it to her lips. "Drink, fortify yourself, for the night is still young and I have much more to teach you."

CHAPTER XXVIII

Kiera sat in the garden day dreaming about the night before. Her hair blew in the warm spring breeze. She was dressed in her amethyst gown with lavender trim. Her hair braided with ribbons of the same color. She was becoming accustomed wearing gowns instead of her tunic and britches. She ran her hands down the sleeves, the fabric was smooth to her touch.

She hugged herself remembering Erik's sweet kisses and soft words the night before. He made love to her most of the night. True to his promise, she had learned a great deal. She smiled to herself, Erik may not love her, but she knew he cared. She was breaking through the wall that protected him. She could feel it crumbling with every touch and every kiss.

She picked a rose as red as any ruby and brought it to her nose. She breathed in its sweet scent. A commotion in the bailey brought her out of her revelry. She walked out of the garden and to the front of the keep to see what was happening.

An army of men on horses filled the bailey. Her mouth dropped open, when she looked up and saw a pair of golden amber eyes staring back at her. His hair was the same color as the sun, with white streaks of age running through it. His frame and stature was familiar to her. He wore the Alastair emblem of the hawk in flight across his armor. It was Erik's father.

He looked down at her. "Are you going to stand their gawking girl or are you going to tell me where my son is?" he said gruffly.

Before she had time to answer she heard Erik come up behind her. "I'm here father," he said in a flat toneless voice. She turned to see him descending the Keep's stairs, his shoulders were straight and his face looked as hard as granite. Kiera felt a pang of regret. For days she hadn't seen that face.

His father dismounted his horse to meet him on the last step. "It's good to see you son," his father said holding out his hand.

Erik looked at it for a moment then, politely took it. "Is it?" he said stiffly. There was an uncomfortable silence that stretched between them.

"Thank you," Erik said blandly.

Kiera could feel Erik slipping behind his walls of indifference. She quickly walked to his side, slipping her hand in his. He looked down at her as if he just realized she was there. "Kiera, I would like you to meet my father, Alexander, the Earl of Kentwood. My Lord this is Kiera, Lady of Alastair."

She bowed slightly, "My Lord, it's a pleasure to meet you," she said politely.

He bent over her hand and placed a kiss on the back of it. "The pleasure is all mine," he said, giving her a brief smile. He stood turning back to Erik. "So, you have finally taken a wife, it's about time you had an heir."

"Yes," Erik said flatly.

Her skin prickled with the tension between them. "Would you care to come in for some refreshments, my lord?" she asked, trying to lighten the air around them.

"Thank you, I have traveled most of the night to get here, I could use a good ale."

Erik stepped aside as his father started to climb the stairs, and said nothing to him as he passed by. Kiera could feel the tension in Erik's body. Her heart went out to him. She put her hand on his shoulder, he shrugged it off. Kiera was shocked by his action. She followed Alexander up the Keep stairs leaving Erik to follow behind.

She quickly ordered the servants to bring ale, bread and stew. Erik's father sat down at the table, she sat next to her father-in-law, while Erik took a seat across from him. He drank his ale without saying a word.

"What brings you to Alastair my lord?" She asked, trying hard to relieve the tension in the air. It only grew worse.

"Erik sent me a message asking me to come," he said looking directly at Erik.

"I asked for your men, not you," he said coldly.

Alexander jolted with the venom in which his son spoke. "I came because I thought you needed my help," he said gruffly.

"I need your men, not you,"

"Erik!" Kiera shouted, "He's your father."

He stood up abruptly knocking over his chair. "He hasn't been my father for twelve years," Then left the Great Hall.

She watched Erik leave the hall in great strides then turned to her father-in-law, "You must realize the turmoil Erik is in. You have been gone for twelve years. Your turning up here is somewhat disconcerting to all of us. We need your armies, but if you have come here to pass judgment on us, then you can take them back with you. I'll not let this wound be opened."

"I haven't come here to cause trouble to my son. I have come to join him in battle, nothing more," he said sadly. After he was done with his stew he rose to leave the Hall. "Thank you for the meal, I'll tend to my men now." He walked out of the Hall leaving Kiera with mixed emotions. On one hand she was angry at Alexander for abandoning his son, on the other she saw a man coming to his son's needs.

She sighed, the next few days were going to be difficult. She sat drinking her wine and pondered it when she heard Isabella walking into the Hall. "Is it true? Is my father really here?" she asked anxiously.

"Yes, it's true," she said holding out her hand to Isabella and pulled her into the seat next to her. "How do you feel about it?"

"I don't know," she said shrugging her shoulders, "I guess I feel a bit nervous seeing him again. I'm worried about what this is going to do to Erik. How did he react when he saw him?"

Kiera turned back to her wine, "Guarded," she said, taking a sip.

"If I know Erik, it was worse than that. How did father act?"

Kiera turned back to Isabella, "Rather gruff, but I sense something more."

"Such as?" Isabella asked.

"I feel that you father is here for more than the battle at Dunsmore." Kiera shook her head, "Maybe I'm all wrong. I was with him such a short time."

Isabella grabbed her hands, "Oh, Kiera! I hope you're right. Erik's bitterness has to end."

"What about you Isabella? He abandoned you as well."

"It was never as hard with me as it had been for Erik. I was very young when he left and Aurelia was always there for me."

"Can you forgive your father?"

"If he came here to make peace with Erik, then I could forgive him anything," Isabella said firmly.

"That's good, because the two of them are going to need our help if they're ever to come together."

"I'll do everything I can," she said.

They carefully planned the evening meal together making sure every detail was taken care of. If the men were sitting down to a good meal, it would be difficult to feel any animosity toward each other.

They were wrong.

When it was time for the evening meal, Erik's mood was blacker than she had ever seen it. She made several attempts to bring him into conversation, but all she got were monosyllable answers. Alexander made no attempt to talk to him, he just sat quietly sipping his ale.

Dominick decided to take matters into his own hands. He turned to Erik, "Erik, how about a hunt tomorrow? With all these men to feed we'll need some fresh meat."

"Fine," Erik said sipping his wine.

Dominick was undaunted, "Lord Alexander we would be honored if you would join us."

Alexander looked over at his son, Erik silently challenged him to agree. "It will be my pleasure," he said never taking his eyes off Erik.

Erik drank deep of his wine, then he abruptly rose, bidding Kiera and the others good night. He gave his father a curt bow.

She was startled by his abruptness. She thought it would take time for Erik and his father to reconcile.

Isabella looked over at her father." She patted Ian's hand then crossed the room to where Kiera and her father were sitting. She sat down in an empty chair in front of them.

"You've turned into a beautiful woman, Isabella. You have my eyes but everything else is your mother's." he said.

"Thank you," she said quietly.

"I understand that you're married. Are you happy?"

"Very, he's a good man," she said looking over at Ian.

"As I recall he was a very good boy. He and Erik were inseparable."

"In many ways they still are. Ian is like a brother to Erik."

"I remember you always tagging along with them."

"I was in love with him even then," she smiled.

"Good, then it's as it should be," he said smiling. He put his hand on top of hers.

She looked down at it. "Why are you really here, father?"

Alexander sighed, "Your brother sent me a message asking for five hundred men to do battle with Dunsmore Castle. I thought he needed me," he said, "I guess I was wrong."

"No, you're not wrong. Erik does need you, not for your men, but for you," she said placing her hand on top of his. "You made him feel like an abomination and that he wasn't worthy of your love."

"Isabella I have learned that there are many mysteries in this world, Erik possesses just one of them. My son is not evil. It's I who was wrong for abandoning him when he needed me most."

"You have got to convey that to him."

"How? He won't even talk to me."

"Keep trying, and don't stop trying until you get through. I believe deep down Erik wants to listen."

He clamped both her hands in his, "I'll do my best." He smiled at her, "How did I get a daughter so wise, when her father is so foolish?"

"Like you said, I take after mother." She stood smiling down at. "I'm glad you're here."

"So am I daughter, so am I."

Her eyes glistened, she bent down kissing him on the cheek. "I'll see you tomorrow."

"Tomorrow."

As Isabella left the Hall she realized that her sister-in-law had a great capacity to love and forgive. A trait she wished her husband had.

She toward Alexander. "You have more than just the battle with Dunsmore. You have to battle through your son's barrier and reconcile what has passed between you." He stood to retire for the evening.

"You're right and I have a battle to prepare for."

"Stay strong, my lord."

There was only one candle lit in their chamber when Kiera entered. She undressed quietly, and pulled the braid and ribbons from her hair. She slipped into bed and blew out the candle. The shutters were open and the moon's light spilled into the room. Kiera could see Erik's eyes were open as he stared at the ceiling. She placed her hand upon his chest. He visible flinched and moved away. This was the second time Erik had shunned her touch. The hurt speared through her heart.

"Erik...." she said softly.

He rolled away from her, "I'm tired Kiera. It's has been a long day. Just go to sleep."

She watched his back for a long time. She thought the door between them was beginning to open and realized it had just closed with her on the outside. Now she had her own battle to wage against that door.

CHAPTER XXIX

Chaos rose as the hunting party formed outside in the bailey. Hawks screeching, dogs barking, horses whinny. As they rode out of the palisades gate Randolf pulled up beside Erik. They both looked at the meadow, now filled with tents and campfires of the men who joined in their battle.

"Good God Erik! It looks as though Alastair is under siege," he said with a chuckle.

"I feel as though I'm under siege."

"With all these people around you, I don't doubt it."

They regrouped just outside the forest. Erik saw his father pulling up beside him. He pretended to be deeply involved with his hawk.

"She's beautiful, what do you call her?" his father asked.

"Celeste," Again, there was that uncomfortable silence. Erik watched his father from the corner of his eye. He closed his eyes and stroked the bird's feathers and connecting with her. She squawked and he returned with a similar sound. He turned to see his father's face for any sign of condemnation, but he was surprised to see none.

"What did she say?"

Erik was surprised by his question but didn't let on. "She's anxious for the hunt to begin."

"Like us all."

Erik unexpectedly felt uncomfortable. He was prepared for his father to say something derogatory, but he didn't. He took off Celeste's hood and released her into the cloudless sky. She immediately took down a dove. When she came back to Erik's arm she was rewarded for her efforts with fresh meat. They went deeper into the forest.

Other hawks did similar things, while dogs were hunting much larger prey. Four deer were brought down in the first hour, along with two boars one of which Alexander speared singled handily. Erik was silently impressed.

Throughout the day Erik constantly communicated with his animals, making the hunt more efficient. His hawk flew overhead spotting deer, geese, pheasant and rabbits. By the end of the day the hunting sacks were full and the hunters ready to go back to the Keep.

As they were heading back to the Keep, Ian rod up beside him. "It was a good hunt today, don't you think?"

"Celeste is always good on a hunt," he said solemnly.

"Yes, and you made a point of connecting with her every time your father was looking."

"I don't know what you mean, I always connect with her on a hunt."

"Yes, but not like today. It was as though you were challenging him."

"That wasn't my intent, I won't hide who I am." He heard the sharp edge in his own voice, but wasn't compelled to apologize.

"He seemed undaunted by your powers. Do you think he could be trying to make amends?"

"It's too late for that."

"It's never too late, my friend. Open your mind, it may open your heart."

"I have no heart, I'm the devil's son, remember?" He urged his horse forward away from Ian and away from the conversation.

The hunting party was subdued as they headed back to the Keep. There wasn't the usual revelry that accompanied a good hunt. They rode in through the palisades gate, and left their kills with Olaf to prepare. Erik deliberately avoided Kiera in the bailey. He went straight into their chamber, quickly bathed and changed for the evening.

The evening meal was another quiet affair for Kiera and Erik. Frustrated, she gave up trying to bring him into a conversation. Eventually she turned to Isabella and talk to her, keeping her hurt feelings to herself. The only time she would see him talk to someone was when Marcus and Jordan were in the room. Then they would go off to a corner somewhere and talk.

At one time when Erik wasn't monopolizing his time, Marcus came to talk with her. "How are thing with you, my girl," he asked.

She sighed, "Not very good," she said looking down at her hands. "Erik is farther away from me than ever."

He put his arms around her, "He has a lot on his mind," he said gently.

"Why won't he let me help him?" she said anxiously.

"It's difficult for Erik. Give him time my love, he'll work it out," he said giving her shoulders a squeeze.

She hoped he was right. She went up to their chambers and readied herself for bed. Sometime later she heard him come in. He sat at his desk, going over papers. What was so important, she didn't know. He finally came to bed. He undressed quickly, slipping beneath the covers. She again tried talking to him, but he pleaded fatigue he rolled away from her pretending to go to sleep.

She hadn't seen Erik most of the next day until the evening meal. Kiera didn't even try to talk to him. Their estrangement didn't go unnoticed. Dominick looked ready to pommel Erik to the ground, and his father watched shaking his head. Kiera ate almost nothing that evening. She pleaded fatigue and went to her chambers early. She didn't wait up for Erik this time, she hadn't slept for two nights and she fell into and exhausted sleep.

She woke to the sound of a loud thunderclap. Lightening filled the room. The bed was empty beside her. She frantically searched the room, he wasn't there. She climbed out of bed, and wrapped a blanket around her. Another flash of lightening filled the room and she saw Erik's shadow on the balcony. He seemed oblivious to the rain. She yelled at him but he couldn't hear her due to the violence of the storm.

She pulled the blanket tighter around her and walked outside and yelled his name louder. He finally turned around. "Erik what are you doing? Come back inside," she said pulling on his arm.

He jerked away, "Go inside Kiera, I'm fine," he said fiercely.

"No, you aren't fine, you're are soaking wet." She pulled on his arm one more time.

His eyes glowed with anger. He jerked his arm away, and grabbed her by both shoulders and pushed her against a wall. "I'm fine, I don't need you. I don't need anyone," over the storm's fury.

Her anger leapt into her body. She knocked his hands off her shoulders. Straightening, the blanket fell away from her, the rain soaked her gown. Lightening flashed all around them. She slapped him hard across the face. He stepped forward, his fists clenched at his side, yet he held onto his control. "You selfish, self-centered bastard!" She turned from him and walked back inside of their chambers.

He followed her. His hands clamped around her upper arm, and turned her to face him, "What do you want from me!"

"I want you to knock down those walls that keep you away from me."

"I can't."

"Can't or won't?" His arms dropped back at his sides as he looked away. "What are you afraid of?" She took a deep breath, "I love you, Erik." His eyes darted back to hers and then turned away. Wrapping her arms around him, her cheek pressed against his sodden tunic. "Don't hide from me. I'll be here for you, always."

He broke away from her, "Don't say that."

"Why?" She turned him to face her, "You have tried everything in your power to drive me away, yet I still stand here. Didn't you hear me tell you I love you?"

His face hardened, "There's no such thing."

"Then tell me what it is I feel."

"I don't know what you feel."

"Then how do you know I don't love you?"

"Don't play games with me."

"I'm not playing. If there's no such thing as love, then what is it you feel for your sister, or your aunt?"

"That's different."

"How is it different, Erik, is the only thing you feel for me is lust?"

He looked down at the floor, "No."

"Then what?"

She saw him fighting for the words, "I care about you Kiera, but I'm not sure I know how to love you. I'm not sure I ever will, love is something that happens to other people, not me."

His words pierced her heart, she thought she could die with the pain, yet she squared her shoulders, "I see, then this is all I could possibly hope for."

He couldn't look her in the eyes, "I'm sorry."

"There's nothing to be sorry for, you have been honest with me, that's all I could ask." She turned away from him. Grabbing a drying towel and a fresh nightgown, she pulled off her sodden one drying herself with the towel.

Lightening flashed again, he saw the scars webbed across her back. She suffered so much as a child, she was still suffering because he couldn't give her the love she wanted or deserved. Damn his black heart, he thought, if only he could bring himself to love her. He got out of his wet clothes and climbed into bed. He watched her dry her hair, and left it hang loose. She climbed into bed, blowing out the candle on the bedside table. She turned her back to him, and pretended to sleep. He desperately needed to hold her but he held still. He could feel the distance between them, yet he was unable to cross it.

CHAPTER XXX

Erik woke the next morning and found Kiera's side of the bed empty. She was nowhere to be found in their chamber. He dressed quickly and went down into the Great Hall. Finding Aurelia, he asked if she'd seen Kiera.

"She has already had her morning meal, she's outside I believe on the training field."

Erik let out a breath in relief, it didn't go unnoticed by his aunt.

"Is something wrong?"

"No, I was just wondering where she was."

He could sense Aurelia had something to say and held up his hand to stop her. "Aurelia don't."

"I can't help it Erik, I feel the turmoil in you."

"It will soon pass, as soon as my father leaves."

"Is that what you want, Erik?"

"Yes."

Aurelia stood up and walked around the table to stand in front of him. "Have you asked yourself why he's here?"

"I have many times and can't come up with an answer."

"Maybe I can give you one. Maybe he is here to reconcile with his son."

"After all these years, why would he want to do that?"

"Maybe he didn't know how before, your message might have just given him the answer."

"You still haven't told me why."

"Despite your differences, you're his son, his flesh and blood. He can't turn away from that forever."

"I still don't understand. Why would he care?"

"Your father loves you."

"I think for once you're wrong. No man who loves a child leaves him just because he's different."

"Did you ever ask him why he left? There may be reasons you never thought of."

"His reasoning may be his own. I have nothing to say to him." With that he walked out the door

Erik found Kiera training with Marcus and Jordan. He watched her as she and Jordan fought together. She was fighting furiously, sweat beaded on her forehead, her cheeks were flushed. Jordan countered her every move but he struggled with her speed. Their swords rang in the heavy morning air. The sky was overcast but it had stopped raining. The ground was soft and a few times she slip in the mud, yet she maintained her balance.

Randolf came to stand next to him. "She trains hard, harder than most of my men," he said.

"Probably because being a woman she has more to prove," Erik said. He watched as Marcus stopped her to give her further instructions.

"Probably, but you would think that being your wife she wouldn't have anything to prove." His ice blue eyes were piercing.

"What do you mean?"

Randolf turned fully to him, "I've watched you the last few days, and the two of you have barely spoken. She seems very unhappy, and this doesn't please me. If this estrangement between you continues and she's not with child by the time we leave, I'll be taking her back to Godwin with me."

Erik's back stiffened as though a rod was tied to it. "You'll have to kill me first, before I allow you to take her."

"You are my friend Erik. But my sister has suffered most of her life. I won't see her suffer no anymore. I'll do battle with you or anyone to give her the happiness she deserves." He looked up to the cloudy sky, then back at Erik. "You are her husband, she belongs to you. It's a pity you can communicate with animals, yet you can't with your wife." He walked away.

Erik stood there watching his friend walk away. He thought about Randolf's words. Maybe it would be best for Kiera to leave. He continued to watch Kiera and Jordan spar. He felt an irritation that the two of them should be working so closely together.

Alexander came up beside him. "Is that Kiera?" Erik didn't answer. "Good Lord man! How could you allow your wife to dress like that, training with your men? I've never heard of such a thing."

"What I allow, or not allow my wife to do is none of your concern," Erik said stiffly.

They stood silently for a while, both men watching Kiera and Jordan train. "Where did she learn to fight like that?'

"Marcus taught her from the time she was a child."

"Ah, Marcus, he is married to Aurelia." He paused for a moment, "I thought she would never marry, it's so good to see her happy."

Erik couldn't bring himself to talk to the man. He was too busy watching Jordan and Kiera in a wrestling match. Jordan threw Kiera over his hip, but lost his balance and both of them went down into the mud together. Both were laughing.

Erik crossed the field in long strides. He pulled Jordan off her by the scruff of his collar, then with one punch knocked him back down to the ground. He grabbed Kiera jerking her up. He looked back down at Jordan, "You ever touch my wife again, and I'll kill you." Still holding Kiera's arm, he led her back to the Keep.

The two men looked to each other and smiled. Jordan and Marcus' plan had worked. Jordan flinched holding his jaw.

Ian walked up to Alexander as they both watched the display Erik just put on. "I think my son just hand a temper tantrum," he said with amusement.

Ian smiled back, "Yes. That looked like a real human emotion to me. She's going to kill him for his high handedness."

"After seeing her fight, I wouldn't doubt it."

Alexander walked away smiling.

As Erik dragged Kiera into the Keep he barked orders to Alice to have a bath sent up to their chambers. Kiera tried jerking away but he held firmly onto her arm pulling her up the stairs. Once in their chamber, he finally released her. She jerked away, "What do you think you're doing!"

"I should ask you the same thing," he said crossing his arms.

"I was training, just like all the other times."

"That's not how I saw it. Jordan had his hands all over you."

"We were practicing hand to hand combat!"

"Is that what you call it?" he said in a condescending tone.

Kiera's anger was fueled, "What are you implying?"

"It looked a little too friendly to be called combat," he sneered.

Kiera's hands clenched at her sides, "Jordan is a friend of mine, we have been for years, you know that," she said through gritted teeth.

"Just how good of a friend is he. Kiera?"

Her eyes widened at the implication, "You son of a bitch!" He managed to duck her swing. He tried wrapping his arms around her, but she jammed her elbow into his ribs which forced him to let go. She braced for another attack. He moved toward her and she kicked out, but he stepped aside causing her to lose her balance. He brought her down to the floor. They struggled as he pinned her arms over her head. "Get off me!"

He straddled her limiting any movement. "Let me make one thing very clear. The only child that comes from your body will be mine."

"You're insane!" She tried to struggle away.

"From now on you'll not be allowed to train for combat, you'll wear a gown at all times and conduct yourself as Lady of this Keep. Is that understood?"

"No! That won't ever happen," she said, breathlessly.

"As my wife you'll do as you're told."

"When I'm treated as your wife I might be inclined to do what you say, but since you are not acting like my husband I feel no obligation to obey."

Before he could respond there was a knock on the door. He pulled her up before he bid them in. A wooden tub and buckets of steaming water were brought in. Erik and Kiera said nothing to each other while the tub was being filled. As the servants were leaving he told one of them to wait outside the chamber door. He turned to Kiera, "Give me your clothes." He glared at her.

She raised her head in defiance. "No." Her heart pumped with anger.

"Give them to me or I'll tear them off of you."

"You could try."

He was in no mood to argue. "Kiera, I want your clothes. .now."

Her eyes flashed with anger. "Fine." She pulled her tunic off and threw it at him. He had to dodge her flying boots. Finally, she took off her muddy britches and threw those at him splashing his face with mud. He took them and gave them to the servant waiting outside. "Give these to Alice and tell her to burn them."

"No, wait!" she said as he closed the door behind him.

She walked to the tub and climbed in with her back to him. She washed the mud from her face. He pulled out her scarlet gown and laid it out on the bed. He walked over to the tub and touched her shoulder. She jerked away. "Don't!"

His hand snapped back as though it was bitten, but he couldn't leave the room. He stood as though he were rooted to the floor.

When she was done with her bath she dried off and began to dress. She tried to lace up her gown. He saw her frustration. He went over to help her. She tried to shrug him off.

"Be still, I'm only trying to help."

Her hands clenched at her sides, but she let him lace her up. He turned her to face him and pulled out her medallion from under the gown. He looked down at it for a moment and then looked up into her eyes. "Never forget your vow to me, Kiera." With that said he walked out of the room.

It wasn't enough she thought to herself, the more she loved him the more she needed his love back. She could never be truly happy without it. He touched her face before he left their chambers.

She walked over to the window, looking up to the overcast sky. Will this ache in her heart ever go away, or was she doomed to a half of a life with her the only one loving in her marriage.

She stood for a while contemplating it when a sudden chill swept through her. It made her uneasy. She quickly stepped away from the window and tried to regain calm. She shook her head, trying to shake the uneasy feeling. She decided she needed to work, to take her mind off of things. She left the chamber in search of Aurelia. If anything Aurelia would have a thousand things for her to do.

Murdock and Lacerta walked around the various camps around the Keep. They moved about freely. There were so many soldiers no one gave them a second glance. They were even able to get inside the Keep itself. They talked with several of the servants finding out the Lord and Lady's daily habits. They were even able to watch Kiera train with Jordan. Murdock glowered at Marcus, the man who had taken Kiera away from him. He will surely die. Murdock's hands tightened on his dagger. He fantasized how he would do it. He was brought out of his revelry as Lacerta pulled him into a dark corner of the palisades wall.

"I believe I have found someone here to help us."

"Someone here?"

"Someone who is not so happy with the Lady of Alastair Keep."

"Good, bring him to me at nightfall, we must take Kiera by tomorrow night, before Dominick and Randolf have time to bring their armies to Dunsmore. With her in my keeping I can have it all, Dunsmore and her powers."

"Yes, my lord." Lacerta slipped back into the crowd.

Murdock stayed in the shadows of the palisades wall. From there he watched Kiera's window, waiting for a glimpse of her. Soon, he thought to himself, soon he would have her, and her powers would belong to him.

She came to the window, he stepped further back into the shadows. He heart beat with the knowledge that she would be his once more. She had turned into quite a beauty, he thought. She had her father's coloring with her mother's fine features. Her posture was erect and very noble. Well he would soon cure her of that when she's behind Dunsmore walls. His hand tightened around the whip he carried at his side. He would have her groveling at his feet and beg him to stop, and there was nothing that bastard Dominick could do about it, nor her pitiful husband. He snickered to himself. If he wanted he would hold her hostage until Erik surrendered Alastair Keep, as well.

This was something to ponder. He will think about it when he is safely back at Dunsmore with Kiera. She moved back inside the Keep. Murdock pulled the hood of his cloak further down over his face before he walked back to the palisades gate and back to the forest where he and Lacerta were hiding.

CHAPTER XXXI

Kiera came back to her chambers after what could only be called a very grueling day. She had seen to all the needs of Alastair Keep's guests, helped Olaf with the breads and soups for the evening meal. She had seen to the cleaning of the Great Hall, sweeping and putting down fresh rushes. When she was finished the Hall smelled of fresh wild flowers.

She also made time to play with Derrick and watch him ride his new pony he'd gotten from Erik. The boy's energy was inexhaustible.

All day long she couldn't shake a wariness that seemed to crawl under her skin. She kept looking behind her expecting to see someone there but no one was there.

Her mind turned to the earlier part of the day. She couldn't believe Erik had actually hit Jordan and threatened to kill him. Why should he care if he swears he can't love her?

She quickly changed her gown to her blue one. Her hair was braided down her back. She placed the silver circlet with the sapphire center stone on top of her head. Looking at her reflection, she was pleased with her appearance. This would be her armor for her battle at hand with Erik.

She was ready to go downstairs. Her eyes were drawn to the window. She looked out into the bailey once more but didn't see anything, yet she couldn't shake the uneasiness feeling. Suddenly she no longer wanted to be alone. Quickly she left the chamber nearly running into Erik on the stairs. He caught her before they collided.

He must have seen her urgency. "Are you all right?"

"Yes, I'm fine, just in a hurry to get down to the evening meal." She could barely be civil.

"Are you sure there's nothing wrong?"

"Other than your being an ass, nothing is wrong"

"I'm sorry for this afternoon. I was coming up to apologize."

"Apology accepted. Now if you'll excuse me."

She began to work her way around him when he gently grabbed her arm. "Please, just give me time."

"Fine, I'll give you the time you need, but not indefinitely. I don't know if I have it in me to endure more unhappiness."

"I understand, but I can't let you go."

"Can't or won't?"

He bowed his head and whispered, "Both."

"I'm not your prisoner Erik. If things don't change I'll leave you."

"And I'll find you."

They were at an impasse. They gazed at each other, neither one ready to give up their resolve. "I'll see you in the Hall," she said and walked down the stairs.

Later Erik came down into the Great Hall and sat next to Kiera. They didn't speak, but he felt that they had come to some kind of truce. The anger had left her eyes.

He looked at his father from the corner of his eye. Erik had to set aside his anger and come to some understanding with his him. They had to be allies if they were to take over Dunsmore. Erik cleared his throat turned toward his father "My Lord, would you care to accompany me on a hunt tomorrow?"

Erik saw his father blanch at his son's formality, but for now this was the best he could do.

"Yes that would be quite nice."

"Good, shall we meet at dawn tomorrow?"

"I'll be ready." Erik went to rise out of his chair, when Alexander stopped him. Erik gave him a curious look. "Son, what is your plan for the siege at Dunsmore."

Erik sat back down, at last a common ground that they could talk about. "We are waiting for Ian's men to arrive. When we are all assembled we'll ride against Dunsmore."

"When do you think that will happen?"

"I hope to leave in a few days. I don't want to give Murdock time to prepare for our attack."

"Do you think Murdock knows of the upcoming siege?"

"Yes, I believe he does. He has spies probably in our own camps outside. There are so many men it would be hard to tell enemy from ally."

Alexander thoughtfully rubbed his chin, "I've been to Dunsmore, it's extremely fortified, from what I can remember, this siege could take quite a while."

"I plan to shorten the time. Marcus has told me there's a secret entrance he doesn't think Murdock is aware of. I plan to take some of my men and open the gates from inside. I hope to take the castle in a day."

"What can I do to help you?" his father asked.

Erik was pleased by his father's enthusiasm. "I'll need you on the outside should we be captured."

"Are you sure you have enough men to go inside with you? Perhaps I--"

"No, Erik said emphatically, "too many men will draw attention. A small team may go unnoticed"

"But I can't just stand around and wait."

"I need you on the outside. You'll know what to do should something go wrong."

Alexander put his hand on top of Erik's, "Thank you for your confidence, son."

Erik pulled his hand away. There was an uncomfortable silence between them. Erik rose. "I'll see you tomorrow morning. Tomorrow afternoon there is a meeting with the leaders

of our attack. We'll discuss our plans then."
He bowed to his father, "I bid you good night."

Kiera and Aurelia watched the exchange between Erik and his father. It looked hopeful. Aurelia gave Kiera's hand a little squeeze. "Keep hope in your heart, Kiera."

"I'm nearly out of hope."

"You have to hold on. Erik needs you."

"Erik doesn't need anyone.

"That's where you're wrong." They looked across the room. "See he is drawn to you even now."

He walked up to her. "I saw you talking to your father was it horrible?" Kiera asked.

He turned back toward his father, "Not so horrible." He turned back to her. "We are going for a hunt tomorrow."

"That's good. You should spend more time with your father."

"We'll see." Erik took Kiera's hand and looked into her eyes. His stare made her heart pump faster. "I know I have acted abominably toward you."

"Yes, you have."

"I'm asking for your forgiveness."

"I don't know. You're asking a lot."

"I know."

She pulled away. "I'll think about it. Now if you'll excuse me, I'm very tired." She moved around him and went up the stairs. When she closed the door to her chambers she sat by the fire. She couldn't decide what she was feeling.

It was a combination of anger, sadness, and love. "Could she ever forgive him?"

Alexander watched Erik and his friends. It was like watching them when they were boys. He felt a deep sadness, he had missed so much of Erik and Isabella's lives. His heart beat with regret, but he was here now and he vowed he will never miss another moment in their lives.

The next evening Erik joined his father and Dominick at a side table. He watched Kiera put her hand on Jordan's jaw and heal it. Erik saw his father's body stiffen and his eyes widened as he watched the bruise fade away. He heard the catch in his breathing. "She's a healer." His father's hands trembled.

"Yes, she is." He wouldn't make excuses for her. She was what she was and no one can change that. "Any slight you give her is a slight to me and you can take you and your men with you."

"It just took me by surprise, that's all."

"She is one of the reasons we're ranging a war with Dunsmore. The other is that Murdock took what was rightfully theirs."

"She's hunted by Murdock who believes he can take her power and make himself immortal. He tormented and tortured her as a child. Marcus managed to steel her away from Dunsmore, but they have been on the run ever since. He's an evil man."

"Couldn't you have stopped him before all this?"

"We didn't know of her trouble until a recently," Dominick said. "We didn't know we had a sister until a couple of weeks ago. Since then we have grown very close."

Alexander looked back at her, "This is why she learned how to fight." He turned back to Dominick. "You needn't worry Dominick, I'll treat her as though she were my own daughter. I'll stand with you and my son to avenge her as well."

Erik didn't want a bond between them, but it seemed he had little choice.

Jongleurs started up the music. Kiera was back at his side swaying to the music when Randolf came up behind her and lifted her off the ground sweeping her into a dance. She laughed with delight. She deserved to be happy. But he wasn't sure he could make her happy. His heart was trapped inside the walls he built and couldn't let anything good come inside.

CHAPTER XXXII

Erik and Kiera left the others early. When she walked to the chamber the window her uneasiness returned. Her hair rose on the back of her neck. She searched the night's shadows to look for any sign of trouble.

"What's out there, that has you so deep in thought," he asked.

"Nothing," she lied. "Nothing that's important." She undressed and climbed into bed. This time she turned her back on him. She was through trying to crack the shell he crawled in to.

"I'm sorry I have been such a bastard. These last few days were difficult for me."

"I know but that doesn't change. Go to sleep. As I said, I'm very tired." He rolled away from her and blew out the candle.

She laid in bed wondering if she could forgive him. He made it clear he couldn't, or wouldn't love her. She wondered if she could live in Alistair knowing he didn't love her. Once Murdock was destroyed it would be safe for her to leave, but could she? Most definitely, yes.

Murdock watched her from the palisades wall. He hid deep in the shadows. He could see her wariness, he smiled. It made him feel powerful. Soon she would be back under his control and no amount of armies could take her from him.

Erik woke with a start when Kiera shot out of bed. "What's wrong?"

"The Dragon, is here" she said her tone was flat.

"He can't be. We have done everything to make you safe."

"No, Erik, he's here, I can feel it."

"What makes you so sure?"

"I just am."

"We'll search for him tomorrow. If he's here we'll find him." By the look on her face he was not getting through.

"No you won't. There are so many people that he blends in."

She was right, but that wouldn't stop him from trying. He would take Marcus and comb through the soldier's camp to look for any sign of him. "Come back to bed. You need your rest."

"No, I think I will sit here for a while."

He gazed at her silhouette in the moonlight. Murdock would have to be killed in order for her to feel safe. With all the men outside and inside of the Keep it may things more dangerous for her. She stood at the window quite some time. "I will find him tomorrow and kill him."

Not if he got to him first.

CHAPTER XXXIII

Erik rose before dawn, quietly dressing, so as not to disturb Kiera. He went down into the Great Hall where his squire Albert was sleeping on a pallet near the stairs, he shook him awake, Albert sat up instantly, "Yes, my lord?"

"Albert, I want you to bring my hauberk and sword. You'll help me with it here."

Albert ran to do his bidding, when Erik stopped him. "I also want you to wake Lord Dominick and Sir Randolf as well as Marcus and Jordan." Erik hesitated for a moment, "Wake my father also. Tell them to meet me in here in the Great Hall."

"Yes My Lord," Albert said, running off to do his master's bidding.

Erik paced in front of the great hearth until Albert returned with his armor. As Albert slid on Erik's chainmail, Dominick and Randolf came downstairs.

"What's wrong?" Dominick asked.

"I believe Murdock is here."

"How's that possible?" asked Randolf.

"There are so many people here that they could go about the Keep unnoticed." Albert handed Erik his sword. "I need you and Dominick to go around your soldier's encampments. Make sure everyone is accounted for. Also check to see if they have seen anyone suspicious, or if anyone has been asking questions about the Keep and Kiera."

Alexander came downstairs, with Marcus and Jordan behind him. Alexander took in Erik's appearance. "I thought we were going hunting today."

Erik turned to him, "We are, only we're hunting for spies instead."

"Spies, here at Alastair, from where?"

"Dunsmore," Erik said strapping on his sword.

"What are you planning?"

"We'll go to the campsites of your men and look for anyone you don't recognize."

Alexander straightened, "I'll have my captain organize the men to make it easier to account for each one." Alexander turned to his squire and sent him for his hauberk. When he returned, Albert helped with it, while his squire went to Alexander's captain.

"How can we assist you?" asked Marcus.

"I want you to join me and Alexander in our search. Jordan, you go with Dominick and Randolf. I'm sure if Murdock's men are here you may recognized some of them."

"Why do you think Murdock's men are here?" Jordan asked.

"Kiera is sure he's here."

Soon all the men were ready to leave the, Ian and Isabella joined them. "Erik, what's happening?" Ian asked.

"I suspect Murdock's spies maybe here."

"What makes you think that?"

"Intuition," he said simply.

"Ian, I need you to stay here and search the Keep, you know everyone here as well as I do." Erik turned toward Isabella, "I want you to stay with Kiera all day, don't leave her side. She's anxious and I believe you can keep her busy enough to keep her mind occupied and off of Murdock."

"When will you be back?" she asked.

"I should be back in time for the evening meal." He kissed his sister on the forehead and left the hall with the other men. Soon they were mounted and ready to leave.

They separated and went to their soldier's camps.

Little did Erik know, they were being watched.

Kiera woke later that morning. She could feel that Erik was gone already. She still couldn't get over the uneasiness and it kept her on edge. She dressed in her tunic and britches.

She sheathed her sword and was drawn to the window again. There was nothing. Looking down she saw the same people she saw every day, nothing was different, but in her heart she knew it was, and that she was being watched. She could feel it. She crossed her arms to rub the prickliness from her skin.

She could feel him, he was close. "Not this time Murdock, I'll not be your victim again."

She quickly turned and left her chambers. Isabella was in the Great Hall at the morning meal when she saw Kiera about to leave the Hall.

"Kiera! Where are you going?"

Kiera stopped short of the Hall entrance. "I'm going to look for Murdock."

"Erik is already searching for him."

"Murdock is too clever to be caught."

"There is no place for him to hide, Kiera," she said holding her back.

"None the less, I can't wait here, like a trapped hare."

"Then I'll help you."

"No Bella, I don't want you to get hurt, you're better off staying here."

"No, I couldn't live with myself if anything happened to you. I'm going and that is final."

Kiera saw the determination on her face. "All right, but you stay close to me and run when I tell you. Promise me.

"I promise." Isabella ran to the table reaching for her eating dagger and slipped it under her skirts. The two women left the Hall together.

The first place they searched were the kitchens and asked Olaf if he'd seen anyone unfamiliar.

"How could anyone tell with all the people at the here?" Olaf said exasperated.

"I'm sorry Olaf, please try and think."

Olaf stopped for a moment. "There was a man here a couple days ago asking about meal times and what your favorite foods were."

"Do you remember what he looked like?"

"He was nothing special, average height, brown eyes, stocky build.

Kiera froze, Olaf was describing Lacerta. She quickly ran out of the Kitchen. Isabella was right behind her.

They moved on to the falconer, then the smoke house. No sign of Lacerta or his men anywhere.

They walked into the stables and found Gerald mucking out the stalls. She saw the hatred in his eyes before he had time to mask it. Kiera resisted the urge to take a step back. The two women stepped forward. Her voice took on an air of authority.

"Gerald, have you seen any strangers at the Keep?"

"No, none, my lady," he said, leaning on his pitchfork. His face was almost smug.

Kiera eyed him suspiciously. "You haven't seen anyone?"

A wicked smile crossed his lips, sending a chill down her spine. She heard the creaking of the stable door behind her. With lightning speed she turned and drew her sword. A hooded man lowered the bar locking the door in place. Sensing danger her horse whinnied and stamped his hooves.

Kiera's blood turned to ice. She could barely take a breath as he pulled his hood away. She stared unbelieving in to his gray eyes. Standing before her was the man of her nightmares, the Dragon.

His smile was evil as he approached her. "How very convenient that you should come looking for us here."

"Draw your sword Murdock, for I intend to kill you," she said, positioning herself for battle.

"Tsk, tsk, that's all you have to say to your uncle after all these years?" He stepped closer.

"You're not my uncle. You're the devil himself and I plan to send you back to hell," she growled. She heard Isabella scream behind her, she turned to find Gerald holding a dagger to her throat.

"Drop your sword Kiera, or I'll slit her throat," Gerald said, pressing the knife to Isabella's neck.

She could see the fear in her eyes. She struggled against her capture. "No Kiera, don't!" She looked at her with resignation. The sword hit the ground. In seconds Murdock's captain was upon her and pinned her arms behind her back. Murdock came closer. She flinched as he reached up and rubbed his knuckles along her cheek.

"Poor child, look what you have been reduced to, a woman who thinks she's a warrior." His menacing face was only inches from hers. She could feel his foul breath with every word he spoke. "We'll get you back home where you belong."

She spit in his face. He stepped back and wiped his face, and with one swift motion he backhanded her across her cheek and cut it with his ring.

Isabella struggled against the vice like grip Gerald had on her but to no avail. "You son of a bitch, leave her alone!" she shouted.

Murdock turned sharply toward Isabella and Gerald, "Gag her we don't want her bringing any guards down upon us." Lacerta pulled out a rag tying it around Isabella's mouth.

Kiera struggled against Lacerta's punishing grip. Murdock turned back toward her. She glared at him with contempt. She turned the healing on to herself and the skin knitted together. She wouldn't be intimidated. He patted her now healed face. "Lacerta was right, your powers have grown stronger."

"Strong enough to destroy you," she said through gritted teeth.

"We shall see My Dear, we shall see." She followed Murdock's gaze to see Gerald raise his dagger to Isabella's throat. Kiera watched in terror.

"No! Please don't," Kiera cried.

Murdock smiled, he had found her weakness. "You'll cooperate with us or your friend will die." He handed leather strips to Murdock. She stood helpless never taking her eyes off Isabella as Lacerta tied her hands behind her back, then bound her feet as well. Gerald and Murdock loaded her onto a wagon. A rag was stuffed into her mouth. She watched as Isabella was tied and loaded into the wagon next to her. Picking up her sword Lacerta threw it into Snow's stall. He must have figured no one will find it in time to save them. He and Murdock climbed in the wagon next to them, one on each side. Gerald laid a blanket over the top of them then covered it with hay.

Kiera prayed, Erik and her brothers would soon realize she and Isabella were missing and come after her before it was too late. A tightening came in her throat, as long as Murdock held Isabella, she couldn't fight. He would use Isabella to manipulate her into doing what he wanted. The nightmare had begun.

She heard the doors to the stable being opened, and felt the wagon rock as Gerald climbed in. He clicked his tongue signaling the horse to go. They moved with a jerk, Lacerta's arm came around Kiera's waist. She tried moving away but he held her firmly in place.

They stopped at the palisades gate, Lacerta pulled her closer to him, "Make one move and I'll kill her," he whispered.

Kiera remained still, listening to Gerald speak to the guard.

"What have you got there Gerald, more muck from the stables? I swear we must have the cleanest stables in all of Briton."

"Well you know our lord, he demands the animals well taken care of."

"I suppose your right. Hurry up about it, Lord Erik has left strict orders, no one in or out."

"I won't take long." Gerald's voice was deceptively light.

She closed her eyes, there was nothing to stop them now. She felt as though she would suffocate under all that hay.

They rode for what seemed to be hours, the sun was high and it became sweltering underneath all that hay.

The wagon stopped suddenly. She could hear horses gathering around them. Lacerta pulled the blanket off them. The cool air revived her, and made her more alert for any chance of escape. Looking around, she saw twenty soldiers surround them. Kiera looked around her in despair at seeing such numbers.

Murdock reached for his horse and mounted and threw off his peasant cloak, to reveal his lordly attire with the familiar dragon displayed across his chest. Her childhood fears came flooding back. When she was placed on Lacerta's horse, he whispered in her ear, "Try to escape and I'll cut your friend in half."

Isabella was loaded onto a horse with one of Lacerta's soldiers.

Murdock led the way through the forest. They rode fast and hard until nightfall then moved to the main road. They traveled well into the night before stopping to make camp.

Tents were set up, camp fires started. In an hour's time it looked as though they were in a small village. Kiera was sat down next to a tree along with Isabella.

Kiera moved closer to her. "I'm so sorry I got you into this, Isabella," Kiera felt heavy with remorse.

"This isn't your fault, you mustn't blame yourself."

"But it's my fault. If I hadn't come to Alastair none of this would've happened."

"Kiera you are the best thing that has ever happened to Alastair, and my brother. You brought him back to life, you made him whole. I'm glad you came. Don't worry, we'll figure a way out of this, we're not completely helpless."

"I wish I had your optimism. I've seen Murdock's evil. It's beyond what you can imagine."

Kiera became silent as Lacerta approached with one of his guards. He pulled her off the ground and wrapped his arms around her waist and pulled her hard against his chest. To her disgust, with her hands and feet bound she fell into him. "How would you like sleeping in my tent tonight?" he sneered, "You might enjoy it," he mocked, running his hand over her breast. "I know I would."

She tried struggling away, "I would rather sleep in a bed filled with snakes."

He grabbed the back of her hair and forced her to look into his eyes. "Have it your way. I'd probably like that more. You'd be begging me to stop."

"Lacerta!" Murdock bellowed, "She is not yours to play with. She and Lady Isabella will be sleeping in my tent," he paused, "heavily guarded."

Her capturer growled, and shoved her to the ground. Lacerta walked back into his tent.

Another guard lifted Isabella off the ground. Kiera and Isabella made eye contact. She saw Isabella's struggling with something behind her. In a flash Isabella's hands were free and she elbowed the soldier in the stomach then threw him over her hip. In an instant she slammed her dagger into the man's chest. Kiera's eyes widened with surprise. Kiera saw Murdock going after her and threw herself in front of him, knocking him to the ground.

"Run Bella! Run!" she shouted.

Isabella didn't hesitate. She picked up her skirts and ran into the darkness of the forest.

Guards stood with their mouths gapping. "After her you idiots! Bring her back!" he shouted. Half the soldiers grabbed torches, running into the forest after her.

Kiera smiled with profound relief. They would never find a slip of a girl in the forest in the dead of night, especially one as clever as Isabella. She began to laugh. Murdock's eyes flared with anger.

"Why are you laugh?" he growled.

"You're a fool, Murdock. I can just see your men in the forest tripping over themselves trying to find her. It really is quite comical if you think about it," she said chuckling.

Murdock's temper was lost. His arm swung wide and slapped her hard across the face. She stopped laughing yet still maintained a smile. It clearly unnerved him. She wasn't the frightened child he knew. He pulled his whip from his side. Her smile faded. She held her breath as he slowly uncoiled it. He wrapped it around the back of her neck and pulled her close to him.

"You'll pay for what your friend has done. And when she's found I'll do the same to her," he snarled.

"I'll kill you first."

"Brave words my dear niece." He pulled sharply on the whip. She felt it burn around her neck. "Let's see how brave you are when I'm finished with you." He turned to the guard, "Tie her to that tree."

Kiera was sick with fear. Nausea started to rise as her hands were bound around a tree. Her legs no longer supported her. Her belt was removed, her tunic torn down her back and moved off her shoulders. She pressed her forehead against the bark of the tree and prepared for what was to come. She heard the snap on the ground beside her.

"Bring back fond memories, Kiera?" He snapped the whip again. "How brave do you feel now?" There was no answer. He ground his teeth snapping the whip on to her back. She made no sound, he struck her again. The whip cut through her skin like a fiery torch. She bit her lip to keep the scream from escaping her mouth. He stuck again, but she wouldn't scream. His anger flared, each stroke became harder. He struck again and again. Finally, he threw away the whip in frustration. His men dodged it as if it were a snake. Storming toward her, he grabbed her by the back of her hair and wrenched her head back.

She smiled, "Go to hell," she croaked, before blacking out.

CHAPTER XXXIV

All day long Erik and his father searched the camps of his men but to no avail. No one had seen anything or anyone unusual. They searched the forest beyond the meadows. Right to the borders of Alastair and found nothing.

Alexander rode next to him, "What do we do next?"

"We go back to Alastair and start again in the morning."

"What if you're wrong, and Murdock and his men aren't here?"

"Then we'll head out past our borders. Even to Dunsmore if we have to."

Alexander didn't say anything for a while as they rode back to the Keep. "Have you tried connecting with your animals to see if they had seen something out of the ordinary?"

Erik turned toward him in surprise, "Why would you suggest that? You're obviously are afraid of them."

"I'm not afraid anymore. You're my son. I'm sorry my religious fanaticism separated us. I was unable to deal with your gift at the time. I see clearer now, I was wrong."

"My gift," Erik smirked, "I was a pariah to you then and now you are calling it a gift.

"I can't change what I've done in the past,
I only ask to be given a chance to make up for
the wrong I've done in the past."

"I'm not sure that's possible," Erik said
quietly.

"I understand." Alexander paused. "I have
decided to stay at Alastair for a while." Erik
remained silent. "I have missed so much of
Isabella and your lives. I wish to make up for
that grave mistake. I want to see you and
Isabella happy. See my grandchildren, watch
them grow."

"We'll see," he said simply. He wasn't sure
he wanted his father that close. There were too
many bad memories and he wasn't sure he could
work through them.

The sun was setting when they reached the
meadow before the Keep. Erik saw Ian riding
hard and fast with three guards at his side.
Dread twisted his gut. Something was very
wrong.

"Erik! Thank God you've returned. I was
coming after you."

"What happened?"

"It's Isabella and Kiera, no one has seen
them since this morning. I've had the Keep
thoroughly searched but they're not to be
found."

Panic filled his mind. He rode past and set
his horse into a dead run to the palisades
gate. The guard eyed him warily. "Has anyone
been in or out of the Keep since I left this
morning?"

The guard shook his head violently, "No, My Lord, no one went in or out, just as you ordered."

"Are you sure." Erik glared at the man.

"Yes, My Lord, the only one who left today was Gerald. He had a load from the stables.

The tightening in Erik's stomach grew worse. "Is Gerald back now?"

"Yes, My Lord, he came back just a few hours ago."

Erik and the others rode into the bailey going directly to the stables. Gerald was cleaning out a stall when he heard the men enter. "Good day My Lord," Gerald said calmly.

Erik removed his gauntlets "Have you seen Lady Kiera and Lady Isabella today?"

"No My Lord, I have been here all day and I haven't seen them."

"You've been here all day? The guard at the gate said you left earlier today."

Erik's struggled to keep his voice calm. Gerald became wary. "Well, yes My Lord, I did take a load of hay out of the Keep."

"Really, and how long did that take you?"

"Not long."

Erik's attention was drawn away when Snow whinnied, and stamped his hoof on the ground. "Hello, my pretty," he said, and stroked Snow's great neck. Closing his eyes he made contact with the animal. He pulled away from his anger and fear so as not to frighten the animal. He saw clearly what had transpired in the stable that morning. As he broke from their connection panic ripped through him. He took deep breaths to calm himself not allowing the others see his fear. Out of the corner of his eye he spotted Kiera's sword. He picked it up and stared at the blade. Anger burned in his gut but forced to push it away just like he did in battle.

Turning to Gerald, he felt the cold blood of murder. Gerald started to back away. "Please, my lord forgi--in one swift thrust Erik sent the sword through the man to its hilt. "In Kiera's name I send you to hell." He withdrew the sword, and Gerald fell dead on the ground.

He turned toward Ian, his face hard as stone, "Murdock has them both." Walking out of the stables, Erik mounted his horse in a single leap, Ian right behind him along with Alexander and Marcus.

The others had returned and he met them in the bailey. "Murdock has Kiera and Isabella, I'm going after them, gather your men and mine. I'll see you at Dunsmore. Marcus, Ian, Jordan, you come with me."

"I'm coming with you," Alexander said.

Erik and his father held each other's gaze. Erik nodded.

Albert ran into the bailey, "Albert, find the two men I sent to Dunsmore, tell them I need them now."

Aurelia and Eleanor came out with sacks of provisions. Eleanor went to her husband's side. He reached down lifting her off the ground pulling her up against him. I know you'll bring her back safely," she said.

He kissed her passionately, "I love you," he said, touching her face.

"You pick the oddest times to become romantic," she chuckled softly.

"Say it woman before I leave," he demanded.

"You know I love you with all my heart and soul," kissing him again. "Be careful, I'm counting on your return."

Olaf came out of the kitchen. "My Lord, please let me come with you."

Erik could use Olaf's strong arm. "Bring your sword." Olaf ran inside to get his sword. A few minutes later they were all ready to leave.

He called upon the wolves to guide them through the night. There pace never slowed down. Ian at his side, both men terrified at what may happen to their wives.

Alexander watched his son. The cold clarity of his purpose was written plainly on his face. He showed no sign of emotion, yet he could feel the turmoil within him. Alexander sighed, this is how his son had lived for the past twelve years. He hid from his emotions and pushed them deep inside. But Alexander knew better. Those feelings were on the surface ready to explode. He pitied him, for when they finally erupted there will be no stopping them.

Hours later the sky paled with the morning light. The clouds were heavy with impending rain. Celeste let out a loud cry. Someone was coming out of the forest some distance away. He moved in closer. In an instant they recognized Isabella. Both men bounded toward her. She ran toward them shouting Ian's name. Before he reached her he was out of his saddle and ran to her picking her up in his arms. They both cried as they held each other tightly.

Marcus and Jordan pulled up beside Erik. He had Celeste search the forest. She wasn't there. Closing his eyes he reached out to her with his mind. If she were dead he would know it. He felt some comfort that she was still alive.

"Kiera?" Marcus asked nearly choking on his question.

Isabella broke loose from Ian's hold. "Murdock still has her."

Erik took in his sister's appearance. Her face had small cuts from the thorns and bushes in the woods, otherwise she wasn't harmed. "I'm thankful you're safe," he said reaching down to touch her face.

"How did you manage to escape?" Ian asked

"The magic trick, Erik taught me when we were children."

"I don't follow you," Ian said puzzled.

"Erik taught me how to escape from ropes when I was eight. I used it last night along with what Kiera taught me about hand-to-hand combat. I told you it would be useful," she said and hugged Ian tight. "I was able to take my captor by surprise and escape into the woods. They couldn't find me in the darkness. The stupid men looked for me all night and I was no more than twenty feet away from their camp." Isabella looked down at her hands and her eyes pooled with tears.

Erik watched her, his belly felt as though it were filled with lead. "There's more, isn't there?" he said flatly.

Tears ran down her cheeks, her amber eyes were shinning back at his, "He beat her, Erik." Isabella covered her face with her hands sobbing for her friend. Ian wrapped his arms around her trying to comfort her.

The bile rose in his throat along with his pent up rage. Storm stamped his hooves on the ground bobbing his head up and down, sensing his master's turmoil.

Erik tried with all his human strength to put out the fires but the black rage consumed him. "Kieraaaaaa!" His horse reared as Erik screamed out her name toward the bleak morning sky.

The volcano of emotion had erupted in him. He bolted for the forest, but Jordan caught up with him and knocked him to the ground.

Erik was like a mad man, it took all of Jordan's strength to keep him on the ground. The others quickly jumped down from their horses to aid him in restraining Erik. Yet he still managed to get to his feet.

Ian kept shouting his name desperately trying to reach through his tortured mind, but to no avail. Isabella stood with her hands on her lips watching her brother in horror.

His father came up behind him wrapping his arms around him like two steel bands. Erik struggled against him but couldn't throw him off. "That's it son, spend your rage, let it go," he said.

"I'm not your son, and you're not my father," Erik said through gritted teeth, struggling to break free.

"I'm your father," Alexander said, jerking his arms tighter around him, "and you'll always be my son. I made a mistake twelve years ago, a mistake I'll regret for the rest of my life. I tortured myself over and over again for leaving you, but I didn't know how to come back, not until that miraculous day you sent your message." Erik struggled harder. "I was wrong for leaving you Erik. I lived in hell without you and your sister. Know this son, I loved you every day of those twelve years. I never lost sight of that." Erik stopped struggling. Alexander continued, "Spend your rage now, then clear your mind, for you'll do her more harm running into Dunsmore like a crazed bull. What do you think Murdock will do to her if you're captured? You are her Achilles heel. She'll be completely at his mercy. Think, boy, think!"

Erik heard his father through his rage. Reason began to spread through his mind and felt the fire of rage turned to coals. He relaxed and his father let go. Erik's head slumped forward. Isabella ran to him and wrapped her arms around his waist holding him tightly. His mind became clearer. His arms came around his sister. He held her tight. She was a balm to his fear. He could hold it back. He looked up to find his father watching him intently.

"We can't make up for the past, but we will work for the future," Erik said, holding his hand out to his father.

Alexander took his son's hand and grasped it firmly. "To our future," he said.

Erik looked toward Ian still holding his sister in one arm. "We'll wait here for Dominick and his men, then we'll formulate a plan to get Kiera back and bring Murdock down." He looked down at his sister, "I'll have some of my men escort you back to the Keep."

Isabella stood away from him. "I'm going with you."

"The hell you are," Ian said.

"Bella it's not safe for you," Erik said.

"I don't care. Everyone I love will be at Dunsmore. I'll not wait to hear word if someone I care about has been killed or wounded. I'm going with you and that's final."

The men looked at each other. Ian and Erik knew too well Isabella was determined. He knew she would follow them alone and put herself in more danger.

Erik nodded his agreement. Ian grasped Isabella's shoulders firmly. "If you go, you'll do as I tell you without question or hesitation, is that understood?"

"I promise," she said sincerely. "Thank you," she hugged him gratefully.

Erik moved to his father, "Let's set up camp, Dominick should be here by nightfall." He turned toward Jordan, putting his hand on his shoulder. "Thank you, my friend."

Jordan smiled back at him then left to help the others set up camp.

Erik turned back toward the trees looking deep into the forest. He felt a hand on his shoulder, he turned to find Marcus standing there. "Kiera is a warrior my son, she will survive until we reach her."

"I know she will but to think she's in the hands of that monster is nearly unbearable," he said looking toward the ground.

"We'll be there soon enough and we'll avenger her suffering."

Marcus went back toward the others. Erik looked back into the forest, "Hold on Kiera, I'm coming."

Kiera willed herself to surface from the pool of her unconsciousness. Her limbs felt heavy. Her back felt as though it were on fire. She opened her eyes to find herself in the Great Hall of Dunsmore Castle. She was lying on a small palette in a corner. When she sat up quickly two guards stood on either side with their swords drawn. One was pointed at her throat.

There was a collar around her neck attached to a chain that Murdock held.

"Ah, you're awake," he said as if he were talking to an honored guest. "Come, join me. I'm sure you must be hungry," he said all too pleasantly. "I do recommend you move slowly though, my guards are a bit jumpy and I don't believe you can heal decapitation.

Slowly she rose to her feet never taking her eyes off the guard pointing his sword. Sometime during the night her tunic was changed. She moved her hand to her chest. Her mother's medallion was still there.

As though reading her mind, "Yes Kiera, you still wear that whore's medallion. You'll still be wearing it when you die." His voice sent tentacles of ice through her veins, yet she refused to show any sign of fear.

"It's not I who shall die Murdock, it will be you along with your twisted love for other peoples suffering," she said with venom.

"You're wrong," he said popping a grape in his mouth. "Do you think I fear your bastard brothers? They're no match for my men, or this castle."

"My brothers are not bastards, and well you know it. They have the documents to prove it. You have committed a crime My Lord Murdock. How do you think the King will feel when he finds out that his most loyal vassal and trusted friend was cheated out of his birthright and his parents murdered? Not only will you have the wrath of my brothers, but that of the King, as well."

Murdock was visibly unnerved. Watching her uncle's discomfort Kiera felt a great sense of satisfaction. She walked to the table without fear, took a cup of wine and drank it down in one gulp and slammed it down on the table. She sat in a chair opposite him and pick up a piece of bread and tore it, then she confidently popped it into her mouth.

"You forget one thing, my arrogant little niece. I have you, and as long as I have you they won't do anything."

"You're wrong Murdock, they're coming and there is nothing you can do to stop them." She leaned in closer. "Your time is up Murdock and your tyranny is over."

His eyes smoldered with anger, he pulled hard on her chain to where his face just inches away. "You won't be so smug when I'm finished with you.

Kiera's mind flashed with hatred. "Your cowardice upon women and children no longer frighten me. If it were just you and me, you would be dead with one stroke of my sword. You pathetic old man."

Murdock's face turned purple with rage, he shoved Kiera hard nearly knocking her backward over her chair, but her speed and balance helped her to keep from falling.

He pointed to his guard, "Clasp her in irons!" he shouted. Two guards moved toward her. In a blink of an eye she kicked back her chair and grabbed an eating dagger from the table, and tossed it toward the guard to her left. He screamed in agony as it penetrated his shoulder. She quickly turned and grabbed the guard on her right by his tunic and pulled him toward her bringing her knee into his groin and at the same time grabbed his sword as he went down. Another guard approach. She took her stance ready to fight him.

She aggressively moved toward the guard. Their swords rang loudly within the stone

walls. She swung with precision and speed. Two
more guards came running into the hall, swords
drawn. She fought all three. The swords
clashing was deafening. Kiera managed to keep
the three men at bay. She struck one in the arm
forcing him to drop his sword. The other two
moved in. She made a long sweeping motion
across their midriff forcing them to jump out
of harm's way. Kiera felt confident she was
winning the battle until she felt the jerk of
her chain and was knocked down to the hard
floor Murdock had a dagger at her throat. She
felt the blood trickle down her neck she became
motionless.

"Drop the sword," Murdock growled. He
pressed the dagger harder against her throat.
She had no choice. The sword fell with a clang
on the stone floor.

"That was most entertaining. You're skill is
quite amazing. He looked toward his guards.
"Now, cast the bitch in irons!" he shouted. The
guards scrambled to get her in the shackles. He
yanked it hard on her collar and jerked her
forward. "Now let's see how proud you are." He
pulled the chain forcing her to her knees. She
struggled against it. "Here you'll eat, and
here you'll sleep. Maybe after a few nights
sleeping on a cold stone floor you'll learn to
keep a civil tongue in your mouth."

"You forget Murdock, I'm no pampered maid
there is nothing you could do to me that would
make me civil to you. Not even your whip could
make me cower in your presence."

Murdock yanked harder on the chain his dagger raised in the other, "Shut up wench, or I'll cut your tongue out!"

Lacerta stopped him. "You forget, My Lord, she is all that stands between her brothers and us. She must be kept unharmed."

In a fit of temper he threw his dagger across the room. "Chain her to the floor, she will be given nothing to eat, only water. Maybe hunger will improve her disposition," he growled as he left the room. The guards chained her to a metal ring in the floor used for the dogs.

She pulled at them in desperation. Lacerta crouched down on his haunches, pulling her jaw to face him. "Not so high and mighty now, are you?"

"I could be on my belly in a pile of muck and not be as low as you are, scum," she said, jerking her head away.

He pulled hard on the collar around her neck, nearly choking her. "You and I will have our day and when I'm through you'll be begging me for my favor."

"I'll be begging for death before I ever let you touch me," she said, meaning every word.

He gave her a wicked smile, "I hope your husband comes to rescue you soon." He stood towering over her, "I'll enjoy killing him before your very eyes."

"A peasant like you could never defeat my husband," she said sweetly.

He pushed her to the floor. Clearly he wanted to strike her, but knew it wouldn't scare her. He turned to the guards, "Watch her!" he commanded before stalking off.

CHAPTER XXXV

After what seemed like hours, Murdock entered the Hall. He gave her a hateful glare as he sat down at the table closest to her. "Say something nice to me," he said far too sweetly.

"Rot in hell!" she spat with venom.

He was calm. Too calm. It made her wary. She leaned away from him. He grabbed the chain of her collar and pulled her closer. He reached for his eating dagger, and cut across her upper arm.

It burned like fire. Her hand went over it to stop the bleeding.

Murdock smiled, "Just a little sting. A sample of what is to come if you don't cooperate with me."

"I'm not here for your entertainment Murdock."

"Oh, but you are my dear. I can do anything I want with you."

Her eyes became deadly, "I look forward to seeing you under my husband's boot heels," she said through clenched teeth.

"But that won't happen, will it?" He crooked his finger under her chin. "Not as long as I have you under *my* boot heels."

She jerked her head away, "Your arrogance will be your undoing, Murdock."

He reached for a loaf of bread, speaking as though he hadn't heard her. "I'm in quite a generous mood today," he said as he broke off a piece of bread and handed it to her.

She pushed his hand away. "My brothers are coming for me."

He looked into her eyes intently. "I'm counting on it."

"You can't defeat them."

"Oh but I can my dear. I have built one of the finest armies in all of England and I have the best captain, with the fiercest reputation."

"Lacerta is nothing but a butcher."

"Yes, but a cunning butcher."

"Don't put all your faith in him. He's not all that he appears. He's as much of a coward as you are."

Murdock jumped out of his chair, "Still your lying tongue, or I shall have it ripped out of your mouth.

His anger fueled hers. "You can't change what is a fact. My brothers will avenge our parents' murder and the steeling of their birthright. You have already lost Murdock. The Dragon will be slain!"

In a fit of rage, Murdock over turned the table. "Enough!" he shouted, grabbing her by the collar. "I have had enough of your insolent mouth. When I'm through with you, there will be little left to save." He pointed to a wooden

beam in the middle of the hall, shoving her
toward two guards. "Tie her to that beam."

Kiera tried hard not to be afraid. In her
mind she pleaded for Erik to come. As she was
tied to the wooden support, she told herself,
"One more time, just one more time. Soon the
Dragon will be dead."

A guard went to tear away her tunic, but
Murdock stopped him. "No! I'll flay the fabric
off her back, as I will her hide."

Kiera resigned herself to the beating. She
only hoped Erik would get to her in time. The
room went deathly quiet as they heard the
howling of wolves outside the castle walls. It
was an unearthly sound. The two guards were
clearly unnerved and drew their swords.
Murdock's hand stilled. The howling continued.
Murdock looked around him, "What unholy sound
is that?"

Kiera laughed with relief, "That is the
sound of your doom, my dear uncle."

A soldier ran into the hall. "My Lord, we
are under attack, come quickly."

Murdock went to Kiera pulling her chin to
face him. "Don't think I'll forget your
punishment. I'll be back to show you who is
master of Dunsmore Castle." he said, jerking
her head away before he left the hall.

He walked to the tower wall and leaned
against the parapet. Staring out into the
night, his blood turned cold. Surrounding the
castle was a thousand men outside the castle
walls. Each heavily armed carrying torches

shadowing them like ghostly figures in the night. He was prepared for battle against an army, but not like this one. Not this many men. His forces couldn't withstand such an assault.

"Damn their eyes." He growled to himself. "How could they have built such an army in such a short amount of time?" His fist hit the stone wall. "She did this," he ground through his teeth. "She is responsible for bringing those bastards to my castle. She will pay." He turned shouting Lacerta's name. His captain appeared in an instant. Murdock grabbed him by the front of his tunic. "If one man gets through I'll see you hanged. Is that clear?"

Lacerta's face turned to stone, "Perfectly, My Lord," he said coldly.

"Good," Murdock said, shoving him back. "I have some unfinished business to attend to."

Kiera's head pounded from her hunger. The crust of bread did little to ease it. But she felt hope. Soon her suffering would end. Her brothers were here. They came to claim their birthright and to kill the Dragon that had killed their parents, and took their land.

She heard the wolves howl again. Erik was close, she could feel him near her. She almost laughed hearing the wolves cry. It would make them wary and uncertain about the battle ahead. Some may even desert, giving Dominick and Randolf a better chance.

She heard a movement behind her. Thinking it was Murdock. She held her breath. She turned her body as much as she could and saw two hooded servants cleaning up the mess that Murdock made. She breathed a sigh of relief. But it was short lived, Murdock walked in within a few seconds.

"Now, my dear, we will continue with your lessons."

The door to the castle was opened by Erik's men. And his armies streamed in forcing Murdock's men to fight for their lives. Erik fought his way to the Great Hall. When he saw Kiera tied to a beam and he fought with more vigor. His only thought was to get to her. When he killed the last man standing in the hall he saw Murdock run to Kiera and placed a sword on her neck.

"Make one move and I'll sever her head from her body."

Erik became very still. He gazed into Kiera's eyes. She showed no fear, and he swallowed his own. A man stood next to Murdock. Cut her down, Lacerta. The man cut the rope from the beam while Murdock continued to hold the sword at her neck

With the speed of a serpent Murdock dropped the sword and grabbed an eating dagger from the table and pressed it to her throat. He pulled her back against him, and held her firmly, not giving her room to move. Marcus came in behind him. Erik never took his eyes off of hers, in hopes of letting her know he wouldn't let any harm come to her.

Murdock pulled her out of the hall and up the stairs to the high walls of Dunsmore. Erik matched them step for step. He moved with purpose. Marcus fought Lacerta behind him, covering Erik's back.

Murdock looked toward Marcus. "Ah Marcus is here. How appropriate. You will die together by daylight.

"You'll be the only one dead, Murdock," Erik growled.

"I think not," he said as he pressed the knife closer into Kiera's throat. Drop your weapons or she will die."

Erik he knew if he tried to fight, he would endanger Kiera's life. There was nothing he could do but lay down his sword. Marcus did the same.

"No Erik!" She struggled against Murdock but with the collar she couldn't break his hold.

Lacerta nodded to his guards. Four soldiers set upon them. Their hands were bound behind them. Lacerta and Erik exchanged glances. Lacerta's expression was smug. Erik swore he would erase that smile permanently. His eyes quickly went to Kiera. Murdock was still holding the dagger to her throat, "Take them to the dungeon, I'll deal with them later." Lacerta shoved Erik hard toward the tower stairs. He saw her eyes pool with tears.

Murdock pulled her to the edge of the parapet wall. He looked down at the ensuing battle. He easily picked Dominick out of the. He smiled to himself. So much like his father in height and brawn. It was like watching his brother's ghost. He watched Dominick and his brother make short work of the men they were fighting and plowed their way toward the gatehouse.

Murdock shouted from the tower wall, his voice carrying through the night and over the shouts and screams of battle. All activity stopped. Eyes were cast upward to see Murdock forcing Kiera to the wall's edge. She struggled against him but her movement was limited with the dagger at her throat. He felt a trickle of warm blood drip down his hand.

Murdock's voice carried down to Dominick. "Lay down your sword or your sister will die." Stressing his point he grabbed the back of Kiera's hair and forced her head back to display the dagger at her throat.

Dominick shouted out, "Know this Murdock the murder of our parents will be avenged. If you should harm our sister, there is not a stone in this castle that won't be torn down to get to you." He held up his sword. "I swear it on my father's sword. Dunsmore land will be returned to me. And your crimes against my family, won't go unpunished."

Murdock smiled, "No bastard son shall take these lands from me!" Jerking Kiera toward him. "But I have Kiera, I have her powers therefore, *I'm* immortal. I'm a man you cannot kill. "

"You'll be dead before the next moonrise," Dominick said with a chilling growl. "She won't save you."

"She will. For I have what she holds dear. She will do exactly as I say. Now tell your men to drop their swords and surrender, or I shall kill her."

"Don't take me for a fool Murdock. I would never allow myself to become your prisoner. Nor am I fool enough to believe that you would kill her. You need her to survive." Dominick shifted in his saddle, lowering his sword at his side.

I'll make a bargain with you. Surrender Dunsmore, and my sister. And I may have mercy. If not.....God help you, for I will tear you apart.

Lacerta shoved Erik down the tower steps. He fell the last few steps to the floor. He glared up at Lacerta. The man just smiled down at him. "Don't worry about Kiera, I'll take good care of her. When I'm through with her, you'll be nothing but a memory."

"You'll never have the opportunity," Erik said between his teeth. "I'll kill you this very night."

"Brave words for a man about to be executed," he said picking Erik off the stone floor. As soon as he was on his feet, Erik jerked away from him. Two guards stepped forward. One holding each arm. They guided him toward the steps leading down to the dungeon.

Suddenly Erik was pulled out of one guard's grasp one direction. He quickly looked up to find Jordan dressed as one of Lacerta's men. Without hesitation Erik swung his shoulder and shoved the other guard toward Jordan impaling him on Jordan's sword. Erik looked back at him. Jordan gave him a sly wink then quickly turned

Erik around and slid his sword between his hands and cut his bonds and handing him the sword. Erik's heart pumped with adrenalin. He moved on instinct, and disposed Lacerta's men as they rushed down the stairs.

Surprised, Lacerta was slow to react. Finally, he drew his sword. More men came running up from behind Lacerta. Erik saw his father come out of the shadows and fight the two men at once.

Erik ducked just as Lacerta was about to sever his head from his shoulders. He swiftly swung his sword up to stop Lacerta's next blow.

Jordan had quickly cut Marcus out of his bonds and Marcus grabbed one of the dead soldiers swords and ran to help Alexander dispose of the two guards he was fighting. Hearing the commotion, more guards came running down the dungeon stairs. Jordan moved forward, with one thrust after another, forced the men back into a corner.

Erik and Lacerta were in mortal combat. Lacerta was fighting for his life. Erik had little opportunity to move in. Lacerta fought aggressively and swung his sword with all his might. Yet Erik was unfazed. He wasted no movement. He was precise. He left no opening for Lacerta to strike.

Erik bided his time. Lacerta began to make mistakes. He swung wide, Erik jumped out of the way. He came at him with a downward stroke and Erik dodged it. Erik swung and Lacerta took a step back. He was on the defensive. Again Lacerta raised his sword and in a flash, Erik's foot came up and slammed into his chest. Lacerta lost his balance. His arms flayed in the air because there was nothing to hold on to. He fell off the edge of the stairs that led down to the dungeon.

He heard the Lacerta's neck snap when he hit head on the stairs before his body fell to the dungeon floor. His blank dead eyes stared back at him. Erik looked down at the body with satisfaction that the man could never hurt his wife again.

Jordan came up behind him. "That was Kiera's move."

Erik smiled back at him, "I know."

Erik turned to his father and Marcus. "I'm going after her. Help Dominick and his men take over the castle. "

Marcus and Jordan ran off. Alexander stayed behind. He clasped his son's shoulders. "Be careful. This man is evil, don't underestimate him."

"Don't worry, I'll take care."

To his surprise, his father wrapped him in his arms, in a great hug, then went off to secure the castle. His thoughts turned to Kiera, and he quickly ran up to the Great Hall.

When he reached the top of the stairs, he heard the cry of battle just inside the bailey walls. His was filled with satisfaction. They had successfully taken over the castle.

He ran into the Great Hall to find it empty. It wasn't until he heard Kiera scream that he realize it was too late.

Murdock saw Erik run into the Great Hall. He pulled on Kiera's collar and held his hand over mouth before she could shout out a warning. With her in tow, he followed Erik into the Great Hall. His large hand nearly suffocated her as she struggled to get free. With one hand, he quietly lowered the bolt to the Hall door. He found a crossbow on a nearby table. Kiera saw his intention, and fought with desperation. She stomped down on Murdock's foot and he was forced to let her go. It didn't matter anymore. Erik was going to die.

"Noooo!" Kiera screamed and ran toward Erik. He turned, but it was too late.

Murdock lowered his crossbow, and with a dead calm fired it at him. The arrow pierced through his chest and he crumbled to the ground.

Kiera ran to his side. The wound was mortal. She looked into his golden eyes. They stared back at her with longing and regret. "Kiera, please," he croaked, "Please don't touch me. For your safety, swear to me you won't try to heal me."

She was overwhelmed with desperation. "Erik, I can't let you go."

"Swear to me!" He went into a fit of coughing.

Her broken heart constricted in her chest. She nodded unable to answer.

His eyes faded into unconsciousness. "Erik! Erik no!" she pleaded.

She heard a sinister laugh behind her. Her blood ran cold, her spine stiffened. "You're mine now." Murdock laughed." There is no one left to interfere. Let your brothers come. As long as I have you no one will dare to attack me. And above all else I'll have your power and I'll become immortal."

Kiera stood slowly, her fear turning into anger and then to fierce rage. A smoldering fire hate was ready to burst into flames. She slowly turned to face the Dragon. The monster that murdered her parents, that tortured her as a child, hunted her like and animal, and haunted her dreams. Now he murdered her husband.

Murdock looked into her smoldering eyes. He took a step back. She saw his fear. A wicked smile spread across her face. The energy ran through her veins and the air began to charge around her. The wind swarmed around the room. She slowly walked toward him. Cups and plates rattled on the tables as she walked by.

"Mother of God." he said breathlessly, "What's happening?"

She smiled at his fear. "My power, uncle. You said you wanted it, so here you have it." Never taking her eyes off him, she flicked her wrist. A cup went flying toward him and struck his shoulder. Kiera kept walking toward him. Plates and cups kept flying toward him. He ducked and dodged them, flinging his arms, trying to swat them away. Soon the air around them was filled with debris.

As she moved closer the energy charge around him. His robes swirled about. Kiera was no longer smiling. With a jerk, she extended her arm. His body flew through the air, hitting a wall behind him, knocking the wind out of him. He fell to the floor in a heap.

Kiera kept walking toward him. Her body hummed with power. He raised his hands to ward her off. "What's the matter, Uncle, you said you wanted my powers," she said sweetly. She cocked her head to one side. "Maybe I haven't entertained you enough."

"No, Kiera please!"

She raised both her arms again and the energy picked him up She moved her arms toward another wall and Murdock's body slammed into it. Her rage made her stronger. She tossed him through the air and he hit another wall, and then another. She didn't stop until she heard the snapping of bones and his head cracked against stone. He was dead before he hit the ground. She stared down at his broken body. It was over.

Her anger was spent and the debris hit the ground with a clatter.

She turned toward Erik. Stumbling weakly she ran to him and kneeled beside him. Uncontrollable tears ran down her face. She touched his forehead, his body was still warm. She closed her eyes. He was spiraling toward the blackness. She knew what she had to do. There was no fear in her. "Forgive me Erik, but I can't live without you. I can't keep my word." She could hear the battle beyond the doors of the Great Hall. Her brothers had won. Dunsmore Castle was now theirs. She was happy for them. A wrong was now righted.

She looked down into Erik's chalky complexion. She pulled the arrow out of Erik's chest. She watched the blood pour from his wound. She gently placed her hand on the wound. She jolted from the impact of the pain, throwing her head back, screaming out her agony.

Erik found himself standing in the darkness. A blue mist moved around him like a fog. He turned but there was no direction to follow. He stopped for a moment. He felt her presence even before he saw her. He watched her break through the mist and wrapped her in his arms. "I thought I lost you," he said pulling her away to look into her face. She smiled sadly. He wanted to ask why, but was afraid. He looked around them. "What is this place?"

"It's the blackness," she answered.

"It's very quiet here," he said, looking around. She touched his hair. "Where are we?"

"We're in a place where souls meet before they separate."

He held her hand. "Then we're dying." he said. He felt no fear.

She held her hand to his face. "No Erik, you are not dying." She held hands. "Already you feel the pull of life. A force that's strong and you can't pull away."

Something was pulling at him, and it was growing stronger. A growing panic filled his chest. He held her hands tightly. "Come with me."

"I can't, Erik, it's too late for me. I can't save us both. You have go on without me."

He tried desperately to hold on to her, but like the mist around him she kept slipping through his fingers. "I forbid you to stay behind." She drifted further away. "Kiera no! Kiera come back to me!" he shouted.

"I don't know how. I love you Erik. I always did." Her voice echoed in his mind. Tears streamed down her face, she blew him a kiss goodbye, and drifted further into the mist, until he no longer saw her.

"Kieraaaaaa!" he shouted. He heard pounding in the distance and growing louder.

He opened his eyes to see a stone ceiling above him. The pounding continued. He turned his head in the direction it was coming from. The door shuttered with every beat. He quickly turned to find Kiera's lifeless body lying beside him. He sat up and pulled her into his arms. His heart was filled with fear. He looked down at her pale face. Tears ran down his cheeks as he gently ran his fingers over her lips. He couldn't stop the flow of emotion that crashed through his walls. "Kiera!" he shouted in agony as he held her tight, sobbing into her hair. "You promised you would never leave me."

He heard the crash as the door to the Great Hall gave way. But he paid no notice. His heart had been shattered. The men came crashing through the door.

Dominick slowly walked over to Kiera's lifeless body. He knelt on one knee and reached out to her to feel for a pulse. The look in his eyes told him there was none. Tears pooled in Dominick's eyes, as he looked to the others. They knew from his expression, she was gone.

He turned back to Erik. Erik shook his head violently "No, she's not gone. She promised she would never leave me."

"I'm sorry Erik," he placed his hand on Erik's shoulder. Erik knocked his hand away. He laid her back down on the floor. "Kiera! Hear me now! Come back to me." There was no response. He shook her hard. Randolf went to step in, but Dominick held his hand up to stop him. "He can do her no harm," he said sadly. Tears ran down their cheeks as they helplessly watched Erik. Isabella stood beside her father sobbing at his side.

"Kiera I know you can hear me. Follow my voice," he shouted. "Kiera hear me, he sobbed. He held desperately to her tunic, shaking her wildly, with no response. He felt the medallion under her tunic. He pulled it out. Taking her hand he wrapped her cold fingers around it. "You swore on this, on our wedding day that you would never leave me. You swore! I hold you to that now." He bent over her body, his face only inches from hers. "Do you hear me, Kiera? If I have to follow you in death, you will not leave me!" There was no response. His tears fell upon her lips. He scooped her up and rocked her in his arms.

As the tears flowed he gently kissed her cheek. "I love you, Kiera. You are the very beat of my heart. I'm sorry, I never told you before. Forgive me. Please don't leave me. I don't want to live this life without you." He held her tightly. The room was silent except for Isabella's sobbing. All hope for his happiness was gone. The men bowed their heads in mourning.

Erik wouldn't let go of his precious Kiera. For a brief moment he thought he felt her warm breath upon his neck, but he had to be wrong. Then he felt it again. His heart slammed against his ribs. He felt the temperature in her body start to rise. He looked down into her face. Her lips were no longer blue. Her color was coming back into her face. He began to laugh with joy. The others looked at him as though he had lost his mind, until they saw her face. They all looked at her with wonder.

"That's it Kiera, follow the sound of my voice. Come back to me." He said firmly. Her eyes began to flutter. "Come to me Kiera."

The others shouted her name, picking up on what Erik was trying to do. They were encouraging her to wake up. Her eyes finally fluttered open. They all shouted with joy. Kiera's bright blue eyes looked into his. Joy filled him to capacity.

She raised her hand and wiped his tears away. He grabbed it and brought it to his lips, kissing her fingers reverently.

"I dreamed you said you loved me."

He smiled brightly, tears glistening in his eyes. "I did say I love you. And I'll say it again. I love you, Kiera. I'll say it for the rest of our lives. You'll never doubt it again."

She saw the love in his eyes. She wanted to look into them for the rest of her life. She turned to see Murdock's dead body lying on the floor. She was free. She was truly free. She looked at the people standing around her. They were her family. The wounds from the past were healed. She looked back into her loving husbands eyes. She touched his cheek and ran her hand over his lips. "Thank you for bringing me back. I love you."

He kissed her fingertips, "I love you too, with all my heart."

She smiled, "I want to go home now."

He held her tightly, "As my lady wishes." He lifted her off the ground and carried her outside, into the bright sunlight. His squire quickly hurried to bring their horses. "The lady will ride with me," he said to Albert. He turned back to Dominick and reluctantly he handed her to him while he mounted his horse.

Dominick held her for a moment before releasing her back into Erik's arms. He kissed her on the forehead. "I'll see you in a few days. As soon as I have everything settled here." He gave her a squeeze before handing her back up to her husband.

She looked over at Randolf, blowing him a kiss. He returned it. She waved to every one as they headed back to Alastair Keep. She nestled against Erik's shoulder. She was finally going home.

EPILOG

It was springtime. The sun was shining brightly. Kiera held her head up to the sun letting it warm her face. She sat in the garden, her favorite place to be. The fragrant flowers always lifted her spirits. She brought one to her face, and gently rubbed velvety petals over her cheeks and chin. She was at peace.

After Dunsmore Castle was returned to her brothers, Dominick gave it and its land to Randolf. Randolf took it reluctantly. He never wanted to be tied down to any land or castle. But Dominick insisted it was his duty. He had Godwin, which was enough for one lord to handle. He didn't want to manage Dunsmore as well. Dominick felt it was only right that Randolf have their birthright and gave him no choice. Kiera was thrilled. Her brother was only three days ride from her. He visited often.

Randolf was grateful for what Jordan had done for his sister all the years he spent protecting her, he gave him a substantial piece of land that he could build his own Keep on.

Marcus was made Captain of the Guards at Alastair. He and Aurelia lived very happily in their Keep. Marcus trained Erik's men with vigor and had the finest trained army in all of England.

Isabella and Ian were expecting their first child that was due in the fall. She received that wonderful news the day before. Ian's chest was puffed up with pride, like a stuffed turkey.

Kiera thoughts turned to Erik. It made her smile. He rarely left her side. When he was close, he never failed to touch her in some way. Often she would find him staring at her as though she would vanish before his very eyes. She would kiss him, to reassure him she was still there. He was learning to share his feelings with her. They spent hours talking about their politics, crops to plant, and the villagers. As well as husband and wife they were great friends.

Erik had learned to trust his father. He visited often. Reassuring Erik he hadn't left for good. Every time Alexander returned, they would greet each other in a great hug. He too had come for the Spring Festival. Alastair was filling up. But it wasn't complete.

She heard the commotion of visitors arriving in the bailey. Her brothers had finally arrived. She struggled to her feet, adjusting herself for her great girth. She was in her last month of her pregnancy. Erik swore if she got any bigger she would burst. He spent every night talking to their child inside her, then kissed her stomach, before he wrapped her in his arms to go to sleep.

She waddled into the bailey to see Dominick dismount from his horse. Derrick was on a pony next to him. He quickly dismounted his horse and ran up to his aunt. "Aunt Kiera, you're huge!"

"Thank you Derrick, it's nice to see you too," she said with a smirk. She held her arms out to him and he hugged her tight squeezing her with all his might. In protest, the baby gave Derrick a kick. His hands went to her stomach.

"I felt it move!" He turned to his father, "Papa, I felt it move!"

Dominick helped Eleanor down from her horse and held her hand as they walked up to Kiera. Dominick gave his sister a great bear hug and kissed her cheek. Eleanor did the same.

"When is this baby going to make its arrival?"

"Hopefully, soon. There's no more room in here," she said as she rubbed her belly.

Randolf walked up, and kissed his sister on the cheek. He placed his hand on her belly. "It feels to be a fine strapping boy."

"I don't care what it is, just as long as it comes soon. Aurelia says it will be any day now. I have a feeling she knows what it is, but she's not telling."

"You'll know soon enough little sister," Dominick said.

"You're right. I'm just tired of being this big." She smiled at her brothers then she wrapped her arms in each of theirs and walked them toward the Keep. "How was your journey?"

"Uneventful," Randolf said with despair.

Kiera didn't miss the boredom on Randolf's face. "Aw, poor baby. Being a landowner isn't all that exciting?"

"No it's not. All I seem to do all day is handle disputes between the villagers. Who has who's sheep, or the cook is having problems with his kitchen help, or the stable boy getting stepped on by a horse. Or the women throwing themselves at me to get my attention." Kiera stopped to look at him. He blushed. "Well that part isn't so bad."

"I didn't think so," she said smiling back at him. "Don't worry Randolf it will get better.

He smiled down at her. Then a pain ripped through her stomach. Her nails dug into his arm. She bent nearly in half. "Kiera, what is it!"

Dominick didn't hesitate. He scooped her up in his arms and turned to Derrick, "Go find your uncle." He took the steps to the Great Hall two at a time. Eleanor and Randolf right behind. He shouted for one of the serving girls to find Aurelia.

The pain finally eased. Kiera was able to breathe again. "I'm fine Dominick, you can put me down now, the pain is go......." Another pain engulfed her. Her fingers dug into his shoulders. "I guess the baby wanted to wait until his uncles were here to see him," she said as the pain finally eased.

Dominick carried her up to her chambers and laid her gently on the bed. Eleanor was there to hold Kiera's hand as another contraction took hold of her. Eleanor looked up at the two men helplessly staring down at Kiera. "Dominick, go outside and see to our things. Randolf go find Erik, then see to whatever task he was doing and finish it for him." Kiera knew Eleanor was giving them something to do so they wouldn't worry.

Aurelia ran into the room followed by two servants. One was carrying in a small tub, the other with buckets of water. Aurelia had a small bowl of cool water in her hands. She laid it on the table near the bed.

"The pains are coming on very quickly," Eleanor said.

"She is in fine shape. Training for all those years should make the birthing go quick and easy."

"Easy!" shouted Kiera, "this is not easy."

"It won't seem so now, but afterwards you won't remember the pain." Aurelia looked into her eyes. She knew she could trust Aurelia, but she needed Erik now. In that instant he burst through the door.

"How is she?" he said breathlessly.

"It's her time," Aurelia said with a smile.

Erik ran to the bed and held Kiera's hand. She smiled until another contraction came. She squeezed his hand tightly. "Hold on Kiera. Hold on."

"You should leave now, Erik it's nearly time for the baby to come," Aurelia said.

He looked at his aunt, "I'm not leaving." His jaw set with determination.

Eleanor smiled. "Dominick had done the same thing."

"Then help me get her comfortable," Aurelia said to him.

The three of them helped Kiera out of her dress and into a nightgown in between contractions. Kiera was nearly blind with pain. They were coming on stronger. She didn't think she could take anymore, but Erik wouldn't let her give up. When it was time to give birth he held her hand, as she bore down. Eleanor, gently pulled the baby out of Kiera's womb. "It's a boy!" Eleanor said. Erik cried with joy, as Aurelia wrapped him in a blanket and handed him his son. Tears streamed down Kiera's cheeks as she looked down into her son's face.

To her surprise another pain gripped her. "Erik!" she cried.

"Aurelia! I thought you said this would be over. What's happening?"

"It's another child," Aurelia said calmly.

Eleanor and Aurelia were too busy to answer any more questions, for the second child had already crowned. Kiera bore down one more time. Eleanor was there, to help with the birth of their second child. "It was a girl!" Eleanor shouted. Aurelia bathed her and wrapped her in a blanket. Then she handed her to her father. Kiera could see that Erik was overwhelmed with emotion. He cried like a baby over his two children. He bent down, kissing the tops of their downy heads. Then he kissed his wife firmly on the lips. "Thank you, my love. Thank you for my wonderful gifts."

Kiera smiled back at him. She kissed the tiny blessings. "Thank you for giving me a life to cherish. I love you."

His amber eyes looked back into her icy blue ones. Kiera felt the intensity of his emotion. "I love you."

About the Author

Victoria Craven discovered her love for storytelling in her sophomore year of high school. Those teenage adventures always had a romantic happy ending, and they still do today. She enjoys writing thrilling contemporary suspense, or paranormal historical romance.

Having lived most of her life in Western Michigan, Victoria re-located to the suburbs of Chicago where she lived with her husband, who is the love of her life. She has three beautiful daughters, and two toddler grandsons who keep her busy, especially since she returned to Michigan where she is happiest among those she loves.

Supported by her friends and family, she has now left a career as a media account executive to pursue a career doing what she's passionate about, writing happy endings that she can share with others.   When Victoria isn't writing or revising, she is playing with her grandsons or curled up with a good book and a vat of hot chocolate.

Tell-Tale Publishing would like to thank you for your purchase. If you enjoyed this book by Victoria Craven and would like to read another by her or another of our fine authors, please visit our website:

www.tell-talepublishing.com